KT-213-867

British Fiction of the 1990s

Edited by Nick Bentley

Routledge
Taylor & Francis Group

LONDON AND NEW YORK

**BLACKBURN COLLEGE
LIBRARY**

Acc. No. ...BB.68.490....

Class No. UCL823..914.BEN

Date ..Oct..2019.........

First published 2005
by Routledge
2 Park Square, Milton Park, Abingdon, Oxon, OX14 4RN

Simultaneously published in the USA and Canada
by Routledge
270 Madison Ave, New York, NY 10016

Routledge is an imprint of the Taylor & Francis Group

© 2005 Editorial matter and selection Nick Bentley

Individual contributions © 2005 the contributors

Typeset in Baskerville by RefineCatch Ltd, Bungay, Suffolk
Printed and bound in Great Britain by
TJ International Ltd, Padstow, Cornwall

All rights reserved. No part of this book may be reprinted or
reproduced or utilised in any form or by any electronic,
mechanical, or other means, now known or hereafter
invented, including photocopying and recording, or in any
information storage or retrieval system, without permission in
writing from the publishers.

British Library Cataloguing in Publication Data
A catalogue record for this book is available from the British Library

Library of Congress Cataloging in Publication Data
British fiction of the 1990s / edited by Nick Bentley.
  p. cm.
  Includes bibliographical references.
  Contents: Introduction : mapping the millennium : themes and trends in
contemporary British fiction / Nick Bentley – From excess to new world
order / Fred Botting – "Refugees from time": history, death and the flight
from reality in contemporary writing / Andrzej Gasiorek – Science and
fiction in the 1990s / Patricia Waugh – British science fiction in the 1990s :
politics and genre / Roger Luckhurst – The McReal thing : personal/
national identity in Julian Barnes's England, England / Sarah Henstra
– Cyberspace and the body : Jeanette Winterson's The.powerbook / Sonya
Andermahr – "Fascinating violation" : Ian McEwan's children / Peter
Childs – "Tongues of bone" : A.L. Kennedy and the problems of
articulation / Helen Stoddart – Mr Wroe's virgins : the "other Victorians"
and recent fiction / B.E. Maidment – Pat Barker's vanishing boundaries /
Lynda Prescott – Singular events : the "as if" of Beryl Bainbridge's Every
man for himself / Fiona Becket – Iain Sinclair's millennial fiction : the
example of slow chocolate autopsy / Julian Wolfreys – Hedgemony?
surburban space in the buddha of surburbia / Susan Brook – Iain Sinclair :
the psychotic geographer treads the borderlines / Peter Brooker.
  1. English fiction–20th century–History and citicism. I. Bentley, Nick.
  PR881.B7235 2005
  823'.91409–dc22.
                        2005002575

ISBN 0–415–34256–2 (hbk)
ISBN 0–415–34257–0 (pbk)

Contents

Contributors

Sonya Andermahr is Senior Lecturer in English and women's studies in the School of Arts at University College Northampton. Her publications include *A Glossary of Feminist Theory* (Edward Arnold, 1997), co-authored with Terry Lovell and Carol Wolkowitz, and *Straight Studies Modified: lesbian interventions in the academy* (Cassell, 1997), co-edited with Gabriele Griffin. She has also published work on Sarah Waters's *Tipping the Velvet*, Sarah Schulman's *Empathy* and women's science fiction.

Fiona Becket is Senior Lecturer in the Department of English at Leeds University. Her publications include *D. H. Lawrence: the thinker as poet* (Macmillan, 1997), *Ireland in Proximity: history, gender, space*, edited with Scott Brewster, Virginia Crossman and David Alderson (Routledge, 1999), and *The Complete Critical Guide to D. H. Lawrence* (Routledge, 2002).

Nick Bentley is Lecturer in twentieth-century literature at Keele University and also an Associate Lecturer for the Open University. His main research areas are in post-1950 British literature and literary theory. He has published articles on Sam Selvon, Julian Barnes and Zadie Smith, and on subcultural fictions of the 1950s: Richard Hoggart, Stuart Hall and Colin MacInnes. He is currently working on a book on British fiction and culture of the 1950s and on a monograph on Martin Amis.

Fred Botting is Director of the Institute for Cultural Research at Lancaster University. His research interests are in Romantic and Gothic writing, contemporary fiction and literary theory. His publications include *Making Monstrous: Frankenstein, criticism, theory* (Manchester University Press, 1991), *Gothic* (Routledge, 1996), *Sex, Machines and Navels: fiction, fantasy and history in the future present* (Manchester University Press, 1999), *Bataille* (Palgrave, 2001), *Tarantinian Ethics* (Sage, 2001) and *Essays and Studies: the Gothic* (D. S. Brewer, 2001). He is also co-editor of *Gothic: critical and cultural concepts*,

(Routledge, 2004) and has a monograph nearing completion on Gothic (post)modernities, romance, consumption and technology.

Susan Brook is Assistant Professor in twentieth-century British literature at Simon Fraser University in Vancouver. She did her Ph.D. at Duke University (2001), and has also taught at the University of Manchester and at Staffordshire University. Her research interests lie in post-war and contemporary British literature and cultural studies, and in feminist and gender theory. Her book, *Angry Young Men, Women and the New Left: literature and cultural criticism in the fifties*, is forthcoming from Palgrave in 2006. She is currently writing an introduction to post-war literature and culture for Continuum and is also working on a new project on representations of suburbs across a range of media in twentieth-century Britain.

Peter Brooker is Professor of literary and cultural studies in the Post-graduate School of Critical Theory and Cultural Studies at the University of Nottingham. His publications include *Bertolt Brecht: dialectics, poetry, politics* (Croom Helm, 1988), *New York Fictions: modernity, postmodernism, the new modern* (Longman, 1996), and *A Glossary of Cultural Theory* (Arnold, 1999). He is also editor of *Modernism/Postmodernism* (Longman, 1992). His book, *Modernity and Metropolis* (Palgrave, 2002), contains an extensive discussion of Iain Sinclair's works of the 1990s. His most recent book is *Bohemia in London: the scene of early modernism* (Palgrave, 2004).

Peter Childs is Professor in English at the University of Gloucestershire. His books include *An Introduction to Post-Colonial Theory* (Harvester, 1996), co-authored with Patrick Williams, *The Twentieth Century in Poetry* (Routledge, 1998), *Modernism*, New Critical Idiom Series (Routledge, 2000), *Reading Fiction: opening the text* (Palgrave, 2001). His most recent publication is *Contemporary Novelists: British fiction 1970–2000* (Palgrave, 2005).

Andrzej Gąsiorek is Senior Lecturer in English at Birmingham University, specializing in nineteenth- and twentieth-century literature. His doctoral thesis explored the nature of experimental fiction in post-war Britain and was published as *Post-War British Fiction: realism and after* (Edward Arnold, 1995). The main focus of his research over the past five years has been literary modernism, and he has published a book on Wyndham Lewis for the Writers and their Work series, which appeared in 2002. He has recently completed two further books: a monograph on J. G. Ballard, forthcoming in 2005 in the new Contemporary British Novelists series published by Manchester University Press, and a collection of essays titled *T. E. Hulme and the Question of Modernism*, co-edited with Edward J. Comentale, forthcoming in 2005 and published by Ashgate.

Sarah Henstra is a Post-Doctoral Fellow at the University of California at Irvine. She has published articles on Angela Carter, Katherine Mansfield, Djuna Barnes and Doris Lessing. She is now completing a book entitled *Solicited Voices: the interview in art and life*, which theorizes the 'genre' of the interview across various literary, political and pop-cultural contexts.

Roger Luckhurst lectures in nineteenth- and twentieth-century literature at Birkbeck College. He is the author of *"The Angle Between Two Walls": the fiction of J. G. Ballard* (Liverpool University Press, 1997) and *The Invention of Telepathy* (Oxford University Press, 2002). He has co-edited *Literature and the Contemporary: fictions and theories of the present* (Longman, 1999), *The Fin de Siècle: a reader in cultural history, c.1880–1900* (Oxford University Press, 2000) and *Transactions and Encounters: science and culture in the Victorian era* (Manchester University Press, 2002). He co-edited 'Remembering the 1990s', a special issue of *New Formations* for 2003, and his most recent book is *Science Fiction* (Polity Press, 2005).

B. E. Maidment is Professor of English in the School of English, Sociology, Politics and Contemporary History at the University of Salford. His research interests include mass-circulation and popular literature of the nineteenth century, especially periodicals and graphic images, writing by Victorian working men and women, including regional writing, Ruskin and Victorian publishing history. He is the author of *Reading Popular Prints 1780–1870* (Manchester University Press, 1996).

Lynda Prescott is Senior Lecturer in literature and Staff Tutor in arts at the Open University. She has also taught at the universities of Bradford and Nottingham. Her publications include Open University teaching materials on Conrad, Kipling and Pat Barker as well as articles on Bernard Shaw, V. S. Naipaul and J. G. Farrell. Current projects include a study of the travel writings of Graham Greene and Evelyn Waugh.

Helen Stoddart is Lecturer in English at Keele University. She has research interests in the Gothic and in the history, representation and influence of the modern circus. Her study of the modern circus, *Rings of Desire: circus history and representation* (Manchester University Press, 2000) gives a particular emphasis to the use of circus representations and metaphors in film and literary fiction. Currently, she is working on a book-length study of Angela Carter's *Nights at the Circus*, to be published in 2005. She has contributed to a number of edited collections and published articles in the *Modern Language Review*, the *Glasgow Review* and *Screen* and is also on the editorial board of *Continuum: Journal of Media and Cultural Studies*.

Patricia Waugh has published extensively in the field of modern fiction and criticism. She is the author of *Metafiction: the theory and practice of self-conscious fiction* (Routledge, 1984), *Feminine Fictions: revisiting the postmodern* (Routledge, 1989), *Practising Postmodernism: reading modernism* (Arnold, 1992), *The Harvest of the Sixties: English literature and its backgrounds 1960–90* (Oxford University Press, 1995), *Revolutions of the Word: intellectual contexts for the study of modern literature* (Oxford University Press, 1997). She has also edited a number of collections and anthologies of modern literary theory and postmodernism including *The Arts and Sciences of Criticism*, co-authored with David Fuller (Clarendon Press, 1999).

Julian Wolfreys is Professor of English at the University of Florida. His teaching and research is concerned with nineteenth- and twentieth-century British literary and cultural studies, literary theory, the poetics and politics of identity and the idea of the city. His recent publications include *Thinking Difference: critics in conversations* (Fordham University Press, 2004), *Critical Keywords in Literary and Cultural Theory* (Palgrave, 2004), *Occasional Deconstructions: poetics, politics, responsibilities* (State University of New York Press, 2003), *Victorian Hauntings: spectrality, haunting, the Gothic, and the uncanny in literature* (Palgrave, 2001), *Readings: acts of close reading in literary theory* (Edinburgh Universtiy Press, 2000), *Peter Ackroyd: the ludic and labyrinthine text*, co-authored with Jeremy Gibson (Macmillan, 2000), *Deconstruction: Derrida* (St Martins Press, 1998) and *Writing London: the trace of the urban text from Blake to Dickens* (Macmillan, 1998). He has, in addition, edited and co-edited numerous books, most recently, *The J. Hillis Miller Reader* (Stanford University Press, 2004), *Glossalalia: an alphabet of critical keywords* (Edinburgh University Press, 2003) and he is General Editor of the *Edinburgh Encyclopaedia of Modern Criticism and Theory* (2002).

Acknowledgements

I would like to thank the following people for their help and advice in producing this book: Fiona Becket, Fred Botting, Peter Brooker, Shaun Richards, Karla Smith and Barry Taylor. I am grateful for the useful comments provided by the readers of the initial proposal, especially Jago Morrison. I would also like to thank Liz Thompson, Diane Parker and Polly Dodson at Routledge for their advice and patience through the various stages of the book's production. Finally, thanks to Kenneth Bentley, Dorothy Bentley and Karla Smith for their continued support and encouragement.

Introduction: mapping the millennium

Themes and trends in contemporary British fiction

Nick Bentley

Trying to identify the defining characteristics of any period of literary history is a difficult task, especially when the period under question is close to us. However, even from our relatively short distance from the 1990s, it is possible to begin to map out some of the dominant trends within the fiction of the period. Two things can be said with relative certainty: first, that the period is one of healthy production of narrative fiction seen by the vast number of novels produced in Britain during the past decade or so and fuelled by the rise of the literary-prize culture (Todd 1996). As Jago Morrison has argued, the novel of the 1980s and 1990s has fully recovered from the fears of its 'death' and 'end' in the decades immediately following the end of the Second World War (Morrison 2003: 3–4). The second main characteristic of 1990s fiction is its sheer diversity. Examples of novels can be identified that address issues of provincialism and globalization, multiculturalism and specific national and regional identities, experimentation and a reengagement with a realist tradition, as well as renewed and reinvigorated interest in a range of differing and overlapping identities: nation, gender, class, ethnicity, sexuality and even the post-human.

Within this diverse range, the relationship between fiction and historical context has been of central concern. On the one hand, the British novel in the 1990s responded to contemporary social and cultural movements within the decade, whilst on the other, there was a concentrated focus on the place of historical legacies and genealogies. Writers such as Martin Amis (1995), J. G. Ballard (1996, 2000), Pat Barker (2001), James Kelman (1994), Courttia Newland (1999) and Will Self (1992, 2000) explored the social and cultural Zeitgeist of the period. Bestsellers by Helen Fielding (1996) and Nick Hornby (1995, 1998) were involved in re-mapping discourses of femininity and masculinity in the post-feminist 1990s, whilst Jonathan Coe (1994) was concerned to offer satirical commentary on the politics of the 1980s and 1990s. Irvine Welsh (1993), Nicholas Blincoe (1995, 1997) and Niall Griffiths (2000) tripped through contemporary underworld, drug and club cultures, whilst Jeff Noon (1993, 1995) and Jeanette Winterson (2000) examined the shifting perceptions of identity and corporality in the new medias of virtual selves, computer-gaming and the Internet. But alongside this response to contemporary issues, there was a continued interest in our relationship to the historical past. Part of the *fin de siècle* focus of the British novel has been to revisit the narratives and genealogies of the past, continuing a trend in British fiction for what Linda Hutcheon has described as 'historiographic metafiction' (Hutcheon 1988). Novelists central to the decade such as Peter Ackroyd, Martin Amis, Pat Barker, Julian Barnes, A. S. Byatt, Beryl Bainbridge, Louis de Bernières, Kazuo Ishiguro, Ian McEwan and Alasdair Gray (and many others) have all produced novels that engage with the complexities of our relationship with history.

Attempting to periodize literary history is a process that is always fraught with difficulties, and the 1990s is no exception. In many ways the 1990s represent a continuation of central themes and concerns of the post-war novel, although many have argued that the period from the mid-1970s onwards represents a different phase in British literature to that of the earlier decades of the post-war period. Philip Tew, for one, identifying the rise of Thatcherism in particular, suggests, 'it must be remembered that the world after the mid-1970s is as significantly different from the preceding twenty-five post-war years, as the 1920s of flappers and boom-and-bust global crisis would have been from the [. . .] world of the late Victorians' (Tew 2004: 36). I would extend Tew's division of literary periods by suggesting that there are recognizable differences in British society and culture between the 1980s and 1990s that are reflected in the fiction of the period. Two international events, standing at either end of the 1990s, had a crucial political and symbolic resonance for British culture.[1] At one end was the fall of the Berlin Wall and the subsequent dismantling of the Communist regimes of eastern Europe and the Soviet Union. This rapid process marked the end of the Cold War and produced a significant shift in power relationships in world politics that inevitably impacted on British culture. The 'end of history' debate was one legacy of this shift, signalled by Francis Fukuyama's book *The End of History and the Last Man* (1992). According to a popular (mis)reading of Fukuyama's work, the collapse of the Soviet Union represented a final victory of the forces of capitalism, with the USA and the West emerging as the dominant ideological forces in the new world order. The removal of the spectre of communism meant the end of the historical dialectic that had set it against the advance of capitalism during the previous two centuries. But in turn this signalled fears amongst left-wing intellectuals concerning the end of an adequate political resistance to the global advance of Western capitalism. As Andrew Gibson has argued, the 1990s witnessed a culture of mourning for this lost position of resistance (Gibson

2003). This was explored in Jacques Derrida's influential and provocative book *Specters of Marx*, which attempted to balance the sense of loss of Marxism(s) (Derrida pluralizes the concept) with its tenacity as a haunting legacy within contemporary cultural politics (Derrida 1994). It must be said, however, that alongside this culture of mourning amongst certain intellectuals and academics, left-wing politics on the ground in Britain continued to fight on national and international issues, most notably in forcing the Conservative government to back down on the poll tax in the early 1990s.[2]

At the other end of the 1990s, or at least close enough to represent a symbolic shift in world politics, were the events in New York and Washington on 11 September 2001 (9/11). The symbolic power of the collapse of the Twin Towers of the World Trade Center reverberated around the world, and has had a particularly profound impact on British culture. Some recent fiction has begun to address the effects of this on British society, for example, Monica Ali's *Brick Lane* (2003) and Jonathan Coe's *The Closed Circle* (2004). The impact of 9/11 is probably too close to see clearly in a cultural perspective, nevertheless the subsequent 'War on Terror' has already been represented as a 'resurrection of history', with the West's ideological and symbolic enemy now shifted away from Marxism and towards an Islamic fundamentalism, which, in an often highly manipulated and mediatized way, threatens to undermine the hegemony of Western capitalism – so much so that certain cultural and political commentators (usually neo-conservatives) such as Charles Krauthammer have spoken of the 1990s as a 'holiday from history' (Krauthammer 2003; Will 2001; see also Žižek 2004). The 1990s, therefore, can be seen as the only decade in the twentieth century, except perhaps the Edwardian decade (1900–10), that the possibility of global war has not had a significant effect on the cultural imagination, and this is despite the abundance of regional wars during the 1990s in the Balkans, Africa and the Middle East. Politics in Britain responded to the shift in the new world order by a move away from the entrenched left-versus-right ideological divisions of the 1980s with a gradual return to consensus politics marked by New Labour's shift from the left to the centre. This process was started by Neil Kinnock, leader of the Labour Party from 1983 to 1992, and completed by Tony Blair who in 1997 became the first Labour prime minister for nearly two decades.

The relationship between fiction and reality is central to an understanding of 1990s culture. The importance of celebrity and the media, of so-called reality TV, the culture of 'spin'[3] and the concentration on the form in which information is communicated to the public are all aspects of this anxiety with the nature of the 'real'. The influence of fiction, therefore, moved beyond literature: fictions were perceived to encroach on all aspects of culture, and much critical theory of the period was interested in the way in which many aspects of life relied heavily on fictional forms. Hayden White's work on history and fiction became increasingly influential, though contentious amongst historians, generating the interest in Britain of 'postmodern history' (Jenkins 1997; Munslow 1997, 2003).[4] The news media was also seen to rely on a complex web of fictional devices, so much so that Jean Baudrillard was able to claim (provocatively) that the 1991 Gulf War only really happened on television (Baudrillard 1995), whilst the form and style of 'news' was parodied by satirical British television shows such as *Have I Got News for You* and *Brass Eye*. Science also began to rely on narrative forms in its attempt to communicate itself to a mass audience, as Patricia Waugh shows in her chapter in this volume. In fact, fictions were everywhere in the 1990s.

This blurring of the boundaries between fiction and reality relates to an important trope within literary and cultural theory during the 1990s: postmodernism. Many critics have suggested that the 1980s represented the high point of postmodern theory (Tomlinson 2003; Sheppard 2000), however, its often provocative and contentious philosophical positions continued to fascinate cultural theorists and novelists alike in the 1990s. Richard Sheppard has argued that there are two distinct phases in postmodernism: the first representing an 'oppositional, anticapitalist, and antiestablishment' stance, whilst during the second its status became 'much more problematic' (Sheppard 2000: 351). In terms of critical theory, we might say that the first phase corresponds roughly to the 1960s and 1970s, and the second to the 1980s. In the 1990s there was an increasing scepticism towards postmodernism amongst literary and cultural theorists: Fredric Jameson (1991), bell hooks (1991), Seyla Benhabib (1992), John O'Neill (1995) and Terry Eagleton (1996) all questioned the value of the various theories attached to postmodernism and postmodernity (see also Tew 2004: 19–23). Patricia Waugh (2001 [1998]) took a more balanced view on postmodernism, distinguishing between a 'strong' and 'weak' variety, the former being less supportive to the articulation of subject positions (Waugh was particularly interested in the relationship between postmodernism and feminism). However, whilst the liberatory potential of postmodernism's scepticism towards grand narratives was questioned, popular culture seemed to embrace postmodern forms. In fact the 1990s could be seen as the decade of popular postmodernism in that its fascination with parody, pastiche, retroism, a knowing self-awareness of previous forms and its general scepticism towards grand narratives seemed to become the prevailing attitude in the popular culture of the period. Brit Pop bands such as Blur, Oasis and Pulp recycled the sounds, styles and fashions of the 1960s and 1970s as retro became the latest thing, whilst television about television abounded (for example, *Tarrant on TV*, *Brass Eye* and Channel 4's *100 Greatest TV Moments*).

Postmodern pastiche proliferated from *The Simpsons* to *Sim City*. The fictionality of so-called real life and the interplay between reality, fiction and
recognized genres were important elements in some of the most memorable
films of the decade such as *Total Recall* (1990), *Forrest Gump* (1994), *Pulp
Fiction* (1994), *Twelve Monkeys* (1995), *Scream* (1996), *Trainspotting* (1996), *The
Truman Show* (1998), *The Matrix* (1999), *Fight Club* (1999) and *The Blair Witch
Project* (1999). One of the reasons for the academic backlash against postmodernism, therefore, was its wholesale incorporation into the institutional
forms of popular culture. Any avant-garde or radical agenda that it might
have claimed in the 1960s and 1970s appeared, by the 1990s, to have been
undercut by its relatively painless incorporation into the films and shows
produced by mainstream institutions such as Hollywood and, in the case
of *The Simpsons*, the Fox Network – hardly recognized hotbeds of radical
politics or experimental aesthetics.

The relationship between fiction, literary theory and popular culture
has always been uneasy, especially since the explosion of 'Theory' in the
1950s and 1960s. Novelists often occupy the middle ground between literary
theory and popular culture. Many writers such as Angela Carter, Salman
Rushdie, Martin Amis, Julian Barnes, Jeanette Winterson, A. S. Byatt and
Jonathan Coe continued to explore the uses of self-reflexive forms, historiographic metafiction and intertextual reference as ways of representing the
relationship between text and world. Newer novelists such as Adam Thorpe,
Irvine Welsh, Alan Warner, A. L. Kennedy, Caryl Phillips and David
Mitchell also used techniques associated with postmodernism for varying
ideological as well as formal purposes. But, as Philip Tew has argued, realism
continued to have a significant influence in British literature of the period,
often as a reaction to postmodernism (Tew 2004: 10). Later 1990s texts such
as Zadie Smith's *White Teeth* (2000) and Courttia Newland's *Society Within*
(1999) seemed to emphasize the realism of their narratives in terms of both
form and content. Newland's desire to record black (sub)cultural experience
in 1990s Britain is a good example here. In his collection of interconnected
short stories, *Society Within*, one character, a struggling novelist who lives
on the urban housing estate that forms the main setting for the book,
encapsulates Newland's realist approach. After receiving a number of
publisher's rejections for his novel, the main character in the story
'Rejection', Michael, considers ditching his literary aspirations and turning
to crime as a more immediate way out of poverty. However, after witnessing
a gun battle from his high-rise window (a battle in which he was nearly
involved) he returns to his typewriter:

> Lynette led Michael to his computer table and made him sit down . . .
> '[N]ow do you see?' she told him . . . [M]ichael sat gazing at the

monitor for a long time, finally nodding his head and starting to type. Lynette watched him for a moment longer – then slowly headed for the front door to greet the police.

(Newland 1999: 251)

The role of the writer in this story emerges as a duty to record authentic marginalized experiences of the kind Michael witnesses. Newland, therefore, decides to reject the potential metafictional possibilities of having a fiction writer as a character in a work of fiction by emphasizing the realist aims of the writing itself.

Nineties fiction, then, represents a complex relationship with the traditions and genealogies of British literary history. In attempting to identify the dominant literary styles of the period, perhaps the most valuable approach is that suggested by Andrzej Gąsiorek (Gąsiorek 1995: 1–17; see also Head 2002: 224–33). He argues that the traditional way of reading post-war British fiction as a struggle between two literary camps – the realists and the experimentalists – represents a false division, and it is far more fruitful to identify a dialogue between realism and experimentalism (or in the 1990s, postmodernism) operating within individual novels. Dominic Head develops Gąsiorek's position by arguing that postmodernism in a British context should be seen as a 'reworking of realism, rather than a rejection of it' and suggesting that a distinctly 'British postmodernism' can be identified (Head 2002: 229). This definition provides a useful way of thinking about much British fiction in the 1990s.

Despite the complexity and variety of forms and subject matter, it is still possible to identify core themes within the fiction of the period. This volume attempts to map out these themes by a division into four sections: 'Millennial anxieties', 'Identity at the *fin de siècle*', 'Historical fictions' and 'Narrative geographies'. It must be said at the outset, however, that the categories suggested by these headings should not be regarded as fixed, and there is clearly much interplay between each of them with regard to any individual writer or novel.

Millennial anxieties

With the end of the Cold War, history played a trick on *fin de siècle* sensibilities in that the most immediate vehicle of apocalypse – global nuclear war – seemed to have evaporated. Millennial anxieties were thereby channelled into a proliferation of alternative forms: from global warming to wayward asteroids to millennium bugs. The 'end of history' debate extended beyond Fukuyama's original political context and connected with other discourses and narratives of endings: the end of ideology, the end of opposition to the market economy and globalization, the end of alternative futures, the end of idealism, the end of culture, the end of value and the end of meaning. These various narratives and discourses of exhaustion and closure represented a form of millenarianism adapted for postmodernity, and fuelled the concerns of many novelists in the 1990s. Despite the claims of the demise of postmodernism, the theoretical ideas explored by Baudrillard, Lyotard, Derrida and Foucault still haunted much of the literary criticism and fiction of the 1990s.[5] The uncertain relationship between the real and the unreal, and the past, present and future that challenged a teleological and rational model of historical progress resulted in many narratives that engaged in self-reflection, and the transparency (or opacity) of writing.

The chapters in the first part of this volume cover general concerns and tendencies in the fiction and culture of the period. The anxieties they identify clearly interrelate with issues of identity, history and geography that form the focus of the other parts of the book.

Fred Botting explores a series of these anxieties as approached in Zadie Smith's novel *White Teeth* (2000). One of these is the appropriation of the politics of multiculturalism and difference by the forces of global consumerism: a form of multiculturalism in which difference is subsumed in 'a new plain of sameness' (p. 22). Botting also contrasts anxieties about the economic and individual excesses of the 1980s: a culture of 'self, spending, sex, shopping, style' (p. 23), as articulated in the fiction of Martin Amis and Julie Burchill, with Zadie Smith's reduction of crucial 1980s events (such as the fall of the Berlin Wall) to mediatized souvenirs, drained of political meaning. Botting goes on to discuss the way in which Smith's novel contrasts various teleological grand narratives with an accidentalism that evades closure and predestination.

One of the contradictions of 1990s culture is that whilst anxieties about the end of history proliferated, there was a continued and sustained interest amongst British writers in the legacies of historical events and ideas. Andrjez Gąsiorek identifies the latter tendency amongst a group of contemporary novelists in their desire to recuperate a sense of the value of historical narratives in coming to terms with our position at the end of the twentieth century. Gąsiorek focuses in particular on the work of Andrew O'Hagan, Jim Crace, J. G. Ballard, W. G. Sebald and Rachel Lichtenstein.

Patricia Waugh explores the trend in 1990s scientific theory towards biology and genetics and how the 1960s 'two cultures' debate was readdressed in the last decade of the century. She identifies a tendency in popular scientific works to use narrative techniques and forms normally associated with literary fiction. She compares the works of popular science writers such as Richard Dawkins and Stephen Hawking with the more sceptical and self-reflexive fiction of Ian McEwan's *Enduring Love* and Salman Rushdie's *Haroun and the Sea of Stories* where a balance between scientific rationalism and literary explorations of subjective emotions appears as the most reliable way of articulating the human condition at the end of the millennium.

Roger Luckhurst argues that science fiction (SF) in the 1990s offered a potential literature of resistance to the new hegemonies of the consensus politics of 1990s Britain. Luckhurst shows that whereas the 1980s saw a distinct oppositional role for art and literature, the 1990s represent what he calls a cultural regulation, whereby significant cultural forms, such as Brit Pop and Young British Art (for example, the works produced by Damien Hirst and Tracey Emin) were leached of any radical or anti-establishment position. Given this climate, Luckhurst shows the way in which critically neglected forms, such as SF, can offer a point of resistance to this cultural regulation. Luckhurst discusses this with respect to fiction by James Lovegrove, Gwyneth Jones and Alan MacLeod.

Identity at the *fin de siècle*

One of the most distinctive elements in 1990s cultural theory was the focus on identity politics. Identity became the main concept by which individuals mapped out their relationship with society and often provided a way of producing narratives of empowerment across a variety of marginalized subject positions. The novel, in particular, provided a fruitful space in which the politics of identity could be explored. A complex web of identity categories were articulated, dramatized and theorized. Some identity categories seemed to be more central to the decade than others. Although class continued to be a central issue in much of the fiction of the period, for example in the work of James Kelman, Martin Amis, Alasdair Gray and Jeanette Winterson, it tended to be eclipsed by seemingly more pressing issues such as gender, sexuality, race and nation. In relation to gender, the debates about the validity and politics of a post-feminist discourse became a central focus, and were addressed in works as different as A. S. Byatt's *Babel Tower* (1996) and Helen Fielding's *Bridget Jones's Diary* (1996). Explorations of sexuality also provided material for many writers during the period, especially in narratives that explored and articulated gay and lesbian identities. Writers such as Jeanette Winterson and, towards the end of the decade, Sarah Waters provided texts that concentrated on lesbian experience, whilst Hanif Kureishi's *The Buddha of Suburbia* (1990) and Alan Hollinghurst's *Spell* (1998) explored bisexuality and gay cultures.

The focus on sexuality paralleled an increasing interest in the 1990s with the politics and aesthetics of the body: the body as the space in which identity locates itself, but also as a site for performance, empowerment, spectacle and the intimate expression of power relationships. The politics of the body also extended into issues of the post-human and the virtual body: of cyborgs and the anonymity of virtual identities constructed through web spaces. Theoretical work by Donna Haraway and Sadie Plant underpin much of the critical analysis of these issues during the period. In this volume, Sonya Andermayr discusses the way in which computer technology, virtual environments and the new textual form of e-mail provide material for Jeanette Winterson to explore the construction of virtual identities in cyberspace in her novel *The.PowerBook*. Andermayr assesses the critical reaction to Winterson's novel and, through reference to Haraway and Plant, discusses the relationship between cyberfeminism and the potential of cybercommunication to produce post-gendered forms of identity.

The politics of identity was particularly influenced by a politics of difference during the 1990s. The decade saw the increasing importance of post-colonial theory, which in turn offered new ways of interpreting Britain's relationship with its colonial past, and the make-up of contemporary ethnic, racial and religious identities. This fed into a new focus on 'black' British writing as a distinct literary identity. However, the category of 'black British' was itself problematic in that it tended to homogenize a variety of writing that might include figures as diverse as Salman Rushdie, V. S. Naipaul, Caryl Phillips and Courttia Newland. Such a categorization is in danger of homogenizing the very difference that it attempts to articulate. Nevertheless, the importance of writers whose ethnic backgrounds deviated from what appears on institutional forms as 'white British' was one of the most visible features of British writing in the 1990s. Rod Mengham sees cultural hybridity as having a 'decisive importance in British fiction' since the early 1980s, whilst Peter Childs comments, 'the 1990s might be most readily drawn in terms of post-colonial themes such as decolonization and diaspora' (Mengham 2003: 5; Childs 2005: 13).

The process of devolution, argued about for most of the 1990s and achieved to a certain degree after 1997 when Scotland and Wales were given their own regional parliaments, underpinned a renewed concern with the articulation of national identity in the British novel. There has been something of a renaissance in Scottish fiction during the period, with many of the most important writers coming from north of the England-Scotland border. Alasdair Gray (1992) and James Kelman (1994), publishing throughout the 1980s, continued to produce influential texts in the 1990s that were concerned with articulating a sense of Scottish identity; whilst a newer generation of Scottish writers emerged that offered more ambivalent engagements with the discourses of the nation: writers such as A. L. Kennedy, Alan Warner and Irvine Welsh. These later writers tended to approach national identity through association with youth cultures and subcultures; the same connection can be made with Welsh writing of the period. The 1990s renaissance of Welshness was most visibly articulated through popular cultural forms and, in particular, the celebration of Welsh national identity by bands such as the Manic Street Preachers, Catatonia and the Stereophonics, as well as the re-imagining of Cardiff as a cosmopolitan European capital represented symbolically by the new Millennium Stadium. The focus on youth culture and Welshness was articulated in the writing of Niall Griffiths, and in the early 2000s by John Williams. In Northern Ireland, the continuing 'Troubles' and the politics of the 'Peace Process', with its attempts at reconciling divisions in the community, were most often articulated in poetry and drama, rather than fiction, although *Reading in the Dark* (1996) by Seamus Deane and *Grace Notes* (1997) by Bernard MacLaverty are notable exceptions. English identity also attracted increasing attention over the decade, fuelled by nostalgic reconstructions of the myths of Englishness in the political rhetoric of the Conservative Prime Minister John Major, as well as in the continuing influence on the English psyche of devolution, post-colonialism, the end of empire and the emergence of multiculturalism and difference as an alternative model of the nation. Novels such as Adam Thorpe's *Ulverton* (1992), John King's *England Away* (1998) and Julian Barnes's *England, England* (1998) place some of these issues at their centre.

Anxieties surrounding the deconstruction and pluralization of the self have resulted in an interest in models of hybridity and inbetweenness, of identities that reside on the borders between, and *in* between, traditional categories of identity. This has led the novel to investigate questions of ontology often expressed as an uncertainty about the relationship between the real and the unreal, between simulacra and simulations, about authenticity and fakery, as well as nostalgia for lost or displaced selves and organic communities. Here, themes of memory and identity become important as a source for both personal and public histories. Sarah Henstra's chapter discusses the representation of these issues with respect to Barnes's 1998 novel *England, England*. As the title suggests, this is framed within a focus on national identity, but it is also concerned with the relationship between personal and national histories. Henstra is also keen to show how memory, although vital to the construction of identity, can often be involved in distorting the past. The discussion of national identity centres on the meaning of Englishness in a post-colonial world and the commodification of the nation in terms of the 1990s emphasis on heritage culture.

Much 1990s fiction explored the ways in which literary techniques and forms have been used to articulate or represent identity. The abundant use of self-reflexive narratives in contemporary fiction reveals a concern to question the relationship between fiction, reality and the construction (or writing) of identity. The role of narrative and storytelling thereby becomes crucial in how identities are communicated to us and to others. Helen Stoddart explores the way in which A. L. Kennedy addresses the relationship between writing and identity through a focus on the materiality of written language. As Stoddart argues, Kennedy's experimentation with a variety of textual forms reveals certain anxieties about the adequacy of writing to articulate meaning. Through reference to Roland Barthes, Stoddart examines the way in which Kennedy's fiction explores the intimate relationship between writing, identity and the body.

The 1990s also saw a number of novels that were concerned with youth culture and subcultures, the most visible of which was Irvine Welsh's *Trainspotting* (1993). Anxieties about the effects of drugs, sexuality and the effects of consumerism on youth have, of course, been around from (at least) the 1950s and the invention of 'the teenager', but the 1990s saw particular concerns about the extension of adolescence downwards and upwards. The content of teen magazines and sex-education lessons were criticized (and defended) for the dissemination of sexual awareness to ever-younger teens, while adolescence as a lifestyle seemed to expand to include twenty- and even thirty-somethings, as seen in the popularity of the extended *Bildungsroman* of the type produced by Helen Fielding and Nick Hornby.[6] Peter Child's chapter in this volume is concerned with the place of the child in contemporary culture and with the way in which children have become a theme in much British fiction of the past decade. Childs looks at fiction by Martin Amis, Pat Barker and Kazuo Ishiguro, but concentrates on the figure of the child and the representation of childhood in Ian McEwan's novels.

The diversity and plurality of fiction that focuses on issues of identity shows the importance of identity politics for 1990s British culture and society. However, separate identities were as often as not in conflict with one another despite attempts in cultural theory to link together marginalized identities – most notably in the increasing influence in the 1990s of Gayatri Spivak's 'subaltern studies', and Laclau and Mouffe's post-Marxist 'chain of equivalence' between different subject positions (Spivak 1988; Laclau and Mouffe 1985; see also Sim 1998).

Historical fictions

Part III of the volume recognizes the importance of historical fiction in the 1990s as a part of a continuing trend in the post-war British novel, especially from the 1960s onwards. This feature of the contemporary novel is expressed in the relationship between the past and the present, between our ancestors and ourselves, and in the relationship between fiction, history and genealogy.

One emphasis here is on the relationship between private and official history. This has two elements: first, there was a concentration on alternative, marginalized and unofficial experiences that offered alternative and often competing perspectives on official histories. This was marked by an interest in underworld and carnivalesque narratives often informed with post-Freudian readings of novels set in pre-Freudian times, for example, Peter Ackroyd's *Dan Leno and the Limehouse Golem* (1994), and the later 1990s fiction of Sarah Waters. Second, there was a focus on narratives of violence, catastrophe and war as many writers reflected on the major conflicts of the twentieth century. Novels such as Pat Barker's *Regeneration* trilogy (1991, 1993, 1995) and Sebastian Faulks's *Birdsong* (1993) take the First World War as their historical setting, whilst the Second World War forms the backdrop for Faulks's *Charlotte Gray* (1998), Louis de Bernières's *Captain Corelli's Mandolin* (1994), sections of Martin Amis's *Time's Arrow* (1991), W. G. Sebald's *The Emigrants* (1996) and Zadie Smith's *White Teeth* (2000). The continued place of these traumatic periods in our collective imagination underlies the focus on the relationship between the past and the present. Certain decades also provided the historical setting for novels, such as the 1960s in A. S. Byatt's *Babel Tower*, the 1970s in Hanif Kureishi's *The Buddha of Suburbia* (1990) and Jonathan Coe's *The Rotters' Club* (2001) and the 1980s in Coe's earlier novel *What a Carve Up!* (1994). A focus on colonial histories was particularly important in the 1990s and continues to be one of the main trends in contemporary fiction. This was exemplified in several works such as Caryl Phillips's *Cambridge* (1991) and *The Nature of Blood* (1997), Salman Rushdie's *The Moor's Last Sigh* (1995) and *The Ground Beneath Her Feet* (1999), Arundhati Roy's *The God of Small Things* (1997), David Dabydeen's *The Intended* (1991) and *Disappearance* (1993), Vikram Seth's *A Suitable Boy* (1993) and, again, Zadie Smith's *White Teeth* (2000).

The writers discussed in the third part of this book reveal the fascination with the past. Lynda Prescott emphasizes the importance of the twentieth century in Pat Barker's writing generally and, in particular, in the last of Barker's First World War trilogy, the Booker Prize-winning *The Ghost Road* (1995). Prescott investigates Barker's interests in the liminal and the shifting boundaries between past and present, masculinity and femininity, and fact and fiction. Prescott also shows how Barker manages to articulate the presence and immediacy of the war despite its historical distance.

The relationship between fact and fiction and between real and symbolic events is also of central interest in Fiona Becket's analysis of Beryl Bainbridge's *Every Man for Himself* (1996). Becket explores the sinking of the *Titanic* as a singular event that echoes across the twentieth century, which carries with it symbolic, social, cultural and historical significance. She also emphasizes the way in which the *Titanic* continues to speak to the present. Through reference to Paul Ricoeur's theories on the phenomenology of fiction, Becket explores the representation of the loss of the *Titanic* in Bainbridge's novel. In particular, she discusses Bainbridge's interest in the interrelationship between a real historical event, the place that event holds in the popular imagination, and the fictionalizing of that event in *Every Man for Himself*.

The 1990s, of course, were not only the last decade of the twentieth century but also of the second millennium, and recent historical fiction has delved deeper into the cultural genealogies and 'psychogeographies' that intimately connect our presents/presence with the past. Peter Ackroyd has continued to produce a writing that moves the reader between historical epochs, for example in his 1993 novel *The House of Doctor Dee*, which juxtaposes a twentieth-century plot line with a fictionalization of the eponymous real-life Elizabethan alchemist. Julian Barnes's *A History of the World in 10½ Chapters* (1989), Adam Thorpe's *Ulverton* (1992), David Dabydeen's *A Harlot's Progress* (1999) and Caryl Phillips's *The Nature of Blood* (1997) are further examples of novels that have revisited pre-twentieth-century histories from a contemporary perspective.

B. E. Maidment's chapter in this book traces a recent resurgence in novels revisiting the nineteenth century back to what he identifies as the 'moment' of Victorian studies in the late 1960s and early 1970s. The emphasis during this period was on recovering a 'history from below' which concentrated on a study of Victorian culture and society that engaged with issues of class, gender and sexuality, by representing the experiences of the 'other Victorians'. Maidment suggests that Victorian sexuality continues to fascinate contemporary writers and identifies 1990s fiction on this theme by A. S. Byatt, Alasdair Gray, Peter Ackroyd, Victoria Glendinning, Matthew Kneale and Sarah Waters. He develops his discussion through a close analysis of Jane Rogers' *Mr Wroe's Virgins* (1991).

Narrative geographies

Much contemporary British fiction has been concerned with the imaginative construction of contemporary spaces and with the relationship between history, geography and identity (Middleton and Woods 2000). This has been seen in the importance of representing social and cultural environments in fiction in terms of class, gender, ethnicity, sexuality and the nation. The rise in the influence of a number of cultural theorists and geographers has fuelled this interest in contemporary spaces, in particular the work of David Harvey, Charles Jencks and Edward Soja, and the reassessment of the representation of cultural geographies in Marx, Michel Foucault and Henri Lefebvre.

The nature of the postmodern city has provided fruitful ground for much contemporary fiction. London, in particular, has been the subject of many British novels – usually concentrated on themes of fragmentation, multiplicity, hybridity and reinvention. A form of psychogeography, the mapping of the psychological effects produced on the individual by physical environments, has been especially noticeable. This has been expressed in fiction in ways that open up the concept of urban geographies to other fields, and there has been a particular focus on writing the city, the role of the postmodern *flâneur*, and the city as event. Concerns with surfaces and appearances have been contrasted with models of the city that emphasize it as a network of hidden narratives from the past, especially in the work of Peter Ackroyd and Iain Sinclair. This is accompanied by an interest in identifying and dramatizing the city's spectres and ghosts, its underworlds and countercultural narratives.

One of the most important contemporary writers on London is Iain Sinclair, and two chapters in Part IV of the book examine his work. Julian Wolfreys investigates the way in which Sinclair's collaboration with Dave McKean, *Slow Chocolate Autopsy* (1997), responds to millennial interests, fantasies and texts. Through Sinclair, Wolfreys traces the relationship between the millennial, excess, writing and temporality in the ghosts that haunt London, and also Sinclair's engagement with an English millenarian tradition. In particular, Wolfreys focuses on the representation of the millennial with respect to three themes: editing, autopsy and surveillance.

Peter Brooker takes a broader overview of Sinclair's corpus, taking the 2001 work *Landor's Tower* as the point of reference. Brooker is interested in the representation of otherness, difference, estrangement and newness in Sinclair's writing. In *Landor's Tower* Sinclair travels out of the metropolis and beyond the suburbs, moving outwards (and backwards) to his childhood origins in the Welsh borderlands. Brooker explores the renegotiation of Sinclair's psychogeographies with respect to this shift away from London – the urban environment that saturated his 1990s novels.

In between the metropolis and the country lies the suburbs, and Susan Brook takes this often-neglected social space as the focus of her chapter. By reassessing the theoretical awareness of contemporary space she explores the way in which postmodernity is experienced in the suburbs, rejecting the conventional reading of them as dry, stultifying and reactionary. Through analysis of Hanif Kureishi's *The Buddha of Suburbia* she identifies the ambivalent and changing representation in that novel of suburban space with particular reference to issues of class and sexuality.

Although each of the chapters in this volume offers its own perspective on 1990s fiction, many connections will be found between them. The reader is invited to select the ones that are of particular interest to them, or to read the whole as a way of engaging with the dominant themes and characteristics of the period. Research into 1990s British fiction has, of course, only just begun and this volume offers an early intervention in the process of crystallizing and defining this fascinating period of literary history. Whether the novels and authors covered are still being discussed in twenty, or even fifty years, remains to be seen, but what the following chapters do provide is a critical engagement with our current understanding of the fiction produced in Britain in the last decade of the second millennium.

Notes

1 John Tomlinson also refers to the events in Berlin in 1988/9 and in New York and Washington in September 2001 as symbolic events that usefully mark of the 1990s as a decade, as perhaps more accurately a 'long' 1990s (Tomlinson 2003).

2 The 'poll tax' was the popular name given to Margaret Thatcher's Conservative government's attempt to revise the way general tax rates were calculated in Britain. It was implemented in Scotland in 1989 and in England and Wales in 1990. It was deeply unpopular and poll-tax riots were seen in London in March 1990, contributing to the downfall of Thatcher later in the same year. (John Major took over as the Conservative Party leader and Prime Minister in November 1990.) The poll tax was eventually replaced by a new council tax in 1993.

3 'Spin' was a term adopted by journalists and political commentators in the 1990s to describe the way politicians would colour the truth and avoid difficult questions by using rhetoric. It was a term taken from cricket and refers to the way in which a bowler manipulates the flight of the ball by spinning it with a twist of the hand.

4 Hayden White suggests that both historical and fictional discourses tend to use similar narrative structures and conventions, thereby blurring the distinction between the two (White 1978).

5 Two examples from British fiction are Patricia Duncker's *Hallucinating Foucault* (1996), and Julian Barnes's *England, England* (1998), which include, respectively, references to Foucault and a character whose ideas are remarkably similar to those of Jean Baudrillard.

6 '*Bildungsroman*' is a German word that refers to a 'novel of development' and traditionally deals with the transition of a character from childhood to adulthood.

References

Ackroyd, Peter (1993) *The House of Doctor Dee*, London: Hamish Hamilton.
—— (1998) [1994] *Dan Leno and the Limehouse Golem*, London: Vintage.
Ali, Monica (2003) *Brick Lane*, London: Doubleday.

Amis, Martin (1991) *Time's Arrow or The Nature of the Offence*, London: Jonathan Cape.
—— (1995) *The Information*, London: Flamingo.
Bainbridge, Beryl (1996) *Every Man For Himself*, London: Abacus.
Ballard, J. G. (1996) *Cocaine Nights*, London: Flamingo.
—— (2000) *Super-Cannes*, London: Flamingo.
Barker, Pat (1991) *Regeneration*, London: Viking.
—— (1993) *The Eye in the Door*, London: Viking.
—— (1995) *The Ghost Road*, London: Viking.
—— (2001) *Border Crossing*, London: Viking.
Barnes, Julian (1989) *A History of the World in 10½ Chapters*, London: Jonathan Cape.
—— (1998) *England, England*, London: Jonathan Cape.
Baudrillard, Jean (1995) *The Gulf War Did Not Take Place*, trans. Paul Patton, Bloomington, Ind.: Indiana University Press.
Benhabib, Seyla (1992) *Situating the Self*, Cambridge: Polity Press.
Blincoe, Nicholas (1995) *Acid Casuals*, London: Serpent's Tail.
—— (1997) *Jello Salad*, London: Serpent's Tail.
Byatt, A. S. (1996) *Babel Tower*, London: Chatto & Windus.
Carter, Angela (1992) [1991] *Wise Children*, London: Vintage.
Childs, Peter (2005) *Contemporary Novelists: British fiction Since 1970*, Basingstoke and New York: Palgrave Macmillan.
Coe, Jonathan (1994) *What a Carve Up!*, London: Viking.
—— (2001) *The Rotters' Club*, London: Viking.
—— (2004) *The Closed Circle*, London: Viking.
Dabydeen, David (1991) *The Intended*, London: Secker & Warburg.
—— (1993) *Disappearance*, London: Secker & Warburg.
—— (1999) *A Harlot's Progress*, London: Jonathan Cape.
Deane, Seamus (1996) *Reading in the Dark: a novel*, London: Jonathan Cape.
de Bernières, Louis (1994) *Captain Corelli's Mandolin*, London: Secker & Warburg.
Derrida, Jacques (1994) The *Specters of Marx: the state of the debt, the work of mourning, and the New International*, trans. Peggy Kamuf, London and New York: Routledge.
Duncker, Patricia (1996) *Hallucinating Foucault*, London: Serpent's Tail.
Eagleton, Terry (1996) *The Illusions of Postmodernism*, Oxford: Blackwell.
Faulks, Sebastian (1994) [1993] *Birdsong* London: Vintage.
—— (1998) *Charlotte Gray*, London: Hutchinson.
Fielding, Helen (1996) *Bridget Jones's Diary*, London: Picador.
Fukuyama, Francis (1992) *The End of History and the Last Man*, London: Hamish Hamilton.
Gąsiorek, Andrzej (1995) *Post-War British Fiction: realism and after*, London: Edward Arnold.
Gibson, Andrew (2003) 'Oublier Baudrillard: melancholy of the year 2000' *New Formations* 50: 123–41.
Gray, Alasdair (1992) *Poor Things*, London: Bloomsbury.
Griffiths, Niall (2000) *Grits*, London: Jonathan Cape.
Haraway, Donna (1990) 'A manifesto for cyborgs', in Linda J. Nicholson (ed.) *Feminism/Postmodernism*, London and New York: Routledge, pp. 190–233.

Harvey, David (1990) *The Condition of Postmodernity*, Oxford: Blackwell.

Head, Dominic (2002) *The Cambridge Introduction to Modern British Fiction, 1950–2000*, Cambridge: Cambridge University Press.

Hollinghurst, Alan (1998) *Spell*, London: Chatto & Windus.

hooks, bell (1990) *Yearning: race, gender, and cultural politics*, Boston, Mass.: South End Press.

Hornby, Nick (1995) *High Fidelity*, London: Gollancz.

—— (1998) *About a Boy*, London: Gollancz.

Hutcheon, Linda (1988) *A Poetics of Postmodernism: history, theory, fiction*, London and New York: Routledge.

Jameson, Fredric (1991) *Postmodernism*, London: Verso.

Jencks, Charles (1991) [1977] *The Language of Post-Modern Architecture*, 6th edn, London: Academy editions.

Jenkins, Keith (ed.) (1997) *The Postmodern History Reader*, London and New York: Routledge.

Kelman, James (1994) *How Late It Was, How Late*, London: Secker & Warburg.

King, John (1998) *England Away*, London: Jonathan Cape.

Kureishi, Hanif (1990) *The Buddha of Suburbia*, London: Faber & Faber.

Krauthammer, Charles (2003) 'Holiday from history', *Washington Post*, 14 February 2003.

Laclau, Ernesto and Chantal Mouffe (1985) *Hegemony and Socialist strategy: towards a radical democratic politics*, London and New York: Verso.

MacLaverty, Bernard (1997) *Grace Notes*, London: Jonathan Cape.

Mengham, Rod (2003) 'General introduction: contemporary British fiction', in Richard J. Lane, Rod Mengham and Philip Tew (eds) *Contemporary British Fiction*, Cambridge: Polity Press, pp. 1–7.

Middleton, Peter and Tim Woods (2000) *Literatures of Memory: history, time and space in post-war writing*, Manchester: Manchester University Press.

Morrison, Jago (2003) *Contemporary Fiction*, London and New York: Routledge.

Munslow, Alan (1997) *Deconstructing History*, London and New York: Routledge.

—— (2003) *The New History*, London: Longman.

Newland, Courttia (1999) *Society Within*, London: Abacus.

Noon, Jeff (1993) *Vurt*, London: Serpent's Tail.

—— (1995) *Pollen*, London: Serpent's Tail.

O'Neill, John (1995) *The Poverty of Postmodernism*, London: Routledge.

Phillips, Caryl (1991) *Cambridge*, London: Bloomsbury.

—— (1997) *The Nature of Blood*, London: Faber & Faber.

Plant, Sadie (1997) *Zeroes + Ones: digital women and the new technoculture*, New York: Doubleday.

Rogers, Jane (1991) *Mr Wroe's Virgins*, London: Faber & Faber.

Roy, Arundhati (1997) *The God of Small Things*, London: Flamingo.

Rushdie, Salman (1996) [1995] *The Moor's Last Sigh*, London: Vintage.

—— (1999) *The Ground Beneath Her Feet*, London: Jonathan Cape.

Sebald, W. G. (1996) *The Emigrants*, trans. Michael Hulse, London: Harvill Press.

Self, Will (1992) *My Idea of Fun*, London: Bloomsbury.

—— (2000) *How the Dead Live*, London: Bloomsbury.

Seth, Vikram (1993) *A Suitable Boy*, London: Phoenix House.

Sheppard, Richard (2000) *Modernism – Dada – Postmodernism*, Evanston, Ill.: Northwestern University Press.

Sim, Stuart (ed.) (1998) *Post-Marxism: a reader*, Edinburgh: Edinburgh University Press.

Sinclair, Iain (2001) *Landor's Tower or The Imaginary Conversations*, London: Granta.

Sinclair, Iain and Dave McKean (1997) *Slow Chocolate Autopsy: incidents from the notorious career of Norton, prisoner of London*, London: Phoenix House.

Smith, Zadie (2001) [2000] *White Teeth*, Harmondsworth: Penguin.

Soja, Edward W. (1989) *Postmodern Geographies: the reassertion of space in critical social theory*, London and New York: Verso.

Spivak, Gayatri (1988) 'Can the subaltern speak?', in Cary Nelson and Lawrence Grossberg (eds) *Marxism and the Interpretation of Culture*, London: Macmillan, pp. 271–313.

Tew, Philip (2004) *The Contemporary British Novel*, London and New York: Continuum.

Thorpe, Adam (1992) *Ulverton*, London: Secker & Warburg.

Todd, Richard (1996) *Consuming Fictions: the Booker Prize and fiction in Britain today*, London: Bloomsbury.

Tomlinson, John (2003) 'The agenda of globalisation' *New Formations* 50: 10–21.

Warner, Alan (1995) *Morvern Callar*, London: Jonathan Cape.

Waters, Sarah (1998) *Tipping the Velvet*, London: Virago.

—— (1999) *Affinity*, London: Virago.

Waugh, Patricia (2001) [1998] 'Postmodernism and feminism?' in Philip Rice and Patricia Waugh (eds) *Modern Literary Theory: a reader*, 4th edn, London and New York: Arnold and Oxford University Press, pp. 344–59.

Welsh, Irvine (1993) *Trainspotting*, London: Secker & Warburg.

White, Hayden (1978) *Tropics of Discourse: essays on cultural criticism*, Baltimore, Md.: Johns Hopkins University Press.

Will, George F. (2001) 'The end of our holiday from history', *Washington Post*, 12 September 2001.

Winterson, Jeanette (2000) *The.PowerBook*, London: Jonathan Cape.

Žižek, Slavoj (2004) 'Welcome to the desert of the real!' Available online at <http://www.peoplesgeography.org/žižek.html>, accessed 1 December 2004.

Part I
Millennial anxieties

1 From excess to the new world order

Fred Botting

They got the same shit over there as we got over here, but . . . there it's a little different

In 2001, the year *White Teeth* appeared in paperback, a global burger corporation ran a series of commercials on British television. The format was the same for each in the series. Recognisable urban landmarks signifying London, Newcastle and Liverpool, were accompanied by a soundtrack of appropriate popular songs: 'Maybe It's Because I'm a Londoner', 'Fog on the Tyne', 'Ferry 'Cross the Mersey'. Sung tunelessly and heavily marked by local dialect, the songs underlined familiar regional differences of place, class and popular culture. Multinational advertising, it seemed, recognised national and regional differences. There was a further twist of conventional advertising expectations as the commercials panned down from their respective cityscapes to present the singers in their usual urban context: all came from Asian ethnic backgrounds. Sound and vision, which up to that point had been stereotypically concordant in matching traditional popular song with a familiar image of a city, might have jarred somewhat in the adding of a perfectly accurate, if normally under-represented, image of British urban identity. Chirpy Cockneys, canny Geordies and Scouse scallies all come in a variety of colours.

Of course, it was part of the project that the expectations and assumptions of a white viewing majority, lured by familiar locales and accents, be disturbed by a mild reminder of the racism embedded in habitual associations. Stereotypes, usually promoted by advertising, provided the basis for a reversal and interrogation of white norms and attitudes. In the process, perhaps, the corporation sought to step upwards on, if not the moral, then the differential high ground: its highlighting of often-occluded differences not only raised questions of norm and race but also foregrounded heterogeneity to combat increasingly firm associations of fast food with the homogenising tendencies of global consumer culture. In celebrating a multicultural and regionally diverse Britain, the global burger chain was reacting to the swell of political criticism and protests levelled at the practices of transnational corporations in the 1990s (Klein 2000): it was now selling itself as a socially and culturally aware business attuned to the nuances of political correctness and able to articulate national, ethnic and local differences in its global frame.

All was not harmonious, however. Discord and dissonance were quite painfully audible in the singing of the songs. Though there was no attempt to teach the world to sing in perfect harmony, an avoidance of the, by then discredited, sickly sentimentalism of triumphant marketing that idealised global unity under the sign of the commodity, discordance was not an acknowledgement of underlying cultural tensions. Tuneless, accented singing, like the unglamorous urban scenes, emphasised the realism of the commercial: it celebrated, not so much an ideal multiracial unity promised by a supposedly colour-blind and liberal consumer capitalism, but the actual integrated and yet diverse cultural composition of Western nations. Artificial presentations of imagined unity cede to the material and identifiable differences of contemporary multicultural society. Ideas of national, regional or ethnic purity and distinctiveness have been invalidated in a changing world of, for the advertisement, the associated pressures of multiculturalism and transnationalism.

Difference, though privileged and authenticated in its regional diversity, was still circumscribed by the golden arches, markers of a new order of sameness. The object of consumer aspiration and satisfaction purveyed in the commercials was a 'Tikka Burger', a concoction based not on authentic regional Indian, Bangladeshi or Pakistani cooking, but on the 'Tikka Masala', a dish invented by immigrant chefs to suit an English palate. It is a fabrication of a fabrication. Clearly the realism and the authenticity promoted by the commercials' images occlude an underlying artifice. That artifice, moreover, pertains to ideas of nation. By the time the commercials appeared, Chicken Tikka Masala was regularly topping consumer polls of the nation's favourite dishes. As the commercials registered, English national identity had changed. But they also implied that national, liberal, multiracial ideals, whether based on (imagined) notions of tradition and authenticity or not (Cool Britannia) had been replaced by the unifying force of the global franchise. Away from global, abstracted and homogenised consumer norms and towards national, cultural and regional differences, the commercial introduced a different plane of sameness: the return executes an imperative to assimilate and incorporate difference in terms of (saleable and profitable) differences. Welcome to the new world order. Enjoy the difference!

Uuummmm, that's a tasty burger

'There used to be a third-generation Italian restaurant across the road: it had linen tablecloths and rumpy, strict, black-clad waitresses. It's now a Burger Den. There is already a Burger Hatch on the street. There is a Burger Shack, too, and a Burger Bower' (Amis 1985: 70–1). *Money* is one of the fictions from the 1980s that registers the impact of the new world order in terms of its effects on urban geography, social attitudes, economic habits and traditional family, cultural and class alignments. The discomfort of its arrival is evident in the crude satire on branding attempted in the naming of fast-food outlets. In the novel, it is more vigorously embodied in the protagonist's – John Self's – wasteful immersion in the unproductive and excessive expenditures of consumer culture: during 'a ninety-minute visit to Pepper's Burger world' he 'had four Wallies, three Blastfurters, and an American Way, plus a nine-pack of beer' (1985: 29). John, both punter and toilet, assumes gross shape as the every-Self of contemporary culture: an East End working-class boy from a dysfunctionally oedipal family, made good and wealthy as a director of TV commercials, he eats, smokes, drinks, pops, wanks, fucks and deludes his way from London to New York and back again, celebrating the period's economic exuberance and delirium, its abundant money and free-market morals, its plethora of desires, images, commodities and fantasies. In the novel, a 'suicide note', it is a destructive, delusional but irresistible itinerary which imprints psyches and communities with the new economic imperatives of a 'money culture'. The transformations are extensive, nationally, socially and individually:

> You flew 3,000 miles to witness exotic business behaviour: procrastination and learned digressions from port-drinking, Cuban cigar-smoking, bowler-hatted Englishmen. What do you get? Effectively, a guy in a baseball hat eating a McDonald's hamburger who processes you as efficiently as if you were some Eurobond sausage.
>
> (Lewis 1991: 159)

Changing national identity forms one of the outcomes of the neoliberalism advanced so militantly by Reagan's and Thatcher's governments: the heady freedoms of market, enterprise, investment, credit spending, uninhibited individualism ('greed is good') introduced new practices and commodities that broke up existing industrial and social orders organised along state boundaries.

Aesthetics and aspirations also changed. Self, spending, sex, shopping, style (mediated by brands) became imperative. In Julie Burchill's S&F

(Shopping and Fucking) novel *Ambition*, the heroine – screwing her way to the top – enjoys a New York trip:

> On Madison Avenue, at the soft-tech, Italo-Japanese, black beige Armani shop, she bought black label, and at Krizia she bought sportswear that would have had a nervous breakdown if one did anything more rigorous than hail a cab. She avoided Walter Stieger but did succumb to a pair of pewter, lace and plastic Vittorio Riccis for Zero. She snapped up a brace of six-hundred-dollar sweaters at Sonia Rykiel and half a dozen pairs of cashmere tights at $178 a throw at Fogal. . . .
>
> (Burchill 1990: 252)

The list of designer stores and excessive spending on useless overpriced goods continues for a page. In Peter York's assessment of the 1980s, everything from property prices and interior decor to dress and dining becomes subject to the rule of spending. One gave oneself up to the delirious flows of capital, a cipher of the incessant circulation of money/desire. Ultimately one was little more than an 'ambulatory kidney', an organ defined by its role in the circulation and expulsion of waste products (Lieberman 1993: 246–7). This is not a world in which restraint, reason, morality or utility held sway. The basic tenets of bourgeois economy – deferral, reserve, rationality and production – ceded to patterns of consumption, luxury and wastefulness, distinguishing postmodern capitalism as it created and exploited apparently inexhaustible desire (Goux 1990). Aesthetics followed economics: the eclecticism of postmodern lifestyles and art was regulated not by any value but by the 'anything goes' of money (Lyotard 1984).

Documenting the 'cultural revolution' that took place at the end of the twentieth century, Eric Hobsbawm notes how the rise of 'new libertarianism' in the 1970s and 1980s took as its justification 'the unlimited autonomy of individual desire'. For him it succeeded in 'breaking the threads which in the past had woven human beings into social textures'. The result was a generalised 'traumatic insecurity' or 'incomprehension' (Hobsbawm 1994: 334–5). In fictions of the 1980s, trying to depict and grasp the extent of social transformations that are everywhere so brashly conspicuous, both a sense of trauma and incomprehension are evident. Anxiety accompanies excess in Amis's fiction. Traditional class hierarchies are brashly trampled in both *Money* and in Caryl Churchill's *Serious Money*. The latter's *Top Girls* charts the irreconcilable political differences cutting across and within gender and family relations. Indeed, 'right-wing radicalism did more to change that very particular British class and value system than decades of leftist post-war social engineering' (York and Jennings 1995: 173). But York, in his retrospective on the decade, also acknowledges how the wealth did not trickle down: unemployment, urban riots and political protest punctured the financial euphoria. Even the 'counter-jumper', John Self, observes how 'England has been scalded by tumult and mutiny, by social crack-up in the torched slums' (Amis 1985: 66). Salman Rushdie concurs: 'looking at smoking cities on my television screen, I see groups of young people running through the streets, the shame burning on their brows and setting fire to shops, police shields, cars' (1983: 117). In *Shame*, as the novel moves from its fantastic political geography of familial and post-colonial conflicts to social conflagrations in the heart of the old imperial power, the underlying violence becomes more localised and ever more specific: 'not so long ago, in the East End of London, a Pakistani father murdered his only child, a daughter, because by making love to a white boy she had brought such dishonour upon her family that only her blood could wash away' (1983: 115). If shame and shamelessness, for Rushdie, form 'the roots of violence', its source is not only attached to internal tensions of different value systems and intercultural conflicts: its outbursts, a violence bound up with repressions and oppressions, is also given vivid, sticky and global form in the image of a soft-drinks vending machine overflowing the plastic cup with its tooth-rotting fizzy liquid (Rushdie 1983: 122). New divisions and tensions accompanied rapid economic change; new world fears, ecological and nuclear, shadowed the globalisation of the transnational corporate enterprise. Apocalypse hung heavy and imminent, like the regular and portentous weather reports, over the prescripted murder plot of Amis's *London Fields* (1990), condensed in names like 'Little Boy', 'Enola Gay', 'El Niño' and the 'Greenhouse effect'; its pervasiveness is alluded to in recurrent mentions of 'the Crisis'. In *Waterland*, also, an all too literal nuclear end of history forms the awful focus of 'feeear! feeear!' (Swift 1984: 288–9).

Accidents happen . . . what a wonderful philosophy

Apocalypticism, with its awful and desirable certitude, is countered by accidentalism in *White Teeth*'s interlinked stories of imperial, cultural and generational movement, climaxing, in fatefully aleatory fashion, on the second millennium's eve. Apocalyptic aspirations are, on the whole, reserved for the religious groups, like Hortense Bowden's Jehovah's Witnesses, eagerly counting down to the Last Day: 'Revelation is where all the crazy people end up'. They are carried on the 'nutso express' and are 'ceaselessly teetering on the precipice of total annihilation' (Smith 2000: 396). The excessive intensity of fundamentalist religion, as in the case of the acronymically challenged Islamic group ('KEVIN'), is undercut by comedy. The apocalypse, in *White Teeth*'s 1980s and 1990s, has become little more than joke. Or a children's game of boyfriend selection: 'the whole bleedin' world has been hit by the bomb . . . An' all the good-lookin' men . . . they're all dead.' So Clara Bowden is left with Ryan Topps, 'the Last Man on Earth' (Smith 2000: 29). Even 'political apocalypse, meltdown' – the end of the Berlin Wall – is a televised event ('history on TV') which, for all its global historical significance, leaves its audience 'bored shitless' or heading down the pub (Smith 2000: 238–41).

In contrast, it seems that accidents keep open a space of everyday liberalism, ordinary possibility and gradual social change against forces, divine or scientific, that would eliminate randomness with awful certitude. Archie's coin-flipping, which begins the novel and enables its key and repeated historical event, staves off millennial anxieties and tempers the overbearing pressures of broader social tensions and historical excesses with gentler freedoms provided by chance and its usually little differentiations: things happen; people get on with their lives. There is, it seems, the act of coin-flipping itself ceding any capacity to decide, no grand plan: little people's little stories unfold without, or in a different realm to, the orchestrations of major historical events; these happen elsewhere, on TV perhaps or, in allusion to the Rushdie fatwa, a book-burning somewhere in the north of England. As in *Waterland*, grand narratives of revolution or world war, which nonetheless roll on somewhere, give way to the ebbs and flows of family stories. The major repeated event of *White Teeth*, the saving of a geneticist with a Nazi past, for all its potentially world-shattering implications, is an '*incident*' that, having served as a bond between two men for forty years, '*will keep us going for the next forty years*' (Smith 2000: 533).

At the start of the novel, determined, on the toss of a coin, to die, chance intervenes again, and Archie's day is transformed 'by means of the entirely random, adventitious collision of one person with another' (Smith 2000: 23). He meets his wife-to-be, Clara Bowden. Chance seems tied to human relations. It is also linked to the accidental movements and migrations of peoples: in contrast to east London with its National Front gangs, north London seems 'more . . . more . . . liberal' because 'there was just not enough of any one thing to gang up against any other thing' (Smith 2000: 59, 63). Small groups, small stories and little accidents make up the everyday family histories of *White Teeth*'s Willesden. Accidents ensure a relatively human and liberal existence, detaching social relations from the weight (and violence) of too much history and tradition. Roots, as Rushdie's *Shame* declares, pull two ways, their bonds and belonging also a binding and burden to be countered by flight (Rushdie 1983: 85–6). For *White Teeth*'s faded father figure, Samad, accidentalism does leave the paternal authority of religious and ethnic identity in question: if belonging and birth come to be seen as accidental, if 'everything is an *accident*', then what does one do? Where does one go? 'What does anything matter?' (Smith 2000: 407). If culture wins out over biology in the shape of Samad's twin sons (one, sent to Bangladesh to be immersed in tradition, turns into a 'pukka Englishman', while the other, remaining amid the corrupting Western temptations of north London, becomes a 'fundamentalist terrorist'), then culture, divested of traditional anchors, cedes to rootlessness and diaspora threatens any identity with disappearance.

Countering 1980s apocalypticism with an accidentalism that foregrounds the lives and social relations of particular families also offers a broader response to the excesses of that decade. When that excess, the de-collectivization, fragmentation and individualism of the period 'was all getting too much', according to York, a tendency to 'cocoon' became evident: rather than embrace social existence, a tendency towards homely units and interiors manifested itself in response to an increasingly dangerous and uncertain external environment (York and Jennings 1995: 159). The 1990s, moreover, did not see a return to a gregarious and outgoing idea of society. The shift in political perspectives from society to individualism was accompanied by various forms of identity politics, not as cogent engagements with economic and social crises, but as 'cries for help' (Hobsbawm 1994: 342). *White Teeth* certainly plays with these identifiable turns in the political environment: the parent-governor scenes, with their arguments over observing religious festivals, the lesbian 'niece of shame', the white liberal doses of therapy for all the family, Islamic challenges to democracy (KEVIN), adolescent animal-rights activism, the intermixing of immigrant and indigenous families, and the question of who wears the trousers in Samad's and Alsana's home place identity (sexual, ethnic, religious and species) and political correctness in the foreground. Like those TV programmes full of lists and nostalgic images, these features only serve as familiar souvenirs of the times. So, too, the novel's references to the big storm, consumption, food and brands. There are mentions of ethnic variations in curry (Smith 2000: 54), its popular homogenisations ('Chicken Jail Fret See wiv Chips, fanks', 2000: 58) and corporate food retailing: 'I'm the sympathetic side of the service industry, I'm service with a fucking smile, I'd wear a little red tie and a little red hat like them fuckwits in Mr Burger if my fuckin' head weren't so big.' So says Abdul-Mickey, proprietor of O'Connell's, 'an Irish pool house run by Arabs' (Smith 2000: 183–4). The corporate domination of the economic and social landscape happens only in passing, passing like the Nike trainers Millat finds 'so beautiful ... it made you want to kill yourself' (Smith 2000: 167) or, later, as the 'gigantic swoosh' impression left by him and his gang, dressed up in gold, bandanas and, of course, completely outfitted in branded sportswear (Smith 2000: 232). These are just signs of those times, divested of the intensities and concerns with which 1980s fiction registered social transformation.

There are, nonetheless, many echoes of 1980s fiction in *White Teeth*. From the dentistry that so preoccupied Amis to the shame that has become a child's insult ('shame, shame, know your name', Smith 2000: 164), to the first letters of the twins' names recalling *The Information*, to the opening suicide attempt that resonates with the 'suicide note' that is *Money*, to that novel's feast of masturbation and Samad wanking away with an ardour 'that even a fifteen-year-old boy living in the Shetlands would find excessive' (Smith 2000: 140), to the weather and forecasts in *London Fields*, the move that subordinates apocalypticism to accidentalism is repeated in a general tempering of any excess or anxiety. 'We're all English now, mate', says Abdul-Mickey; 'no one was more liberal than anyone else anywhere anyway', states Alsana (Smith 2000: 63, 192). She is 'as liberal as the next person' which, of course, means that she remains prone to liberalism's anxieties in respect of 'other enjoyment', in her case, the 'fun' attached to homosexuality (Smith 2000: 285). A victorious, homogenising liberal Englishness emerges. The novel's north London seems to embody one version of the thesis that accompanied the major event closing the decade: the fall of the Berlin Wall prompted the claim, and also a chapter title in the novel, that the 'end of history' had been reached. With the victory of liberal democracy, ideological strife is finished; humans, having their material needs satisfied by technologically enhanced powers of capitalism, also wish to satisfy a desire for recognition, a wish embodied in freedom and democracy (Fukuyama 1992). Even the emerging cultural tensions, noted by Fukuyama in his citation of Samuel Huntington's 'civilizational clash', seem reduced (Fukuyama 1995: 3). *White Teeth*'s north London, with its mixed families, everyday consumption and low-level tensions outside the family, seems to have resolved questions of cultural difference and tension in its end of history. Religious and cultural tension, indeed, is little more than a family affair, an instance of intergenerational, quasi-oedipal tension, rather than outright hostility.

But I saw some shit this mornin' made me think twice

At the end of history, an end Baudrillard locates in the 1980s, 'things began to run in reverse' (1994: 10). *White Teeth* cruises through decades and historical moments as though in a gallery's retrospective show. Its main narrative sections, except one, go backwards: 'Archie 1974, 1945', 'Samad 1984, 1857', 'Irie 1990, 1907'. The novel closes in a historical loop, by accident and repetition, which folds back upon events in 1945. It barely seems to move forwards, except, in the final section, from 1992 to 1999. Twin studies, twin events: Archie, warned in 1945 of the oedipal dangers of one's actions returning to haunt one, repeats his act to 'save a man twice' (Smith 2000: 540). If 'every moment happens twice', it does so to complete the frame of modernity and close its story (Smith 2000: 532). Archie repeats. Dr Perret escapes death a second time. The law cannot decide between Magid and Millat, so lightly sentences them both, doubling and dividing punishment, fair and unjust at the same time. Irie cannot decide who is the father of her child, having slept with both twins within hours of each other. She ends up in the Caribbean with a surrogate family of Hortense, Joshua and her unnamed daughter composing postcards to two fathers and no father, writing to a good uncle and a bad uncle. Events close with a 'historic moment': O'Connells lifts its gender bar and allows two couples to see in the millennium together (Smith 2000: 541). Divisions, doublings, endings. History ends, the novel ends. In repetition. Almost.

The narratives have moved back to move forward, charting patterns of empire and its decline, diaspora and disappearance, roots and migrations, identity and its loss. The movements present the *fort-da* of modernity: a (hi)story of human emergence, progress, development from empire, war, revolution, all mapped onto so many little stories of family, culture and generation. Modernity appears, as if from nowhere, and is gone. It repeats to close its loop, end its (hi)story, pressed by something it can neither explain nor represent. Something sublime, unnameable, perhaps. *White Teeth*'s 1970s, 1980s and 1990s bring out the second book-end of modernity to keep the latter on the shelf: Jerome Christensen has compared the contemporary 'commercialist hegemony' of global liberalism with the period after Waterloo as scenes of 'imperial break-up, ethnic crack-up, and commercialist mop-up' (1994: 453–4). Repetition, return. Before modernity, at its birth, some thing; after it . . . away, and back. And away again. Modernity's *fort-da* is played out in *White Teeth*. The equation is given in the novel to account (for the failure to account) for time wasted in O'Connell's: 'why would one keep returning, like Freud's grandson with his *fort-da* game, to the same miserable scenario' (Smith 2000: 244). The futile (ir)rationalisation of the question turns on time itself, time doggedly refusing the possibility of adequate exchange, remaining, insisting, persisting, beyond the circuits of economic calculation and reason and, even, pleasure: 'after you've spent a certain amount, invested so much of it in one place, your credit rating booms and you feel like breaking the chronological bank. You feel like staying in the place until it pays you back all the time you gave – even if it never will' (Smith 2000: 244). Credit, boom, breaking the bank, the pattern, mimicking the 'casino capitalism' of 1980s economic exorbitance, presents an overinvestment of aspirations underpinned by a widening gap in the possibility of knowing one's desire. This is enjoyment in its full psychoanalytical sense (Lacan, Žižek, Wilson). Its excesses, in bourgeois economic terms, make no sense, nor they do accord with categories provided by reason, use or morality, but introduce a pathological element that, in the shift from models of production to consumption, become the norm (Goux 1990). Enjoy!

The *fort-da* plays out an old motif of the 'sins of the father', a game between an Eastern father and Western sons. It is a repetition, a rerun, 'like watching TV in Bombay or Kingston or Dhaka, watching the same old British sitcoms spewed out to the old colonies in one tedious eternal loop.' Immigrants, 'particularly prone to repetition', moving West to East, East to West, even on arrival keep 'going back and forth' in some kind of 'original trauma' (Smith 2000: 161). Trauma, beyond the pleasure principle and the paternal principle, remains the place to which one returns. Samad, Archie, both curiously unpaternal fathers, end up – like the novel, almost – in O'Connell's. Movement returns to the same place as in the *fort-da* game, one of the examples, cited by Freud, of a drive that may not be explained by the pleasure principle (Freud 1984). Enjoy! A return to loss, traumatic experience, culture, modernity. A rerun, almost, of sins and father figures. Away and back, disappearing and returning. Movement, then, never really moves, like the novel. Its histories and stories, of empire and the Indian subcontinent, of migration, diaspora and return never go anywhere: all the action occurs in London. The illusion of departure, of movement, staged in the narrative's temporal displacements and loops, barely hides the immobility, the hypostasis of its setting. Eternal recurrence of the same: *White Teeth*'s topos is simultaneously atopic, its chronologies and histories, even, subsumed by the place it never leaves. Magid, sent away to recover a past and tradition that was never his own, returns even more the same: rational, liberal, legalistic, almost a sterile figure in his impossibly white suit and superclean lifestyle, a hyperbolically 'pukka Englishman', that is, even more English than the English, even more English than, for Abdul-Mickey, the Englishness defining everyone as being 'all English now, mate'. Family meals with Magid are 'like sitting down to breakfast with David Niven' (Smith 2000: 424). It's all TV.

All English and never English. The school music lesson embracing different cultural forms defends difference on the grounds that it is not nice to make fun of another's culture: 'how would *you* like it, Sophie, if someone made fun of Queen?' Sophie wouldn't like it, of course, 'because Freddie Mercury is from *your culture*'. And Samad, watching, silently reflects on rumours of a 'very light-skin Persian called Farookh' who went to school in Panchgani near Bombay (Smith 2000: 155). Samad, however, also believes in 'protecting one's culture' (Smith 2000: 235). His wife is less convinced. She cites from the *Reader's Digest Encyclopaedia*: 'Indo-*Aryan* . . . it looks like I am Western after all.' Despite original trauma, there are no authentic origins: the more one moves back in search of purity and authenticity the less easy it is to recover: 'do you think anybody is English? Really English? It's a fairy tale!' (Smith 2000: 236). At the end of history, the end of myths of national identity. And their virulent fundamental return. The fairy tales play, it seems, on the eternal loop of sitcom reruns. And so does the end of history: watched, passively, on TV, where it can be replayed and replayed forever, the collapse of communism and the Berlin Wall is a historic event that can be switched off. The viewers are bored like Fukuyama's last men at the end of history, condemned to a life of consumption that is 'in the end, boring' (Fukuyama 1992: 314). History ends. It goes nowhere. Consumed.

In Julian Barnes's story of paradisiacal, post-mortal utopia of 1980s consumption ('The Dream' in *A History of the World in 10½ Chapters*), things seem to be getting better and better – better breakfasts, better sex and sporting performances, a better class of dead celebrity encounter – until, finally, the escalation of improvements exhausts desire and aspiration: things become boring. The dream from which the story arises ('I've just had it', says the narrator) also ends it: 'I've just had it' (Barnes 1990: 283, 309). Worn out, fed up with repetition–escalation–exhaustion, the narrator has simply had enough of it all, wanting only the good old-fashioned final consumption of real death. At the end of history, however, things do not end with a bang, with finitude and finality, as in the good old nuclear apocalyptic fantasies of the Cold War. Repetitions and reversals accelerate chaotically and without end: the reunification of Germany starts 'a reverse rewriting of the whole of the twentieth century' (Baudrillard 1993b: 98). As things move backwards and flip over like a coin spinning in the air, history, nation and modernity expire:

> *So there is not even the end of history*. We are faced with a paradoxical process of reversal, a reversive effect of modernity which, having reached its speculative limit and extrapolated all its virtual developments, is disintegrating into its simple elements in a catastrophic process of recurrence and turbulence.
>
> (Baudrillard 1994: 11)

Without history yet permanently awash in historicisms and retrospectives, the future becomes old-fashioned and consumption holds sway. Baudrillard's 'last man' is 'the end-user of his own self and his own life, the terminal individual, with no real hope of either descendants or transcendence' (Baudrillard 2002: 67). Irie's daughter, without name or father, is a puppet whose strings have been severed and is, for that reason, as free as any 'last man'. No strings, no walls: an untied existence beyond boundaries, roots and filiations. Where the Cold War sustained the comforting illusion provided by opposition that, because of tyranny there must be freedom and democracy, because of political oppression there must be progress and perfectibility, its collapse discloses repetition and turbulence – without end. Where East and West, as political blocs, were 'bonded together', 'stabilised', by a 'transnational economy, which neither could control' and 'by the strange interdependence of the Cold War power system', both were thrown 'into disorder when it collapsed' (Hobsbawm 1994: 418). The 'historic irony', for Hobsbawm, lay in that fact that a fashionable neoliberalism 'triumphed at the very moment when it ceased to be as plausible as it had once seemed. The market claimed to triumph as its nakedness and inadequacy could no longer be concealed' (1994: 343). Modernity, repeating itself beyond the end, closes in upon itself, goes into reverse and implodes.

Was an instant of purity worth a lifetime lie?

White Teeth, in repetition, with its twin events, closes on itself. Almost. Something escapes, along with its heroic little mouse. While it might appear that modernity has looped back on itself in repetition, closing with twin sentences, family resolutions and marital millennial celebrations, the reversal of history and ending of the novel occurs in the one section that declares a forward chronological movement: 'Magid, Millat and Marcus 1992, 1999'. Mmmmodernity does not simply fold back on itself; its end of history discloses another momentum, a momentum, an undercurrent, pulsing from the Second World War in the figure of the genetic scientist: Perret is mentor to Marcus and a shadowy figure confirming the 'scary' 'neo-fascist tabloid fantasies' that circulate, so the latter's encounter with a reader of his work suggests, between popular receptions of technical innovation, science fiction and science (Smith 2000: 419). Looking back, reading techno-scientific advances as a return of the same old racist and eugenicist fantasies, the reader, an unnamed Asian woman, exemplifies for Marcus the persistence of popular fears and fantasies far in excess of anything science can realise. Nonplussed, as she leaves for her departure lounge and he goes to meet Magid's plane, he speculates on the gulf separating the identical twins, proof for him of the ill-informed and ungrounded nature of popular fears; proof, also, sublime, uncanny, incredible, of nurture winning out over nature, of culture overcoming genetic determinism: Magid would 'have the same genetic code as a boy he already knew, and yet in every conceivable way be different. He would see him and not see him' (Smith 2000: 422).

If culture wins out over nature, splitting the twins more surely than their original egg, confounding and separating appearance and identity, inside and out, it also gives way to another, imaginary and chimerical twinning, one based on identification, ideas, minds: 'Magid and Marcus. Marcus and

Magid' (Smith 2000: 423). Of one mind, an über-mind, Marcus, sharing rational, benevolent, humanistic principles with Magid, seems fairly liberal in his scientific outlook and practice: he works for 'humanity', believing in the 'perfectibility' of all life and the twin aims of 'social and scientific progress' (Smith 2000: 312). A nineteenth-century scientific humanitarian, perhaps, focused on the objectivity of his innovations and untainted, like Magid, by religious or sentimental scruples. But his mentor has a past. And Marcus's own comments and press releases claim a different history and future: 'you eliminate the random, you rule the world', 'the FutureMouse© holds out the tantalising promise of a new phase in human history where we are not the victims of the random but the directors and arbitrators of our own fate' (Smith 2000: 341, 433). This is, as a journalist notes, 'scary shit'. But it is also Magid's position: his letters to Marcus, the basis of their (post-)-ideological twinning, speak of eliminating the random; his reflections against his own birth, as he watches every stage of Marcus's mouse experiment, build in a crescendo of negations towards another kind of certainty and purity (Smith 2000: 366, 489).

> No random factors. [. . .] No doubt as to when death will arrive. [. . .] No question about who was pulling the strings. [. . .] No question of a journey, no question of greener grass, for wherever this mouse went its life would be precisely the same. [. . .] No second-guessing, no what-ifs, no might-have-beens. Just certainty. Just certainty in its purest form.
> (Smith 2000: 489–90)

This event-creation, as witnessed by Magid, has moved beyond anything that might have been considered human or natural, a rewriting of life and death and all the accidents, surprises, uncertainties in between. From the techniques of modernity, another phase, neither human nor natural history, emerges.

The novel, of course, views such claims with suspicion. Marcus's and Magid's anti-accidentalism is associated with other kinds of apocalypticism: Magid is an incredible figure, pathologically clean, overbrushing his teeth and ironing his underpants; the Chalfens, like Hortense, have a quaintly 'nutso' quality to their Chalfenist convictions. The ending, too, seems to celebrate accidents and chance, a victory for the aleatory over the controls, certainties and apocalyptic fantasies articulating religious and scientific fundamentalism, which have, since Darwin at least, become a repetitively familiar bickering old couple. As the human drama of gunshot, bullet, slow-motion instinctive reactions and blood unfolds, the mouse's glass prison is smashed and the little creature escapes the grasp of his desperate captors to disappear into an air vent. '*Go on my son!* Thought Archie' (Smith 2000: 541).

Silently cheering on the underdog, Archie's gaze on the disappearing mouse offers a simple identification as a reading: an underdog, like the mouse, this small man with an inconsequentially everyday existence has again played a heroic part in world events. A habitual coin-tosser, practitioner of chance and indecision, yet accidental and unwitting agent of change, Archie stands for an everyday, almost unconscious, liberalism, one bound up with ordinary humanity and its gradual, accidental changes, its unexpected conjugations, its slow generational natural-cultural evolutions. Things will carry on, by habit and accident, doing their thingy thing with a few surprises and events happening along the way. Archie's gaze on the disappearing mouse offers a very human, even anthropomorphic, take on its escape. The mouse is like him, an undermouse; its drama, a human drama. His gaze duplicates that of most of the audience, divided, as if by consumer survey, into two groups: 'those whose eyes fell upon a bleeding man, slumped across a table, and those who watched the getaway of a small brown rebel mouse'. The mouse, curiously, flashes a 'smug look' (Smith 2000: 541). The gaze, then, is split between human and transgenic mouse, a mouse masquerading in the unbloodied eyes of the onlookers as human, heroic criminal and rebel, while all the time being a being of a resolutely different order of post-natural creation.

Everything is split at the end of the novel between two gazes. Doubling: a division and multiplication. Not only is there the instinctual act of Archie's repetition, saving a man twice. The two twins are punished, one justly and the other not, since the law, its procedures and witnesses, are unable to identify the culprit: individual responsibility, suitably enough in a novel advocating accidentalism, has been rendered undecidable. It is an 'impossible case'. The law divides, a cloned law: two are sentenced for the act of one. Irie's daughter is another curious genetically undecidable creation with two fathers and none: writing her postcards to two father/uncles, she 'feels as free as Pinocchio, a puppet clipped of paternal strings' (Smith 2000: 541). Beyond the anchors, names and injunctions of paternity lies her freedom, yet she is compared to an artificial, mechanical creation who has been given life. At the end, the novel's celebration of the last days of paternal order – its traditions, laws, history, science, religious and family values – bears witness to the birth of a stringless being, unbonded and unbounded by paternal roots, laws or genes. Looking back on modernity, playing out its *fort-da* narrative, the novel moves forward, cutting the strings tying the grandchild to the reel of nature and culture.

This shit doesn't just happen

The ambivalence of the ending remains, returning to a humanity of family, modernity, liberalism, of a natural and cultural evolution of gradual change, randomness and accidents. At the same time, almost imperceptibly and looking the same, everything has moved to a hyper-modern phase. The mouse that escapes by happy accident is a being already programmed to be beyond chance and nature. Its escape, for all the quiet support of the accidental Archie, is not a victory for random modernity but a simulation of accidentalism that offers a consoling opposition to an apocalypticism that has already occurred, but in different form – a quiet yet relentless apocalypse. Simulation repeats and supercedes modern relationships: appearing to regress, it moves forward, re-establishing relationships on another plane, a plane enabled by, and supplementing, the economic and techno-scientific imperatives of post-war modernity. It looks back, and simulates, the split gaze of the novel on a humanity that remains in confusion and blood and on a transgenic mouse that slips away.

Discussing different orders of the simulacrum in terms of information and code, Baudrillard notes a transition from a productive nineteenth-century symbolic economy to the hyperreality of simulations. Genetic science, depending as it does on biological and digital code, reflects 'the ambiguity of all contemporary science':

> Its discourse is directed at the code, that is, at third-order simulacra, but it still follows second-order 'scientific' schemata such as objectivity, the scientific 'ethic' of knowledge, the truth-principle and the transcendence of science, and so on.
>
> (Baudrillard 1993a: 84)

Working, it seems, according to modern notions of science, like Marcus in *White Teeth*, information and code point in a new direction. The combination of genetic research and ever more efficient technological systems engenders a hitherto unimaginable transformative power associated with a 'post-disciplinary rationality'. Nature, biology and organisms are no longer subject to random, gradual change but become objects of wholesale transformation: 'the object to be known – the human genome – will be known in such a way that it can be *changed*' (Rabinow 1992: 236). Knowledge and power are conjoined, modern distinctions are confounded and erased, as techno-science moves to a theory/practice which means that 'nature will be ˙known and remade through technique and will finally become artificial, just as culture becomes natural' (Rabinow 1992: 242). Simulation, through information and code, identifies the point at which all distinctions and oppositions are rewritten and supplanted:

> When *episteme* and *techne* are seen as intertwined (thus rejecting the Greek logocentric legacy), the time-honoured dichotomies between

theory and practice, discovery and intervention, and observer and phenomenon are blurred. Technology and theory generate each other; epistemic things become technical things and vice versa, as Hans-Jörg Rheinberger has shown.

(Kay 2000: 36)

Techno-science thus introduces a new level of mastery, one in which natural accidents and the desire for apocalyptic certainties shadowing modernity, as Haraway suggests, find themselves elided (Haraway 1997: 10). Technological capacities, beyond culture and nature, deliver a new 'genomic biopower' that 'promises new levels of control over life through the pristine metalevel of information: through control of the word, or the DNA sequence' (Kay 2000: 327). This is, indeed, a new order of things, a different stage, as suggested in the novel's accounts of genetics: the struggle to eliminate the random has, it seems, moved into an entirely new phase.

In *White Teeth*, a short scene encapsulates the move from chance and human indecision, associated with the accidents of nature and culture, to another order. Pressed, significantly by Magid, to make a decision about meeting his twin, Archie, predictably enough, resorts to a toss of a coin. It spins through the air to land, not on one side or the other, but directly in the slot of a gambling machine: 'what are the chances of that, eh?' (Smith 2000: 457). The machine lights up as the coin falls in its slot, indecision and chance suddenly given over to a mechanised apparatus of randomness, a game of simulations, chance no longer playing out in either a human or natural arena. Who decides when even the polarised options of chance are taken away? An Other, a neutral space? At the end of the novel, nothing, it seems, is left to chance. The room – a 'new British room' – where FutureMouse is to be presented to the world offers a new kind of space, one familiar and adequate to the presentation of the little rodent celebrity. The presentation venue is the 'same room', a 'final space', a 'corporate place', locus of a 'clean slate': it is 'a virtual place where their business (be that rebranding, lingerie or rebranding lingerie) can be done in an emptiness' (Smith 2000: 517). Vacuous, hollow, its design is carefully colour-co-ordinated, its atmosphere market-researched: 'renamed, rebranded, the answer to every questionnaire nothing nothing space please just space nothing please nothing space' (Smith 2000: 519). Unpunctuated, the void-room of rebranding, empty forms, tick-box spaces, is also a projective blankness, 'just like TV': familiar, a space to be filled, a recognisable void, the presentational hole of the new world order, evacuating everything before it while leaving everything simulated, a consumer-friendly, predictable, programmable, saleable sameness. Desire and difference have been emptied out, in order that they can be returned without blood, chance, uncertainty, a managed vacuity fully assimilated and homogenised according to the imperatives of a mediatised, marketised, corporate order of simulation. It is a space where migration and diaspora meet the blank homogenisation of corporate existence, multiculturalism and multinationalism indistinguishable in the rebranding and neutralisation of difference.

The 'Exhibition Room' is where culture meets corporations, identities meet the delicatessen, difference served up on the platter of the same, consumption, control, communications, excellence, filling the void they repeatedly empty out. If such a void cannot quite yet be filled, as Marcus notes, by the techniques of a science still lagging behind the fictions and fantasies of a culture in the throes of change (though FutureMouse scurries in that direction), other forms of engineering have already got the process underway. In the novel, there are plenty of signs of its emergence across the commodified cultural and social datascape. In O'Connell's, Abdul-Mickey has a 'new bible': '*Food for Thought: A Guideline for Employers and Employees Working in the Food Service Industry – Customer Strategy and Consumer Relations*' (Smith 2000: 184). At Glenard Oak secondary school, 'this was the age of the league table' (300). Consumption and education are redefined in the same manuals, guidelines, audits, reviews, consumer charters, all operating according to the same performative imperatives and placing all judgements and activities on the same tabulated forms (Lyotard 1994; Readings 1993). These forms, the voids of so many questionnaires, operate in the same fashion as the 'Exhibition Room': empty, evacuated spaces where all taints of history have been obliterated-simulated, places of ruination and clearings for the (no/new/neu)future, they become blanks where things can be created anew, neutral, neutered sites of recreation, imagination, projection, presentation and identification. Marcus, of course, didn't just make things, make money or sell things, 'he created beings' (Smith 2000: 311). The room, an exhibition–presentation–projection space serves as a fantasy screen, like the television set it resembles for Archie and Millat. The latter, 'unfazed', about to act, has seen it all before on TV (Smith 2000: 526). He's worn it and played it out on the street, had its simulations on his bedroom walls, its images on his video cassettes. Half Muslim, half Hollywood gangster, Millat is torn, his very identity opened to the global signs, images and brands that have made him. For Irie, the clear space of re-imaging and rebranding occurs in another context: 'she *wanted* to merge with the Chalfens, to be of one flesh; separated from the chaotic, random flesh of her own family and transgenically fused with another. A unique animal. A new breed' (Smith 2000: 342). In the decade of the wannabe, what does she want, really, really want . . .? Desire and identification flatten her future on an imagined screen that, in its simulation-revelation, overcomes origins and accidents; her projections fall on the unreal, cloned, fantastic Chalfens, a race apart, beings disconnected from the socius which made them, familiar aliens extrapolated on a curiously hyper-liberal, hyper-middle-class, hyper-English plane: OncoEnglish™. FutureClass©.

I used to be you . . . then I evolved

'What do you get when materialism meets the underclass meets technology?' There is no punchline to York's summary question of the 1980s: the absence of supposed trickle-downs of wealth led to new class divisions, paranoid security consciousness and 'imagined dystopias' like those of *Blade Runner* (York and Jennings 1995: 171). Where the style revolution in property and interior decor still fuels the demand for urban living loft apartments, designer eating and seating, other leftovers of the 1980s also linger in the calls for incessant renovation and innovation. To renovate requires the ruin and supercession of old arrangements; to innovate demands the creation of new technologies and commodities. The ruins of future dystopias, imagined in the 1980s, are ruins to be remade, replicated, according to new corporate imperatives: 'more human than human' is the slogan of the Tyrrell corporation. Social, cultural and bodily spaces are readily refashioned. With their 'good genes', the Chalfens are replicants, their 'purity' a mark of being 'more English than the English' (Smith 2000: 328). 'Clones of each other', narcissistically designed creations of 'mirrored perfection', their sameness played out on a plane of simulation–repetition–exhaustion: for them 'the boredom was *palpable*' (Smith 2000: 313). More English than English, more human than human, the repetition signals a logic of replication; it throws them into the world of consumer simulations, a world of heritage repackaging in which the familiar past is remade elsewhere in the pattern of *England, England*: the 'original' nation has its most recognisable and marketable features extrapolated in a theme-park nation that becomes, of course, more real than the original, better than the real thing. The latter, in its turn, turns into a retrograde backwater (Barnes 1998).

The 'new British room' from which FutureMouse escapes and the world into which it leaps are samespaces that have already been reconditioned from familiar modern fragments and remodelled in tune with a corporate, techno-scientific post-humanism. Divested of material and natural anchors by biotechnological innovation, humanity can become mobile: the Chalfens are 'unblocked by history, *free*'; Irie anticipates 'a time, not far from now, when roots won't matter any more' (Smith 2000: 319, 527). Mobile, disembodied, immaterial and replicable also means saleable: 'when bodies are constituted as information, they can be not only sold but fundamentally reconstituted in response to market pressures' (Hayles 1999: 42). This is what happens when biology, information technology and corporate capitalism combine: 'the species becomes the brand name' (Haraway 1997: 12).

Haraway's account of the emergence of the 'New World Order, Inc' identifies a turn away from the transuranic elements of Cold War nuclear stand-off, embracing instead the possibilities of transgenic relations in 'transnational enterprise culture' (1997: 52–3). Patenting, branding, research and development, the loosening of state controls and opening up of commercial incentives throw life on the mercy of the market. While different social relations, based on something other than blood, kinship and family may be made possible by biotechnology, the pressure brought to bear by the 'corporatization of biology' presses in a more homogenising direction (1997: 93). Haraway's examples of life in the new world order include OncoMouse™, a creation of DuPont NEN Products that is simultaneously a system for cancer research, a living animal (raising issues of rights) and a commodity to be marketed. Questions of race, human and ethnic, are paramount. Another example of the new world order, for Haraway, is a 1993 cover image of *Time* magazine entitled 'The New Face of America'. Composed of morphed database images of several representative racial types, the face depicts the alignment of biotechnology and consumerism. Haraway finds the 'utter homogenization' quite 'numbing'.

Writing of the various images used in the morphing programme, all, of course, baring bright white teeth, Haraway comments: 'these figures of the new humanity look like I imagine a catalog of replicants for sale off-world in *Blade Runner* might look – young, beautiful, talented, diverse, and programmed to fulfil the buyers wishes and then self-destruct' (Smith 2000: 264). Sanitised, assimilated, the future has landed on the present. In multicultural and racial terms, such a future present finds other exemplary image-created beings who begin to turn race from a struggle against historical 'pain' into a 'recipe for being' (Smith 2000: 264). It becomes something like a fashion accessory, incarnated, Haraway notes, in the 'morphing practices' of Michael Jackson (Smith 2000: 261). A mouse, a pop star, the same, same screen of celebrity creation and consumption. For Baudrillard, Jackson is more than a 'solitary mutant': he is 'a precursor of a hybridization that is perfect because it is universal – the race to end all races' (Baudrillard 1993b: 21). A veritable last man. For every FutureMichael™ there will be a FutureMickey™: given that 'The New World Order is a Disneyish order', 'there is no real reason why Disney should not buy up the human genome . . . to turn it into a genetic attraction' (Baudrillard 2002: 151–2).

'Thriiii-ller!' sang Millat, in the politically correct school music class (Smith 2000: 156). A smug look is the genetically designed FutureMouse's only comment as it slips away at the end of the novel. A cartoon moment. Stumbling over the novel's modern retrospections to move forwards to the new, new millennium, *White Teeth*'s 1990s register that 'pluralization' and its 'fragmented effective and concerted opposition' have been, as transnationalism replaces state authority, superseded by an 'incessant desire for the new integral consumer capitalism' (Waugh 1995: 213). Consumption, however, is not only fully mediated, a thoroughly televisual affair, it has also become transgenic. Magid, Millat, Marcus . . . Mickey Mouse, Michael, McDonald's. Mmmm!

References

Amis, Martin (1985) *Money*, London: Penguin.
—— (1990) *London Fields*, London: Penguin.
Barnes, Julian (1990) *A History of the World in 10½ Chapters*, London: Picador.
—— (1998) *England, England*, London: Jonathan Cape.
Baudrillard, Jean (1993a) *Symbolic Exchange and Death*, trans. Iain Hamilton Grant, London: Sage.
—— (1993b) *The Transparency of Evil*, trans. James Benedict, London: Verso.
—— (1994) *The Illusion of the End*, trans. Chris Turner, London: Polity Press.
—— (2002) *Screened Out*, trans. Chris Turner, London and New York: Verso.
Burchill, Julie (1990) *Ambition*, London: Corgi.
Christensen, Jerome (1994) 'The Romantic Movement at the End of History', *Critical Inquiry* 20: 452–76.
Freud, Sigmund (1984) *On Metapsychology*, Harmondsworth: Penguin.
Fukuyama, Francis (1992) *The End of History and The Last Man*, London: Penguin.
—— (1995) *Trust*, London: Penguin.
Goux, Jean-Joseph (1990) 'General economics and postmodern capitalism', *Yale French Studies* 78: 206–24.
Haraway, Donna J. (1997) *Modest_Witness@Second_Millennium. FemaleMan©_Meets _OncoMouse™*, London and New York: Routledge.
Hayles, N. Katherine (1999) *How We Became Posthuman*, Chicago, Ill.: University of Chicago Press.
Hobsbawm, Eric (1994) *The Age of Extremes*, London: Penguin.
Kay, Lily E. (2000) *Who Wrote the Book of Life? A history of the genetic code*, Stanford, Calif.: Stanford University Press.
Klein, Naomi (2000) *No Logo*, London: Flamingo.
Lacan, Jacques (1992) *The Ethics of Psychoanalysis 1959–60*, trans. Dennis Porter, London: Routledge.
Lewis, Michael J. (1991) *The Money Culture*, London: Hodder & Stoughton.
Lieberman, Rhonda (1993) 'Shopping Disorders', in Brian Massumi (ed.) *The Politics of Everyday Fear*, Minneapolis, Minn.: Univiersity of Minnesota Press, pp. 245–65.
Lyotard, Jean-François (1984) *The Postmodern Condition*, trans. Geoff Bennington and Brian Massumi, Manchester: Manchester University Press.
Rabinow, Paul (1992) 'Artificiality and enlightenment: from sociobiology to biosociality', in Jonathan Crary and Sanford Kwinter (eds) *Incorporations*, New York: Zone, pp. 234–52.

Readings, Bill (1993) 'For a heteronomous cultural politics: the university, culture and the state', *Oxford Literary Review* 15: 163–99.

Rushdie, Salman (1983) *Shame*, London: Jonathan Cape.

Smith, Zadie (2001) *White Teeth*, London: Penguin.

Swift, Graham (1984) *Waterland*, London: Pan.

Waugh, Pat (1995) *Harvest of the Sixties*, Oxford: Oxford University Press.

Wilson, Scott (2004) 'The Joy of Things', in Ivan Callus and Stefan Herbrechter (eds) *Post-Theory, Culture, Criticism*, Amsterdam and New York: Rodopi, pp. 167–88.

York, Peter and Charles Jennings (1995) *Peter York's Eighties*, London: BBC Books.

Žižek, Slavoj (1993) *Tarrying with the Negative*, Durham, NC: Duke University Press.

2 'Refugees from time'

History, death and the flight from reality in contemporary writing

Andrzej Gąsiorek

In 1990, at the cusp of the last decade of the second millennium, the journal *New Literary History* put together a special issue on recent developments in theories of history. The emphasis in most of the ensuing essays typically fell on the so-called 'linguistic turn' that allied contemporary historiography with postmodern scepticism. The irrecoverability of the past and the lack of isomorphism between any possible accounts of it and the experience of the events themselves produced what Michael S. Roth described as the shared view 'that History has been undone' (Roth 1989/ 90: 242). This alleged 'undoing' had implications not simply for the discipline as a scholarly enterprise but for all teleological conceptions of process and development, as Roth's use of the capital made clear. And while some worried that the briefly topical New Historicism (arguably a by-product of a new end-of-millennium Decadence) was complicit with a retrogressive formalism characterized by 'subtle denials of history' (Porter 1989/90: 253), others, most notably the neo-conservative Francis Fukuyama, made the preposterous post-Hegelian claim that history itself had effectively been completed and had now come to an end by way of the triumph of free-market capitalism and Western liberal democracy.[1] In his acute analysis of various related *post-histoire* theses, Lutz Niethammer considers post-history to be 'a symptomatic sensibility' rather than 'a developed theory' (Niethammer 1992: 138), and he rightly describes its shared features as cultural pessimism, loss of belief in the existence or viability of any collective subject as a possible motor of history, recognition of multiple forms of life (pluralism), and emphasis on the individual's sense of powerlessness in the face of social institutions and processes (a prevalent theme in New Historicist writing). For Niethammer, the 'postmodern modernity' we inhabit is marked by a reflexivity that has nonetheless dispersed the various hopes previously associated with a nascent modernity, with the result that a temporal stasis is attributed to social existence, seen now as 'a mortal life lived without any seriousness or struggle, in the regulated boredom of a perpetual reproduction of modernity on a world scale. The problematic of posthistory is not the end of the world but the end of meaning' (Niethammer 1992: 3).

A striking feature of some of the most interesting writing in Britain over the past decade is that it has refused to accede to these often simplistic and almost always defeatist conclusions. Some writers (J. G. Ballard is probably the best example) have taken absence of belief in emancipatory social schemes (impossible to project onto a blank future) and loss of faith in the possibility of meaningful communal life as points of departure for explorations of the alienated personal life in a depthless, dehistoricized present. But others (Andrew O'Hagan, Rachel Lichtenstein, Iain Sinclair, and the German writer W. G. Sebald, to name but a few) have sought to grasp the ongoing pressure on the present (as influence, as legacy, above all as trauma) of a historical past that continues to shape the private and public life. Ballard's recent work in novels such as *Cocaine Nights* (1997), *Super-Cannes* (2001), and *Millennium People* (2003) treats all ideas of the future as a horizon of expectation towards which the present might strive as a long-abandoned fantasy; his characters exist in a terminal present drained of time, a dead zone destroyed by a globalized, technology-driven system that pulls everything into the tyrannic embrace of the ever-same now. In contrast, the writing of O'Hagan in *The Missing* (1995) and *Our Fathers* (2000), Lichtenstein and Sinclair in *Rodinsky's Room* (2000), and Sebald in *The Emigrants* (1997), *The Rings of Saturn* (1998), and the extraordinary *Austerlitz* (2001) witnesses to a tragic past in which appalling events have far-reaching consequences in the present. In Ballard's writing the past offers neither any principle of continuity between then and now nor any values in relation to which individuals can locate or define themselves, with the result that the temporal dimension is etiolated in his fictional worlds, to be superseded by an overriding concern with the category of space. Marc Augé's observation that concern with space has recently assumed importance because loss of belief in teleological conceptions of human life make it difficult to treat time as 'a principle of intelligibility, let alone a principle of identity' (Augé 1995: 25) indicates where the pressure point lies, but it is precisely against the seeming inexorableness of such conclusions that the other writers mentioned here are reacting. Sebald, referring to the 'in some respects genuinely admirable reconstruction' of Germany after the Second World War, describes its 'creation of a new, faceless reality' as 'a reconstruction tantamount to a second liquidation in successive phases of the nation's own past history' (Sebald 2003: 7), a liquidation that his entire oeuvre attempts to resist, while Sinclair, assessing Lichtenstein's quest for Rodinsky, views her passion for filling the gaps of an unfinished life as motivated by a desire 'to complete whatever it was that Rodinsky had begun: to pass beyond ego, and all the dusty particulars of place and time, into a parallel state' (Lichtenstein and Sinclair 2000: 4).

Andrew O'Hagan's novel *Our Fathers* offers a useful point of departure here because it so thoughtfully captures the dissonance between a disappointed, patricidal present and an over-optimistic, utopian past, while insisting that the latter cannot simply be obliterated. Obliteration features prominently in this text since it focuses in detail on Glasgow's 1960s slum-clearance programme, which aimed to rebuild the city almost from scratch by putting up numerous affordable tower blocks; the narrator's grandfather (Hugh) is depicted as a major proponent of this creation ex nihilo, while thirty years later the narrator himself (Jamie) is busy pulling down the poorly built and unsafe high-rises that had been erected with laudable socialist aspirations in mind. Hugh's uncompromising stand represents one form of disavowal: the past associated with exploitative landlords, crippling rents and appalling housing conditions is seen as irredeemably corrupt and thus to be destroyed before a new, more equitable, future can be put in its place. But Jamie's equally intransigent revolt against this aspiration is another form of disavowal, since it in turn bulldozes not just the buildings his grandfather has put up but also the ideals that underpinned them. The latter's return journey to Scotland and Glasgow to be with his grandfather at his deathbed is then an act of filiation of sorts. It signals a willingness (after a long refusal) to confront the legacy of a deeply troubled familial and national history, which, it transpires, can no more be evaded or obliterated than the problem of social justice can be solved by starting from a mythical ground zero.

The missing link in *Our Fathers* – a classical narrative of oedipal revolt – is the father, that violent, grief-loving and alcohol-suffused stand-in for the nation's most destructive inner tendencies. In this narrative, oedipal rage is baked in the blood and then passed on down the generations. The father's hatred of his father (Jamie's grandfather) is not only a refusal of political idealism but also a failure to come to terms with social change, to accept the burdens of domestic responsibilities and to acknowledge his own weaknesses. His turning away from self, family and nation ultimately manifests itself as a longing to escape temporality itself, a theme that also permeates Sebald's work: 'Robert didn't want to be young – he wanted to be past everything. He wanted to live out of time' (O'Hagan 2000: 10). Robert's desire to evade time reflects a radical self-hatred, a division at the core of his being, which originates in repeated historical treacheries and aligns him with nationalism's perennially disappointed hopes. In a Scotland perceived as 'lashed, betrayed, forgotten', a profoundly destructive melancholia sets in: 'Our fathers were made for grief. They were broken-backed. They were sick at heart, weak in the bones. All they wanted was the peace of defeat. They couldn't live in this world. They couldn't stand who they were'

(O'Hagan 2000: 8). Filiation is blocked in this scenario, offering the son the two possible paths of repetition or rejection, each of which is damaging in a different way: the first continues to play out, without in any way working through, a traumatized response to familial-national history, while the second attempts to bypass that history altogether, in blind ignorance of the ways in which it inevitably exerts pressure on the present.

In tracing the family's history the novel subtly works its way through various revisions. The grandfather's overweening idealism is both subjected to critique and sympathetically presented as a valuable attempt, at a specific point in the time of a particular society, to remake it anew, so that Hugh's tower blocks come to resemble 'great catacombs of effort' that 'stand for how others had wanted to live, for the future they saw, and for hopes now abandoned' (O'Hagan 2000: 68). The father emerges from his angry destructiveness to acknowledge his inability to live up to Hugh's dreams for him. And the son, accepting his dependence on the example of his grandfather, grasps that their shared disease was the demand that the world answer to them and recognizes that a fantasy of plenitude lay behind this utopian dream: 'We couldn't complete the world or ourselves. We could only live, and look for small graces, and learn to accept the munificence of change' (O'Hagan 2000: 146). But what this also means is that the chastening of experience that enables the narrator to accept finitude and incompleteness demands in turn a rapprochement with the history that has hitherto been rejected, even if that history can never fully be assimilated or known. Reflecting on Hugh's life, Jamie concludes that it belongs to a history in which he is inescapably embroiled: 'We were all lost in the past he cared for. And I'll always say it: being lost in his time made my own time clearer. I wanted my own day, but not at the expense of every day that preceded my own' (O'Hagan 2000: 221).

Hugh's passing away in *Our Fathers* is described in bleakly naturalistic terms as 'the geology of death asserting itself' (O'Hagan 2000: 232). The preceding narrative has insisted that continuities between present and past must be established if the lineaments of contemporary social life are to be understood, but the finality of death calls the validity of this project into question. Hugh is reduced to a 'skinful of animal fibres' (O'Hagan 2000: 232) before his identity is finally dissolved into nothingness. Death is in *Our Fathers* offered as a brute datum, but in Jim Crace's *Being Dead* it is elevated to the principle of a metaphysic. Everything in this text is considered in terms of the human organism's corporeality and its inevitable disintegration. That we are within a post-religious frame of reference is made clear at the beginning of the novel, when the brutal murder of the two central protagonists – Joseph and Celice – leads to reflection on different practices of mourning. A hundred or so years ago these deaths would have been commemorated by a quivering in which reminiscence and recollection would have recreated their lives in an attempt to rescue them from the exigencies of time. Quiverings, however, took place in 'optimistic times' when 'death was an ill-lit corridor with all its greater rooms beyond' (Crace 2000: 3), whereas ours 'are hardly optimistic or sentimental times', and for these characters there is 'nothing after death . . . but "death and nothing after" '(Crace 2000: 4). But if death closes all horizons, the lives that precede it can be retold from the end back to the beginning; the narrative in which these murdered protagonists exist can run against the tyranny and eventual closure of clock-time, thereby once again reaffirming the dreams and aspirations that have been curtailed so sharply. If the supernatural frame of reference belongs to a form of life that no longer compels assent then a resurrection of sorts may be achieved by means of a different kind of quivering – that of fictional narrative. It is within and through the category of the aesthetic, in short, not that of theology, that these lives may be redeemed, and in keeping with this shift the direction of the narrative must run backwards from death to life rather than forwards from the dissolution of corporeality to any possible existence beyond it:

> It might be fitting, even kind, to first encounter them like this, out on the coast, traduced, spreadeagled and absurd, as they conclude their lives, when they are at their ugliest, and then regress, reclaiming them from death. To start their journey as they disembark, but then to take them back where they have travelled from, is to produce a version of eternity. First light, at last, for Joseph and Celice. A dawning death. And all their lives ahead of them.
>
> (Crace 2000: 4–5)

This strategy asserts the value-conferring power of art as perhaps the sole means by way of which an otherwise pointless existence (which is programmed for death from the outset) can be given any meaning at all. And while the undoubted beauty of Crace's limpid prose (the pleasure of the text) goes some way to making good on this claim, his uncompromising insistence that life is little more than an over-long prelude to decay and nullity tends to undermine it. In spite of the text's resurrection of Celice and Joseph, this narrative act, like the wider aesthetic of which it is a small part, is implicitly presented as a form of escapism from unpalatable truths: 'It's only those who glimpse the awful, endless corridor of death, too gross to contemplate, that need to lose themselves in love or art' (Crace 2000: 37). The paradox at the heart of *Being Dead* is that the novel doesn't just contemplate this grossness but revels in it, while at the same time it tries to recover its protagonists from that grossness by tracing their lives back from their deaths. There is little local detail here, and even less cultural texture. Celice and Joseph, perhaps fittingly for two zoologists, are seen less in relation to human history or social life than to natural history and the life cycle of the biological organism. Thus we are simply told that: 'The plain and unforgiving facts were these. Celice and Joseph were soft fruit. They lived in tender bodies. They were vulnerable. They did not have the power not to die. They were, we are, all flesh, and then we are all meat' (Crace 2000: 12). And this narratorial statement merely confirms what Celice – professor of zoology – has always taught, namely that preachers and scientists alike 'want to give life meaning only because it clearly has none, other than to replicate and decompose' (Crace 2000: 40).

If aesthetic pleasure, despite being tainted by the charge of escapism, offers one possible response to this bleak truth in *Being Dead* then love, for all its fragility, offers another. The novel seeks to redeem Celice and Joseph from death by depicting their bodies as a *tableau vivant*: 'For while his hand was touching her, curved round her shin, the couple seemed to have achieved that peace the world denies, a period of grace, defying even murder. Anyone who found them there, so wickedly disfigured, would nevertheless be bound to see that something of their love had survived the death of cells' (Crace 2000: 12). It is hard to know how to read this, given the text's earlier rejection of sentimentalism and its insistence elsewhere that nothing survives of human life forms, except the memories they bequeath to others and the artefacts they leave behind. The love invoked here inevitably struggles to withstand the logic of this position. Joseph's touching fingers, which reach across to his dead wife in a final act of conciliation, hint at the lover's desire to propitiate the beloved – to atone for love's disappointments – but all that can survive the smashed bodies lying lifeless on the sand is the gesture itself. Moreover, the love described here, as the novel goes on to show, has hardly been inspiring and, as in O'Hagan's *Our Fathers*, it has occasioned a generational conflict, which leaves the rebellious daughter in self-imposed exile from her parents' lives. For her, salvation from the stifling restrictiveness of their impoverished emotional existence lies not in love but in a vitalist philosophy that celebrates the hard, gem-like flame of an all too short existence. Thus she asserts in modern idiom the values urged a hundred years earlier by Strether to Little Bilham in Gloriani's garden:

> The world's small, breathing denizens, its quaking congregations and its stargazers, were fools to sacrifice the flaring briefness of their lives in hopes of paradise or fears of hell. No one transcends. There is no future and no past. There is no remedy for death – or birth – except to hug the spaces in between. Live loud. Live wide. Live tall.
>
> (Crace 2000: 171)[2]

O'Hagan's *Our Fathers* and Crace's *Being Dead* confront the inescapable fact of death by refusing to blink in the face of the destruction of the physical organism and the dissolution of the conscious identity. In *Our Fathers* this terminus offers those who still live the opportunity to reappraise their commitments in relation to a shared, if always problematic, history, and this in turn enables them to move beyond the reactive language of revolt. *Being Dead*, less concerned with a wider social and historical context, focuses primarily on the human entity as a form of biological matter and depicts generational conflict as the supercession of one way of life by another that thinks of itself as more robust, while all the time the novel celebrates the emotional depths and passionate obsessions of lives that are nonetheless deemed to be pointless. In short, the absence of some overarching telos in terms of which a human life might be conceived as an unfolding project forces the attention onto its finitude and its corporeality, while denying significance to any possible guiding metanarrative. But another way of looking at this predicament – in which the future has no meaning except as the extension of a blank present – is to focus on the exorbitation of the present under the sign of excess, and this is precisely what one finds in Ballard's work.[3] For Ballard, the loss of the future as a horizon towards which one looks in the hope that present-day aspirations may be fulfilled there has transformed the here-and-now into a succession of meaningless events; hence his claim that we have 'annexed the future into the present, as merely one of those manifold alternatives open to us', a situation in which 'we live in an almost infantile world where any demand, any possibility, whether for life-styles, travel, sexual roles and identities, can be satisfied instantly' (Ballard 1995: 4).

A socio-cultural milieu in which choice is perceived as an unassailable right and the gratification of desires is promoted as an indisputable good, while scant attention is paid to how the rhetoric of choice is bound up with free-market ideologies and economics, may indeed be described as infantile. Ballard has long been interested in tracing the ways in which an increasingly technologized society shapes and controls human subjectivities, but what is of particular interest in his recent work is that he focuses so intently on the colonization of daily life by systems that progressively erode the possibility of human agency. Human beings are, in novels such as *Cocaine Nights*, *Super-Cannes* and *Millennium People*, systematically subordinated to the urban and technological environments that dwarf them. In this version of postmodernity as terminal zone, time ceases to have meaning and the future is construed solely in terms of a further domination of space: more road networks, business parks, retirement pueblos, shopping malls. Thus in *Millennium People* an advancing estate (symbol of unstoppable urban sprawl) is described as 'the future moving towards you' (Ballard 2003: 133), while the pristine corporate estate of *Super-Cannes* is 'a huge experiment in how to hothouse the future' (Ballard 2001: 15). Alienation and anomie are the most striking features of what passes for communal life in these texts, and the characters who play out puppet-like lives in exurban environments are synthetic products of the culture that has manufactured them as its most typical exemplars. As the temporal dimension is gradually hollowed out in these texts, to be replaced by a preoccupation with the ways in which space determines identity, the novelist's attention once again falls on the problem of subjectivity in a world no longer able to conceive an alternative to an interminable, unchanging and self-regulating present. Politics, a character blithely remarks in *Cocaine Nights*, 'is over . . . it doesn't touch the public imagination any longer' (Ballard 1997: 245).

Ballard's exploration of this version of post-history construes the subject as either a machinic entity or an untrammelled id. In the first variant the cross-breeding of bodies and machines is foregrounded, the human organism being regarded as a programmable bio-robot, a prosthetic entity, a piece of hard-wired technology. Identity is depicted as a functional mechanism that can be engineered, plugged in, coded. Seen as a conduit or a point in a circuit, the subject is no longer in any sense a self-authoring agent, thus the notion that a life may be granted meaning by being situated within a narrative (as, say, *Our Fathers* and *Being Dead* in different ways suggest) is called into question. For what might it mean to construct any such narrative when it has always already been written? Ballard's late novels suggest that meaningful agency (understood as the capacity for autonomous thought and action) is scarcely possible when a technocratic bureaucracy arrogates to itself the functions previously allotted to citizens who once participated in social life. Thus the corporate estate in *Super-Cannes* represents a neo-fascistic fantasy of the perfectible system:

> An invisible infrastructure took the place of traditional civic virtues . . . The top-drawer professionals no longer needed to devote a moment's thought to each other . . . There were no town councils or magistrates' courts, no citizens' advice bureaux. Civility and polity were designed into Eden-Olympia.
>
> (Ballard 2001: 38)

Designed according to a view of humans as automata, the world view hard-wired into the estate sees individuals as monads whose relationships with others are entirely instrumental and holds that civic responsibilities are best handled by computer systems and managerial elites. As *Super-Cannes* has it: 'We're breeding a new race of deracinated people, internal exiles without human ties but with enormous power. It's this new class that runs our planet' (Ballard 2001: 256).

When the human being is conceived as a cybernetic organism which exists in a depersonalized space characterized by affectless relationships, then resistance to this reductiveness may take the form of a return of the repressed, in which authenticity of being is identified with the unleashing of desire. A counterblast to the notion of the machinic subject (all circuits and interfaces), this id-driven atavism asserts the value of drives, instincts and emotions. In *Cocaine Nights, Super-Cannes* and *Millennium People* powerful enchanter-figures attempt to break down the social restraints that are supposedly constraining the texts' central protagonists in order to liberate them from repression. Criminality, violence and psychopathology are defended not only as the paths along which a truth of self may be discovered, but also as the sole means of resisting a streamlined and controlling polity. The rhetoric of transgression is offered here as the jargon of authenticity. This rhetoric, which draws on romantic-expressivist philosophies, equates psychic health with 'deviant' behaviour, and of course in an administered and seemingly meaningless world celebrations of the instinctual self are bound to carry a good deal of weight. As Charles Taylor suggests, 'the moral energy and excitement attending the naturalist rejection of religion and traditional ethics comes from this sense of empowerment, of releasing nature and desire from a stultifying thraldom, releasing them to a fuller affirmation' (Taylor 1992: 343). An unillusioned view of human nature, as Nietzsche never tired of insisting, is the basis of this perspective: the untrammelled subject, impelled by its drives and instincts, expresses its truth through the free enactment of desire.[4]

In both *Cocaine Nights* and *Super-Cannes* transgressive acts are small-scale events; they function as little homeopathic doses delivered to the social organism for its greater good. But in *Millennium People* a far deeper revolt is in play. It is not an overly administered and eventless society that is the target here but rather an absurd and indifferent universe. This is a metaphysical revolt whose roots lie in nihilist and existentialist modes of thought, which is articulated in the form of a millenarian gospel of dread: 'Sadly, life is worth nothing . . . The gods have died, and we distrust our dreams. We emerge from the void, stare back at it for a short while, and then rejoin the void . . . the universe has nothing to say. There's only silence, so we have to speak' (Ballard 2003: 261).[5] In this novel transgression takes the form of a terrorism whose pointlessness represents an attempt to outbid the meaninglessness of the contingent universe, while at the same time (in a real *reductio ad absurdum* of expressivist thought) its violence proclaims 'a fierce authenticity that no reasoned behaviour could match' (Ballard 2003: 182). On this view, terror becomes the source of a negative sublime through which arbitrary violence comes to represent 'an empty space larger than the universe around it' (Ballard 2003: 176), and the individuals enthralled by this destructive grandeur rage against a world from which meaning has been expunged. This is less Nietzsche's philosophical realm beyond good and evil and more Freud's account of the id as that which 'knows no judgements of value: no good and evil, no morality' (Freud 1975: 107). Terror refuses all moral obligations, all social restraints; its acts of blind destructiveness proclaim an unceasing revolt against humanity itself. If 'meaningless violence may be the true poetry of the new millennium' and 'only gratuitous madness can define who we are' (Ballard 2001: 262), as one of Ballard's protagonist's speculates, then we must surely read this credo as a desperate response to the machining of subjectivity, the final act in a drama that can only end with an irrationalist negation of the symbolic realm.

A marked feature of Ballard's explorations of identity is the extent to which he depicts characters as actors inhabiting prescripted personalities, as ciphers going through the motions of life. There is a disconcerting sense of distance from the affects in his novels, a dissociation of sensibility in which characters observe themselves emoting even as they recognize that they are not really inhabiting their feelings. Identity is always precarious in Ballard's work, always one step away from being exposed as a complete sham. And its flimsiness is systematically related to the simulated nature of contemporary social existence, wherein the visual media are decisive presences in most people's lives. In texts such as *Cocaine Nights*, *Super-Cannes* and *Millennium People*, all of which are preoccupied with contemporary visual culture, the issue at stake is less the 'influence' of the mass media and more the decisive role they have played in transforming people's ways of perceiving reality and of understanding themselves. In these novels it is not just that identity appears to be little more than a mediated phantasm, a scripted role in an imaginary (cinematic? televisual?) spectacle, but that characters willingly enter into the spectacle precisely because they cannot conceive of an existence lived outside its validating norms. It is the camera alone that can provide the sense of reality required for identity to sustain itself. As *Cocaine Nights* has it: 'There's a kind of amnesia at work here – an amnesia of self. People literally forget who they are. The camera lens needs to be their memory' (Ballard 1997: 262).

Andrew O'Hagan offers a very similar reading of the determining role played by the visual media in contemporary culture in his 'Afterword' to *The Missing* (1995), his powerful account of abduction and murder in postwar Britain. O'Hagan emphasizes the ubiquity of surveillance and the obsession with celebrity in his reading of the present. Drily observing that in this media-saturated society people mistake 'the process of watching for the machinery of thinking' (O'Hagan 1995: 248), he suggests that we are witnessing profound changes in our conceptions of selfhood and identity, the emptiness of celebrity being lapped up in bizarre fashion as 'an enlargement of our own mentalities' (O'Hagan 1995: 260). Thus for O'Hagan: 'Reality, so far as TV and the tabloids are concerned, is the slow, watchable business of people being themselves becoming famous. When they stop being famous they also stop being themselves: they have no self. Game over' (O'Hagan 1995: 261). What is interesting here is that O'Hagan links the relentless presentism of this version of reality (nothing exists beyond *this* moment, *this* immediate performance of self) with a disconnection from the past, as though only the here-and-now could have any possible meaning or validity. This is the amnesia of self described in *Cocaine Nights*, where the emptying out of time manifests itself in thralldom to satellite TV, a retreat from public space and a disconnection from the historical past. *Millennium People*'s alienated protagonists, in turn, choose to inhabit 'zones without meaning' in which 'there's no past and no future', precisely because they are 'in flight from the real' (Ballard 2003: 133).

Given this persistent association of televisual culture with the hollowing out of identity, it is worth pausing over the completely different response to the still photograph in the work of W. G. Sebald and Rachel Lichtenstein. For what is at stake in the contrast between responses to the simulations of the moving image and the otherworldliness of the sepia-tinted picture is an entirely different practice of thinking, which is orientated to the legacy of the past in a profoundly reflective way, and which seeks to combat the amnesia identified by Ballard and O'Hagan by tracing the skeins of history. In *The Emigrants* the narrator's discovery of a photograph album of his mother's, in which he finds family portraits from the Weimar period, prompts in him 'a growing need to learn more about the lives of the people in them' (Sebald 1997: 71), while Lichtenstein in *Rodinsky's Room* responds to her grandfather's death by rescuing his suitcase 'full of old clock parts, certificates, photographs', which she pores over 'for hours' in the realization that 'with him was buried the key to [her] heritage' (Lichtenstein and Sinclair 2000: 19). The obvious remoteness and the plangent unknowability of these mementoes from a bygone age seem to compel their possessors to engage with the vanished reality they so precariously betoken. The work of both these writers is thus motivated by an ongoing sense of a debt to the past, not simply because it continues to press upon and shape their lives in the present but because it has a significance (as burden and legacy) that must be attested. In marked contrast to the affectless amnesia prevalent in a culture that remorselessly promotes the value of contemporaneity, there is here a commitment to remembrance and memorialization, as well as a passion for identifying complex historical causalities. As *The Emigrants* phrases it: 'And so they are ever returning to us, the dead' (Sebald 1997: 23). Aware that all accounts of the dead (whether in the form of fiction, memoir or history) are always reconstructions, Sebald and Lichtenstein are nonetheless moved by what Paul Ricoeur describes as 'the vow to do justice to the past' (Ricoeur 1984: 26), a vow that for Ricoeur, as for Lichtenstein and Sebald, 'must not lead us to give more value to the verbal power invested in our redescriptions than to the *incitements* to redescription that come from the past itself' (Ricoeur 1984: 34).[6] *Austerlitz*'s way of passing on a knowledge that makes extraordinary unexpected connections embodies this imperative, in that it becomes 'a gradual approach to a kind of historical metaphysic, bringing remembered events back to life' (Sebald 2001: 14).

Sebald's writing returns again and again to the shattering of identity brought about by the experience of historical trauma, principally that of the Holocaust, and by the sense of impotence it engendered in those who were not interned and murdered in concentration camps but whose lives could not escape the evil unleashed by the Second World War. The desolation of identity among survivors is a recurrent theme in Sebald's work, which in *The Emigrants* and *Austerlitz* is inextricably bound up with the inability even to *think* the horrific events of the recent past, an inability that extends to his own writing project: 'I am well aware that my unsystematic notes do not do justice to the complexity of the subject, but I think that even in their incomplete form they cast some light on the way in which memory (individual, collective and cultural) deals with experiences exceeding what is tolerable' (Sebald 2003: 79). In *The Emigrants* and *Austerlitz* the intolerability of experience leads to complete withdrawal from the world, the consummation of the self by inner desolation, radically split identity, internal exile. Unable to confront dreadful experiences and memories, the self becomes evanescent and unreal; thus Sebald writes of Bereyter's sense that 'with every beat of the pulse, one lost more and more of one's qualities, became less comprehensible to oneself, increasingly abstract' (Sebald 1997: 56).[7] In the case of Ambros Adelwarth, a man 'filled with some appalling grief' (Sebald 1997: 111), this inner desolation culminates in the 'longing for an extinction as total and irreversible as possible of his capacity to think and remember' (Sebald 1997: 114), while Austerlitz's lifelong inability to confront the memory of his pre-refugee life in Prague leaves him feeling 'as if [he] had no place in reality, as if [he] were not there at all' (Sebald 2001: 261).

But reality of sorts, however tarnished or broken-backed, is granted to these figures, as it is to David Rodinsky, through these texts' acts of witness and testimony. Rachel Lichtenstein's quest for Rodinsky takes on a symbolic significance, and her narrative becomes a form of *kaddish* for the unnumbered victims of anti-Semitism. Like the 'caretaker communities' she encounters in Poland, those who 'have chosen to remain, guarding the decaying remains of their heritage' (Lichtenstein and Sinclair 2000: 228), her text participates in a process of remembrance that refuses to break the bonds of the past. This process will always be partial and always motivated by present-day concerns and needs. Casting its shadow over Lichtenstein's and Sebald's work is Proust's *A la recherche du temps perdu*, with its insistence on the impossibility of re-experiencing the past except in memory. It is because Marcel recognizes that the desire for a return to the past is inseparable from fantasy, and that his attempts to recreate childhood experiences in adult life will never reproduce them in anything other than a radically altered form, that the book is so saturated with the imagery of dreams – the source of its melancholia. Marcel's awareness that he is 'not situated somewhere outside Time, but [is] subject to its laws' (Proust 1989: 520) attests the lag in time between experience and memory, which Slavoj Žižek sees as constitutive of the self in time: since 'temporality *as such* is sustained by the gap between apprehension and comprehension: a being able to close this gap . . . would be a noumenal *archetypus intellectus* no longer constrained by the limitations of temporality' (Žižek 2000: 43). The gap is irreducible, unbridgeable. But the tension between recognition of this fact and the desire to resist its brute intransigence produces haunting elegies to a past always at the edge of being forgotten. This writing has no patience with those who fly from the troubling reality of history, but the conflict between lucid testimony and nostalgic longing continues to mark it.[8] For Sebald, the 'ideal of truth inherent in its entirely unpretentious objectivity . . . proves itself the only legitimate reason for continuing to produce literature in the face of total destruction' (Sebald 2003: 53), yet nagging away at this laudable goal is the equally potent desire of an end to exile, a redemptive homecoming, a return to an idealized past that is to remain as it was remembered in childhood fantasy, and this dream is most poignantly expressed by Austerlitz's hope 'that time will not pass away, has not passed away, that I can turn back and go behind it, and there I shall find everything as it once was' (Sebald 2001: 144).[9]

Notes

1 See Fukuyama's *The End of History and the Last Man* (1992); for a critical discussion, see Burns (1994), *Francis Fukuyama and his Critics*.
2 Thus Strether:

> All the same don't forget that you're young – blessedly young; be glad of it on the contrary and live up to it. Live all you can; it's a mistake not to. It doesn't so much matter what you do in particular, so long as you have your life. If you haven't had that what *have you* had?
>
> (Henry James, *The Ambassadors*, pp. 139–40)

> There are, of course, Paterian echoes both here and in *Being Dead*. See Pater 1990: 152.

3 See, for example, Marc Augé's suggestion in *Non-Places* that what he calls *supermodernity* is characterized above all by the principle of excess.

4 Thus Nietzsche, in *Beyond Good and Evil*, asserted that beneath all the mistaken theories of human psychology 'the terrible basic text *homo natura* must again be discerned' and his assumption of the task 'to translate man back into nature' (Nietzsche 1990: 162).

5 Compare the similar sentiments of *Being Dead*: 'She was too young to need the death-defying trick of living in a godless and expanding universe, its gravity dispersing by the second, its spaces stretching and unspannable, its matter darkening. Life is. It goes. It does not count' (Crace 2000: 170).

6 See also Dominick LaCapra's valuable injunction that because 'the documentary record is itself always textually processed before any given historian comes to it' historians 'are confronted with phenomena that pose resistances to their shaping imagination and that present complex problems for their attempt to interpret and reconstruct the past' (LaCapra 1985: 35). For Sebald's preoccupation with such questions, see *The Emigrants* (1997: 29, 230), as well as 'Air war and literature: Zürich lectures', the opening essay in *On the Natural History of Destruction* (2003); for Lichtenstein, see Lichtenstein and Sinclair 2000: 240, 242, and 323–4.

7 The allusion to Robert Musil's *Der Mann Ohne Eigenschaften* indicates that this loss of self is inseparable from a corresponding inability to connect with, or situate oneself in relation to, reality itself: 'And since the possession of qualities assumes a certain pleasure in their reality, we can see how a man who cannot summon up a sense of reality even in relation to himself may suddenly, one day, come to see himself as a man without qualities' (Musil 1997: 13).

8 See, for example, Lichtenstein's description of a crass 'art performance' in which prayer books and synagogue records are ripped up and strewn upon the floor of a nightclub (Lichtenstein and Sinclair 2000: 37–40), or Sebald's anxiety about 'the mental impoverishment and lack of memory that marked the Germans' (Sebald 1997: 225).

9 The bleak corrective to this hope is provided by Sebald's account of his own homecoming, and his recognition that his memories ignored the devastating historical events then taking place. See Sebald 2003: 71–2.

References

Augé, M. (1995) *Non-Places: introduction to an anthropology of supermodernity*, trans. John Howe, London: Verso.

Ballard, J. G. (1995) *Crash*, London: Vintage.

—— (1997) *Cocaine Nights*, London: Flamingo.

—— (2001) *Super-Cannes*, London: Flamingo.

—— (2003) *Millennium People*, London: Flamingo.

Burns, T. (ed.) (1994) *Francis Fukuyama and His Critics*, London: Littlefield Adams.

Crace, J. (2000) *Being Dead*, Harmondsworth: Penguin.

Freud, Sigmund (1975) *New Introductory Lectures on Psychoanalysis*, trans. J. Strachey, Harmondsworth: Penguin.

Fukuyama, F. (1992) *The End of History and the Last Man*, London: Hamish Hamilton.

James, H. (1979) *The Ambassadors*, Harmondsworth: Penguin.

LaCapra D. (1985) *History and Criticism*, Ithaca, NY and London: Cornell University Press.

Lichtenstein, R. and I. Sinclair (2000) *Rodinsky's Room*, London: Granta.

Musil, R. (1997) *The Man Without Qualities*, trans. Sophie Wilkins and Burton Pike, London: Picador.

Niethammer, L. (in collaboration with D. Van Laak) (1992) *Post-histoire: has History come to an end?*, trans. P. Camiller, London: Verso.

Nietzsche, F. (1990) *Beyond Good and Evil*, trans. R. J. Hollingdale, Harmondsworth: Penguin.

O'Hagan, A. (1995) *The Missing*, London: Faber & Faber.

—— (2000) *Our Fathers*, London: Faber & Faber.

Pater, W. (1990) *The Renaissance: studies in art and poetry*, ed. Adam Phillips, Oxford: Oxford University Press.

Porter, C. (1989/90) 'History and literature: "after the New Historicism" ', *New Literary History* 21: 253–72.

Proust, M. (1989) *Remembrance of Things Past* (Vol. I), trans. C. K. Scott Moncrieff and Terence Kilmartin, Harmondsworth: Penguin.

Reck-Malleczewen, F. (2000) *Diary of a Man in Despair*, trans. Paul Rubens, London: Duckbacks.

Ricoeur, P. (1984) *The Reality of the Historical Past*, Milwaukee, Wisc.: Marquette University Press.

Roth, M. M. (1989/90) 'Introduction', *New Literary History* 21: 239–51.

Sebald, W. G. (1997) *The Emigrants*, trans. Michael Hulse, London: Harvill.

—— (1998) *The Rings of Saturn*, trans. Michael Hulse, London: Harvill.

—— (2001) *Austerlitz*, trans. Anthea Bell, London: Hamish Hamilton.

—— (2003) *On the Natural History of Destruction*, trans. Anthea Bell, London: Hamish Hamilton.

Taylor, C. (1992) *Sources of the Self: the making of the modern identity*, Cambridge: Cambridge University Press.

Žižek, S. (2000) *The Ticklish Subject: the absent centre of political ontology*, London: Verso.

3   Science and fiction in the 1990s

Patricia Waugh

In the year 2000, the Human Genome Sequencing Consortium completed its report, describing the genetic composition of the species *Homo sapiens*. Rather like the relation of a fictional character to those real people who have passed through its author's life, the human genome was a composite extrapolated from information obtained from fifteen different members of the species. The scientists seemed to have intensified their labours in the last year of the century, submitting the completed book of life – comprising some three billion entries – well ahead of schedule, to coincide with the global festivities marking the human entry into the new millennium. Journalists could not resist the apocalyptic appeal. Even the *Observer*, a respectable broadsheet not normally enamoured of the sensationalist subheading, carried a banner across its front page on 11 February 2001: 'Revealed: the secret of human behaviour'. Furthermore, and demonstrating just how far Western democracy had moved on from the elite science and shrouded mysteries of Bacon's laboratories in that first scientific utopia, *The New Atlantis* [1627], the very next edition of *Prospect* magazine offered unfettered access to this blueprint of all human life. Piled neatly on the newsagents' racks, alongside the bulky shrink-wrapped classical-music glossies, the heavy-metal magazines and the PC guides with their complimentary disks, every copy of *Prospect* also carried a free CD-ROM. This was a disk carrying the recipe for the human species. Like the voices of the long-dead divas and the up-and-coming rock starlets, the 'code of life' had now been digitally remastered and made available at the click of a mouse. Incapable of resisting the symbolism, I bought it. After a century that had witnessed the worst intra-species violence, tribal bloodshed, and political conflict in its entire history, maybe this latest scientific grammar of creation might spell out who we are and what are our purposes on this earth. Surveying the disk in its shiny plastic wallet and trying hard to resist the millennial hype, I thought about those famous words of Charles Darwin which had provided the conclusion to *The Origin of Species* some 150 years previously:

> In the distant future I see open fields for far more important researches.
> Psychology will be based on a new foundation, that of the necessary
> acquirement of each mental power and capacity by gradation. Light
> will be thrown on the origin of man and history.
>
> (Darwin 1996: 394)

I rushed eagerly home, under the darkening sky of the winter afternoon, to
play my disk.

The disk seemed the perfect symbol for the year 2000. For here was the
entire string of three billion letters, arranged in the various combinations
and repetitions with difference of the four-letter alphabet, proclaimed as
the recipe for creating a human being. It seemed somehow appropriate too
that the recipe might only be accessed through a CD-ROM, for it was the
mathematician Alan Turing, at Bletchley Park in 1943, who first insisted
that numbers could compute numbers so that a computer, Colossus, could
then be built to break another code and crack open the encoding machines
of the Nazis. At exactly the same time, in 1943, and only a few hundred
miles away, in Dublin, a Nazi refugee, Erwin Schrödinger, was delivering a
series of lectures entitled, 'What is Life?', proposing that chromosomes
carry some kind of code-script containing the message that is the secret of
life. Even before Crick and Watson's momentous discovery of the code of
DNA, reported in *Nature* in 1953 as a writing that carries the genetical
information, the combined insights of Turing and Schrödinger had already
made possible the understanding of life as a kind of stored digital programme. As one more versed in literary than scientific theory, however, I
couldn't help also remembering that 1953 was the year that the French
literary theorist Roland Barthes published his *Writing Degree Zero*, a critical
text that similarly called for a new materiality of writing and that would also
lead to a concerted assault on notions of design, intentionality, authorship
and selfhood. By the year 2000, therefore, scientific assertions that might
have produced appalled responses from humanists thirty years or so earlier,
seemed in a curious sense seamlessly continuous with the world-picture
being assembled in much contemporary literary and cultural theory. Matt
Ridley's definition of 'life' in *Genome*, for example, also written in 2000,
might have stepped out of a postmodernist textbook: 'anything that can use
the resources of the world to get copies of itself made is alive; the most
likely form for such a thing to take is a digital message – a number, a script
or a word' (Ridley 2000: 15). The idea that the human self is written
was hardly news to anyone who had spent the past twenty-five years in the
literary academy. The notion that writing, or the digital, is more fundamental than carbon, or the cellular, took equal possession of both the
humanities and the sciences in the 1990s. If life is no longer 'stuff' but rather

'bytes and bytes of information', to quote Richard Dawkins, then digital information on a computer disk might indeed be life: 'what lies at the heart of every living being is not fire, not a warm breath, not a spark of life. It is information, words, instruction' (Dawkins 1986: 112). Yet as I sat before my computer screen staring with mild disappointment at the incomprehensible runs of variations on C A G T, the syntax of life, it was difficult trying to imagine how anyone might extract from this library of Mendel anything remotely resembling a semantics of the human self. If the textualism of the postmodernists seemed to evacuate the warm breath of the living body, then the digital information refigured by the scientists seemed even further removed from the Promethean fire.

However, the discovery and then 'breaking' of the code of DNA in the 1950s had certainly introduced a new wave of interest in evolutionary biology, intensifying throughout the 1990s in the lead-up to the completion of the genome report at the end of the decade. For in spite of my bewilderment as I stared at the alphabet soup on my computer screen, scientists such as E. O. Wilson, Stephen Pinker and Matt Ridley had indeed, throughout the decade, taken Darwinism out into politics, ethics and questions of human behaviour, with a steady flow of popular books which mixed respectable science with scientistic speculation. Given the oracular nature of the claims, it is hardly surprising that such books had been the publishing sensation of the past fifteen years, nor that they were written and authorised by an expanding universe of distinguished research scientists gifted with the narrative verve of a P. D. James or the stylistic virtuosity of a Martin Amis. Looking at the buoyant sales figures and their rhetorical styles of presentation, it often seemed as though these books constituted a new middle-brow fiction, vying not so much with other kinds of reference book, but with popular novels such as *Jurassic Park* and *The Day of the Triffids*. Writers such as Richard Dawkins, Stephen Jay Gould, Daniel Dennett, Steven Pinker and E. O. Wilson, for example, producing books with metaphorically resonant titles such as *Life's Grandeur, The Language of the Genes, The Selfish Gene, The Blind Watchmaker* and *The Blank Slate*, have served, rather like Nellie Dean in *Wuthering Heights*, as conduits, simultaneously, for both the domestication of science and, at times, its over-expansion and sensationalisation. And yet the scientific community could not dismiss these books. Dawkins' *The Selfish Gene* was probably the most scientifically influential interpretation of evolution since *The Origin of Species* and, although a best-seller, it was also required reading for every first-year university student of biology. In 1995, the literary agent for many of these writers, John Brockman, published his own book entitled *The Third Culture*. The title deliberately appropriated a term first used by F. R. Leavis, in the context of his own 'two cultures' debate with C. P. Snow in the 1960s, to refer to his ideal of a collaborative-creative literary criticism. Such a criticism would bridge the liberal divide between public and private, so that literary studies might become a discipline which genuinely mediates between the strictly 'objective' and the merely 'subjective' in the service of a communitarian and shared practice of knowledge, informed by a secure sense of cultural value. Brockman, however, begins his book by dismissing the claims of literary studies and declaring that the new intellectuals are the scientists. For an education in Freud, Marx and modernism is now defunct, and the reactionary and useless knowledge peddled by literary intellectuals is simply the 'marginal disputes of a quarrelsome mandarin class chiefly characterised by comments on comments, the swelling spiral of commentary eventually reaching the point where the real world gets lost' (Brockman 1995: 17). Scientists are now not only busy making the world a better place, but even democratising access to that knowledge, encouraging public debate through popularisation and responsible science journalism.

For scientists in the 1980s and 1990s had begun to write like novelists, spinning fascinating stories, creating mysterious characters and manipulating point of view so that readers could feel transplanted into strange new worlds. Hard-line ultra-Darwinists such as Richard Dawkins became adepts at narratological compositions that played on what would seem to be a deeply ingrained human tendency to project its own creaturely attributes onto both animals and non-organic life (for why else would we enjoy novels, become engrossed in computer simulations, weep at Disney movies or be amazed at the antics of selfish genes or the cleverness and con-artistry of extended phenotypes?). His immensely influential reorientation of Darwinism, so that natural selection becomes a process operating at the level of the gene rather than that of the individual or group, is brilliantly effected in his book *The Selfish Gene* (Dawkins 1976) simply through the control of point of view. Like any novelist, Dawkins has understood that the readerly experience of inhabiting a single point of view for an entire fiction achieves two important effects: one is to produce sympathy for the character whose perspective is so represented (like Jane Eyre or Holden Caulfield, for example), and the other is that unless there is a change of perspective, the reader usually comes to conflate that particular epistemological perspective with the ontological totality of the world of the fiction. Through point of view, Dawkins will persuade the lay reader of the vacuity of readings of natural selection which emphasise cooperative group-level activities, or of those which provide alternative perspectives to his ultra-adaptationism (such as Gould's suggestion that although natural selection might constitute the main driving force of evolution, many of its by-products persist as autonomous entities with no relevance to the evolutionary imperative). It seems no coincidence that the book appeared during the high point of the Thatcher years. Dawkins' gene, positioned like a Jamesian ficelle, intelligent but unknowing, is caught up in a Hobbesian world of atomistic and competing entities, none of which is able to grasp the entire plot. Like the view provided by James's free indirect discourse however, the perspective of Dawkins' gene is conveniently both limited and omniscient, for the gene carries the code of DNA, and, both architect and architext of the plot, fashions algorithmically out of the unnameable, the primary soup of chaos, the entire order of nature. We might think that we are intentional agents of our own destinies. But just as culture writes the self in much of the literary theory of the 1990s, so in the biological sciences, DNA catches chance on the wing and palimpsestically builds the script for that lumbering robot which will facilitate its own replication in a fantasy of mechanical autogenesis and anamnesis, to build ever more replicating machines, organisms who are, precisely, 'bytes and bytes of information'. In an appendix to Dawkins' book, *The Extended Phenotype* (1999), Daniel Dennett praises the logic of Dawkins' thinking and its relevance for 'others in the social sciences and even in the physical sciences and in the arts' and notes his brilliantly creative demonstration of the genome as consisting of 'mechanisms of breathtaking deviousness and ingenuity – not just molecular copyists, and proofreading editors, but outlaws and vigilantes to combat them, chaperones and escape artists and protection rackets and addicts and other devious nanoagents, out of whose robotic conflicts and projects emerge the marvels of visible nature' (Dawkins 1999: 266). Dawkins' picture of the self as endlessly written, reprogrammable, downloadable, deferred, reiterated and decentred, a virtual body emancipated from its organic counterpart begins to sound uncannily like the 'subject' of much contemporary theory, but further enhanced with the substantial characteristics, plot function and unique point of view of a character in a fast-paced novel.

Science in the 1990s therefore quickly came to seem even sexier than in the 1980s, even if the latter was the decade of the Big Bang, of theoretical physics and of chaos, catastrophe, indeterminacy, fractals, and all that non-linearity talk which served as both the (Procrustean) bed and the source of (fore- ?) play for the postmodern imagination. For, as J. B. Haldane once observed in the 1920s (the crucial decade for biology which created the 'modern synthesis' of Mendelian genetics and Darwin's theory of natural selection), if physics is a heresy, then biology is a perversion (Haldane 1921). Biology is knowledge turned the wrong way, the forbidden knowledge that will inevitably break the so-called modern settlement of Baconian science which had promised axiomatically to separate questions of means, whose answers are written in the book of Nature, from those questions of ends and purposes, whose answers are to be found only in the book of God. Those working in the biological sciences, attuned to the new market in popular-science publication, were not slow to recognise the seductive lure of a perfect circle, this 'perversion' shining out of the latest utopia of mathematised knowledge. For if science could reveal 'the secret of human behaviour' then it would not only account for the body but also for the emergence of mind out of the algorithmic drive of natural selection. For as well as being the decade of the body, the 1990s were dubbed the 'decade of the brain' by none other than the President of the United States. For, in claiming to describe consciousness, science might thereby achieve the ultimate condition of closure where that unique instrument of knowledge, the human mind, turns in on and arrives at an account of itself, thus closing the gap between third- and first-person accounts of knowledge and experience. A scientific explanation of mind would destroy forever the assumption that consciousness is ontologically subjective and therefore outside the remit of an objective and scientific third-person account. If the mind is the brain and emerges out of body, then mind is equally a product of evolution and, far from representing a 'blank slate' or even the Kantian transcendental categories, mind too has been hard-wired by the evolutionary process. If science could now account for mind within the terms of a strictly causal materialism, then it would appear that science is also able to break out of incompleteness and arrive at a final theoretical closure which includes in its account of the material universe an account of itself. The very undecidability borrowed from Godel, teased out in Russell's set-theory paradoxes, and placed at the heart of postmodernism as the centrepiece of its refutation of positivism, would be overcome.

Biology in the 1990s therefore takes the kind of creationist turn familiar in theoretical physics of the 1980s. Matt Ridley's *Genome*, subtitled 'the autobiography of a species', opened with a bare-faced parody of Genesis which replaces the all-creating Logos with the auto-poetics of the gene which will eventually shape chaos into the script for mind. Indeed, scientists had come to regard themselves as approaching the last frontiers of knowledge, empowered to give an account of beginnings and ends whilst continuing to insist that the methods of positivist science are the only avenue to knowledge of the world. Physics had already, in the 1980s, begun to indulge in expansionist and epic vocabularies, grand narratives with titles such as GUT (grand unified theory) and TOE (theory of everything) reflecting Pythagorean dreams of describing the entire universe, including the mind which describes, in the terms of a mathematical intelligibility encompassing matter, force, space and time and, for Steven Hawking at least, the mind of God. In the 1990s, however, the biological sciences displaced physics as the visible cornerstone of this evolutionary epic, this grandest of narratives, partly because the mathematisation of biology and the emergence of biochemistry and molecular biology facilitated their inclusion within the reductionist paradigm where all 'true' sciences can be analytically broken down to the fundamental level of physics and mathematics. Not content with claiming authority within the terms of positivist reduction, biologists such as E. O. Wilson began, in the 1990s, a campaign for a new 'consilience' (the title of his book of 1998), where an expansionist science would build from the certain ground of mathematics to claim:

> People need a sacred narrative. They must have a sense of larger pur-
> pose, in one form or other, however intellectualised. . . . If the sacred
> narrative cannot be in the form of a religious cosmology, it will be
> taken from the material history of the universe and the human species.
>
> (Wilson 1998: 295)

In other words, Wilson is calling for an end to the modern settlement which had rested positivist science upon the axiomatic separation of facts and values; now science will not only provide secure knowledge in an age of postmodern epistemological doubt, it will draw upon that knowledge to provide a foundation for values and purposes, the traditional demesne of the humanities in the post-Enlightenment world.

Not surprisingly, therefore, whereas the novel in the 1980s had reflected the more pervasive cultural preoccupation with physical theories of the universe, novels of the 1990s most certainly show a marked orientation towards and engagement with the biological sciences. As A. S. Byatt has suggested, 'the stories we tell ourselves take form from the large para-digmatic narratives we inhabit' (Byatt 2000: 65). Novelists engaging with Darwinian ideas in the decade included Ian McEwan, Doris Lessing, A. S. Byatt, Graham Swift, Penelope Fitzgerald, Fay Weldon, Jim Crace and Jeanette Winterson. The decade began with the publication of a savage interrogation of the relation between the biological sciences and ethics in Amis's *Time's Arrow* (1991) and ended with the writing of David Lodge's pedagogic comic novel of (partial) consilience, *Thinks . . .* (2002). Indeed, for some reviewers the infatuation with science had gone too far. In a review of Ian McEwan's *Enduring Love* (1997), Cressida Connolly complained that

> You can't pick up a novel these days without being bombarded
> by Heisenberg's Uncertainty Principle, or the latest theories on Dar-
> winism. Popular science now occupies ample shelf-room in every book-
> shop and a prominent place in best-seller lists. Novelists should tell us
> stories, not recite particle physics.
>
> (Connolly 1997)

The review then goes on to suggest that McEwan is guilty not only of casting his line into overfished waters, but also of drowning his individuality in a sea of science rather than stories. 'He gives us a world', Connolly suggests, in which 'logical positivism rules', and she goes on to call for an 'immediate, worldwide moratorium on novelists reading works of science. Like oceans plundered of whales, science books have become overfished by voracious, imaginative writers' (Connolly 1997). Connolly reveals not only her own literary prejudices, however, but also a rather disturbing ignorance about debates within contemporary science, where an expansionist naturalism has more threateningly displaced most vestiges of logical positivism. Consequently, she thoroughly fails to appreciate both McEwan's artistry, his own knowledge of current scientific debate, and his moral seriousness in writing the novel. She compares the work unfavourably with Thornton Wilder's novella *The Bridge of San Luis Rey*, another fiction that begins with a human tragedy involving a dramatic fall. McEwan is praised for the vivid quality of his opening scene, breathtaking in its audacity, where a hot-air-balloon accident pierces the sleepiness of a spring morning in an English village and brings together two random passers-by whose lives will then be changed forever by the chance encounter. The opening incident propels the mood and pace of the novel out of bucolic charm and into the tense plottedness of a psychological thriller, for one of these characters, Jed, a religious maniac, becomes obsessionally fixated on the other, Joe, whose preoccupation with truth is bound up with a mid-life crisis about the inauthenticity of his occupation as a popular-science writer, and the scientific career that he failed to pursue. Joe's correspondent fascination with Jed therefore as a rare scientific 'case' (a sufferer from De Clerambault's Syndrome), leaves the reader uncertain about the final location of the psychological obsession. It is this uncertainty which seems to bother Connolly, and McEwan is compared unfavourably with Wilder as an author who abandons events to contingency, whereas Wilder's plot is read as a theodicy where the opening disaster is finally revealed as part of a divine plan. McEwan is condemned as the advocate of a world in which logical positivism rules, and Connolly's hidden assumption seems to be that fictional plots had better be consolatory and redemptive as if that were the main function of fictional stories. But the theme of McEwan's novel, if carefully read, is the potentially dangerous effects of the human desire for premature closure, the desire to read into nature redemptive plots and, in the absence of a theology, the human tendency to look to secular explanatory systems like science for such consolation. Throughout, Joe's attempts to describe with scientific precision the course of events and the nature of Jed's malady, are counterpointed with the perspective of his partner, Clarissa, a literature teacher writing a critical work on John Keats. The intellectual momentum of the novel is in the play between Joe's evident defensive rationalisations and resort to science as a means of avoiding his own complex emotions, Clarissa's fallible but more openly emotional and humanistic interpretation of events and Joe's paranoid take on things which functions as a kind of parody of a teleological and divine omniscience and omnipotence. For the designer of this universe is equally and self-consciously fallible, equally struggling to reconcile humanistic, scientific and divine accounts of ends and origins, in an attempt to understand the nature of human love from religious, evolutionary, Romantic, pathological and medical and literary perspectives. What Connolly entirely fails to appreciate is that McEwan *ironically* dramatises the paradox of a fortunate fall (the balloon incident) that will test and finally prove the love of his protagonists. Moreover, Joe and Clarissa have had to come to terms with their inability to reproduce, so that their love, like Jed's for Joe, is entirely at odds with the ultra-adaptationist explanations of human behaviour that are eventually recognised by Joe at the end of the novel as supplying only a limited perspective. The more sombre vein of an 'enduring love', love as not only joy but also an acceptance of the burden of responsibility toward the other, takes the place of Romantic innocence after the newfound and tentative understanding gleaned through the tragic turn of events. In the process, McEwan certainly tries to demonstrate ways in which scientific knowledge can enhance human understanding and, indeed, was subsequently quoted in another headline banner running across the review section of the *Guardian* newspaper on 9 June 2001, to the effect that 'literature and science, two distinct forms of investigation, are natural allies in the exhilarating quest to understand the human condition'. But *Enduring Love* suggests that they will not become allies until both recognise the limits of their own and each other's mode of understanding, and both also see the dangers of imperialism and overreaching. The sceptical rationalism of science is a counterforce to dangerous dogma, but science may also become dangerous dogma in its own right if it is regarded as a system of natural law sanctioning and guiding human ends and purposes. Science cannot obviate the need for complex human judgement and personal immersion in the messiness and contingency of circumstances and relationships.

For as science has crept increasingly onto the public agenda, the earlier metafictional energies of the novel in the 1970s have been revived and turned inwards again towards an interrogation of the relative epistemological status and value of the understanding of life, the 'stories', offered by scientists, on the one hand, and humanistic understanding on the other. Two important perspectives, in particular, emerge from McEwan's novel: one is that he presents an alternative picture of human consciousness which is not incompatible either with that of the traditional humanities or with some of the scientific alternatives to the ultra-adaptationist position that has become the popular image of evolutionary theory; secondly, he presents a picture of human existence which demonstrates the final inadequacy of any reductionist evolutionary account but without therefore capitulating to the postmodern evacuation of knowledge and judgement. Joe's attempts, from the beginning, to position every event in relation to some shibboleth of the grand narrative of current ultra-Darwinism, is undone again and again by McEwan's plot. But McEwan also cleverly shows how Joe looks to science in every instance as a means of avoiding his own emotional promptings. Within the first few pages of the novel, for example, he is seen to invoke the Hamiltonian equation (the argument against altruism which was the mathematical justification for Dawkins' selfish-gene theory), in an attempt to justify his own failure of heroism and to displace his mounting sense of guilt over the death of the character Joseph who continued to hold onto the wayward balloon in an attempt to save the child within. McEwan sees that to invoke the third-person perspective of science, as positivists such as Russell or Wells had so often insisted, might be a means of escape from solipsistic blindness, but it might equally function as a means of disavowing personal responsibility or displacing the difficulty of judgement with a fatalistic or deterministic perspective. Again and again, McEwan's novel suggests the need to sustain a Popperian perspective on the world, an attitude of sceptical reason and rigorous testing of any hypothesis, but he also demonstrates the ease with which science may degenerate into scientism. Science requires the same kind of rigorous scepticism turned on itself that it turns on everything else. As Joe slowly learns to integrate feeling and logic in order to cope with his circumstances, he discovers human reason as a mode of practical wisdom, that functioning of consciousness that has, presumably, always played an important role in the evolutionary survival of the species. Towards the end of the novel, as he crouches in the undergrowth observing the roundworms and giants of the underworld, it comes to him that humans are part of this natural dependency, that we are, to use the philosopher Alasdair MacIntyre's phrase, 'rational dependent animals', and he reflects that although 'some people find their long perspectives in the stars and galaxies; I prefer the earthbound scale of the biological'. Immediately after, however, he reveals that he has abandoned the comforts of ultra-Darwinism. As 'rational' dependent creatures, we are no longer simply 'in the great chain. It was our own complexity that had expelled us from the Garden. We were in a mess of our own making' (McEwan 1998: 206). McEwan's novel brilliantly alerts the reader to the scientism of ultra-Darwinism, the way in which intentionality is evacuated in order to maintain the third-person perspective; the way in which scientism may only be resisted if we exercise our judgement and insist on our moral freedom to choose. On the other hand, he also shows how evolutionary theory can temper a complacent liberalism which all too easily invokes the positivist separation of facts and values, and the Kantian separation of reason and feeling and knowledge and natural necessity, to insist on a freedom from biological constraints and imperatives which finally arrives at the subjective plasticity and emptiness of the postmodern.

For McEwan, like other novelists of the 1990s who engage with science, is writing in a tradition of British fiction that has always sought to subject scientific claims of epistemological exclusivity to its own broader conceptualisation of knowledge, reason and understanding. Iris Murdoch's insistence that 'we are men and we are moral agents before we are scientists' is central to her belief that literature is as much a valid form of human knowledge as science, for there can be no knowledge or understanding without moral concepts already shaping what we take a situation to be (McEwan 1998: 207). Interestingly, the work of contemporary neurobiologists such as Antonio Damasio, who have demonstrated the absolute dependency of reason on emotion and the body, appears to uphold Murdoch's conception of the relation between emotion, reason and value. Other writers, either familiar with his work or sympathetic to such a materially grounded but non-reductionist idea of consciousness, are Doris Lessing, A. S. Byatt, Ian McEwan and Martin Amis as well as the erstwhile friend of Murdoch, the philosopher Philippa Foot. Damasio's insistence that emotion is 'integral to the processes of reasoning and decision-making' and his suggestion that self emerges as 'the feeling of a feeling' (both substantiated by his work with brain-damaged patients) appears to give scientific legitimation to the more generous understanding of knowledge in the humanist tradition of the novel (Damasio 2000: 31). Kazuo Ishiguro's novel of 1989, for example, *The Remains of the Day*, although not explicitly 'scientific', is similarly preoccupied with a sense of how adherence to an impoverished model of reason that separates thought from feeling produces moral and spiritual blindness. For Stevens, the butler, has been brought up in an atmosphere of the stiff upper lip. Its nearest philosophical equivalent must either be the Kantian concept of the categorical imperative or the Stoical concept of a Natural Law understood as a model of the rational intelligibility of the order of things which requires the strict extirpation of feeling for its comprehension and execution. Cultivating detachment and rationality in the belief that emotional connection to things or people leaves the self thereby vulnerable to forces beyond instrumental control, Stevens is absolutely dutiful and blindly obedient to his profession of butlering and his Nazi-collaborating master. Only when he recognises, belatedly, his love for Miss Kenton, does he glimpse genuine moral knowledge and recognise his complicity in the inhuman treatment of his father and his collaboration with Fascism. Ishiguro allows the insight to resonate not only as a means of understanding the kind of blind obedience which facilitated the 'banality of evil' which was National Socialism, but also in the context of contemporary managerialism and bureaucratisation, where a scientifically reductionist concept of rationality is allowed to guide the formulation of means as well as ends.

By the 1990s, however, the growing tendency of some scientists to pronounce on areas well beyond their traditional domain produced a self-reflexive questioning in novelists about the nature and value of their own kinds of storytelling. For the question which permeates much of the fiction which engages with science is that posed by Haroun to his father, the storyteller Rashid, in Salman Rushdie's *Haroun and the Sea of Stories*: 'What's the use of stories that aren't even true?' (Rushdie 1991a: 27). The answer to the question is pursued through a fable of the two cultures which involves the gossipy and storytelling land of Gup in its war with the authoritarian and scientific land of Chup, whose sovereign, as in Hobbes's scientistic blueprint of an ideal society, *Leviathan*, has issued a moratorium on fanciful talk and is slowly poisoning the source of the sea of stories. Rushdie uses the parable in order to expose not only the dangerous fancifulness of much contemporary science but also its inauthenticity in insisting on passing off its more speculative claims as absolute truths. Two years earlier, he had written a review of Stephen Hawking in which he notes the general scientific turn towards the grand narrative:

> These days the creation of Creation is primarily the work of scientific, rather than literary or theological, imaginations. It's a hot story, and Professor Hawking's book, *A Brief History of Time*, is only the latest of a string of popularising bestsellers on the subject – fascinating books – full of exclamations.
>
> (Rushdie 1991b: 262)

Pointing out that physicists seem to be victims of their own notion of an anthropic principle in that they have created a universe that begins with the biggest exclamation of them all, Rushdie maintains a perspective of ironic and bemused distance on such claims as, indeed, on the postmodernist infatuation with a liberatory reading of the New Physics. His land of Chup is an explicitly ironic take on what he clearly regards as animistic nonsense: for Rushdie recognises the atavistic tendencies all around him to look to scientific (or any monologic or totalising) accounts of nature in order to sanction and legitimise human values.

Chup is a kind of ghost world, a synthetic mythical realm limned out of all those attempts by theoretical physicists in the previous decade to account for the strange behaviour of matter at the subatomic level. Chup is a quantum world, but instead of promising the kind of liberatory freedom from determinism celebrated in the postmodern version of the New Physics, Chup is a dark and scary world whose saints and good citizens have sewn up their lips; where shadow selves have split from their material bodies and live and act at a distance with independent wills of their own; and where light has disappeared into a permanent black hole into which Haroun and his co-questors are dragged by powerful superstrings. (Anyone who has read any of the popular quantum books of the 1980s will readily pick up the allusions.) Chup is an authoritarian technocracy that has banished stories, but its existence allows Rushdie to explore the answer to Haroun's question. By showing how stories not only keep alive our sense of wonder, but also sharpen our sceptical faculties in a world where much that is pure story is passed off as truth, the tale justifies its own existence and that of all fictional tales. Haroun's question sounds defensive to begin with, for what exactly is the place of the 'pure' story in a world where even W. H. Auden, confronted with a roomful of scientists, professed to feeling like 'a shabby curate who has strayed by mistake into a drawing room full of dukes' (Auden 1963: 81). Rushdie suggests though that stories are a mode of critique and understanding as well as of fantasy and imagination. Fictions, as H. Vaihinger argued at the beginning of the century, are for finding things out, but we need to be conscious of the distinction between a pure fiction and a scientific hypothesis, for example, for as the former is not available for empirical testing, its imposition on the world of history might be only too tragic (Vaihinger 1924).

Yet expansionist science also makes claims that are not open to testing. Moreover, popularisation intensifies this tendency: the desire, for example, to enthral your reader with a tale of the quest for, or the cracking of, the DNA code; or to suggest hugely significant implications for the organisation of human lives or beliefs. But as science grows more theoretical and more unavailable for testing in a laboratory (the origins of the universe or life, for example), so it becomes more dependent on narrative presentation and the use of rhetorical tropes such as metaphors. The enormous market in popular science is partly created as the gap between theory and data grows ever wider and the need for plausible bridging narratives correspondingly more acute. Yet a science that threatens to impinge on human life not merely in the form of technology but also in the shaping of values and public policy, needs to be as vigilant as possible about the status of its evidence and the effects of narrative transmission. Many of the novels mentioned above seem to recognise a new role for fiction in reflecting on the need to discriminate between different kinds of stories. Their interrogation of knowledge claims are often more Socratic than the popular science books of the decade with their infatuation with controlling metaphors which begin life as placeholder terms for ambiguities and mysteries in the scientific data, but often take on a misplaced concreteness of their own. One of the ways in which Rashid's stories are shown, from the beginning, to be useful, is that 'everyone had complete faith in Rashid, because he always admitted that everything he told them was completely untrue and made up out of his own head'. So the politicos, who everyone knows, never tell the truth but never admit that they are telling stories either, 'needed Rashid to help them win the people's votes' (Rushdie 1991a: 20). In an interview with Brian Aldiss in the early 1990s, Doris Lessing insisted that:

> This fantasising and dreaming must have a use of some kind; otherwise we'd have lost it. From the time that we know anything at all about history we were telling stories to each other. Why is the brain organised in this way? And why do we dream? What we're doing when we dream is telling ourselves stories; it's the same pattern.
>
> (Lessing 1996: 171)

Sometimes, though, we need to realise that the story being told to us is some version of the 'noble lie', for in a culture where science has made exclusive claim to knowledge, then scientists are likely to try to play the role of Guardians. Which is why we also need stories that expose the stories that are told to us, by the scientists 'for our own good'. These are the critical stories, the epistemological fictions, which many of our best novelists have been telling in their engagement with science in the 1990s.

What Rushdie detects in contemporary science is a new fundamentalism. Biology seems to be moving imperialistically into the arena of human value, human behaviour and human consciousness, (in other words) the traditional domains of the novel. Several writers, such as Fay Weldon in *The Cloning of Joanna May* (1989), explore ways in which postmodern anxieties about gender and identity can be related to new biotechnologies and their global organisation. Like her earlier novel, *The Life and Loves of a She-Devil* (1983), this novel too plays with the feminist possibilities of the cyborg in defying the nature/nurture split which has functioned within patriarchy to control the minds and bodies of women. Joanna's replicated self functions as a comic version of fashionable postmodern accounts of 'fluidity', but the novel is also a reminder that although the cyborg might function as a useful philosophical conceit, the reality is that biotechnologies such as cloning, genetic modification and engineering, have become essential processes in global capital and in themselves hardly intrinsic instruments of liberation. However, biotechnologies and genetic engineering, though the visible face of science's impact on society, are not the only scientific threat to cultural values. The threat from new 'sciences' such as evolutionary psychology is more subtle and insidious. In the past decade, the postmodernisation of academic literary studies has drawn literary theory into a complicitous relation with the new anti-humanist scriptoral and digital vocabularies of biotechnology. At the same time, the relativism and aestheticisation arising from its insistence on viewing all narratives as 'stories' has rendered it incapable of interrogating knowledge claims or distinguishing truth from fiction in the expanding universe of the new science-writing. Whilst post-modernists continue their infatuation with cyborgs and Uncertainty whilst waging their wars with actual science, novelists have conducted a much more open but also critically engaged dialogue with current debates within the biological sciences. Those writers such as Rushdie and, more recently, Jeanette Winterson in *Gut Symmetries* (1997), who have also drawn on meta-phors from the New Physics, have tended to engage them with more ironic intent. Winterson's novel, for example, explores the imperialistic claims of contemporary physics as akin to those of Renaissance alchemy, but she is also aware of the powerful investment of human desire in the projection of and yearning to believe in a correspondent universe. The nostalgia for the lost narrative is not dead. And the expansion of the biological sciences, and with it a new oracular expansionism in the nature of scientific claims, is one of the major reorientations of intellectual culture between the 1980s and the 1990s. Certainly it changed the nature of relations between scientific and literary cultures. The 1980s saw postmodernism gradually encroaching on the ground of more and more academic disciplines, displacing a cogni-tive model of understanding with an aestheticist one and even appropriat-ing the newest physics in order to subvert physics and realist science as the paradigm for all knowledge. However, the shift towards the biological sciences in the 1990s produced a stream of 'consilience' books by promin-ent scientists which represented clearly imperialistic moves by science, in turn, to appropriate those areas of cultural value, such as questions of human purposes and ends, traditionally reserved for the humanities. In the 1980s, it had seemed for a time as if postmodernism was having it all its own way. The New Physics had not only furnished a useful armoury of epistemological concepts such as Uncertainty, Complementarity and Indeterminism, but further speculation by scientists themselves (Neils Bohr, for example), on free will and liberation from determinism, became meat and drink for postmodernists eager to cut science down to size and at the same time borrow some of its glamour and authority within the modern research academy. With grand narratives safely disposed of, all that was required of postmodernism was to demonstrate how science itself was sim-ply another story or, as Richard Rorty had memorably put it, that 'poems are the same as protons' (Rorty 1991: 83). It became evident, however, by the 1990s that postmodernists had spoken too soon. Not only did theorists such as Lyotard wilfully exaggerate the abandonment of grand narratives, but his insistence that even the 'nostalgia for the lost narrative' had been lost, and the postmodern obsession with some of the more fantastical thought experiments of theoretical physics, woefully blinded them to the grandest of all epic and cosmological narratives being doggedly and collectively built by biologists and disseminated through the popular accounts flooding the bookshops throughout the decade.

For, on the one hand, evolutionary biology seemed to fortify a picture of human nature hard-wired not so much by the Kantian categories, but much more substantially by the genes: so that one could think of genes as 'theories of existence' arrived at over aeons through trial and error and effectively destroying for ever any culturalist assumptions of the human mind as a blank slate. It would not be pushing the analogy too far to see a kind of Aristotelian picture of the species returning where, much like his notion of the Final Cause, each individual, through the genes, potentiates and seeks to fulfil his essence, arriving at what he is, and therefore at the good, in the fulfilment of his purpose. Interpreting the genome, for the evolutionary psychologists at least (and this was one of the fastest growing and most influential interdisciplinary discourses in the 1990s), meant arriving at a much more profound knowledge than hitherto of human needs and proclivities and one which might in the future, therefore, shape the formulation of human rights and the provision of law, welfare and health care. Francis Fukuyama's *The Post-Human*, for example, argued that the insights of the evolutionary biologists would become crucial in strengthening an understanding of human need and therefore human rights in order to resist the displacement of the human by the post-human of biotechnology. Yet, for the literary reader at least, the assumption that because the genes carry our biological legacies, we should therefore shape our social policies in accord with what they seem to tell us, sounds all too like Huxley's poor old savage John who, unable to renounce the old ways or understand the new, the culture that has chosen 'machinery and medicine and happiness', crucifies himself at the end of the novel quoting Shakespeare on human nature to the very end. Presumably few people would want to live in the utopian world of Mustapha Mond, but fewer still would want to live with John in the Savage Reservation (Huxley 1955: 183). Any reader acquainted with *Brave New World* (or, indeed, G. E. Moore's *Principia Ethica* [1903]) might see the flaw in the evolutionary psychologist's arguments: just because we have inherited certain behavioural patterns is hardly an argument for their necessary enhancement and implementation. As T. H. Huxley saw, in his passionate essay 'Evolution and Ethics' of 1892, there are all kinds of behaviours, part of our evolutionary legacy, which we may feel it is better, in the interests of the social good, to moderate, reorient or even repress.

Yet there are important ways, as we have seen in the writing of novelists of the period, in which the softening of the fact/value distinction has had the important effect of expanding ideas of human reason and reclaiming for art a cognitive status even though that knowledge is very different from that of science. The problem of how to come to terms with a scientific realism which builds a picture of nature entirely unable to legislate for or sanction human ends is one which haunts the British novel from the moment that T. H. Huxley published his essay. The problem engages modernists from Hardy, through Conrad, Lawrence and Woolf, and is at the centre of critical debates passed on from I. A. Richards, with his accounts of scientific and emotive language, to F. R. Leavis, with his concern to establish a cognitive aesthetics founded on an idea of the 'tacit' where knowledge is always involved with judgements of value. However, it is also the case that since the Snow–Leavis debate, literary culture has itself divided: literary studies within the academy becoming more professionalised and defensive about its knowledge status. Far from representing an homogenous cultural group (criticism largely conceived as the handmaid to literature), there is now probably more of a stand-off between novelists and academic literary criticism than there is between novelists and contemporary scientists. It is far from unusual to find contemporary novelists writing endorsements for the front covers of popular-science books, but rare to find a literary critic appearing even on a back cover. The two cultures debate in the 1990s has bifurcated. On the one hand, it has become a much more narrowly focused 'turf war' between academic scientists and literary intellectuals that is ultimately about the function and composition of the modern academy and the value and defence of disciplinary boundaries. But, on the other hand, when one moves outside the academy, the debate is more genuinely open and Socratic, less defensive and certainly more temperate in tone. Novelists tend to be much less exclusive and proprietorial about knowledge than academics, though perfectly ready to defend their own particular ground when necessary. One area that has come under recent scrutiny, for example, is that of consciousness. Philosophers such as Thomas Nagel are insistent that science will never manage to describe what it actually feels like to be inside the mind of a bat, though such imaginings are the very lifeblood of the novel. But scientists have been trying to colonise the account of consciousness too. And whereas the creative mind within a Romantic paradigm was famously a repetition in the finite world of the infinite I am, for the contemporary scientist such as Daniel Dennett, writing in 1995, mind is simply a parallel processing machine built out of the algorithms of evolution, 'an impersonal, unreflective, robotic . . . scrap of molecular machinery [which] is the ultimate basis of all agency, and hence meaning, and hence consciousness, in the universe' (Dennett 1995: 203).

Just as the Darwinian account of natural selection could dispense with a Designer, so the neo-Darwinist account of mind can eliminate intention. In this account, authors are no longer required. The similarity between this kind of thinking and that of the literary theorists has not escaped the contemporary novelist.

David Lodge's *Thinks* ... is a meditation on such paradoxes of the contemporary two-cultures debate, conducted through a Romantic plot involving a novelist and creative-writing tutor, Helen Reed, and a cognitive scientist, Ralph Messenger, who is engaged on a project to build an intelligent robot. Much of the narrative is taken up with their ongoing debate on the nature of consciousness and about whether it is possible for a computer to acquire personhood with or without emotions or a human body. Secure in his detached third-person perspective on the world, the somewhat predatory and emotionally arrested Messenger tells Helen, 'you're a machine that's been programmed by culture not to recognise that it's a machine' (Lodge 2002: 101). Helen, a widow recovering from the loss of her husband, and all too humanly an emotional participant in, rather than rational observer of, the world, feels not only personally threatened by Ralph's projective identification, his scientistic reduction of her selfhood to a machine. She recognises the reasons for his investment in this picture of the self: for if a human is a machine, a very complex computer, then computers might become the equivalent of persons; and if material substance ceases to matter, then silicon life might become indistinguishable from carbon life. Then science will have created a person. But she feels professionally threatened too as a writer of fiction and one who also deals in the creation of human simulations: 'I sort of resent the idea of science poking its nose into this business, my business. Hasn't science already appropriated enough of reality? Must it lay claim to the intangible invisible essential self as well?' (Lodge 2002: 62). However, Lodge reintroduces into this novel the postmodernist literary academic Robyn Penrose from his earlier 1980s novel *Nice Work* (1988), to illustrate the point that literary theory has already 'poked its nose in'. Helen listens to a lecture given by Robyn which draws on scientific metaphors to underpin a post-structuralist conceptualisation of the self and notices a

> queer kind of correspondence between what she was saying and what Ralph Messenger says. Both of them deny that the self has any fixed identity, any 'centre'. He says it's a fiction that we make up; she says it is made up for us by culture. It's alarming that there should be so much agreement on this point between the most advanced thinking in the sciences and the humanities.
>
> (Lodge 2002: 225–6)

One can't help feeling that Lodge the novelist and erstwhile literary academic shares his character's alarm and is concerned to distance the novel both from the academic culture of the scientist and that of the contemporary literary critic and defend its place in an ongoing liberal or radical humanist tradition.

In the end of course, it is Lodge's novel at the level of *discours*, rather than the *histoire* it narrates, which effects a kind of rapprochement between the two cultures, although Ralph becomes more empathetically human and Helen somewhat more Stoical and capable of detachment. (She manages to teach him the importance of the first-person voice and she learns from him the usefulness of the third.) For *Thinks* . . . is itself a pedagogic attempt, conducted in Socratic fashion, to educate the lay reader into awareness of the latest scientific theories and to find ways to bridge the two cultures divide without abandoning humanistic understanding.

If anything, and in spite of the shared obsession with codes and writing, relations between scientists and literary intellectuals have become even more combatative since the Snow–Leavis debate. The 1990s was the decade of the so-called 'science wars' which culminated in the infamous Sokal hoax of 1996, where the physicist Alan Sokal published a spoof article, 'Transgressing the boundaries: towards a transformative hermeneutics of quantum gravity', deploying both authentic and deliberately mangled scientific ideas to support an irrationalist and supposedly 'postmodern' and radically 'uncertain' conception of self, society and the physical universe (Sokal 1996: 217–52). Sokal later exposed the spoof and justified its publication by insisting that the postmodern displacement of facts and evidence with a pervasive relativism, subjectivism and fictionality was – aside from American political campaigns – the most pernicious manifestation of anti-intellectualism of our time. Embarrassed by the subsequent attempt to co-opt him for the anti-Enlightenment Right, Sokal insisted that the hoax had been written not to attack political radicalism but to show that the intellectual confusions of the current humanities constituted a self-defeating apostasy of a culturalist left bent on destroying those very intellectual resources, symbolised by the scientific paradigm of knowledge, which protect from dangerous conflations of science with pseudo-science and the return to authoritarian dogmas. The message of his later co-authored book, *Intellectual Impostures*, is unambiguous:

> the link between postmodernism and the left constitutes, prima facie, a serious paradox. For most of the past two centuries, the left has been identified with science and against obscurantism, believing that rational thought and the fearless analysis of objective reality (both natural and social) are incisive tools for combating the mystifications

promoted by powerful – not to mention being desirable ends in their own right.

(Sokal and Bricmont 1998: 187)

What most infuriates physicists such as Sokal and Bricmont and biologists such as Richard Dawkins, is that postmodernists, unlike novelists, claim to share the same epistemological ground as scientists, but seem intent on destroying its intellectual credentials. Literary theory is therefore dismissed as a manifestation of post-positivist science envy and insecurity about the disciplinary integrity and authority of the humanities in a techno-scientific culture. Yet Lodge is not the only novelist to note the complicity between the discourses of ultra-Darwinism, biotechnology and postmodernism which, between them, seem to have constructed primal myths of the pre- and post-human as a means of both articulating and displacing anxieties about who or what we are at the beginning of the twenty-first century. And indeed, to read both Richard Dawkins *and* Jean Baudrillard, paradoxically, is to encounter selves reduced to collision sites of codes through which endless messages pass and flow and where the virtual body seems entirely emancipated from its organic counterpart. A flight from experience, from the lived body, into an intertextual dematerialisation of the real, seems to preoccupy postmodernists, scientists and multinational financiers alike. Which is why the fictional meditation on that condition in the 1990s, whether in the comic mode of Lodge, for example, or in the savage indictment of a model of reason which abandons feeling and reduces the body to waste, to shit, as offered by Martin Amis in *Time's Arrow*, should be part of the education of all of us.

References

Amis, Martin (1991) *Time's Arrow, or, The Nature of the Offence*, London: Jonathan Cape.

Auden, W. H. (1963) 'The poet and the city', in *The Dyer's Hand*, London: Faber & Faber.

Barthes, Roland (1968) *Writing Degree Zero*, trans. Annette Lavers and Colin Smith, New York: Hill and Wang.

Brockman, John (1995) *The Third Culture: beyond the scientific revolution*, New York: Simon & Schuster.

Byatt, A. S. (2000) *On Histories and Stories*, London: Vintage.

Connolly, Cressida (1997) 'Overfished waters', *Literary Review*, September.

Damasio, Antonio (2000) *The Feeling of What Happens: body, emotion and the making of consciousness*, London: Vintage.

Darwin, Charles (1996) *The Origin of Species*, ed. Gillian Beer, Oxford: Oxford University Press.

Dawkins, Richard (1976) *The Selfish Gene*, Oxford: Oxford University Press.

—— (1986) *The Blind Watchmaker*, Harmondsworth: Penguin.

—— (1999) *The Extended Phenotype: the long reach of the gene*, Oxford: Oxford University Press.

Dennett, Daniel (1995) *Darwin's dangerous Idea: evolution and the meaning of life*, London: Allen Lane.

Foot, Philippa (2001) *Natural Goodness*, Oxford: Clarendon Press.

Fukuyama, Francis (2003) *Our Posthuman Future: consequences of the biotechnology revolution*, New York: Picador.

Gould, Stephen Jay (1992) *Life's Grandeur*, London: Vintage.

Haldane, J. B. S. (1921) *Daedalus, or, Science and the Future*, London: Kegan Paul.

Hawking, Stephen (1998) *A Brief History of Time*, London: Bantam.

Huxley, Aldous (1955) *Brave New World*, Harmondsworth: Penguin.

Ishiguro, Kazuo (1989) *The Remains of the Day*, London: Faber & Faber.

Lessing, Doris (1996) *Putting the Questions Differently: interviews 1964–94*, London: Flamingo.

Lodge, David (1988) *Nice Work*, London: Secker & Warburg.

—— (2002) *Thinks . . .*, Harmondsworth: Penguin.

Lyotard, Jean-François (1984) *The Postmodern Condition: a report on knowledge*, Minneapolis, Minn.: Minnesota University Press.

McEwan, Ian (1998) *Enduring Love*, London: Vintage.

Moore, G. E. (1903) *Principia Ethica*, Cambridge: Cambridge University Press.

Ridley, Matt (2000) *Genome: the autobiography of a species*, London: Fourth Estate.

Rorty, Richard (1991) *Objectivity, Relativism and Truth*, Cambridge: Cambridge University Press.

Rushdie, Salman (1991a) *Haroun and the Sea of Stories*, London: Granta.

—— (1991b) *Imaginary Homelands*, Harmondsworth: Penguin.

Sokal, Alan (1996) 'Transgressing the boundaries: towards a transformative hermeneutic of quantum gravity', *Social Text* 14 (spring/summer): 217–52.

Sokal, Alan and Bricmont, Jean (1998) *Intellectual Impostures*, London: Profile.

Vaihinger, H. (1924) *The Philosophy of As If: a system of the theoretical, practical and religious fictions of mankind*, trans. C. K. Ogden, London: Routledge & Kegan Paul.

Weldon, Fay (1983) *The Life and Loves of a She-Devil*, London: Hodder & Stoughton.

—— (1989) *The Cloning of Joanna May*, London: Collins.

Wilson, E. O. (1998) *Consilience*, London: Little, Brown & Company.

Winterson, Jeanette (1997) *Gut Symmetries*, London: Granta.

4 British science fiction in the 1990s

Politics and genre

Roger Luckhurst

For some of us, there was a curious bifurcation of the experience of literary culture in the 1990s. Cultural theory often adopted an apocalyptic tone, and proclaimed the end of history, the end of the subject, or, in Jean Baudrillard's case, the end of the end. Postmodernism stubbornly survived its origins in the 1980s and many ratcheted up the rhetoric of cultural pessimism. No more political art. The exhaustion of the avant-garde. In Sven Birkets' view, new digital technologies prophesied the end of Literature and its mode of civilised acculturation through reading. These discussions filtered into angst on the literary pages about the decline or death of the English novel: was Martin Amis, along with his teeth, finished? Could we confess that Salman Rushdie was writing terrible books yet? Was Zadie Smith the saviour of the tradition or an empty emblem of multiculturalism? Yet at the same time as these enervating debates there was a remarkable renaissance going on elsewhere, in different kinds of genre writing. Detective fiction, fantasy, Gothic, horror and science fiction entered phases of extraordinary vitality in the 1990s, all the more striking for being surrounded by the language of entropic decline and millennial gloom.

Critics have largely ignored this renaissance, which suggests that the claim that the postmodern is marked by an erasure of the boundary between high and low art is spurious. This short intervention will focus on only one genre: science fiction (SF). I want to argue that there is an intrinsically cultural-political reason for the resurgence of 'lowly' genres in the 1990s, relating to the development of a new kind of cultural politics that has been called 'cultural governance'. I will explore this political context before reading a number of recent SF works by James Lovegrove, Gwyneth Jones and Ken MacLeod.

Cultural politics: from opposition to governance

Cultural politics in 1980s Britain was marked by strongly demarcated ideological divisiveness encouraged by the three governments led by Margaret
Thatcher between 1979 and 1990. The approved version of Culture
became Heritage: the deep English traditions of castles, country houses and
costume dramas (John Major bathetically added warm beer and village
cricket to this vision in 1992). Certain aspects of 'high' culture could find
sanction, but the lower-middle-class fraction from which Thatcher (and
Major) emerged suspected cultural pretensions and favoured resolutely
middle-brow artists: Rudyard Kipling, Edward Elgar, Anthony Trollope
(Major's favourite author). Suspicion of culture was of a piece with the
hatred of intellectuals in the cultural establishment. This cultural sphere
was confronted by a policy of punitive withdrawal of state support, opening
up allegedly inefficient institutions to the free market. This recognised that
opposition to Thatcherism was increasingly *cultural*, since the parliamentary
Labour party was in disarray, left-wing local governments had powers progressively reduced, and union power was broken. Where political routes for
opposition were legislated away, cultural moments of resistance multiplied.
We might list the cinema of Derek Jarman, Alan Bleasdale's portrait of
unemployed desperation in *Boys from the Blackstuff* (1982), Troy Kennedy
Martin's anti-nuclear series *Edge of Darkness* (1985) or Tony Harrison's film-
poem, *V*, a cause célèbre in 1985 in which populist Thatcherites squared up
to the liberal literati. Instances could be multiplied: as Suzanne Moore
recalls, by the late 1980s culture was 'the only space that true opposition to
Thatcherism could come from' (Moore 1998: 17).

This confirms Stuart Hall's analysis of the centrality of culture to any
understanding of contemporary social formations. Hall identifies three distinct levels for analysis of this effect. First, he looks at substantive changes to
cultural institutions, suggesting that the global explosion of communication
technologies, such as television, satellite and Internet links, and the escalation of a fully mediated apprehension of the world in general has pushed
cultural logics to the centre of analysis. Where Culture, narrowly defined,
used to be peripheral to the more serious study of economy and society,
Hall now suggests that 'cultural industries have become the mediating
element in every other process' (Hall 1997: 209). Second, Hall suggests that
the category of culture has moved increasingly to the centre of critical
epistemologies – that politics, sociology and the loosely defined region of
'critical theory' all identify culture as central for analysis and critique.
Third, Hall notes 'the centrality of culture to issues around social regulation, morality and the governance of social conduct in late-modern societies' (Hall 1997: 227). One reading of the anxieties Thatcherism expressed

about culture was that it expected the ravages of the deregulated market to be managed or alleviated by salve of Art, that culture worked as the sort of moral cement in the way favoured by Matthew Arnold. Alarms rang when cultural institutions seemed to oppose the political centre, so that if they would not regulate change they would be subject to regulation. Hall notes that we need to attend to regulation *by* culture as much as regulation *of* it, and this is integral to reading the shifts in cultural politics in the 1990s.

The internally divided Major governments, which survived for seven years between 1990 and 1997, occasionally renewed the adversarial rhetoric of Thatcherism with regard to cultural policy. Yet Major marked a change in strategy in managing the unpredictability of cultural production with the formation of the Department of National Heritage (DNH). Andrew Taylor suggests that the DNH constitutes the key instance of a new kind of cultural governance of the 1990s. The formation of the DNH was a manifesto pledge by Major in 1992. Implementation increased its power: cultural policy was to have a full cabinet member for the first time. This reflected the importance now given to the financial and symbolic capital of heritage, media and the arts. The DNH also became the test-bed for a mode of governance built on a small central core that was to steer a complex set of apparently autonomous institutions. The ministry was to devolve budgets down to some forty-five separate bodies, including the Arts Council, museums, libraries and galleries. Advocates of this management theory idealised the prospect of minimal state intervention and autonomous networks that would regulate themselves. Andrew Taylor's analysis, however, showed that this model dictated conformity to the ideological vision of the political centre through policy reviews, financial and managerial audits. Central government could point to their distance from the cultural sphere, yet use the networks of funding to exert control. What happened was an abandonment of oppositional confrontation with a recalcitrant cultural sphere; instead, the pressure of managerialism would bring it into line.

These factors help explicate the very different sense of cultural politics in the 1990s. Across different cultural arenas, the opposition that had characterised the 1980s began to dissolve into forms of complicity with the dominant culture. Let me give two examples: popular music and fine art. In music, the punk aesthetic of do-it-yourself independent labels and distribution had developed by the 1980s into a full-scale countercultural movement that opposed music corporations. The 'indie' scene was uniformly opposed to the dominant commercial culture, if only occasionally explicitly anti-Thatcherite. In the early 1990s, the distinction between 'independent' and 'corporate' labels began to dissolve, and the anomalous hybrid form of what Joe Brooker has termed the 'corporate indie' began to emerge (Brooker 2003). Independent labels were swallowed by large corporations, who sought to hide their multinationalism behind the cachet of the local authenticity. The apotheosis of this captured youthful disaffection was the Brit Pop phenomenon, and the 'Battle of the Bands' between Blur and Oasis in the summer of 1995. Both derived from once-independent labels: both now measured their success purely in commercial terms.

Similarly, the Young British Artists dominated the British cultural scene in the 1990s with an avant-gardism that was evacuated of any political sense. Art schools contributed successive generations of oppositional culture in Britain. This group, emerging from Goldsmith's College, instead imbibed lessons about self-promotion and successfully sold their work to the art collector and Conservative party advertising guru, Charles Saatchi. As Stallabrass notes, this group deliberately abandoned the language of art theory and postmodernism that had dominated the 1980s, and adopted an aggressively anti-intellectual demotic. The 'pervasive and disabling irony' with which art like this was presented (Stallabrass 1999: 95) also pointed to the way in which the languages of conceptualism and tabloidese had been collapsed into each other. The high point of the Young British Artists was Saatchi's 'Sensation' exhibition at the Royal Academy of Arts in 1997. This was presented as Young Turks transforming the bastion of the English fine-art tradition in England; what it embodied was the emptying out of avant-gardism into general mainstream culture.

Pop culture and British art were the leading cultural phenomena that were incorporated into the cultural governance operated by New Labour in the late 1990s. As an emblem of a young, populist government, Noel Gallagher, the guitarist with Oasis, was invited to a 10 Downing Street reception in the autumn of 1997. Simultaneously, the 'Sensation' exhibition was drawing large crowds to the Royal Academy. This was the season of 'Cool Britannia', the claim that British culture – in music, art, fashion and urban 'cool' – led the world. The Department of National Heritage was renamed as the less conservatively freighted Department of Culture, Media and Sport. When its new minister, Chris Smith, published a collection of speeches called *Creative Britain* in 1998, Damien Hirst designed the cover. These synergies mark a further extension of the praxis of cultural governance.

At first, New Labour appeared to believe it could be post-political. The much-vaunted 'Third Way' was meant to transcend old ideological divisions of Left and Right and to marry the best practice of European social-democratic parties with neo-liberal economics. Disarmingly, Anthony Giddens confessed in the introduction to *The Third Way* that 'in spite of their electoral successes social democrats have not yet created a new and integrated political outlook' (Giddens 1998: 24). In other words, Giddens hoped to provide a framework for an as yet empty project. For Giddens, the key issue for any social democratic party was 'what should its orientation be in a world where there are no alternatives to capitalism?' (Giddens 1998: 24). Giddens noticeably placed heavy emphasis on the role of civil society in encouraging active citizenship, social inclusion and cultural belonging to ameliorate what he acknowledged in passing was the 'culturally destructive power' of global markets (Giddens 1998: 65). Culture once more provided the possible ground for cohesion. It could be harnessed to produce subjects fit for Cool Britannia. An essay by Perri 6 (the research director of the New Labour think tank Demos) called 'Governing by Cultures' argued that 'government is essentially in the business of changing the cultures of its own staff, the organizations that cluster around it . . . and the wide public' (Perri 6 1997: 262). He encouraged all governments to 'think of its policies in cultural terms' (Perri 6 1997: 274), because Thatcherism had proved that markets alone did not foster social trust or cohesion. Only culture, Perri 6 stated, could enable 'a viable capitalist social order to organise and sustain itself' (1997: 275).

If there is some considerable slippage in these discussions between different conceptions of culture – between aesthetic activities, managerialism and the anthropological sense of culture as a 'way of life' – then that is a deliberate reflection of the interpenetration of economic, social and cultural spheres. As Alan Finlayson comments, 'in a context where "everything" is now "cultural" everything becomes available as an object of government policy' (Finlayson 2003: 197). Finlayson convincingly suggests that the ultimately determining instance for all activity within New Labour is the free market, and that policy aims to 'break down the old divisions between social sectors, such that the economic impulse is free to roam throughout the social organism' (Finlayson 2003: 187). The central government might adopt a rhetoric of devolution and the dispersal of power to localised agencies, but this model of governance enforces conformity. Culture might not just build a sense of community in otherwise purely economic monads, it might also create 'the true reflexive individual, possessing a kind of permanently revisionist self; an empowered and mobile subject . . . who is his/her own entrepreneur of selfhood' (Finlayson 2003: 194).

Whilst political protest has revived and proliferated in diverse forms in post-1997 Britain, the 'cultural industries' appear to have been further incorporated into the work of governance. As the minister Chris Smith stated only twenty-two days after the 1997 election: 'The arts are not optional extras for government; they are at the very centre of our mission' (1998: 42). The strategy was simple: culture becomes an *industry*, with a £50 billion annual turnover. Each sector (film, publishing, fine arts, music) can produce profit and import/export balance sheets, and is praised for adding economic value. Cultural-political questions are annulled by economism.

Indeed, 'controversial' art is likely to generate a greater profit margin, whilst issues of aesthetics are sidestepped for vague statements about the need to include all tastes. Although Chris Smith regularly invoked Matthew Arnold to emphasise that economic value must be considered with the 'intellectual, spiritual and social value' of culture (Smith 1998: 15), this very sanction was routed through the project of New Labour. The arts were 'to assist in the regeneration of areas of deprivation' (Smith 1998: 19) or 'to ensure social inclusion' (Smith 1998: 24). Is Culture thereby inoculated into an inoffensive populist mainstream, a vector for a wider exercise in cultural governance?

Science fiction under New Labour

My contention is that the genres undergoing energetic reinvention in the 1990s – notably the Gothic, SF and fantasy – experienced such a revitalisation because they could still find spaces outside the general de-differentiation or 'mainstreaming' effect sought by the strategy of cultural governance. The low value usually accorded to the Gothic–SF–fantasy continuum allowed these genres to flourish largely below the radar of a cultural establishment often complicit with the new methods of governance. The more literary editors dismissed the limitations of genre-writing or *Granta* magazine's stunt to nominate the twenty best young British writers of the decade explicitly (if inconsistently) rejected genre writers, the more oppositional energy accrued to these genres. I do not want to argue that SF is somehow 'outside' the market or has evaded the profound economic changes in publishing in the 1990s (the end of the Net Book Agreement or the multinational consolidation of publishing houses). This would be an absurd position to defend, since it is a commercial genre. And I also do not want to argue that these genres are somehow intrinsically oppositional – perhaps along the lines that SF is always-already a political literature of 'cognitive estrangement', as Darko Suvin (1979) has suggested (academic SF criticism has sometimes followed this line). More modestly, I propose that if we read these low genres contextually, then relative to the co-optation, complicity or evasion manifested in other cultural forms, these genres become available as potential sites of critique within a particular historical conjuncture.

I have argued elsewhere that the resurgence of a London Gothic in the 1990s is partly because the Gothic tropes of feudal tyranny, ghostly repetition and the oneiric disruption of modernity are readable as a commentary on the mixture of tyranny and farce that constitutes the recent story of London local government. New Labour wanted to restore the elected city government that had been abolished by Thatcher in 1986, but Labour gerrymandered the process of candidature for elected Mayor, backed away from any reform of the self-government of the Corporation of London and stripped the new democratic assembly of substantive power. The Gothic was generated from the fear that modernity was haunted by pre-modern, feudal or Catholic tyranny. The Gothic London imaginary intertextually constructed throughout the 1990s by Christopher Fowler, Kim Newman, Neil Gaiman, Alan Moore and Iain Sinclair overlaid these eighteenth-century horrors with the arbitrary powers being exerted in the contemporary world. These Gothic fictions do not provide a consistent political line: the overdetermined nature of generic tropes allows them to be inflected in many incoherently radical or conservative ways. This is also the case with SF. British SF in the 1990s is fascinating precisely because it avoids obvious didacticism. 'Political' readings, instead, come from attending to the ways in which generic tropes are reconfigured by context. Two narrative formulae especially seem to me to be working through the particularity of 'Cool Britannia': the disaster narrative and the cybernetic subversion of totalities. Let me take these in turn.

It has long been established that the English tradition of SF has heavy investments in the imagination of disaster, from H. G. Wells's delight in demolishing surburban London in *The War of the Worlds* (1898), through John Wyndham's *The Day of the Triffids* (1951), to the fascination with the decline of England envisioned by J. G. Ballard since the 1960s. In the 1990s, Ken MacLeod's *The Star Fraction* was set in a London reduced to self-governing anarchistic cantons, Gwyneth Jones published two novels imagining a post-apocalyptic Britain descending into precarious anarchy, and James Lovegrove's *Untied Kingdom* knowingly revisited the landscapes of southern England that are integral to this domestic disaster tradition.

Such a cluster is unsurprising, given the ferment around New Labour's declared intent to modernise the constitutional arrangements of the United Kingdom. Power was to be devolved to Scotland and Wales; the negotiations between Irish, British and the sectarian parties of Northern Ireland seemed likely to result in a new constitutional settlement; the House of Lords was to abolish hereditary voting rights. As the majority of these proposed reforms were scaled back or compromised disdain grew. In surely one of the most comical documents of the 1997 Cool Britannia era, the Demos think tank indicated the level of thought dedicated to solving this problem of national identity. In *Britain*™ Mark Leonard proposed that 'Britain's corporate identity is weak' (Leonard 1997: 10), and thus needed rebranding. The corporate model was explicit: one section title ran 'Can one brand a country? Lessons from business' (Leonard 1997: 43). 'Few', Leonard said, 'have made the link between the political and cultural aspects of identity and their economic significance – the "identity premium" that flows to businesses when national identity is being managed well' (Leonard

1997: 63). As should be expected, culture was an essential part of this new governance of nationality.

Susan Sontag long ago argued that popular disaster fictions were interesting if ultimately juvenile responses to crisis. But recent disaster fiction shows complex and variegated engagements with questions of national identity. In James Lovegrove's *Untied Kingdom* the imagined context for British decline in the book – Britain is bombed back into the Stone Age by an ill-defined International Community – resonates with Blair's militarised foreign policy, inverting it.

> England wasn't going to be re-admitted into the global fold for some while yet . . . England's plummet from First to Third World status was a salutary reminder of what could happen to any industrialised nation if its leaders were not careful. England was an object lesson in how *not* to handle an economic crisis.
>
> (Lovegrove 2003: 104)

Lovegrove constructs a loose episodic quest, taking his lead character from the generic southern rural village Downbourne to the corrupt metropolis. Within this structure, Lovegrove's account of England becomes increasingly conservative. Our hero's penultimate stop is the country seat of a loveable rogue aristocrat. The dilapidated state of Fairfield Hall reflects government 'taxes on this, taxes on that. At the time, they were treating the landed gentry like a disease that had to be eradicated' (Lovegrove 2003: 267). Lovegrove's tone is difficult to judge, making it unclear whether he is investing fully in this conservative account. Certainly, when the narrative voice praises the aristocratic hall, the terms could almost have been lifted directly from someone like Roger Scruton: 'Something so solid, so sempiternal about the place, . . . What could destroy this? No Act of Parliament, of International Community, even of God, had power sufficient . . . Fairfield Hall had been founded on land and lust, earth and earthiness, and had endured' (Lovegrove 2003: 268). This novel responds to the Blairite reconstitution of Great Britain in a way that retreats into consolatory visions.

The similar reduction of England to primitive conditions by Gwyneth Jones could hardly be more different. For me, her recent books are central instances of work that is able to launch a trenchant critique of Blairism because it stays outside mainstream novel conventions by using a hybrid SF/fantasy form. *Bold as Love* and its sequel *Castles Made of Sand* concern questions of resistance, incorporation and political compromise. They are set in Dissolution Summer, the point at which imperial Britain disintegrates. It is also a moment in which late capitalism collapses – society is downsizing, seeking local sustainable ecologies, and progresses towards a kind of neo-medieval condition. There is a risk of Islamic separatism in the high-density Asian populations in Leeds and Bradford. In the course of the books, communication beyond England becomes virtually impossible as computer technologies are irreversibly corrupted. Within this bleak portrait of decline, Jones is seeking what she calls a 'compromised and *possible* utopia' (Jones 2002a: 140). This is a project she has been exploring at least since *Kairos*, published in 1988, which explores the dissolution of Thatcherite Britain into anarchy. In a recent commentary on that work, she has argued for 'the value of limited solutions': 'idealistic revolutions tend to have depressingly poor results. There's an awful symmetry, whereby the bid for freedom rebounds to a position more doctrinaire, repressive, and harsh than the situation it set out to cure' (Jones 2002b: 179). This takes on even more meaning in the wake of the modernising rhetoric and managerial 'revolution' in New Labour policy.

Taking a cue from the centrality of popular music to politics in the 1990s, the significant political leaders in *Bold as Love* and *Castles Made of Sand* are rock stars. Seeking populist cachet, the government sets up a Counter-cultural Think Tank (which echoes New Labour's Creative Industries Taskforce), only to find itself marginalised by a coup engineered by the Counterculturals. Negotiations with Westminster and the musicians are manipulated by Benny Preminder. This looks suspiciously to me like a sly portrait of New Labour's principal architect and schemer, Peter Mandelson. In a sly comment on Blair, one rock star 'had been sardonically amused, recalling the Think Tank era, when the Prime Minister and the Home Secretary had been so thrilled to be hanging out with rockstars . . . He has to be with the in-crowd' (Jones 2002a: 97). To make this even more explicit, someone passes 'a flash American magazine a month old, with Fiorinda on the cover: *Cool Britannia?* said the copy' (Jones 2001: 289). This references the *Vanity Fair* cover of 1997 that announced the new London 'cool'.

The crisis government is headed by the Triumvirate, three rock stars caught up in a complex *ménage à trois* (these are also books that entwine an investigation into polymorphous sexuality, sexual abuse and domestic violence with the broader treatment of the condition of England). What the Triumvirate seeks is a different kind of politics that owes something to William Morris and the domestic tradition of artisanal socialism, inter-twined with anarchism as it was in the nineteenth century, and yet now more open to Islam, a fair degree of witchery and sustainable New Age technologies. This is not, then, a nostalgic vision of neo-medieval 'green and pleasant' England. Jones does borrow from the actual counterculture of music festivals and the so-called Travellers – significant new political actors in the 1980s and 1990s that refused engagement with the utilitarian-ism and rhetoric of modernisation. Yet Jones is suspicious of claims to recover pre-modern authenticity: the Ancient British Tendency is based in Glastonbury and held to be 'aggressively anti-science and covertly white supremacist' (Jones 2001: 265). The crisis of 'Englishness' is not to be solved by returning to conservative narratives of belonging to some ancient tradition inhering in the land. And this is also Jones's explicit riposte to a trend in English fantasy that invests heavily in myth as guarantor of racial Englishness – J. R. R. Tolkein's Middle Earth before the scouring of the Shire, say.

I am perhaps risking the sense that Jones's work can be comfortably decoded in a straight allegorical way – as if allegory could ever work without a remainder. This would be to simplify texts that are constantly ambivalent and ironic about the fantasy resolutions offered. Yet the ways in which the characters agonise over questions of compromise and resistance, incorporation and rejection, does make this work centrally engaged with the problems of cultural governance in a way few others have addressed.

Let me turn now to the other generic element of SF that I think has been used to produce plots that address contemporary cultural governance. Many cyberpunk fictions basically explore the narrative possibilities of evading or even overthrowing increasingly totalised systems of computerised surveillance and direct control of populations. William Gibson's *Neuromancer* (1984) began by pitting subversive cells of hackers and hardbodies against multinational corporate power; his cyberpunk trilogy ended by finding ghosts, incalculable new entities, populating the machine. Jean-François Lyotard provided the almost perfect commentary on this: any total, inhuman system could never reach complete control, because it would always be haunted by a spectral excess that would resist routinisation within a totality. This is a plot that speaks to an English situation where enforced social inclusion in a post-hegemonic consensus, aided by a 'mainstreaming' of culture, becomes a totality that prompts resistance. SF, that disregarded low cultural form, once more provides a location from which to launch critique. This allows a reading of Ken MacLeod's *Fall Revolution* quartet (1995–9), a linked series of books on resistance to varieties of totalitarianism.

MacLeod's novels utterly resist summary. The density of the writing is itself a mode of defying totality, since the reader only ever understands the whirl of events belatedly. In *The Star Fraction*, published in 1995, the British state has collapsed and a civil war between the rump of the old centre and other armed political factions is allowed to rumble on, monitored by US/ UN forces (in this world the UN has become an arm of the American state). The portrait of London is of self-governing ghettos, 'divide-and-rule replicating downwards in a fractal balkanisation of the world' (MacLeod 1998: 77). Communists, fundamentalist Christians, anarchist libertarians and radical ecologists run mini-states. Across this fractured space, the generic cyberpunk team of resisters seek traces of a software programme, the Star Fraction, which constitutes the Grail of revolutionary possibility. Surveillance system and political containments are short-circuited by our band of heroes, and the virus of revolution is unleashed. It is something of a jolt to realise that this is a science fiction built on rigorous Trotskyist lines, and that the extrapolation lies not in the busy technologies that clutter the foreground but in the social liberation made possible by those technologies.

It is only in the second novel, *The Stone Canal*, published in 1996, that the political ambitions of the sequence really begin to reveal themselves. At once a prequel and a sequel to *The Star Fraction*, MacLeod offers a genealogy of this future, rooting it in the factionalism of the British Left in the 1970s. The future societies MacLeod explores result primarily from the ideologies of two characters, Jonathan Wilde, a left-libertarian anarchist, and David Reid, who starts out as a member of the International Marxist Group, but who moves, over the course of the 1980s and 1990s, towards an anarcho-capitalist and anti-statist stance. Various social formations result from these political positions. Wilde's ideas lie behind the libertarians of London in *The Star Fraction*. Reid builds the anarcho-capitalist New Mars in *The Stone Canal*. That anarcho-capitalist formation confronts the socialist federation of twenty-fourth-century earth in *The Cassini Division* (1998). An alternative trajectory from the Fall Revolution is explored in *The Sky Road* (1999), a stable but uneasy ecotopia in Scotland. 'Thus', John Arnold and Andy Wood observe, 'the four books build, but then interrogate, a large and complex history of human affairs across several centuries; and use this history to explore a variety of ideology, ideas and political practices' (Arnold and Wood 2003: 30).

The Stone Canal presents a historically accurate trajectory of the Left in late twentieth-century Britain. David Reid, in particular, represents how elements of the 'hard left' in the 1970s shifted into a libertarian embrace of the subversive possibilities of capitalism in the 1990s. MacLeod is also, therefore, reflecting on the history of the Left that led to the rise of New Labour in the mid-1990s. Blairism is resolutely centrist because of this history of factionalism, holding that the eighteen years of Labour defeat between 1979 and 1997 was the result both of cleaving to a historically defeated socialist economic theory, and also of the bitter doctrinaire disputes between rival elements of the Left. MacLeod began publishing the sequence as Blair's ideological repositioning of Labour away from socialism was starting to cohere as a social-market doctrine, and also when the first critiques of New Labour were beginning to emerge in journals like the *New Left Review*.

MacLeod's work is a fascinating reflection on this political context because he plays off political theory against fictional play, alternative history and the utopian imagination. Mockingly funny about the arcane disputations of the Left, he nevertheless preserves a commitment to the revolutionary ideal. Indeed, MacLeod seems to construct scenarios in which *any* mode of totality is subjected to subversion – whether it comes from free-market capitalist anarchy, the coercive socialist state or the collective or individualistic modes of libertarianism. Farah Mendlesohn is right to suggest that 'absolute liberty' is the ideal that constantly subverts political organisation in MacLeod's scenarios – that 'the truly successful revolutions in these novels are the social upheavals which derail the revolutions' (Mendlesohn 2003: 18). This shares some similarities with the kind of anarchy explored by Gwyneth Jones, where process, or becoming, is valued over condition, or being. MacLeod has, needless to say, little time for any Third Way post-political fantasies of engineered consensus. MacLeod celebrates, in comic terms, the unforeseeable supplement that wrecks any totalising project.

British SF in the 1990s was part of an energetic cultural-political scene. A new generation of British writers engaged through genre because of its very position in relation to the cultural mainstream: I could extend this study to consider works by John Courtenay Grimwood, China Miéville, Justina Robson, Adam Roberts and others. SF has the leverage of being, to some degree, outside a homogenised and mainstreamed culture. In many ways, this moment recalled American SF in the early 1950s, when figures like Frederic Pohl, Judith Merril and James Blish launched devastating critiques of enforced conformity, consumer capitalism and McCarthyite oppression through SF plots. MacLeod acknowledged this moment in SF history by naming the libertarian space-exploration company after the famous 1953 political satire by Pohl and Cyril Kornbluth, *The Space Merchants*. Pohl has argued that SF is best understood as a 'political cryptogram', which is 'able to say things in hint and metaphor that the writer dares not say in the clear' (Pohl 1997: 12). In the early 1950s, Merril later claimed, 'Science fiction became, for a time, virtually the only vehicle of political dissent' (Merril 1971: 74). The situation was of course very different in 1990s Britain, where the penalties of refusing to conform were less punitive, and with numerous lively and vocal avenues of dissent to the 'post-political' hegemony sought by New Labour. In that sense, there is no point in arguing for some intrinsic superiority or aesthetic value of SF over other modes of writing. This is a conjunctural phenomenon, and is best understood as a product of resistance to the mainstreaming effect that constitutes a central element of contemporary cultural governance. It does mean that to 'read the scene' of the 1990s to proper effect, literary historians have to start integrating lowly genre writing into their understanding of the literary politics of the era.

References

Arnold, John H. and Andy Wood (2003) 'Nothing is written: politics, ideology and the burden of history in the Fall Revolution Quartet', in Andrew M. Butler and Farah Mendlesohn (eds) *The True Knowledge of Ken MacLeod*, Reading: Science Fiction Foundation, pp. 29–46.

Birkets, Sven (1994) *The Gutenberg Elegies: the fate of reading in an electronic age*, London: Faber & Faber.

Brooker, Joe (2003) 'Commercial alternative', *New Formations* 50: 106–22.

Finlayson, Alan (2003) *Making Sense of New Labour*, London: Lawrence & Wishart.

Giddens, Anthony (1998) *The Third Way: the renewal of social democracy*, Cambridge: Polity Press.

Hall, Stuart (1997) 'The centrality of culture: notes on the cultural revolutions of our time', in Kenneth Thompson (ed.) *Media and Cultural Regulation*, London: Sage, pp. 208–38.

Jameson, Fredric (1982) 'Progress vs. Utopia; or, can we imagine the future?', *Science Fiction Studies* 9(2): 147–58.

Jones, Gwyneth (2001) *Bold as Love*, London: Gollancz.

—— (2002a) *Castles Made of Sand*, London: Gollancz.

—— (2002b) '*Kairos*: the enchanted loom', in Joan Gordon and Veronica Hollinger (eds) *Edging into the Future: science fiction and contemporary cultural transformation*, Philadelphia, Pa.: University of Pennsylvania Press, pp. 174–89.

Leonard, Mark (1997) *Britain™: renewing our identity*, London: Demos.

Lovegrove, James (2003) *Untied Kingdom*, London: Gollancz.

Luckhurst, Roger (2002) 'The contemporary London Gothic and the limits of the "spectral turn" ', *Textual Practice* 16(3): 526–545.

Lyotard, Jean-François (1991) *The Inhuman: reflections on time today*, trans. Geoffrey Bennington and Rachel Bowlby, Cambridge: Polity Press.

MacLeod, Ken (1998) *The Star Fraction*, London: Orbit.

—— (1999) *The Stone Canal*, London: Orbit.

—— (2000) *The Cassini Division*, London: Orbit.

—— (2001) *The Sky Road*, London: Orbit.

Mendlesohn, Farah (2003) 'Impermanent revolution: the anarchic utopias of Ken MacLeod' in Andrew M. Butler and Farah Mendlesohn (eds) *The True Knowledge of Ken MacLeod*, Reading: Science Fiction Foundation, pp. 16–29.

Merril, Judith (1971) 'What do you mean Science? Fiction?', in Thomas Clareson (ed.) *The Other Side of Realism: essays on modern fantasy and science fiction*, Bowling Green, Ohio: Bowling Green University Popular Press, pp. 53–95.

Moore, Suzanne (1998) 'The cultural revolution', *Marxism Today* (Nov/Dec): 17–21.

Perri 6 (1997) 'Governing by cultures', in Geoff Mulgan (ed.) *Life After Politics: new thinking for the twenty-first century*, London: Fontana, pp. 260–82.

Pohl, Frederic (1997) 'The politics of prophecy', in Donald M. Hassler and Clyde Wilcox (eds) *Political Science Fiction*, Columbia, SC: University of South Carolina Press, pp. 7–17.

Rhodes, R. A. W (1996) 'The new governance: governing without government', *Political Studies* 44: 652–67.

Smith, Chris (1998) *Creative Britain*, London: Faber & Faber.

Sontag, Susan (1987) 'The imagination of disaster', in *Against Interpretation and Other Essays*, London: Deutsch, pp. 209–25.

Stallabrass, Julian (1999) *High Art Lite: British art in the 1990s*, London: Verso.

Suvin, Darko (1976) 'On the poetics of the science fiction genre', in Mark Rose (ed.) *Science Fiction: twentieth century views*, New York: Prentice Hall, pp. 57–71.

Suvin, Darko (1979) *The Metamorphoses of Science Fiction*, New Haven, Conn: Yale University Press.

Taylor, Andrew (1997) ' "Arms length but hands on": mapping the new governance: the department of national heritage and cultural politics in Britain', *Public Administration* 75: 441–66.

Part II

Identity at the *fin de siècle*

5   The McReal thing

Personal/national identity in Julian Barnes's *England, England*

Sarah Henstra

In today's world of transnational capitalism, what better does England have to offer for profit than its heritage? Such is the thinking behind 'England, England', a Disneyland-like theme park on the Isle of Wight that gathers and replicates English landmarks and traditions for the enjoyment of leisure tourists from around the world. The conception, development, and operation of the island project occupies the bulk of Julian Barnes's 1998 novel, and its satirical treatment challenges our value-laden distinctions between 'original' and 'copy,' 'reality' and 'performance.' But the comedy is bracketed by two shorter sections which pursue with greater seriousness the paradoxes of the *England, England* narrative. The theme-park plot becomes a kind of parable about the fate of a national identity, as Barnes's characters wrestle with doubts about the reliability of memory (both personal and national), the uses of the past, and the possibility of authentic contact with others in a world of simulation and hyperreality. Throughout, the novel is preoccupied with the question of England's collective selfhood in a post-empire age. What fate awaits a 'nation fatigued by its own history' (Barnes 1998: 253)? The future as envisioned by the novel involves a dystopic choice: to trivialize and commodify the trappings of 'Englishness' for profit on the island theme park, or to retire to the increasingly isolated and impoverished mainland, 'Old England,' as it comes to be known abroad – in other words, England must either sell out or declare bankruptcy. Within the context of such futuristic extremes, Barnes explores the psychological mechanisms of desire and longing that comprise identity, using the juxtaposition of private self and public role to highlight the anxious search for authenticity underwriting 'Englishness' at the end of the twentieth century.

The satirical narration of the theme-park story focuses most sharply upon the marketing genius behind the project, Sir Jack Pitman. Introduced as the quintessential Englishman for a modern age, Sir Jack amounts to everything that has gone wrong with the idea of being English. The identity has been usurped by someone without the birthright: Jack's name is rumored either to have been anglicized to disguise Eastern European origins or intentionally cloaked in such a rumour to disguise working-class English origins (Barnes 1998: 33). And the lifestyle of Englishness has been assumed without respect for tradition or taste, so that Pitman House's architectural sophistication is grossly compromised by the boss's self-designed office replete with curtained *faux* windows, coal fires, and reproduction bubble-nosed light switches.

While many of the players in the novel are drawn along such cartoonish lines in the interests of comedy, the character of Martha Cochrane, one of Sir Jack's special consultants, provides the occasion for the text's more serious inquiry into the links between individual and collective identity, between personal loss and national decline. Martha's role as 'Appointed Cynic' on the England, England project (Barnes 1998: 44) expands until she eventually usurps her boss as CEO of the theme park. But its continued success makes her feel increasingly shallow and fraudulent, and after Sir Jack ousts her she retires to the increasingly backward life on the English mainland. From our first glimpse of Martha, her individual identity is linked to that of her country. Her earliest memory is of assembling her Counties of England jigsaw puzzle and of being overwhelmed by 'a sense of desolation, failure, and disappointment in the imperfection of the world' when she discovers a piece missing (Barnes 1998: 5). Her father, it turns out, likes to sneak a piece of the puzzle into his pocket and (re)produce it for her amazement and relief: 'Staffordshire had been found, and her jigsaw, her England, and her heart had been made whole again' (Barnes 1998: 6). The metaphor of the child working on the puzzle literalizes the psychological identification that leads an individual to invest in a national sense of self. And the child bereft by a missing piece (and later, by a missing father) dramatizes how a sense of loss both binds and troubles the emotional connections in group identity.[1] A similar set of images describes Martha's childhood love of the county agricultural show, where livestock, produce, and baked goods compete for prize ribbons. The schedule of prizes book takes on a special significance for the little girl: 'Martha did not understand all the words, and very few of the instructions, but there was something about the lists – their calm organisation and their completeness – which satisfied her' (Barnes 1998: 9). Integral to Martha's sense of security on the fair day is her parents' togetherness. After their divorce, and her ritualistic disposal of her jigsaw-puzzle counties, Martha still clings to her memory of the 'superior justice' of the fair: 'Swung high to the heavens in a place where, despite the noise and the pushing, there was order, and rules, and wise judgment from men in white coats, like doctors' (17–18). Such an image sums up the fusion of Martha's early emotional attachments amongst (absent) father, nation, and discursive law. This pre-lapsarian idyll symbolizes a yearning for wholeness that eventually catches up with Martha. She compares memory to what remains of a dream on waking:

> You dreamed all night, or for long, serious sections of the night, yet when you woke all you had was a memory of having been abandoned, or betrayed, caught in a trap, left on a frozen plain; and sometimes not even that, but a fading after-image of the emotions stirred by such events.
>
> (Barnes 1998: 6)

Early losses compounded by the inevitable failure of recall set the stage for Martha's struggle to reconcile national and personal selfhood, while the suggestion here of indeterminate betrayal and uneasiness directs the reader's attention to a narrative substratum of anxiety and grief.

But for Martha, the problem isn't as straightforward as 'What I loved, I lost.' Memory not only fails to recall faithfully the past; it is also apt to distort past events for its own purposes. Martha notes that what is represented by memory is not 'a solid, seizable thing' in the past, but rather 'a memory now of a memory a bit earlier of a memory before that of a memory way back when' (Barnes 1998: 3). This recursive structure thwarts any attempt to reach unmediated 'truth' about her past; memory is a sign that only ever points back to another sign. In addition, memory is performative rather than strictly commemorative, insofar as most recollections of childhood amount to 'a calculated attempt to take the listener's heart between finger and thumb and give it a tweak whose spreading bruise would last until love had struck' (Barnes 1998: 4). The rhetorical function of memory, in other words, outranks any bid for accuracy. Martha compares personal memory with national history to explain how the means supercede the ends when reconstructing the past: 'It was like a country remembering its history: the past was never just the past, it was what made the present able to live with itself. The same went for individuals, though the process obviously wasn't straightforward' (Barnes 1998: 6).

Rather than grounding identity in a historical reality, memory is discovered in *England, England* to be one performative operation amongst many in the service of the ongoing re-iteration of selfhood.[2]

The kind of comparison Martha draws between national and individual historiography occurs throughout the novel. Dr. Max, the England, England project historian, is at first dismayed to find in the knowledge polls he conducts that most consumers 'remembered history in the same conceited yet evanescent fashion as they recalled their own childhood' (Barnes 1998: 82). But if (historical) memory is about function – a necessary justification for the way life has turned out – then why not turn it to the function of money-making? Marketing English history will require reworking it into a more modern, convenient, consumable format: the plan is to recreate key historical sites and cultural hallmarks in one, central, Pitco-owned and operated location. A half-size Big Ben and Buckingham Palace, Brontë country and Jane Austen's house, Sherlock Holmes and Nell Gwynn, Robin Hood and his Merrie Men – all are replicated in England, England and offered for the visitors' itinerary. Throwing over the traditional virtues of origin and originality means that the entrepreneurs are no longer constrained by the inconveniences of 'factual,' or even remembered, history and are instead free to pander to the familiar, fond, and 'evanescent' versions tourists prefer.

The question of natural versus artificial identity is approached first on the personal level by Martha. Her efforts to become a 'mature, ripened person' (Barnes 1998: 205) are driven by her belief that she must somehow discover and grow into her nature, but she finds herself worrying whether 'this nature was no more natural' than the constructed reality of the theme park (Barnes 1998: 226). And in the end, Martha is faced with the depressing possibility that 'for all a lifetime's internal struggling, you were finally no more than what others saw you as. That was your nature, whether you liked it or not' (Barnes 1998: 259). Martha's discovery that identity is as much externally imposed as inborn or self-built is a proposal defended against from the start by Sir Jack's tourism project. To embrace the reductive, external idea of Englishness so as to sell it back to the foreigners who expect it is to reclaim control over how (and to whose profit) that identity is perceived. One of the ironies mobilized here is the fact that, traditionally, it is 'Third World' (i.e., colonized) countries who are forced to accept and market the 'other's' version of their cultural identity to bring in tourist dollars. The 'historical depression' (Barnes 1998: 39) arising from decolonization and its attendant sense of England's decline can be reversed by a new kind of territorial expansion – the conquest and control of the global tourist trade.[3] Of course, the 'past' that the island project sells to other nations is precisely the superficial, sentimental version that the entrepreneurs themselves disdain. Visitors to England, England shop with farthings and ha'pennies (Barnes 1998: 182) and sip their pints of Jolly Jack ale in the Old Bull and Bush (Barnes 1998: 111). But the island planners realize at the outset that leisure consumers buy their tickets in order to feel affirmed in their ignorance, not to be lectured at.[4] And successfully commodifying something that represents 'real' Englishness, no matter how poor a copy the product might be, helps to buttress the (false) confidence that there is indeed an original behind the replica, a real England behind England, England.[5]

However, this cavalier approach to identity is sobered even within the

'England, England' section of the novel by an ongoing concern with the distinction between reality and appearance, original and replica. Sir Jack launches the first 'brainstorming' session on the theme-park project with the question, 'What is real?' (Barnes 1998: 31). This question is framed throughout the narrative as a uniquely English preoccupation. When the island's creative team quarrels over whether the hired 'peasants' should be required, for the sake of authenticity, to fraternize with the tourists in the pubs after hours, the conflict boils down to the difference between the tastes of the hosts (the English) and of their visitors (the rest of the world). The Concept Developer, Mark, tries to articulate his discomfort with the idea:

> 'Have you ever been to a play and when it's over the actors come off the stage and walk through the audience shaking hands with you – like, hey, we were only figments of your imagination up there but now we're showing how we're flesh and blood the same as you? It just makes me uneasy.'
> 'That's because you're English,' said Martha. 'You think being touched is invasive.'
> 'No, it's about keeping reality and illusion separate.'
> 'That's very English too.'
> 'I fucking *am* English,' said Mark.
> 'Our visitors won't be.'
>
> (Barnes 1998: 111)

Sir Jack's consulting team is still trying to adjust to the notion that the replica is indecipherable from, and superior to, the original. Initially, this idea is pitched to the team in terms of the mastery and control that becomes possible through the re-presentation of reality. The 'French intellectual' (Barnes 1998: 52) brought in to elucidate the theory argues that 'We must demand the replica, since the reality, the truth, the authenticity of the replica is the one we can possess, colonise, reorder, find *jouissance* in' (Barnes 1998: 55).[6] Mark's protests about wanting to maintain the distance between the 'real experience' and the 'show' are silenced by Martha's reminder that to others, Englishness simply *is* a show. Since foreigners are exempt from the collective investment in a myth of 'pure Englishness,' they will not feel anxious for a grounding in 'reality' under the island's simulacra.

Visionary that he is, Sir Jack is the first to see that the whole question of replica versus original will become irrelevant. He dismisses the French theorist – 'He was disappointing, I thought' (Barnes 1998: 61) – preferring to pursue the issue to a much greater extreme. As Sir Jack explains to his baffled employees, the ultimate success is not to copy the real thing but to *create* the real thing:

The lake you discern on the horizon is a reservoir, but when it has been established a few years, when fish swim in it and migrating birds make it a port of call, when the treeline has adjusted itself and little boats ply their picturesque way up and down it, when these things happen it becomes, triumphantly, a lake, don't you see? It becomes *the thing itself.*

(Barnes 1998: 61)

A reality conceived of, established, and fully controlled by himself is Sir Jack's driving fantasy in the island project. But Martha never quite buys the fantasy, not even as CEO of England, England. In the press she praises the ascendancy of 'client choice' on the island as 'empowering and democratic' (Barnes 1998: 182), but privately she 'regard[s] the Island as no more than a plausible and well-planned means of making money' (Barnes 1998: 192). While this cynicism does not prevent her from running the enterprise as well as Sir Jack might have done, it complicates her stance in relation to the phenomena that begin to occur once the island does begin to take on a life of its own and starts to look like 'the thing itself.' When the 'smugglers' housed in the Lower Thatcham cottages begin actually to smuggle – to counterfeit island coins, to import pornography, to distill liquor – Martha coolly invokes clause 13b of their contract and retrains them as 'prisoners' at Carisbrooke Castle (Barnes 1998: 201). But her first impulse on hearing the security report is to respond quite differently: 'Martha suppressed, with great difficulty, the carefree, innocent, pure, true laugh that lay within her, something as incorporeal as the breeze, a freak moment of nature, a fresh-ness long forgotten; something so untainted as to induce hysteria' (Barnes 1998: 199). Sir Jack is closer to the mark than Martha in envisioning how the island would become 'the thing itself'; Martha finds herself astonished at the 'separation – or adhesion – of personality' that keeps prompting the Island employees to become the characters they're playing (Barnes 1998: 197). But Sir Jack has the wrong idea about who will be in charge of the emergent 'thing': the tidy mastery of his plan falls apart under the burgeon-ing on the island of a collective life – a collective identity – beyond the grasp of Pitco's planners.

As suggested in the 'pure, true laugh' to which she succumbs, Martha's witnessing of the identity-adoption happening amongst the actors generates within her a half-acknowledged yearning for the 'freshness' or innocence that would permit her, too, to forget her various roles. Dr. Max gives her a hard reminder of the performative structure of identity when he says, 'Most people, in my opinion, steal much of what they are. If they didn't, what poor items they would be. You're just as constructed, in your own less . . . zestful way, no disrespect intended' (Barnes 1998: 133–4). This bothers Martha because for her, the question has always been to discover, to mature into, her true nature beneath all the constructed behavior: 'Because,' she reasons, 'if you were unable to locate your true nature, your chance of happiness was surely diminished' (Barnes 1998: 226). But what England, England eventually teaches her is that happiness, truth, and genuine contact with the world lie elsewhere than in the ever-elusive realization of one's 'true' identity.

Martha's confrontation with Dr. Samuel Johnson is the turning point in her career as Official Cynic/CEO for Pitco. Hired for the Island Dining Experience to provide visitors with famous English soliloquy, witty repartee, and 'cross-epoch-bonding' (Barnes 1998: 208), the actor playing Dr. Johnson is instead turning up complaints about poor grooming and table manners, racist remarks, irritability, moody silences, asthmatic wheezing, bullying dominance, and shoe fetishism. Far more than a result of method acting, Dr. Johnson's is an identity rehearsed and reiterated into a coherent 'self' – a self whose foibles prove irreconcilably inconvenient to the profit-minded project. Watching this melancholy genius sway and twitch in her office, Martha suddenly finds herself believing in him. Despite all the training which tells her that 'the Johnson regression' is purely an issue of breach of contract, she is moved by his vulnerability:

> The sudden truth she had felt as he leaned over her, wheezing and muttering, was that his pain was authentic. And his pain was authentic because it came from authentic contact with the world . . . By whatever means this vision had been put in front of her, she saw a creature alone with itself, wincing at naked contact with the world. When had she last seen – or felt – anything like that?
>
> (Barnes 1998: 217–18)

The encounter leaves Martha feeling spiritually bereft, 'as if she were less real than he was' (Barnes 1998: 212). It sends her into a tailspin of doubt about the easy binary which, as cynic, she has maintained between her *own* reality and the show; more crucially, she wonders where identity might really locate in relation to such a binary.[7] Facing Dr. Johnson she sees that identity has nothing to do with real versus fake, original versus copy – instead, identity comprises of the particular venue(s) it provides for contact with other people. She sees the way emotion bodies forth the 'self' no matter how artificially that self may be cobbled together; that desire fills out the contours of identity, inhabits it, is fulfilled or thwarted through its operations. Martha begins to feel that her worldly cynicism must be the *least* authentic way to live in the world, and that, as Dr. Johnson declares, she is nothing more than a 'wretched un-idea'd girl' (Barnes 1998: 209).

Only through a symbolic image is Martha finally able to put her finger on what she feels is wrong with England, England, and with her role in it. She recalls the motif of the woman swept off a cliff by the wind, miraculously saved because her billowing skirts slow her fall. Even though Martha herself has helped to (re)invent and commercialize this image (as the island's 'Heavens to Betsy' Bungee Experience), she is now struck by the necessity of honoring the original myth *regardless* of its truth value: 'Part of you might suspect that the magical event had never occurred, or at least not as it was now supposed to have done. But you must also celebrate the image and the moment even if it had never happened. That was where the little seriousness of life lay' (Barnes 1998: 238).

Martha's early loss of faith in the personal and national myths of her childhood does not exempt her, she realizes, from the fear, the desire, and the need for emotional contact that generates such myths in the first place.

To commemorate the original image is a tall order for a country whose national images have been proven not only questionable in content, but historically exploitative in function. Trying to recover a sense of seriousness eventually leads Martha to the British mainland, now referred to as Old England (since the island comprises all that is currently 'English'). There, mass depopulation and economic depression have turned back the clock: villagers subsist on harvesting local crops and digging coal, and the country-side is dotted with windmills, sundials, barge-horses, and hedgerows (Barnes 1998: 255). Citizens of the newly christened 'Anglia' find the resultant poverty and isolation relatively easy to bear 'in the absence of comparisons' (Barnes 1998: 253). Purity returns to nature in the absence of pollution: 'Chemicals drained from the land, the colours grew gentler, and the light untainted; the moon, with no competition, now rose more dominantly. In the enlarged countryside, wildlife bred freely' (Barnes 1998: 255). The village where Martha lives, we're told, is 'neither idyllic nor dystopic,' just bound to the land and its routines. Martha progresses from sentimentality about its quaintness, to depression over its 'incuriosity and low horizons,' to quiet acceptance (Barnes 1998: 257).

Proposed as an antidote to the 'sleek loop' of ironic self-doubt that plagues Martha and her modern world, the 'nut-eating isolationism' (Barnes 1998: 253) of Anglia behaves like a narrative fulfilment of Martha's yearning for wholeness. If doubts fade away in Anglia, however, they continue, significantly, to bother readers of this concluding section of the novel. How could the 'untainted' light and gentle colours belong to anything other than a regressive, nostalgic fantasy? Is the return to days of yore a flat-out denial of modern reality? Does Julian Barnes really endorse the suggestion that Anglia 'was the last realistic option for a nation fatigued by its own history' (Barnes 1998: 253)? One way of interpreting this section might be to read for the same satirical treatment that characterizes the theme-park plot. Anglia is precisely the opposite extreme, as radical as England, England and utterly reliant upon its existence.[8] And certainly, some of Anglia's characters are worthy of Barnesian satire: Jez Harris, the self-styled village yokel – 'formerly Jack Oshinsky, junior legal expert with an American electronics firm' – comes directly to mind (Barnes 1998: 242). But the note of wistfulness that creeps into Barnes's descriptions of the landscape as 'buff and bistre, ash and nettle, dun and roan, slate and bottle' (Barnes 1998: 258), of the Sunday congregation's 'stomachs calling out for the joint of lamb they had given the baker to roast in his oven' (Barnes 1998: 258), tempers the satirical tone and nudges the 'Anglia' section towards something less ideologically straight-shooting.

If the conclusion of *England, England* amounts to nostalgic reverie, it is not without a degree of self-consciousness about its escapism. Martha, for one, scrutinizes her own fascination with the daily lists in the *Mid-Wessex Gazette* of 'items sold by hundredweight, stone and pound for amounts expressed in pounds, shilling, and pence': 'This was hardly nostalgia, since most of these measures had been abolished before she was sentient. Or perhaps it was, and nostalgia of a truer kind: not for what you knew, or thought you had known, as a child, but for what you could never have known' (Barnes 1998: 260).

Martha's interest in such reports is thus characterized as 'artificial without being specious' (Barnes 1998: 260). Here, the text seems to be forwarding a version of nostalgia that might be excused – might be considered 'truer' – because it is knowingly constructed and aware of its idealizing take on the past. This self-conscious nostalgia differs from the kind that prompted England, England's visitors delightedly to purchase their souvenirs with pouchfuls of farthings and half-crowns, because it acknowledges that the object of its affection is not, and possibly never was, the 'real thing.' At the fore of the 'Anglia' section is the question of a return to innocence. Martha watches the children filled with wonder at the village fête: 'Even when they disbelieved, they also believed. The tubby, peering dwarf in the distorting mirror was them and wasn't them: both were true . . . She, Martha, could no longer do that . . . Could you reinvent innocence? Or was it always constructed, grafted on to the old disbelief?' (Barnes 1998: 264).

Does living in Anglia allow Martha to escape her world-weary skepticism long enough to recover from her sense of spiritual bankruptcy? Does the respite from the profit-driven play of signifiers finally offer her the occasion for seriousness, for commemoration, for the honoring of her dead?

Furthermore, and integral to the challenge that *England, England* will leave before its readers, is the question of how this 'constructed innocence' measures up in relation to other attitudes toward an unrecoverable past, whether personal or national. 'Anglia' can be read as a prescription for the anxiety over what is 'real' that runs throughout the novel. The unreliability of memory, the dishonoring and disowning of an imperial past, the sense of personal betrayal linked to national letdown – all of these things complicate and thwart the possibility of authentic identity. In 'Anglia,' Barnes draws a commemorative portrait of England's lost origin, a eulogy for the old myth of organic society. The rhetorical paradox of paying these last respects without (re)idealizing or reinvesting in the myth – the trick of honoring the moment 'even if it had never happened' (Barnes 1998: 238) – makes for a resolution that cannot be called 'successful' except insofar as it calls into doubt the very possibility of success in any such attempt. For Barnes, to celebrate the original moment or myth means somehow to approach it without the agenda of appropriation or mastery, of exploitation or profit. Achieving 'life's little seriousness' can thus only happen by sidestepping or renouncing modern life's driving ideology. The communities in Anglia develop through such a strategy of renunciation: close the borders, silence the media, squelch enterprise, reject the unfamiliar. But this formula is also what prevents the attempt to 'rediscover' an Englishness of old in Anglia from being anything *more* than nostalgic, since it was precisely England's ambition and desire for expansion that defined it (and fated it for modernity).

Perhaps a more accurate appraisal of the conclusion offered in 'Anglia' than 'recovery' is 'retirement': Martha finally retires from her life, chooses to inter herself in the landscape of a lost past. Unable to reconcile her cynicism with her longing for wholeness, Martha instead withdraws from the struggle. This is supported by the claim that in Anglia, Martha eventually reinvests in the collective fantasy of holistic, in-born identity: 'These questions [of how and why Anglia arose] were not debated in the village: a sign perhaps that the country's fretful, psoriatic self-consciousness had finally come to an end. And eventually she herself fitted into the village, because she herself no longer itched with her own private questions' (Barnes 1998: 257).

Here, Barnes imposes a resolution for the problems raised in the text by resurrecting the ideal of unself-conscious identity. Martha leaves behind the self-consciousness that has haunted her since her first experience of betrayal; England rediscovers its 'natural' self in the organic community of Anglia. Such a resolution is bound to fall somewhat flat for readers who take seriously the novel's challenges – as in the character of the island's Dr. Johnson – to the notion of an organic 'self' hiding out beneath the masks called for by modern existence. The withdrawal of the challenge contributes to the sense of retirement pervasive at the novel's close.

Although the novel's last offered glimpse into Martha's thoughts has her musing on how Gibbet Hill would look as an island feature (Barnes 1998:

265), we leave our heroine sitting in the moonlight observing a rabbit 'fearless and quietly confident of its territory' (Barnes 1998: 266). This final image has two rhetorical effects: first, it answers an earlier metaphor drawn by Dr. Max to explain the unmarketability of 'reality':

> The great public [. . .] want reality to be like a pet bunny. They want it to lollop along and thump its foot picturesquely in its home-made hutch and eat lettuce out of their hand. If you gave them the real thing, something wild that bit, and, if you'll pardon me, shat, they wouldn't know what to do with it. Except strangle it and cook it.
>
> (Barnes 1998: 133)

Watching this Anglian rabbit going about its business unreferenced by human desires suggests that a 'reality' has once again asserted its objective existence, or at least that a balance has been restored between that 'reality' and the signifying systems that give it meaning. Second, the image effects another invocation of old myths, for what more could post-empire England hope for than to once again be 'fearless and quietly confident of its territory?' But the questions Martha has silenced in herself continue, significantly, to remain unresolved for readers of the novel. The challenge mobilized in Barnes's satire to the idea of a personal/national 'real thing' presses beyond the borders of Anglia and continues to enliven the paradoxes of collective identity and collective history.

Notes

1 Sigmund Freud examines the psychological workings of group identity in his essay 'Group psychology and the analysis of the ego.' Because of his emphasis on collective emotion rather than collective agreement or collective action, Freud's analysis lays out a useful vocabulary for a discussion of Englishness as a collective, *affective* structure. For Freud, nationalism is based on a common emotional investment in an imaginary sense of wholeness, community feeling, or 'belonging.'

2 This terminology comes primarily from the work of Judith Butler, whose account of identity in *Gender Trouble* maintains that the discursive behaviour by which people are said to 'represent' or 'describe' themselves constitutes rather a performative *production* of those selves. Focusing on gender as a set of performative signifiers, Butler describes a reciprocal relationship in which our biological 'sex' seems to dictate our 'gendered' behaviour, whose primary function is actually to point back at our 'sex,' to re-cite and re-present it as *prior* to gender.

3 Tourism theorist Benjamin R. Barber explicitly links past imperial glory to the modern financial triumph of the theme park: 'As once the sun never set on the British empire, so today, Disney [in its Annual Report] can boast, "the fun now follows the sun around the globe" ' (Barber 1995: 134).

4 Nezar AlSayyad points out that: 'Although tourists generally long to visit

"authentic" places, the authenticity they seek is primarily visual. Thus, their encounter with "real" history remains marked by distance. And while they may wish to meet the world of the "other," they also take great pains to limit its influence on them' (AlSayyad 2001: 10).

5 In the same way, Jean Baudrillard's theory of the hyperreal describes how Disneyland presents itself as an imaginary or fictional space to make us believe that the rest of America is real, 'to conceal the fact that it is the "real" country, all of "real" America, which *is* Disneyland (just as prisons are there to conceal the fact that it is the social in its entirety, in its banal omnipresence, which is carceral)' (Baudrillard 1983: 25). Barnes's novel plays out this idea in that England, England comes universally to be understood as 'England,' while mainland England itself is dismissed as 'Old England' and eventually changes its name to Anglia (Barnes 1998: 253).

6 The 'French intellectual' is an obvious send-up of Baudrillard, who praises 'the emancipation of the sign': 'released from that "archaic" obligation that it might have to designate something, the sign is at last free for a structural or combinatory play according to indifference and a total indetermination which succeeds the previous role of determinate equivalence' (Baudrillard 1988: 125).

7 Erik Cohen explains how, as institutions become increasingly detached from 'reality,' the individual turns into himself/herself in search of the real. The opposition between self and society thus reaches its maximum when 'nothing on the "outside" can be relied upon to give weight to the individual's sense of reality' (Cohen 1987: 373). This kind of opposition, which has allowed Martha to remain 'immune' from the kind of disorientation Mark worries about (arising from confusion between reality and performance), collapses through her encounter with the Dr. Johnson character.

8 Barber draws such an opposition in *Jihad* vs. *McWorld*, positing 'jihad' as the articulation and assertion of identity claims that are vitalized in opposition to (and therefore in total reliance upon) the globalized markets of 'McWorld.' Everyone wants to know, claims Barber, whether the lands of origin that fire his or her imagination can be made real, 'And they gather, in isolation from one another but in common struggle against commerce and cosmopolitanism, around a variety of dimly remembered but sharply imagined ethnic, religious and racial identities meant to root the wandering postmodern soul and prepare it to do battle with its counterparts in McWorld' (Barber 1995: 164).

References

AlSayyad, Nezar (ed.) (2001) *Consuming Tradition, Manufacturing Heritage: global norms and urban forms in the age of tourism*, New York: Routledge.

Barber, Benjamin R. (1995) *Jihad* vs. *McWorld*, New York: Random House.

Barnes, Julian (1998) *England, England*, Toronto: Vintage Canada.

Baudrillard, Jean (1983) *Simulations*, trans. Paul Foss, Paul Patton and Philip Beitchman, New York: Semiotext(e).

—— (1988) *Selected Writings*, ed. Mark Poster, Cambridge and Stanford, Calif.: Polity Press and Stanford University Press.

Butler, Judith (1990) *Gender Trouble: feminism and the subversion of identity*, New York: Routledge.

Cohen, Erik (1987) 'Authenticity and commoditization in tourism', *Annals of Tourism Research* 15: 371–86.

Freud, Sigmund (1955) 'Group psychology and the analysis of the ego', in *Standard Edition of the Complete Psychological Works of Sigmund Freud*, Vol. XVIII, ed. and trans. James Strachey, London: Hogarth, pp. 67–143.

6   Cyberspace and the body

Jeanette Winterson's
The.PowerBook

Sonya Andermahr

'Meatspace still has some advantages for the carbon-based girl.'

(Winterson 2000: 174)

Jeanette Winterson's fiction is well known for its multiple border-crossings and fantastic journeys through space, time, genre and gender. Her fictional universes blur the boundaries between masculine and feminine, past and present, material and magical worlds. Her early novels, *Oranges Are Not the Only Fruit*, *The Passion* and *Sexing the Cherry*, employ diverse intertexts such as fairy tales, Grail legends and biblical stories, and a variety of chronotopes including the Napoleonic wars, carnival Venice and seventeenth-century London. In her latest novel, *The.PowerBook*, Winterson extends her exploration of the familiar motifs of storytelling, travel and time travel, discovery and self-discovery and the reinvention of bodies and selves, through a move into cyberspace.

The.PowerBook is Jeanette Winterson's seventh novel and, according to the author, it completes a cycle or series beginning with her semi-autobiographical debut, *Oranges Are Not the Only Fruit*: 'And they interact and themes do occur and return, disappear, come back amplified or modified, changed in some way, because it's been my journey, it's the journey of my imagination, it's the journey of my soul in those books' (Reynolds and Noakes 2003: 25).

The seven-book cycle consists of what have become, for readers and critics, identifiably 'Wintersonian' features and themes, which are continually reworked: highly self-conscious and self-reflexive first-person narratives; radical temporal shifts and narrative frame-breaks; linguistic game-playing; intertextuality and allusion to myths, fairy stories, the Bible and other books; a preoccupation with questions of identity and selfhood; and her central theme – the transcendent nature of love. In fact, her work has become synonymous with postmodern aesthetic techniques, and is one of the reasons why she is so useful in the classroom: her books are virtually 'how-to' guides to the postmodern text, a point almost parodically reinforced by the recent *Essential Guide* to her work by Margaret Reynolds and Jonathan Noakes. Winterson's admission in the interview conducted for this study that the novel finishes a sequence, leads to the question of whether it is not simply that Winterson has completed some sort of personal journey but whether this mode of writing itself is now in some way exhausted. Is there a point at which postmodern reworking becomes merely repetitive and a kind of *mise en abyme* where the conceits cannot be taken any further? In this case, cyberspace perhaps represents Winterson's 'final frontier' in the exploration of her virtual-worlds theme.

The critics are famously split on the Winterson oeuvre; as Margaret Reynolds flamboyantly puts it, you either passionately love it or hate it (Reynolds and Noakes 2003: 5). Like Lynne Pearce a few years ago,[1] I have to admit to an ambivalence towards Winterson's work: I have loved her work, and I have disliked aspects of it too. While I don't accept the view, reported by Pearce (1998: 39), that her work since *Sexing The Cherry* has deteriorated – indeed, *Written on the Body* matches the power of her first novel in my view – I do find myself occasionally nodding in agreement at some of the characterizations of her work as 'arch', 'solemn' and 'self-important' (Lezard 2001). Moreover, the very familiarity of her themes tells against her and makes them at times seem more laboured than original. Critics of *The.PowerBook* have continued in this divided vein, and I think it is useful to consider some of their responses here for what they say about attitudes to contemporary fiction as well as about Winterson herself.

Elaine Showalter's bruising review for the *Guardian*, entitled 'Eternal triangles: *The.PowerBook* is lost in space', represents the detractors. 'Alas', she says,

> *The.PowerBook* retells the same story of adulterous bisexual love that she has been telling throughout the decade. Her obsession with the Romantic triangle takes place on a higher aesthetic and intellectual level than the obsessions of this year's popular fiction, but like any of the candy-coloured novels about relationships stacked on the tables of London bookshops, it is still literary junk. Despite a capacity for exquisite erotic prose, high intelligence and an inspiring commitment to serious art, Winterson is becoming a mannered artist with nothing to say.
>
> (Showalter 2000)

Moreover, she sees Winterson's work as symptomatic of the English novel at the turn of the century, accusing it of avoiding the big subjects of our time, writing about love instead of money, about sex instead of power, about the past instead of the future, and about cities of the interior instead of real cities. In part this sounds like a plea for less postmodern textuality and more realism, but that would ignore the postmodern stylists who are interested in such 'big' questions such as Martin Amis as well as those realist novelists through the years who eschew the macro for the microcosm. It is true, as Winterson herself admits, that the invented cities of *The Passion* were written during 'the boomtime of the Thatcher years, clock-race of yuppies and City boys, rich-quick, never count the cost' yet make no allusion to them (Showalter 2000).

Interestingly, Winterson was asked about the Showalter review by an online reader who posed an intelligent question about whether the 'reductiveness' Showalter speaks of could be applied to the insularity of queer fiction or whether it was 'a mark of the self-reflexivity your writing inhabits' (Winterson 2000b). However, she claimed never to read reviews and declined any attempt to engage his question seriously, stating that, 'reviewers are often bonkers but readers are totally sane' (Winterson 2000b). Winterson's interview answers, it seems, repeat the operation of her fiction, which is to privilege the author–reader compact, to emphasize 'universals' such as the power of desire and the imagination, and to evade attempts to delimit or specify their meaning. Elsewhere she writes:

> My work sits better in the European tradition of Borges and Calvino, than it does in the Anglo-American tradition of realism and narrative. I like to use invented worlds. I cross continents of history and geographies of time to arrive in a wooded valley and dig up a story. There are always stories – endless stories – but not locked into time and place.
>
> (Winterson 2002: 3)

In another review for the *Guardian*, Nicholas Lezard offers a more generous reading, calling the novel both 'charming and moving' and averring that Winterson 'writes about sensual and erotic life with great understanding' (Lezard 2001). Writing in the *Observer*, Kate Kellaway calls *The.PowerBook* 'witty, original and good', describing the experience of reading the novel as 'like being on a strange package holiday with a wonderfully unreliable guide' (Kellaway 2000). Initially, she admits to being alarmed by the thought of Winterson going 'online', but in the event is won over because, she argues, Winterson is not in fact interested in cyberspace for its own sake but only as a conceit, and the novel is all the better for it:

> It takes no more than a page or two before it becomes marvellously clear that Winterson has no future as a boffin. The computer is, for her, a conceit, an invitation to explore, a way of making narratives come

and go faster than the speed of light. It never holds her up or back. Her writing is graceful, jargon-free, light as thistledown.

Computers are fickle and provisional: suited, perhaps, to the telling of love stories. And yet this is a novel that is in no way 'state of the art'; its heels are in the past, its heart outside time. It is more like a book of spells than a computer manual, written by someone determined to be a witch through words, convinced that lives are transmutable, open to the power of wishes. She believes that we can be the authors of our own lives.

(Kellaway 2000)

Here, Kellaway deftly captures the pleasures of Winterson's writing and her belief in the power of narrative to transport the self. She is also right to claim that Winterson's use of virtual reality is a metaphorical one, enabling her to explore her familiar themes of love, desire and boundaries. Winterson is not really interested in new computer technologies per se; her use of them is a bit like the way trendy vicars use pop music to convey the Christian message.[2] However, in appropriating the image of virtual reality and using it as device to represent the body and explore the meanings of gender and sexual desire, she does engage debates within and about so-called cyber-feminism. The rest of the chapter analyses Winterson's use of cyberspace in the context of cyberfeminism and argues that the novel provides a useful dialogue between disembodied postmodern models of the virtual self and feminist theories of female embodiment, in the process privileging the body in its many forms: physical, textual, erotic, fantastic and virtual.

Kate Kellaway's reference to 'a book of spells' written by a witch in the context of cyberspace brings to mind Donna Haraway's influential mid-1980s essay, 'A manifesto for cyborgs', in which she famously mapped the identity of women in the postmodern world onto the image of the cyborg, and argued that the hybrid female cyborgs populating women's writing destabilized a range of hierarchies, boundaries and identities. Haraway argues, first, that in a postmodern world, all human beings have adopted 'cyborg' identities; second, that cyborg identities are post-gender because they do not rely on concepts of natural sexual difference or origin myths; and third, that women have a particular affinity with cyborg identities because of the historic fragmentation of their identities as both human and non-male simultaneously; and, fourth, that the concept of the cyborg therefore affords feminists new possibilities to articulate a sexual political critique of operations of power in the postmodern world. While, some of these points may seem contradictory, Haraway emphasizes her ironic use of the concept of the cyborg and holds the different claims in playful tension with each other. The cyborg myth is both a dangerous and a potentially liberating one. Above all, her notion of the cyborg is one which blurs the boundaries between organism and machine, between the fictional and the real: 'The cyborgs populating feminist science fiction make very problematic the statuses of man or woman, human, artefact, member of a race, individual identity, or body' (Haraway 1990: 220).

Feminist work in this field in the years since the publication of Haraway's manifesto has sought both to critique male-dominated technology and to enfranchise women through it. Cyberfeminism is by now a familiar if not hackneyed academic concept – there are indeed Readers in cyberfeminism[3] – which refers to a rethinking of the feminist project in the light of new computer technologies, postmodern theory and the opportunities for 'going beyond' gender offered by these. In *Zeroes + Ones*, for example, Sadie Plant tells stories about both the feminine origins of computer technology and its potential to liberate us from gender binarism. Her work is enthusiastic about the possibilities afforded by the new technologies of abandoning gender as the grounding for identity and exploring the self outside this straitjacket: 'Cybernetic feminism does not, like many of its predecessors . . . seek out for woman a subjectivity, an identity or even a sexuality of her own: there is no subject position and no identity on the other side of the screen' (Plant 1997: 116). Instead it facilitates the deconstructive potential that resides in the 'matrix' itself, and draws attention to the ways in which the 'feminine' characterization of new technologies works in favour of women themselves:

> Like woman, software systems are used as man's tools, his media and his weapons; all are developed in the interests of man, but all are poised to betray him. [. . .] Women's liberation is sustained and vitalized by the proliferation and globalization of software technologies, all of which feed into self-organizing, self-arousing systems and enter the scene on her side.
>
> (Plant 1997: 112)

It seems to me that this idealist view of cyberspace ignores the fact that it is very often women who occupy the role of low-paid data inputters in what Donna Haraway has called 'the informatics of domination' and what radical feminists used to call 'white, capitalist patriarchy' (Haraway 1990: 204).[4] And it remains the case that not only are men much greater leisure-users of the web than women, but also that the number of sites containing child pornography has risen by 64 per cent, and that many of those 'playing with' identity on the web are middle-aged men masquerading as twelve-year-old girls.[5] Needless to say, this outcome was not part of the utopian vision of feminist web enthusiasts.

However, cyberfeminist theorists also evince a more cautious and down-beat attitude to the new computer technologies. Zoë Sofia in an essay entitled 'Virtual corporeality: a feminist view', disputes the view that virtual reality represents a utopian space for feminism: 'Virtual worlds and bodies offer pleasurable fulfilment of the defensive and ultimately misogynistic fantasy of escape from Earth, gravity, and maternal/material origins' (Sofia 1999: 65). She makes the interesting claim that women's more instrumental, less affective relation to computers represents a form of 'conscientious objection' to the 'idealist, masculinist and militaristic culture from which computers have come' (Sofia 1999: 64). Similarly, Anne Balsamo reviewing the representation of female cyborgs in popular culture, argues that, on one hand, 'female cyborgs embody cultural contradictions which strain the technological imagination'; on the other hand, 'while challenging the rela-tionship between femaleness and technology, [they] perpetuate oppressive gender stereotypes' (Balsamo 1999: 149). From a feminist perspective then, the ways in which cyberculture gets inscribed are more important than the image of the cyborg per se. As Haraway puts it: 'The cyborg is a kind of disassembled and reassembled, postmodern collective and personal self. This is the self feminists must code' (Haraway 1990: 205).

The.PowerBook certainly seems to have taken to heart the utopian version of cyberfeminism: the novel exhibits Haraway's 'pleasure in the confusion of boundaries' (Haraway 1990: 191), both sexual and narrative, for her central character and narrator Ali/Alix is a variously female and male, sexual chameleon who surfs the web and apparently travels through Europe in search of her married lover, while simultaneously telling the reader a series of stories woven through with history, myth and legend. The novel references numerous heterosexual and gay lovers who are linked into one universal story about love. These include Lancelot and Guinevere from Malory's *Morte D'Arthur*, and Paulo and Francesca who appear in both Boccaccio and Dante. In its mercurial female/male hero-narrator Ali/Alix the novel also alludes to Scheherazade and the *1001 Arabian Nights* tales. 'To avoid discovery I stay on the run', she tells us on the opening page (Winterson 2000a: 3). The resulting e-novel she composes for her lover to read becomes the 'real story' against which the various literary tales are set. Winterson's use of the web as a tool to transcend and evade sexual difference while proliferating and celebrating sexuality therefore answers Haraway's call for texts 'in a postmodern, nonnaturalist mode and in the utopian tradition of imagining a world without gender' (Haraway 1990: 192), and apparently shares Plant's view that computer technology has the potential to liberate us from gender binarism. When asked her sex online, for example, the narrator responds 'Does it matter? This is a virtual world' (Winterson 2000a: 26).

If the stories she tells are literary classics, the form she uses is up to date. Winterson's adoption of the iconography and language of cyberspace has been seen as a gimmick by some reviewers of the novel.[6] The title which resembles a web-site address, the computer manual-type format, the use of computer icons and terms such as 'hard drive' and 'new document' as chapter headings, all suggest an engagement with the new computer technologies which she doesn't deliver. However, as befits a fiction writer, Winterson's use of icons is symbolic – she puns on the religious and aesthetic meanings of the word 'icon', for example – and corresponds to the cyberfeminist notion of hybridizing forms and weaving together the organic and the mechanical, the traditional and the new. Winterson's use of icons extends beyond computer discourse to include symbols such as the tulip, a message in a bottle, the Eiffel Tower, a key, and Mount Everest. The tulip icon, which functions as the online alias of the narrator's lover, is variously pictured as open and closed, and operates in a similar way to the fruity images in *Sexing the Cherry*, which stood in for sexual attributes of the characters.

Significantly, it is e-mail that Winterson selects as her main 'contact' in Roman Jakobson's terms. E-mail, while existing in a virtual space and offering an instantaneous message service, is the closest thing in cyberspace to conventional writing. It is, after all, a written form. It also confers a certain amount of status and control on the author: all e-mail messages are authored – they come with a sender's name attached – and you compose and send any message you like. Clumsier than a conversation in 'real' time, e-mail nevertheless carries a similar element of pleasurable anticipation that a letter does, as the phrase 'you've got mail' suggests. Winterson's e-writer Ali also 'unwraps' her e-mail as she might a present (Winterson 2000a: 3).

The invitation with which the novel begins – 'You can be free just for one night' – combines two devices for self-transformation: first, an old-fashioned costume shop, which hires out clothes with which the client can disguise his/herself; and second, its virtual counterpart, the e-mail fantasy:

You say you want to be transformed.

This is where the story starts. Here, in these long lines of laptop DNA. Here we take your chromosomes, twenty-three pairs, and alter your height, eyes, teeth, sex. This is an invented world. You can be free just for one night.

Undress.
    Take off your clothes. Take off your body. Hang them up behind the door. Tonight we can go deeper than disguise.

(Winterson 2000a: 4)

Winterson strips back the layers of 'the self' beyond both cultural gender and biological sex. The body becomes a garment, which far from representing the essential self may well disguise it: 'But what if the body is the disguise? What if skin, bone, liver, veins, are the things I use to hide myself? I have put them on and I can't take them off. Does that free or trap me?' (Winterson 2000a: 15).

The novel exemplifies Winterson's abiding belief, expressed throughout her work, that 'we think of ourselves as closed and finite, when we are multiple and infinite' (Winterson 2000a: 103). The cyberspace motif allows her to articulate this exemplary statement of postmodern subjectivity in terms of the new technologies, often in insightful and original ways, such as in her comparison of the self to a 'windows' programme:

> There are so many lives packed into one. The one life we think we know is only the window that is open on the screen. The big window full of detail, where the meaning is often lost among the facts. If we can close that window, on purpose or by chance, what we find behind is another view.
>
> (Winterson 2000a: 103)

The novel itself works as a series of windows or vignettes, each adding a layer to the narrative so that reading it is analogous to surfing the web. In a series of metafictional gestures, moreover, Winterson makes the surfing–writing–reading analogy explicit:

> I was typing on my laptop, trying to move this story on, trying to avoid endings, trying to collide the real and the imaginary worlds, trying to be sure which is which. [. . .] When I sit at my computer, I accept that the virtual worlds I find there parallel my own. I talk to people whose identity I cannot prove. I disappear into a web of co-ordinates that we say will change the world. What world? Which world?
>
> (Winterson 2000a: 93–4)

The experience of cyberspace leads to a blurring of boundaries, to a collapse of the distinction between addresser and addressee, self and other, real and imagined, writing and reading:

> Night.
>   I'm sitting at my screen reading this story. In turn, the story reads me.
>   Did I write this story, or was it you, writing through me, the way the sun sparks fire through a piece of glass?
>
> (Winterson 2000a: 209)

And just as the narrator e-mails her lover, so her e-novel calls her into being, creating her identity discursively: 'The story is reading you now, line by line' (Winterson 2000a: 84).

Historically, feminist discourses have tended to either deny the female body in their desire to play down the differences between men and women; or, conversely, they have highlighted and magnified them as the basis for a politics of difference. If once the problem was steering a course between sameness and difference, or social and biological determinisms, now it is one of disembodiment and over-embodiment. Postmodern feminists such as Butler, Haraway and Plant run the risk of the former, while French feminists such as Cixous and Irigaray risk the latter. Either our bodies are entirely contingent and plastic (through cybernetic hybridization, perform-ance or while online) or they are the basis of an essentialized psychosexual economy. This debate has become one of the main sites of contestation in contemporary theory, and one that Winterson's texts can be seen to explore. At first glance, the French feminist body is too saturated in femininity, too biologically based and too maternal for Winterson's purpose. Significantly, there is no reproduction or children in her work. But in seemingly rejecting this model, does the woman disappear in Winterson's texts? I would argue not, because the postmodern body is insistently and continually both degendered and regendered by Winterson.

In her brilliant, simultaneously lyrical and analytical novel *Written on the Body* she utilizes the device of a disembodied genderless narrator in order to celebrate the beloved's body in all its physical beauty and abjection. In cyberfictional terms, 'meatspace' is most definitely privileged in this novel. The female body is explored and excavated, categorized, fetishized and made love to. At times, the narrator is oblivious to her objectification of the beloved; at times she is acutely and ironically aware of her own complicity in Romantic and patriarchal ideologies. At first glance, *The.PowerBook* seems to leave 'meatspace' behind as its refrain 'freedom just for one night' attests. However, bodies are shucked off online only to be gloriously recaptured in a series of erotic e-mail tableaux. My favourite is the opening 'tulip' story, which reworks Virginia Woolf's *Orlando* by utilizing tulip bulbs to effect a fantastic change of sex from female to male:

> When is a tulip not a tulip?
> When it's a Parrot or a Bizarre. When it's variegated or dwarf. When it comes called Beauty's Reward or Heart's Reviver. When it comes called Key of Pleasure or Lover's Dream . . .
> Tulips every one – and hundreds more – each distinctively different, all the same. The attribute of variation that humans and tulips share.
> It was the Key of Pleasure and Lover's Dream that I carried from

Sulyman the Magnificent to Leiden in 1591. To be exact, I carried
them under my trousers . . .

(Winterson 2000a: 9–10)

In *The.PowerBook*, Winterson addresses the body as though it were simultaneously there and not there, embodied and disembodied: the novel is full
of bodies and body parts, but also strangely bodiless. And yet Winterson
insists on the materiality of the body and its desires at every turn. What she
aims to do here as in her other work is reach a point where the story can be
told without reference to gender, where it ceases to matter. She seeks a way
of writing sexuality beyond gender. This is why Mallory's successful but
doomed quest to reach the summit of Everest is perhaps the central love
story of the novel. At times, when she is at her most lyrical and purely
textual, the result is strikingly effective as in this extract from the Lancelot
and Guinevere section of the novel:

Your marrow is in my bones. My blood is in your veins. Your cock is
in my cunt. My breasts weigh under your dress. My fighting arm is
sinew'd to your shoulder. Your tiny feet stand my ground. In full
armour I am wearing nothing but your shift, and when you plait your
hair you wind it round my head. Your eyes are green. My eyes are
brown.

(Winterson 2000a: 69)

Lancelot's identity merges with that of Guinevere; sexual references as well
as pronouns cross over and combine with referents from other registers, so
that eye colour and items of clothing become as significant or insignificant
as sexual body parts in the relationship between the lovers.

Winterson, as a lesbian writer, may be looking for a way to escape what
Haraway has called oedipal origin stories and the ways in which women
have been inscribed as Woman in patriarchal narratives. She exemplifies the
way in which, in Teresa de Lauretis's words,

lesbian writers and artists have sought variously to escape gender, to
deny it, transcend it, or perform it in excess, and to inscribe the erotic in
cryptic, allegorical, realistic, camp, or other modes of representation,
pursuing diverse strategies of writing and of reading the intransitive
and yet obdurate relation of reference to meaning, flesh to language.

(de Lauretis 1993: 144)

At times, Winterson writes in a more specifically 'lesbian' register, like a riff
on Irigaray's 'two lips' (1985):

Sex between women is mirror geography. The subtlety of its secret –
utterly the same, utterly different. You are a looking-glass world. You
are the hidden place that opens to me on the other side of the glass. I
touch your smooth surface and then my fingers sink through to the
other side. You are what the mirror reflects and invents. I see myself,
I see you, two, one, none. I don't know. Maybe I don't need to know.
Kiss me.

(Winterson 2000a: 174)

For those seeking to privilege a 'lesbian' reading of the novel, this is the
passage that is followed by the quotation I've used in the epigraph: 'Meatspace still has some advantages for a carbon-based girl' (Winterson 2000a:
174). Like Irigaray, Winterson plays on and with the Freudian notion of
lesbian love as narcissism. It is a dangerous strategy as it risks fixing lesbian-
ism as a form of self-love or 'twinning', and thus eliding the differences
between women. However, Winterson's allusions are self-consciously playful, as her references to *Alice Through the Looking Glass* and her insistence that
women are simultaneously the same and different suggest.

More commonly the referents are sexually indeterminate:

In this space which is inside you and inside me I ask for no rights or
territories. There are no frontiers or controls. The usual channels do
not exist. This is the orderly anarchic space that no one can dictate,
though everyone tries. This is a country without a ruler. I am free to
come and go as I please. This is Utopia. It could never happen beyond
bed. This is the model of government for the world. No one will
vote for it but everyone comes back here. This is the one place where
everybody comes.

(Winterson 2000a: 175)

In this passage, which characteristically works through aphorism and assertion, Winterson celebrates sexual love and the sense of liberation it affords.
In a series of sliding referents, both metaphorical and metonymical, it refers
to a 'space', which is simultaneously real and fantasized, literal and symbolic, which is inside the body, perhaps specifically inside the female body,
but also between lovers.

Winterson's work exhibits most of the features outlined by Haraway
in her study of women's cyborg texts. However, while goddesses have no
part in Haraway's postmodern universe, the love object at the centre of
Winterson's texts is always idolized and mythologized. Her worlds are full
too of Old Testament-type polarities and dichotomies that don't sit well
with post-structuralist feminisms. In this respect, Zoë Sofia's concept of

'virtual corporeality', an oxymoron suggesting an impossible combination, is extremely useful in thinking about Winterson's use of cyberspace and postmodern concepts more generally. Winterson's texts are peopled with similar impossible combinations: gender and species hybrids such as the Dog Woman in *Sexing the Cherry*, the web-footed Villanelle in *The Passion*, and transsexual time-travellers like Ali/Alix in *The.PowerBook*. In epistemological terms, too, her work represents something of a contradiction: while she is a thoroughgoing postmodern stylist, foregrounding the discursive construction of identity and self, refusing realist techniques of characterization, she is, nevertheless, committed to representing love and Romantic desire as moral – or immoral – absolutes, which stand seemingly outside time and place. She is not so much a biological as an emotional essentialist.

The concept of 'virtual universes' perfectly captures what Winterson creates in her fiction: whether the settings are historical, fantastical or nominally 'realist' as in *Oranges are not the Only Fruit* and *Written on the Body*, her characters are always products of the imagination, fluid and chameleon, cyborgs of the soul. She presents the self as a fictional space of invention by setting up a series of equivalences: self, body, text, story. While, in fact, these things are not reducible to each other, both postmodern chronotopes and the space that is fiction have the effect of collapsing them. In *The.PowerBook*, her genre of choice is not so much cyberfiction as the romance quest, which she returns to its medieval source and presents as the basis of all storytelling. In her version, the genre is about self-discovery and is as relevant now as it ever was. Winterson's message is that reality dissolves into stories and what propels them: desire. E-mail and the web are tools, instruments for the telling of stories, and all reality is 'virtual'.

While *The.PowerBook* has little to say about the new computer technologies themselves, Winterson makes striking use of cyberspace and virtual reality as tropes. Ultimately, Winterson's text is not proffering cyberspace as a feminist utopian space so much as presenting it as an analogous fictional realm in which she and her readers may sport. In this sense, Winterson knows that the true site of morphological transformation is as old as the hills – storytelling itself. As she says, 'This is Utopia' (Winterson 2000a: 175).

The editor of this collection of essays asked me to look at Winterson's treatment of 'identity', to see if it was characterized by 'millennial anxieties' and concerns. In fact, while Winterson's characters represent almost exemplary postmodern selves – fragmented, contingent, discursively constructed – there is always in her texts another presence, another persona, Winterson herself, who seems to exhibit few doubts about identity or anything else and resembles nothing so much as the god-like authorial voice of nineteenth-century fiction. 'Postmodern or materialist?' is the question so often asked of contemporary women's writing. Winterson's work defies categorization, but has leanings in both directions. She remains, too, that not so common thing, a lesbian writer who, without even using the term and, in fact, disavowing it in interview for its obvious limiting connotations, conveys a postmodern lesbian aesthetic consisting of a challenge to compulsory heterosexuality and a celebration of sexual love that references, even as it goes beyond, same-sex desire to include all lovers. Whether in nineteenth-century Venice, twenty-first-century Rome or indeed cyberspace, these are her real subjects. For Winterson there is – or has been – only one story: 'I keep telling this story – different people, different places, different times – but always you, always me, always this story, because a story is a tightrope between two worlds' (Winterson 2000a: 119).

This brings me to the question I raised at the beginning of the chapter: is Winterson's preoccupation with bisexual love in a virtual world exhausted as a topic for the new millennium? Reading the critics, I would say probably, yes. Reading her many – mainly young – fans on her web site, I would say no.[7] For myself, I'd like to see Winterson change tack and find another tale, but tackle the social issues of our day – an Amis-like satire on money, power and the contemporary city? I'm not so sure.

Notes

1 In an article on her changing responses to Winterson's work, Pearce writes:

> What my re-reading goes on to acknowledge, however, is the way these desperate and devious readerly-manoeuvres – made in order to maintain my 'special relationship' with the Winterson texts – could not be sustained indefinitely. As I acknowledge, in my 're-memory', *Written on the Body* was: 'The beginning of the end of my special relationship with "Jeanette" '.
>
> (Pearce 1998: 33)

2 In the interview published in *The Essential Guide*, Winterson elaborates on her attitude to the web:

> I don't think technology can change your attitude. I think it's simply something that you use or not depending on where you live in the world and how you live in the world. The Web doesn't matter to me. What matters to me is that people should go on having creative ideas and go on producing interesting work. How they do it, and how they disseminate it is really unimportant. I don't care if books end up being electronic . . . what matters is what's in them, and not necessarily the form that they take.
>
> (Reynolds and Noakes 2003: 28)

3 And I am indebted to the excellent *Cybersexualities: a reader on feminist theory, cyborgs and cyberspace* edited by Jenny Wolmark for several of the cyberfeminist writings that I discuss here.

4 Haraway writes: 'From one perspective, a cyborg world is about the final imposition of a grid of control on the planet, about the final abstraction embodied in a Star Wars apocalypse waged in the name of defense, about the final appropriation of women's bodies in a masculinist orgy of war' (Haraway 1990: 196).

5 See, for example, 'Child porn websites soar as internet leads to huge increase in sex offences' and 'Soham officer posed as a schoolgirl in chatroom', *Evening Standard*, Thursday 21 August 2003.

6 Showalter, for example, states: 'Designed to suggest the appearance and the technique of virtual reality, with a cover like a computer handbook and chapter divisions of hard drives, icons and documents, *The.PowerBook* is not a playful postmodern experiment or an investigation of the multiple personalities of e-mail' (Showalter 2000).

7 Winterson's official web site can be contacted at info@jeanettewinterson.com. Anna Troberg also runs a readers' site at <http://www.winterson.net>.

References

Balsamo, Anne (1999) 'Reading cyborgs, writing feminism', in Jenny Wolmark (ed.) *Cybersexualities: a reader on feminist theory, cyborgs and cyberspace*, Edinburgh: Edinburgh University Press.

de Lauretis, Teresa (1993) 'Sexual indifference and lesbian representation', in Henry Abelove, Michele Aina Barale and David M. Halperin (eds) *The Lesbian and Gay Studies Reader*, London and New York: Routledge.

Haraway, Donna (1990) 'A manifesto for cyborgs', in Linda J. Nicholson (ed.) *Feminism/Postmodernism*, London and New York: Routledge.

Irigaray, Luce (1985) *This Sex Which Is Not One*, trans. Catherine Porter with Carolyn Burke. Ithaca, NY: Cornell University Press.

Kellaway, Kate (2000) 'She's got the power', *Observer*, Sunday, 27 August. Online. Available HTTP: <http://books.guardian.co.uk/reviews/generalfiction> (accessed 21 July 2003).

Lezard, Nicholas (2001) '*The.PowerBook* by Jeanette Winterson', *Guardian*, Saturday, 12 May. Online. Available HTTP: <http://books.guardian.co.uk/reviews/roundupstory> (accessed 21 July 2003).

Pearce, Lynne (1998) 'The emotional politics of reading Winterson', in H. Grice and T. Woods (eds) *I'm Telling You Stories: Jeanette Winterson and the politics of reading*, Amsterdam and Atlanta, Ga.: Rodopi.

Plant, Sadie (1997) *Zeroes + Ones: digital women + new technoculture*, New York: Doubleday.

—— (1999) 'The future looms: weaving women and cybernetics', in Jenny Wolmark (ed.) *Cybersexualities: a reader on feminist theory, cyborgs and cyberspace*, Edinburgh: Edinburgh University Press.

Reynolds, Margaret and Jonathan Noakes (2003) *Jeanette Winterson: the essential guide*, London: Vintage.

Showalter, Elaine (2000) 'Eternal triangles, Jeanette Winterson's *The.PowerBook* is lost in cyberspace', *Guardian*, Saturday, 2 September. Online. Available HTTP: <http://books.guardian.co.uk/reviews/generalfiction> (accessed 21 July 2003).

Sofia, Zoë (1999) 'Virtual corporeality: a feminist view', in Jenny Wolmark (ed.) *Cybersexualities: a reader on feminist theory, cyborgs and cyberspace*, Edinburgh: Edinburgh University Press.

Winterson, Jeanette (2000a) *The.PowerBook*, London: Jonathan Cape.

—— (2000b) 'The author of *Oranges Are Not the Only Fruit* and *The.PowerBook* discusses gender, identity and why she's a hopeless Romantic', Guardian Unlimited, Thursday, 7 September. Online. Available HTTP: <http://www.guradian.co.uk/Archive/Article> (accessed 21 July 2003).

—— (2002) 'Invented Worlds', from the programme for the stage production of *The.PowerBook*. Devised by Jeannette Winterson, Deborah Warner and Fiona Shaw. Lyttleton Theatre, 9 May–4 June 2002.

Wolmark, Jenny (ed.) (1999) *Cybersexualities: a reader on feminist theory, cyborgs and cyberspace*, Edinburgh: Edinburgh University Press.

7 'Fascinating violation'

Ian McEwan's children[1]

Peter Childs

'But this new element – the innocent child – put his lapse beyond mitigation'

(McEwan 2001: 132)

Since at least the United Nations Convention on the Rights of the Child in 1989, renewed discussion of the status of childhood was markedly evident at the conclusion of the twentieth century.[2] This was accompanied by debate on child abuse and protection, fuelled by media enquiries that stretched from the speculation surrounding the longest criminal trial in US history, 'The McMartin Pre-School Case', on child molestation, concluded in January 1990, to the attention devoted to the murder of two ten-year-old girls by Ian Huntley in the English village of Soham in 2002. In between were vociferous concerns expressed over children's physical and sexual safety from relatives and strangers, their too-fast development into adults, their commodification within consumerist society, their exploitation over the Internet, their increased exposure to and use of drugs and violence, and also their supposed neglect, especially in single-parent families.[3] The Child Support Agency was established to deal with the latter, while analysis of repressed-memory syndrome was said to have unearthed past child abuses. The Catholic Church and foster homes were the subject of scandals, and investigations of infant death started to suspect or detect newly discovered abuses such as shaken-baby syndrome and Munchausen's syndrome by proxy. Media interest in children's bodies also ran a gamut of concerns from anorexia in the early 1990s to obesity at the end. In the UK, the culmination of the 1990s increased interest in protecting the child came in June 2003, when Tony Blair appointed the first minister for children and in March 2004, when the Children's Bill created a children's commissioner for England to champion their rights, after the investigation into the death, at the hands of her carers, of Victoria Climbié in 2000.

In the context of these developments, this essay will consider the figure of the child in contemporary British fiction of the period, with emphasis on the novels of Ian McEwan, from *The Child in Time* (1988) through to *Atonement* (2001). Recent novels have shown a fascination with the violation of childhood through various kinds of encounter with the adult world and I want to contextualise the discussion of McEwan's work by discussing examples by three other authors from the period 1989–2001. These novels reflect dominant fears about child safety and childhood in the 1990s: child murder, child molestation and the influence of childhood trauma on later life. Each of the three preoccupations contains significant traces of deep anxieties picked up in McEwan's fiction about adult identity related to early life experience.

Pat Barker's *Border Crossing* (2001) explores the relationship between a child and a psychiatrist in connection with a case that has clear parallels with the murder of the infant Jamie Bulger in Bootle, Merseyside by two ten-year-olds in 1993. The broad public fascination with the case, evidenced in books such as Blake Morrison's *As If*, Gitta Sereny's *Cries Unheard* and Mark Thomas's *Every Mother's Nightmare*, was less because of the child victim than the child murderers, which raised deeply troubling questions about the responsibility and the 'corruption' of pre-adolescents, particularly as the catalyst for the murder was alleged to be an adult horror video with children and violence at its centre: *Child's Play 2*. David Jackson's *Destroying the Baby in Themselves* (1995) sees the Jamie Bulger murder as a consequence of a childrearing system in which two ten-year-old boys were trying to assert a masculinity they felt they had to live up to. The case and Jackson's reading have much in common with McEwan's *The Child in Time*, discussed below, which explores gendered identity in relation to childrearing and begins with the disappearance of a child from a supermarket, as Bulger was abducted from a shopping centre on Merseyside. In the novel McEwan postulates that a generation is inescapably reflected in its attitude towards the nurturing and education of children. This partly explains the novel's title, which is also an allusion to the various designs on and desire for childhood that run throughout the narrative.[4]

The allegations of sex offences involving minors against pop stars Gary Glitter, Pete Townshend and Michael Jackson, alongside a number of best-selling confessional books which included allegations of childhood abuse, from Dave Pelzer to Billy Connolly, gave such issues a high profile in the press and brought a new language into general currency, including terms ranging from transatlantic watchwords like 'stranger danger', through phrases for technological threats such as 'internet grooming', to clinical concepts like 'recovered memory'. A 1990s cult of frenzied concern for children was subsequently satirised by Chris Morris in a special edition of his *Brass Eye* television programme focusing on media coverage of paedophilia in 2001. Including a simulated lynch-mob attack on a prison in which a paedophile was being held and a campaign to quarantine all children in the nation's sports stadiums at night, the programme itself inevitably created an outcry of the kind it was satirising.[5] The closest to Morris's satire in high-profile literary fiction has been Martin Amis's major novels of the period, *London Fields* (1990) and *The Information* (1996). Both contain elements of child molestation or exploitation, which for Amis is linked to the cultural shift that has seen pornography enter mainstream culture in the West. In one essay from *The War Against Cliché* (2002), Amis writes that pornography's 'industrial dimensions are an inescapable modern theme' (Amis 2002: 161), and this stretches to include children: for example, Marmaduke, Guy Clinch's unruly son in *London Fields*, 'looks as though he is already contemplating a career in child pornography' (Amis 1990: 158), while Keith Talent confesses: '*Got to stop hurting K*, Keith had written, *Just takeing it out on the Baby*' (sic) (Amis 1990: 454). In *The Information* the abuse of children also becomes the last recourse for put-upon adults who, through the torturing of others, attempt to punish something in themselves. It is a constant subject, in the press: 'every other day on the cover of my newspaper there is a photograph of a murdered child' (Amis 1996: 124). It is also at the heart of the novel's chilling climax, when Richard Tull's child Marco is nearly brutally attacked by Steve Cousins (Amis 1996: 478, 492–3). Cousins's own interest in pornography has its roots here:

> many of the actors and almost all of the actresses on the pornographic screen had been abused as children. That meant that he and they formed . . . not a happy family. But a big one. . . . They were all children together in this – this big family. All children, until they weren't. Pornography was the story of his life.
>
> (Amis 1996: 410–11)

By the time of *Yellow Dog* in 2003, where a father is separated from his child because of false allegations of abuse, Amis had taken to characterising the West as simply a 'porno world'. This is in contrast to the militancy of the pre-post-feminist 1980s when campaigns were mounted against chain stores like W. H. Smith for selling soft-core top-shelf magazines, the majority of whose market share moved in the following decade to mainstream publications such as *Loaded* and *FHM*. By the end of the 1990s, 'crack whore' was a slogan emblazoned on the T-shirt of fifteen-year-old singer Charlotte Church and 'porn star' was a successful fashion brand. Child abuse itself was a prominent subject of novels in the decade, up to Gilbert Adair's Hitchcockian revenge thriller *A Closed Book* (1999)

Kazuo Ishiguro's fifth novel, *When We Were Orphans* (2001), is his most explicit investigation to date into the ways in which childhood shapes later life and yet eludes the adult it affects; most importantly, childhood represents in the novel a prelapsarian Eden before the fall into adulthood. For Ishiguro this is a kind of nostalgia for 'a time in your childhood before you realised the world was as dark as it was. . . . A child's logic somehow dictates that when you heal your own past, the whole world will come to be put back together again' (Shaffer 2001: 4). While all Ishiguro's narrators are looking for clues to explain how they have become who they are, it is only in *When We Were Orphans* that he places a professional investigator at the centre of a book. Christopher Banks's search for his missing parents is inevitably entangled with staging the psychological pursuit of his own identity and coming to terms with having been thrust into an adult world when he was suddenly abandoned at the age of ten. At more than one point Banks appears to be on the verge of ameliorating the psychological damage of his desertion in childhood, especially through a possible relationship with Sarah Hemmings, another orphan, but instead his life is marked by repetition. He abandons Sarah, as he abandons Jennifer, the orphan he adopts, and as indeed he once abandoned his childhood friend Akira, replaying his own abandonment by both his parents and his 'Uncle Philip' (Ishiguro 2001). Like Ryder in Ishiguro's earlier *The Unconsoled* (1995), Banks unconsciously turns his deepest personal fear into a universal one: 'After all, the whole world's on the brink of catastrophe. What would people think of me if I abandoned them all at this stage?' (Ishiguro 2001: 212). In *When We Were Orphans* Ishiguro creates in Christopher Banks a figure who centres the world on his own childhood loss, which he spends a lifetime trying to explain to himself.

Abandonment and the lost child are principal themes in McEwan's novels, and this is partly expressed through children's marginalisation or absence from the narratives themselves. His third novel, *The Child in Time* (1988), initially set in the 'last decent summer' of the 1990s, is interested in the intersection of the personal and the official relationships between parents and children. This manifests itself most explicitly in the novel's concern with both individual child care and the interest professionals and the government take in the rearing of children. McEwan explains that he was partly inspired by reading Christina Hardyment's book *Dream Babies* (1983), in which McEwan believed Hardyment was suggesting that child-care manuals accurately indicate 'the spirit of an age':

> You have the intense regulation of the Victorian notion of breaking a child's will, followed by a rather sentimental child-centred Edwardian view, followed by the rather grisly pseudo-scientific notion of childcare

that predominated in the 1920s and '30s, with a lot of input from behaviourists, and then in 1948 . . . Spock.'

(Reynolds and Noakes 2002: 11)[6]

Following this logic through, McEwan thought that under an authoritarian government it was quite plausible that another child-care manual might be in preparation, sponsored by the state. At one stage McEwan considered drafting a parodic manual but finally restricted himself to writing the extracts that preface each of the chapters of *The Child in Time* and which are supposedly taken from the government's *Authorised Childcare Handbook*. The tenor of these extracts reflects the mood outlined by Hardyment at the end of her 1983 book: 'hundreds of experts are now at great pains to tell us exactly what nature allows us to be, and the prospect is bleak' (Hardyment 1983: 293).

One of the most striking aspects of *The Child in Time* is McEwan's decision to set it ten years on from his time of writing. What emerges is a future in which beggars are licensed, the police are armed and ambulance services have been privatised, indicating a society largely indifferent to the care of its citizens. The novel's social context is thus shaped as a projection of the state of the nation towards the millennium if the authoritarianism of Thatcher were to endure – a projection that was partially echoed in the 'Back to Basics' family-values campaign of the Major government in the early 1990s.

For Malcolm Bradbury, probably thinking of *Black Dogs* and *Enduring Love*, McEwan's first novel set in the 1990s also in some ways anticipates the novelist's own future thematic concerns:

> Childhood, always central in McEwan's fiction, is the main theme, but now no longer seen as an angle on a hard adult world from a child's perplexed and ambiguous point of view, but as an element in the ambiguous world of contemporary family life. . . . This was a book that laid down many of the themes of McEwan's fiction of the Nineties.
>
> (Bradbury 2001: 481)

It is *The Child in Time*'s concern with the meaning of childhood that has attracted most attention, but it is common in McEwan's novels since *The Cement Garden* (published in 1978) to find a preoccupation with children becoming adults and adults returning to childhood. The focus on trans-formation is most evident in McEwan's book for children, *The Daydreamer* (1995). The conceit of the seven interlinked stories is that daydreaming is an out-of-body experience where the imagination takes the mind far from the individual's physical environment. Consequently, each of the stories con-cerns metamorphosis: the daydreamer's projection into another kind of body, such as a doll or a cat, a baby or a grown-up, or others' transformations from mother's boy into bully or old lady into burglar. The middle chapter of the book concerns a vanishing cream where the body is cloaked in invisibility, but it is in the final story that McEwan confronts childhood's uneasy relationship with the adult body. In the daydreamer's twelfth year he begins 'to notice just how different the worlds of children and grown-ups were' (McEwan 1995: 130). It is here that McEwan makes explicit his debt to Kafka by transforming the first sentence of *Metamorphosis*: 'The following morning Peter Fortune woke from troubled dreams to find himself transformed into a giant person, an adult' (McEwan 1995: 135). By alluding to Gregor Samsa's overnight metamorphosis into a giant insect, McEwan is suggesting both the importance of childhood and (day)dreaming to the inventions that underpin fiction and also the gulf between 'the worlds of children and grown-ups', physically bridged by the transformation of adolescence.

It is the imagination that bridges this gulf mentally, and this is the principal subject of *The Child in Time*, the novel of McEwan's that is most concerned with the relationship between the child's and the adult's world, but where there is no literal child at all. The presence of children is removed at the start of the novel, when the protagonist Stephen Lewis loses his daughter Kate, and only reintroduced on its closing page, when a new baby is born to Stephen and his wife Julie.[7] *The Child in Time* is thus far more concerned with the child within the adult than with children per se. When Stephen recalls Kate he fondly remembers 'her lessons in celebrating the specific', and asks himself: 'Wasn't that Nietzsche's idea of true maturity, to attain the seriousness of a child at play?' (McEwan 1988: 105–6). By contrast, Stephen as an adult has lost the child within himself: 'He was partly somewhere else, never quite paying attention, never wholly serious' (McEwan 1988: 105). Yet, to return to thinking and behaving like a child, like the publisher-turned-politician Charles Darke, would be a kind of death; thus the novel suggests that the mature individual has to balance the child and the adult, like the ego balancing the demands of the id and the super-ego.[8] The result of authoritarianism is to recreate citizens as children in response to parental control and patronage. Watching television, Stephen, though positioned as a baby-with-a-bottle himself, berates the infantilisation of his contemporary society:

> the wide open faces were those of children . . . infants who longed for nothing more than to be told when to laugh? Stephen tilted his bottle and sucked and was ready to disenfranchise them all. More than that he wanted them punished, soundly beaten, no tortured. How dare they be children!'

> (McEwan 1988: 124–5)

As much concerned with child abuse as Amis's recent fiction up to *Yellow Dog*, McEwan's *Black Dogs* (1998a) purports to be a divagation by an orphan, Jeremy, drawn to and fascinated by the families of others. Overall, the novel is an exploration of the nature of 'evil', which has its counterpart in McEwan's screenplay for *The Good Son* (1993), in which a couple refuse to believe that their son is capable of the acts he is alleged to have committed, until he attempts to kill his own mother. *Black Dogs* also evinces an incredulity towards sudden, seemingly motiveless violent aggression. In a crucial scene that unlocks his own repressed rage, Jeremy witnesses a seven- or eight-year-old boy repeatedly struck by his father at a restaurant table: 'It was impossible, I thought I had not seen it, a strong man could not hit a child this way, with the unrestrained force of adult hatred' (McEwan 1998a: 129). Jeremy attacks the man and is distressed when he realises that his 'elation' at punishing him has 'nothing to do with revenge and justice' (McEwan 1998a: 131). McEwan suggests that violence breeds violence throughout *Black Dogs*, as one act of aggression leads inexorably to another, which may be concealed as political action, sexual passion or self-righteous anger. Jeremy's mother-in-law, who has had an encounter in 1946 with two ferocious black dogs, which have supposedly been trained by the Gestapo to rape as well as savage, tells him: 'these animals were the creations of debased imaginations, of perverted spirits no amount of social theory could account for. The evil I'm talking about lives in us all. It takes hold in an individual, in private lives, within a family, and then it's children who suffer most' (McEwan 1998a: 172).

The child who has suffered most in *Black Dogs* is Jeremy's niece Sally, with whose family Jeremy lived as a teenager after the death of his own mother and father in a car crash. Jeremy much later realises that Sally's parents' 'violence extended to my niece. That she let twenty years go by before she told anyone shows how suffering can isolate a child. I did not know then how adults can set about children, and perhaps I would not have wanted to know' (McEwan 1998a: 16).[9] McEwan alludes here to the willed ignorance of violence that has kept domestic and child abuse hidden from public recognition and yet in the 1990s became the subject of intense public scrutiny. Sally's story is completed later in the book: 'she had married a man who had beaten her and left her with a child. Two years later, Sally had been found unfit, too violent to care for her little boy who was now with foster parents' (McEwan 1998a: 68). Like Ishiguro's novel examined earlier, *Black Dogs* is on one level the attempt of an adult to come to terms with the childhood loss of his parents – both novels' narrators seek out the parental guidance they feel they have lost. This is a loss which has not only created emotional disturbance but also a disorientation which leads both narrators to characterise their lives in terms of the search for an answer that cannot be found: Banks's answer to his childhood abandonment, Jeremy's to the presence of evil in the world, leaving him oscillating between rationalist and metaphysical explanations.

Jeremy also increasingly becomes an image of the novelist, of the observing outsider trying to make sense of the lives and opinions of others – an aspect of the book that links it to *Atonement* (2001). *Atonement* recalls Henry James's *What Maisie Knew* and L. P. Hartley's *The Go-Between* in depicting adults' sexualised behaviour from the perspective of a child, but, as in many discussions of the Bulger case, it associates childhood as much with ineluctable guilt as Romantic lost innocence. Briony Tallis carries a childhood mistake all her life and, having atoned in the only way she feels she can, looks forward to escaping through illness and senility the albatross of an unalterable past to which she can only bear witness.

As a child, Briony considers the moral worth of fiction as she imagines turning into a story an incident she has witnessed unobserved:

> There did not have to be a moral. She need only show separate minds, as alive as her own, struggling with the idea that other minds were equally alive. It wasn't only wickedness and scheming that made people unhappy, it was confusion and misunderstanding; above all, it was the failure to grasp the simple truth that other people are as real as you. And only in a story could you enter these different minds and show how they had an equal value. That was the only moral a story need have.
>
> (McEwan 2001: 40)

This story becomes the substance of the novel itself, rewritten several times over a period of sixty years by the adult Briony.[10] At the start of the narrative, Briony is a solitary, precocious thirteen-year-old girl with a desire for intrigue: 'hidden drawers, lockable diaries and cryptographic systems could not conceal from Briony the simple truth: she had no secrets. Her wish for a harmonious, organised world denied her the reckless possibilities of wrongdoing' (McEwan 2001: 5). Experimenting with drama and fiction has demonstrated 'that the imagination itself was a source of secrets' (McEwan 2001: 6) and writing a story meant Briony's 'passion for tidiness was also satisfied, for an unruly world could be made just so' (McEwan 2001: 7).

When a girl, Briony feels that she will mature through experience of real life, in which the process of becoming involves cutting away 'the sickly dependency of infancy and early childhood . . . She would simply wait on the bridge, calm and obstinate, until events, real events, not her own fantasies, rose to her challenge, and dispelled her insignificance' (McEwan 2001: 74–7). Thinking that she is emerging from 'a childhood she considered closed' (McEwan 2001: 116), Briony has yet to pass over into adult comprehension. Stationed symbolically on the bridge, she stands poised between possibilities, inexperience and experience, childhood and adulthood, fiction and quotidian reality. Consequently, she misses the truths of others' experience and instead conjures the world for herself through 'a trick of her imagination' (McEwan 2001: 177): 'truth was strange and deceptive, it had to be struggled for, against the flow of the everyday' (McEwan 2001: 158). Briony's mother is depicted as thinking that 'Her daughter was always off and away in her mind, grappling with some unspoken, self-imposed problem, as though the weary, self-evident world could be re-invented by a child' (McEwan 2001: 68).

Though set in the 1930s and 1940s, *Atonement* reflects attitudes towards children at the millennium because it depicts a society that enshrines the child in a state of fragile innocence and simple truthfulness at danger from an adult world of sexuality and violence. On the one hand, the children whose parents are about to divorce – the fifteen-year-old Lola, and the nine-year-old twins Jackson and Pierrot – are the ones deemed vulnerable, while Briony's word is considered inviolable despite her overactive imagination. On the other, the working-class young men Robbie Turner and Danny Hardman are thought of as the only possible suspects following the sexual assault on Lola, while the man responsible, Paul Marshall, patronises the policemen on the terrace (McEwan 2001: 175). In Briony, McEwan presents the child and the writer together, in that Briony's story is fictionalised by Briony herself, but also in the sense that the child and the novelist both fashion worlds of their own imagining, are both 'daydreamers' in the novel's terms:

> The very complexity of her feelings confirmed Briony in her view that she was entering an arena of adult emotion and dissembling from which her writing was bound to benefit. . . . [S]he needed to consider Robbie afresh, and to frame the opening paragraph of a story shot through with real life.'
>
> (McEwan 2001: 113)

For Briony, the incident between Robbie and Cecilia has 'made her into a real writer', but for McEwan this is a deeply problematic concept as it involves the presumption that one can know the other by inhabiting 'some god-like place from which all people could be judged alike. . . . If such a place existed, she was not worthy of it. She could never forgive Robbie his disgusting mind' (McEwan 2001: 115). Briony's desire to craft fiction thus gives rise to the story she fabricates for the police, in which reality is fashioned from imagination: 'Her eyes confirmed the sum of all she knew and had recently experienced. The truth was in the symmetry, which was to say, it was founded in common sense. The truth instructed her eyes. So, when she said, over and over again, I saw him, she meant it' (McEwan 2001: 169).

Only much later, after she has come to describe herself as 'unforgiveable' (McEwan 2001: 285), does Briony become a writer able to judge events from others' perspectives and seek to forgive herself for her own mind with its 'joyful feeling of blameless self-love' (McEwan 2001: 177). This is when there is no one else – Robbie, Cecilia or God, 'the Author of everlasting life' (McEwan 2001: 326) – to whom she can atone, confining her to the same position as Ishiguro's Christopher Banks, endlessly circling his own mind to find a way to undo the past.

Finally, though, one novel seems to be about the child and the other not at all. McEwan's 1997 novel *Enduring Love* is in one pertinent way structurally similar to *The Child in Time* in that, despite children's general absence from the narrative, it starts and finishes with them. Insinuating the consolations for death offered by children, the novel ends with the daughter and son of a doctor called Logan who was killed trying to save a child in the first chapter. Also, completing the cycle of events that began with Joe and his partner Clarissa's picnic at the start of the narrative, the book concludes with another picnic, at which Logan is proven innocent of his wife's accusation of adultery and in which his children help to bring the childless couple Joe and Clarissa closer together again (later, they 'successfully' adopt a child) (McEwan 1998b: 242). Indeed, a child's question concludes the narrative: in the novel's final words Rachael Logan pointedly asks Joe to tell her brother 'the thing about the river' (McEwan 1998b: 231). What Joe has told Rachael is to imagine the 'smallest possible bit of water that can exist . . . Two atoms of hydrogen, one of oxygen, bound together by a mysterious powerful force' (McEwan 1998b: 225). Millions of these particles then make up the river, he says. In a novel in which the claims of science and art to explain the world have competed, one analogy here is evidently with the smallest human unit in society, in which two people are bound together alongside a third, their child. Despite the absence of children from the main plot of *Enduring Love*, the ties of love that bind are exemplified in the act of Logan's self-sacrifice at the start of the narrative – hanging on to an air-balloon's mooring rope to keep a child from flying away. The scene exemplifies McEwan's representation of children throughout his fiction of the period, in which numerous adults, from Stephen Lewis to Briony Tallis, feel the need to hold on to and protect a child that has ostensibly escaped them, not least because, as the narrator argues in *Black Dogs*, 'at some level you remain an orphan for life; looking after children is one way of looking after yourself' (McEwan 1998a: 10).

Notes

1 The phrase 'fascinating violation' describes Jack's delight at the prospect of the cement garden in McEwan's first novel (McEwan 1997: 17).

2 For a discussion of this see Patrizia Lombardo (1997). This special edition of *Critical Quarterly*, edited by Lombardo, builds on the foundational work on the subject, Neil Postman's *The Disappearance of Childhood* (1982), which focused on television as the culprit for the end of childhood – a standpoint that twenty years later makes Postman's book itself seem almost nostalgically dated.

3 For an in-depth discussion of the fascination with children and sexuality in the 1990s see the Introduction and final chapter of James R. Kincaid, *Child-Loving: the erotic child and Victorian literature* (Kincaid 1992). Kincaid makes the point that fears in the late twentieth century can be likened to nineteenth-century, and especially Dickensian, fictions about the child.

4 The title is also an allusion to Michael Tippett's 1930s oratorio *A Child of Our Time* with which McEwan became acquainted while writing his own libretto for *Or Shall We Die?* (1989).

5 One of the major reference points of the satire was the filming by the BBC *Panorama* programme of a crowd protesting outside a Bristol police station to which the child-murderer Sidney Cooke had fled for protection in 1998. The Criminal Justice Act of 1991 had made supervision of ex-offenders compulsory, but many released child-murderers such as Cooke had been sentenced prior to the Act and so were unsupervised on release.

6 McEwan is referring at the end to Dr Benjamin Spock (1903–98), an American paediatrician whose theories encouraged mothers to show greater attention towards, and freedom of expression for, their children.

7 Stephen follows the four stages of loss outlined in John Bowlby's work: numbing, searching for the lost figure, disorganisation and reorientation to reality (Bowlby 1991).

8 Darke can be seen as a projection into the future as he represents in extreme form the 'kidult' of the millennium: the Peter Pan adult who wishes to revert to childhood as much as teenagers are thought to wish to escape childhood or anorexics refuse an adult body (literary examples of the blurring of lines between child and adult range from the commitment-phobic 1990s ladlit novels of Nick Hornby to the creation of the *Bookseller*'s 'Crossover' list of best-selling fiction that is bought by both adults and children).

9 This last phrase invokes the novel's epigraph from Marsilio Ficino.

10 'The earliest version, January 1940, the latest, March 1999, and in between, half a dozen different drafts' (McEwan 2001: 369).

References

Adair, Gilbert (1999) *A Closed Book*, London: Faber & Faber.
Amis, Martin (1990) *London Fields*, Harmondsworth: Penguin.
—— (1996) *The Information*, London: Flamingo.
—— (2002) *The War Against Cliché*, London: Vintage.
—— (2003) *Yellow Dog*, London: Jonathan Cape.
Barker, Pat (2001) *Border Crossing*, London: Viking.
Bowlby, John (1991) *Loss*, Harmondsworth: Penguin.

Bradbury, Malcolm (2001) *The Modern British Novel, 1878–2001*, rev. edn, Harmondsworth: Penguin.

Hardyment, Christina (1983) *Dream Babies: child care from Locke to Spock*, London: Jonathan Cape.

Ishiguro, Kazuo (1995) *The Unconsoled*, London: Faber & Faber.

—— (2001) *When We Were Orphans*, London: Faber & Faber.

Jackson, David (1995) *Destroying the Baby in Themselves*, London: Five Leaves.

Kincaid, James R. (1992) *Child-Loving: the erotic child and Victorian literature*, London: Routledge.

Lombardo, Patrizia (1997) 'The end of childhood?', *Critical Quarterly* 39(3) (autumn): 1–7.

McEwan, Ian (1988) *The Child in Time*, London: Picador.

—— (1989) *A Move Abroad: Or Shall We Die? and The Ploughman's Lunch*, London: Picador.

—— (1995) *The Daydreamer*, London: Vintage.

—— (1997) *The Cement Garden*, London: Vintage.

—— (1998a) *Black Dogs*, London: Vintage.

—— (1998b) *Enduring Love*, London: Vintage.

—— (2001) *Atonement*, London: Jonathan Cape.

Morrison, Blake (1998) *As If*, London: Granta.

Postman, Neil (1982) *The Disappearance of Childhood*, London: Bantam.

Reynolds, Margaret and Jonathan Noakes (eds) (2002) *Ian McEwan: the essential guide*, London: Vintage.

Sereny, Gitta (1998) *Cries Unheard*, London: Macmillan.

Shaffer, Brian W. (2001) 'An interview with Kazuo Ishiguro', *Contemporary Literature* 42(1): 1–14.

Thomas, Mark (1993) *Every Mother's Nightmare*, London: Pan.

8 'Tongues of bone'

A. L. Kennedy and the problems of articulation

Helen Stoddart

Many of the writers who have gained commercial success and critical acclaim in the late 1980s and 1990s have been characterized both by their ability to write about, and through, different media. Martin Amis, Salman Rushdie, Jeanette Winterson and Hanif Kureishi have all dabbled in journalism (personal, political and literary), stage/screenplay writing and have made appearances on television and radio programmes. Those capable of such multi- or cross-media interventions are, perhaps since Angela Carter, no longer exceptional, and contemporary writers are increasingly accustomed to media and celebrity, even if they are not necessary adept or comfortable with it. In this respect then, A. L. Kennedy appears to be contemporary with full media low-down. Although she is primarily known as a short-story writer, through collections such as *Night Geometry and the Garscadden Trains* (1990), *Now That You're Back* (1994), *Original Bliss* (1997), and *Indelible Acts* (2002). She has also written three novels (*Looking for the Possible Dance* [1993b], *So I am Glad* [1996a], and *Everything You Need* [1999]); volumes of film criticism (*The Life and Death of Colonel Blimp*, 1997) and cultural commentary (*On Bullfighting*, 2000); a stage play (*The Audition*, 1993); a radio drama (*Born a Fox*, 2002); a film screenplay (*Stella Does Tricks*, 1996); and is a regular contributor to the *Guardian* and other newspapers, as well as to various radio and television discussion forums. One of her most recent projects is reported to be an animatronic film for children (Curtis 2002).[1] Add to this, contributions to dance/performance productions (*Delicate*, 1995 for Motionhouse Dance Company from which the collection *Absolutely Nothing* [1998] is taken, and *True [Requiem for Lucy Palmer]*, 2000 for Fierce Productions), a musical comedy (*Indian Summer*, 2000/1), a BBC drama documentary (*Ghostdancing*, 1995), an arts documentary (*For the Love of Burns*, 1999) and two six-part television series in collaboration with the poet John Burnside for Canadian television (*Dice* [2001/2] and *Dice II* [2002]), and quite an astoundingly sizeable and, for such a relatively young writer, a uniquely varied body of work emerges. Although, at times, the work has contained a few swipes levelled at the cult of literary/media celebrity and has reflected critically on the language, structures and issues that this culture has fostered, it is prolifically experimental in its encompassing of literary forms and electronic and performative media; perhaps more so than any of her more celebrity-hungry peers.[2]

This extraordinary level of adaptability and output cannot be explained away entirely by the fact of her being a writer who operates (mostly) outside the best-sellers lists who must earn a living in and around fiction. Rather, I think they need to be taken either as the sign of a writer who is driven to explore many kinds of forms and idioms, or, as it sometimes feels, of one who has mounted a campaign of dissatisfied, restless plundering (or itching against) existing literary styles and genres.[3] Her fiction constantly grapples with the possibilities and failures of different forms of language (including physical performance), while at the same time exploring certain specific effects of the media and media technologies but, more specifically, the textures, effects and potential of literary language as a medium. What I want to explore here is the way that Kennedy's work is preoccupied with writing and its product, written language – its materiality as well as its material effects – and the way that this continually leads her to revisit painful or ambiguous forms of inscription and articulation. Often this ambiguity is compounded through geographical spaces dominated by vague or eroded details of time and place, populated with characters who are humiliated either by their invisibility, erasure and inarticulacy or by excessive forms of visibility and legibility, often for the purposes of surveillance or entertainment. In other words, articulation is nearly always a problem in which speech or writing and bodily presence/presentation are equally involved in what amounts to a grappling between abstraction and substance: doubt, disappearance and abstraction on the one hand collide with pain, spectacle and physical presence on the other. Sometimes these sets of terms relate to the writing itself, at other times they describe its contents.

Sarah M. Dunnigan has drawn attention to something very similar in her observations about the striking way in which Kennedy's work moves from what she identifies as a kind of 'ghost writing' that has an ever-present sense of 'desire, memory and loss', to one that showcases an enjoyment of language and the 'sensuality of the word' (Dunnigan 2000: 145).[4] Bharat Tandon has recently described the 'spaces' Kennedy leaves 'around her narrative, into which its nasty jolts and one-liners are allowed to echo' (Tandon 2004: 19). At times, then, an elliptical, Spartan or even cryptic style may be part of an evocation of absence or loss; or figures may seem almost inhuman or characterless because they are in the service of some wider allegorical function;[5] but at other moments bodily sensuality or visceral pain ring through the prose as though the writing was itself involved in an attempt to snag against the very thing it describes. If this begins to sound like a familiar Romantic desire for the word/signifier to embody the thing signified, then it is important to stress that Kennedy's self-consciousness about writing and the act of writing is continually foregrounded in a way that feels modern, and that the frustrations, even pains, presented about articulation and expression always appear to be in the service of communicating the social or political reasons for the relative ineffectiveness of a character's thought or speech, rather than those of the author. It is as though her writing, with its pleasure in the 'sensuality of the word' and in the action of writing itself, draws especial attention to the way language has, following Barthes, become long understood to be 'condemned' to 'silence and to the distinction of signs'. As Barthes asserts, this is because 'there always remains *too much meaning* for language to fulfil a delectation appropriate to its substance' (Barthes 1986: 77). Although Kennedy does not invoke the possibility of a utopian 'rustle' of language that Barthes describes in his essay, nonetheless she does at times indulge both a 'delectation' and a frustration with its 'substance' (Barthes 1986: 77). Each of these reactions feeds into the very common circumstance in her writing wherein a character finds themselves frustrated in speech but then in some way physically emblazoned, often very painfully and, with some form of symbolic (usually non-linguistic) and spectacular signification. In this sense writing within the fiction often becomes literally substantial as it is marked out along the surface of the human body, just at the moment in the narrative when spoken and written language have ceased to be either possible or useful. Added to this, Kennedy appears to capture a particularly 'end of the century' anxiety about the end of writing and meaning. Often these fictions depict moments when writing itself becomes a form of spectacle (when it is fantastically emblazoned on bodies or becomes merely a set of codes or signs) and the human body itself becomes part of the language of signification, though it must either suffer to signify or be transformed through metaphor in the process.

'Spared', the first story in the *Indelible Acts* collection, is a third-person narrative in which the central figure, Greg, provides an example of the way in which (in this case) spoken language misdirects meaning; it also describes a body that offers up signs to be read, although in this case no one reads it. Greg begins an extramarital affair in the queue of a Glasgow cheese shop where he chats up Amanda, who will become his lover. The story begins with this account of what can be read as the determining moment of the affair and is presented as Greg's reflection on his own careful deception during part of their first exchange:

Things could go wrong with one letter, he knew that now. Just one.

'Actually, I moved here ten years ago.'

He had found it so terribly, pleasantly effortless to say, 'Actually, I moved here ten years ago.'

(Kennedy 2002: 3)

The narrative voice that constantly focalizes through Greg's unspoken thoughts and feelings then gives away 'his intended sentence' which was 'Actually, I'm married' (Kennedy 2002: 3). He goes on to lament that in the 'course of one consonant everything had changed', even though there 'had only been a little thickness about the *m*, a tiny falter there that might have suggested a stammer' (Kennedy 2002: 3). The detail and emphasis of this moment are privileged by flashback since, although it heads up the plot, in story terms it occurs a little way into the narrative and mid-way in their conversation.[6] Significantly, Greg displaces moral responsibility for his deceit onto language itself; he claims that 'Things could go wrong with one letter, he knew that now. Just one', as though the letters themselves somehow led to or provoked the 'wrong', rather than the speaker. The result is that we are led to believe that all the narrative action that follows has been triggered by a 'stammer'; one in which a speaker slips in time and position from present declaration ('I am') to past description ('I moved'). Most importantly, it is a course of action that leads not just to an affair and a further set of practised deceptions on Greg's wife Karen, but also results in Greg experiencing a profound 'feeling of extinction' and an apocalyptic sense that he is approaching a millennial 'outbreak of emptiness, of ending' (Kennedy 2002: 21) and possibly 'the end of everything' (Kennedy 2002: 19).

Greg's stammering over the confluence between 'I'm' and 'I moved' allows him to indulge the deception that a similarity in the substance and sound of the words has, itself, the potential to catapult the speaker into a diversion from an original, intended meaning. Although Greg utters the sentence 'Actually, I'm married' later (Kennedy 2002: 18), its first meaning can never be recovered because it has changed from a sentence that might have prevented an affair to a qualification of an affair already gaining in momentum. What is particularly interesting about this, however, is the way that Greg's stammer leads to – is indeed dramatized through – a course of action (the affair) in which speech becomes progressively less possible or meaningful ('It was tricky to speak' [Kennedy 2002: 18]) and communication is conducted increasingly only through bodies during sex. Greg's despair at this substitution of speech for sex culminates in the sodomy that provokes his impending feeling of millennial meltdown and in this sense his predicament is sharply reminiscent of the correlated series of black holes in

Martin Amis's *London Fields* (Amis 1990).[7] On the first of two occasions, this literary echo becomes dramatic when written language, or at least significa- tion, slips onto Greg's body. Amanda writes her telephone number 'on the inside of his wrist' and later this covert location gives his memory of the physical 'tickle' of its inscription an added frisson that propels him to the bathroom for a silent double masturbation, followed by a short dream of an 'undefined apocalypse' (Kennedy 2002: 11). As the letters melt away from distinction they are converted into a compulsive sensuality, but the result is only emptiness and the end of meaning. Later Greg's failure to feel guilt ('He had not felt remotely guilty' [Kennedy 2002: 14]) when lying to his wife is more or less instantly displaced and converted into a 'raw and lumi- nous' rash of shamefully 'crimson pinpricks' on his body that he fears may 'cohere, some morning, arranging itself to spell out Amanda's name' (Kennedy 2002: 15). In both these cases sexual desire and its social prohib- ition conspire to convert a communication that was, in the first instance, sensuously pleasurable into a guilty torment: an indelible writing that is at once a sign of disgrace, of perpetual doubtfulness and of an impending and inevitable ending. After all, the concept of indelibility (registered in the title of the collection) itself invokes two sorts of marking out: external (a form of writing or marking that cannot be erased), and internal (a stain of con- science or disgrace), both of which are mutually complicit in this story and elsewhere in the collection (Kennedy 2002). Greg may feel he is 'spared' as the story ends, but he is not 'saved', nor redeemed in any way that would lend certainty to his continuance. Even his attempt to comfort himself ('*Nothing's going to happen. Nothing's going to leave me, I really ought to be certain of that*' [Kennedy 2002: 22]) has the effect of converting the repeated 'nothing' from a consolation to a sinister threat of negation.

What is striking about the function of stammering in 'Spared' is the way that it precisely illustrates Barthes's claim that indeed all speech 'remains . . . condemned to stammering'. Stammering, he argues, is partly a result of the continuous temporal dimension of speech since, like all live actions, its 'fatality' is that it is 'irreversible', so that mistakes such as Greg's 'I moved here . . .', once uttered, can never be truly erased, only revised sub- sequently through further speech. Hence, stammering is Barthes's term for 'annulation-by-addition' (Barthes 1986: 76). Although he has argued that language harbours the possibility of a utopia, a 'rustle' through which 'the phonic, metric, vocal signifier would be deployed in all its sumptuosity, without a sign ever becoming detached from it . . . without meaning being brutally dismissed, dogmatically foreclosed, in short castrated', it is the stammer which is its habitual and inevitable sound. Thus, the stammer is comparable to a motor's '*misfire*' because it is the 'auditory sign of a failure' as well as the symptom of 'a fear: I am afraid the motor is going to stop'

(Barthes 1986: 76–7).[8] Of course Barthes's point here is that this fear is immanent within the use of all language. What is interesting in Kennedy, however, is the way that her writing is not only acutely aware of this, but also dramatizes the condition in such a way that the fear of stopping – of all things coming to an end – becomes connected not just, as it does in 'Spared', to a sense of millennial anxiety, but also to a punishing view of the human body. Bodies frequently become the vehicles for a displaced and spectacular form of alternative language (for example, the rash) that is at times both abstract and painfully visceral, and only rarely is a utopian fantasy of escape from this indulged.

Perhaps an extreme example of this lies in the *Absolutely Nothing* collection, itself a post-hoc publication of Kennedy's lyrical contribution to a physical performance piece in which the bodies of the performers together with Howard Skempton's musical composition (mainly for cello and percussion) constituted the primary language of communication. The opening lines of the first text in this collection is itself a teasing instruction on the relationship between the body and language:

> Part the mind from the muscle,
> The muscle from the mind,
> Then you can speak.
> You can have tongues of bone now,
> Cartilage, nerve, blood.
>   (Kennedy 1998: 1)

What is striking here is that even as the first line commands a separation between cerebral and physical activity, the alliteration this sets up between the two terms ('mind' and 'muscle') merely demonstrates, through the very texture of the language itself, a correspondence and indeed a tangible over-lap between the two things it would have parted.[9] Only once the mind has removed itself from the burdens of muscle, the next line implies, may excit-ing and forceful articulation be routed back through the body. And yet, although the final two lines here make a form of poetic sense, they do beg the question: what use is a 'tongue of bone'? The added force of a tongue released from the dragging weight of muscle is one that, though meta-phorically forceful, is not only both conceptually impractical, but poetically, the contrasting use of hard consonants ('Cartilage, nerve, blood'), snags at the ear.

Kennedy, then, explores the way in which the physical weight of the body is an impediment to speech through characters whose bodies interrupt or make awkward communication, while at the same time she traces the ways in which communication is transferred onto bodies that become the vehicles for a brutally displaced language of feeling which, by virtue of its displacement, is articulated as a language of suffering. In *Looking for the Possible Dance*, however, Kennedy combines a physically struggling and inarticulate body with a fantasy of one that is released into grace and gracefulness (Kennedy 1993b). The narrative moves between a dominating focus on Margaret's relationship to her boyfriend Colin, and her conversations on a train with a young boy named James who has cerebral palsy. Like many characters in Kennedy's fiction, James is both abandoned and maltreated by his family; parents are the worst (especially mothers), though when kindness is shown it usually comes from either grandparents or aunts and uncles. Characteristically then, James's grandmother is patronizing and will not allow him to use a 'noisy' (Kennedy 1993b: 56) machine that would announce words for him, but she at least shows a concern that is absent in his silent and resentful mother. In these two narratives that both revolve around Margaret, Kennedy sets up an ironic contrast between Margaret's (on/off) relationship with Colin over a period of years and her brief encounter on a train with James. James's body makes it excruciatingly impossible for him to talk; he cannot speak so must write on a piece of paper, though we are told that 'the pen top is hard to hold and hard to pull off, the pen is hard to fit inside a fist. To bring the pen to paper seems to take minutes' and when he does manage to write it is a 'laborious' process during which it appears that the 'letters shiver away from his hand' (Kennedy 1993b: 57). When he does communicate, although he is aggressive, he is nonetheless entirely forthright ('FUC OF TOO'), and their encounter results in a bond of understanding between them. He admits to her (significantly in phonetically spelled words – spelling that follows speech) that 'PEOPLE CAN TALK TO' that she makes him feel 'FUC WON HUNNER PERCEN MEEEEEE' (Kennedy 1993b: 191) and she 'leans and kisses James, just reaching his forehead above one eye' (Kennedy 1993b: 170) as he leaves the train. The connection between them, then, appears to arise almost *despite* written communication, something that is confirmed by the way that James, as he 'struggles out of the blanket to wave back' (Kennedy 1993b: 170), drops the piece of paper on which she, with the promise that they might write to each other, has written her address. Their relationship, however, has been based instead on chat and on physical presence and reassurance that transcend the temporary connections forged by writing.

On James's departure Margaret finds that she has a 'tightness in her throat' (Kennedy 1993b: 170) and this difficulty with speech, especially at moments of intense feeling, pervades the relationships of this novel and others. Margaret remembers that when her father 'hugged her' he 'gave her that silence again. The one that happened sometimes when they touched' (Kennedy 1993b: 67). Though her father likes to talk 'on the move', his stillness and silence are described as having a morbid quality ('she would be frightened that he was dead' [Kennedy 1993b: 58]), and his 'conversations seem to hover and lose themselves as the spaces between the words ran into silence' (Kennedy 1993b: 58). When she and Colin are interrupted by her employer, Mr Lawrence, she feels, when Lawrence leaves them in an atmosphere of embarrassment, that 'she should call something after him, but could think of nothing, no words' (Kennedy 1993b: 197). Clearly this silence and inarticulacy is an indicator of loss and longing rather than of merely stillness or serenity, however, two forms of bodily articulation in the novel step in as alternative but contrasting modes of articulation: dance and torture.

The dance metaphor featured in the book's title works to conjure up an imaginary fullness of communication between individuals or groups who are otherwise uncertain or alienated. While an actual ceilidh proves to be the scene of racist provocation as well as a marital and alcoholic breakdown that is immediately followed by a death, it is important that 'Margaret's last memory' of the event is of waltzing 'with Colin in a room without music, but full of stepping and spinning couples'. The absence of music evokes the physicality and presence of the dancing bodies all the more forcefully ('the slide and stamp of their feet' with the 'steady clapping and someone humming under their breath') and fills Margaret with a warm feeling that 'a familiar mind is watching': familiar because it 'feels something like the small heat of her father's smile'. In turn she links this to her 'flattening her hands against Colin's back and thinking he danced as if he might be family. It would be good if they could all together like that' (Kennedy 1993b: 198). Earlier in the book we are told that Margaret has ditched her youthful and optimistic student activism in which, faced with 'dying, unemployment and embarrassing old age', she and her peers merely 'closed their eyes and they ran and danced' in 'pointless, but glorious gestures'. Now she tells herself that she 'couldn't dance across that distance, couldn't dance away that deathly fucking peace', though she still yearns, 'looking for the possible dance, the step, the move to beat them all' (Kennedy 1993b: 39–40). By the end of the novel, however, when distance and a characteristically stilted, abruptly terminated phone conversation between Margaret and Colin appears to signal reconciliation (of a sort) between them, the final lines of the book constitute a kind of blindingly bright, white, cinematic wipe:

> The late sun outside the station is very strong, and from a distance its doorways seem white, more like curtains of white than ways made through walls into light. Margaret walks to one door and sinks into brilliant air, becoming first a moving shadow, then a curve, a dancing line.
>
> (Kennedy 1993b: 250)

The light forms a 'dancing line' marking the end of the process of narration and bleaching out Margaret's body as she walks into something like a brilliant theatrical curtain through which she escapes the novel's stage. Thus, dancing in this novel is mainly abstract and imagined and, as such, separates off harmonious, loving and fully communicative relationships between classes, family members, lovers and races from the brutal consequences of inadequate, everyday speech, or its absence.

By contrast, Colin's body has articulation forcibly inscribed upon it in a brutally sadistic attack on him by gangsters, punishing him for threatening their extortion business. Though the prelude to their beating involves two men who 'stepped up and beside him, as if they were part of some dance, as if all they ever did was to move in tight beside strangers and not let them go' (Kennedy 1993b: 227), their encounter involves the opposite of dance: the nailing of his body down on the floor. Perhaps inspired by Burgess or Kubrick's *A Clockwork Orange* (1971), the gangsters swap Beethoven for Mozart's Clarinet Concerto. The musical agility of the 'Adagio' as it 'rippled over the boards and through the dust' taunts Colin's broken and kicked body as, no longer able to walk, he is forced to crawl across the same boards to kiss the feet of his tormentors. Though the music is 'carrying words', these culminate on the page without any corresponding 'agility' of (sentence) form:

YOU'LL HAVE
STIG
concentrate   don't go   away   from   us
STIGMATA
JUST LIKE BABY JESUS
. . . . . .
COLIN
Colin
Co
        CHRIST
        LOOK AT THAT.

(Kennedy 1993b: 232)

Certainly this scene might be selected as a further illustration of Sarah Dunnigan's claim that 'Kennedy's fictions construct their own metafictions or metanarratives', something that 'is exemplified not only by their artistic formalism but in the process by which the act of writing is deconstructed by Kennedy's protagonists, usually for its emotionally sacrificial nature' (Dunnigan 2000: 147). Here, the writing is both broken down on the page and capitalized in order to represent the fragmented and violent qualities of the speech as the semi-conscious Colin hears it, but this also has the effect of removing the transparency of language by giving it concrete and spectacular form. At the same time, the words draw attention to Colin's physically sacrificial state; one that has come about just at the moment when verbal communication between him and Margaret has broken down. The 'stigmata' are imprinted on his hands precisely so that they may be read by others, but in a perversion of the function of Christ's scars, they have been placed there to repel and deter others from following Colin's example. What is also significant about this scene is the fact that the spectacular quality of Colin's punishment is tied to humiliation: we are told that he 'felt ashamed when Webster looked at him' (Kennedy 1993b: 233).

A more general predicament of being put on show while in a state of suffering, or indeed being made to watch something uncomfortable, is one to which Kennedy often returns. Indeed, an ongoing fear of spectacle, surveillance and observation, which are frequently presented as exploitative or torturous, seem to go hand in hand with an anxiety about the adequacy of written language and representation. In this sense *On Bullfighting* is an interesting work because it is written about a time when Kennedy feels she may be witnessing the end of her ability to write, or, as she puts it, the 'death of my vocation' (Kennedy 1999: 125). A painful relationship breakdown leads her to make the claim that 'All I found out was that some things have no words for them, so why bother with words' (sic) and to focus instead on her study of the history and meaning of bullfighting. This lack of words, or at least the feeling of the uselessness of words, leads again, then, to an attention to the spectacle of theatrically endangered bodies. There is no more visceral or more dangerous sport or entertainment (aside from the circus) that negotiates with death more flamboyantly or systematically than bullfighting. Yet what Kennedy appears to admire most in the intricate and highly ritualized body language of the matadors' performances, is its resistance to linguistic articulation and narrative. Though she offers accounts of the performances she sees, she admits that 'even the best words can never entirely approach them' (Kennedy 1999: 125) and the 'beauties' of the 'spectacle appear(s) to be photogenic, but not filmic' (Kennedy 1999: 137).[10] Exactly because these moments are live, indeed are about the risk offered only by the energy of a live performance, they cut against forms of continuous representation so that, she suggests, almost nothing of their meaning or force can be spelled out in narrative.

On Bullfighting is also an interesting volume for the way that it forces a readerly negotiation with the intimacies that exist, not only between a writer and their subject matter, but also between an artist or writer and the rituals of language and form through which their work is rendered visible. Kennedy's admission about the influence of the media on her work confirms the importance she attaches to literature's facility expressing interiority and desire: 'Part of my definition of myself and elements of my identity like nationality comes from the media. I believe that writing is the most intimate of the media' (Kennedy 1995: 100). The hovering sense of intimacy and involvement in the writing occasionally make it hard to maintain a rigorous separation between the work and the writer (or at least some apprehension of her); the work constantly slips between different modes of fiction and cultural commentary making it hard to hold on to the division of sorts. Both *The Life and Death of Colonel Blimp* and *On Bullfighting* recount what are offered as highly personal incidences, thoughts and memories from Kennedy's own life, as well as more general reflections on the social and historical meaning of cinema and bullfighting respectively (Kennedy 1999 and Kennedy 1997). Both open with extensive accounts of the mental and physical pain felt by the author on different occasions. In *On Bullfighting*, a decision to abandon a suicidal jump from a tenement window is followed by an investigation into bullfighting that is punctuated by accounts of the author's chronic backache. *The Life and Death of Colonel Blimp* begins with an account of a cold wind in London ('My forehead hurts so much that I want to cry' [Kennedy 1997: 9]) that sets off a memory of childhood and home in which both become defined by brazening out cold, pain and isolation. Indeed, the portrait that emerges of Romantic loneliness, social isolation and the suffering of the artist surely reaches self-parody in *The Life and Death of Colonel Blimp* when four succeeding paragraphs end, 'I was a foreigner', 'I would be a foreigner there, too', 'I was out of time' and 'I was culpably out of place' (Kennedy 1997: 11). What is odd in both these cases is that this appears to be the voice of a writer who, in the first instance is searching out a language in which to describe her social isolation and individual pain, yet the dramatic forms through which she finds the best expression for these are ones characterized by mass, all-inclusive spectacle involving bodies subject to scrutiny, desire and often punishment by spectators in positions of relative safety, and, if not entirely non-linguistic, then certainly non-literary articulation.

The fiction also at times echoes or overlaps with this discursive writing. For example, in an essay in memory of her grandfather (Joe Price) and his experience of boxing she writes about her grandmother's first husband (Jack Peace) whom her grandmother found dead in bed next to her on the morning after their wedding night (Kennedy 2000: 167). This narrative had already been included in an early short story 'Genteel Potatoes' in which a female first-person narrative voice also recounts the death of her grandmother's first husband (Kennedy 1993a: 42–6). Again, 'no one will tell her that her husband has cancer and will die', indeed 'will be dead beside her the morning after her wedding night' (Kennedy 1993a: 46). However, this is qualified by an insistence at the bookends of the story that, because of the gulf of time and experience that divides the female generations of this family, this can be 'no more than a story about Grandmother, because it cannot be the truth' (Kennedy 1993a: 42). The events presented in the 'tale' create and nurture the moments 'before I can begin writing this story' (Kennedy 1993a: 46) and must be recognizably separated out from it because, as the narrator points out, 'as you read this, I am somewhere else. So this is a story' (Kennedy 1993a: 42). The authorial presence appears to be carefully evacuated here as it is overtaken and replaced by the ghostly narrative voice she creates. Ghostliness is then doubled when this voice describes itself as being haunted by the 'lines and lines of women who are nothing more than shadows in my bones'. Here, fiction overtakes and redeploys remembrance. In this sense the voice is at once emptied of presence and yet, in the same move, it is then precisely located and identified in terms of gender and specific genealogical and class developments. So, while the narrative self-consciously foregrounds the hesitancies and failures inherent in the (re)telling of familial narratives ('the detail of her surroundings will be sadly incomplete'), this also works to wrest focus and authority away from the individual, narrative voice in a way that both distils and extends the significance of the story's key scene in which the grandmother, as a young girl, is described as fixing her 'genteel lady' employer with a 'magnificent glare' before dropping the rotten potatoes she has been given to eat in front of her. In this sense the facts of this pre-Second World War family history themselves become the 'shadows' in the 'bones' of the story itself; they form a ghostly echo, but one that lends visibility and priority to a minor domestic servant and thereby articulates a broader gender-specific class confrontation that harbours resonances of the political impact and influence of the potato famine. The same stark narrative event of a husband's sudden death, though it is quite peripheral to the central events of each piece of writing, are lit up in quite distinct ways through the respective contexts of fictional story and discursive essay.

Many writers of the 1980s and 1990s such as Julian Barnes, Angela Carter and Jeanette Winterson have been labelled postmodern for their use of pastiche, treatment of history, fascination with media and media language, subversions of narrative authority and personal biography and their mixing of genres. What is interesting about Kennedy's work is that most of these characteristics are visible across the body of her work, rather than in individual fictions. The focus of this chapter has been on the repeated returns within these narratives to accounts of characters involved in acts of writing or attempts at writing, but rarely do these result in anything other than frustration, pain, humiliation or an absence of meaning. Such problems of articulation are frequently directed towards resolution through forms of bodily and non-literary, even non-linguistic communication, though these either weigh the bodies down, placing them in vulnerable, dangerous or spectacular positions, or else they are abstracted through forms of metaphor, memory or fantasy. The narrator of 'The seaside photographer' in *Night Geometry and the Garscadden Trains* addresses the memory of her (now dead) grandfather with the final words 'All I can do is write you words you cannot read and feel them between us' (Kennedy 1993b: 126) and this sense of language as a consolatory action rather than an act of specific or effective articulation runs throughout these stories. Language, and more particularly the act of writing, in the beauty and force of the sounds, textures and different forms and intimacies it continually makes available, is both its own consolation and also the means through which its inadequacies, losses and absences are traced – though not always spelled out – through characters whose bodies bear the punishing marks of powerful feeling that blisters on the surface of the body.

Notes

1 See the A. L. Kennedy website, <http://www.a-l-kennedy.co.uk>, for more information on, and reviews of, these projects (as well as the author's reviews of the reviews).

2 Famously, Kennedy herself levelled a few swipes at the cult of literary celebrity when she branded the 1996 Booker Prize 'a pile of crooked nonsense'. The winner, she said, was invariably determined by 'who knows who, who's sleeping with who, who's selling drugs to who, who's married to who, whose turn it is'. She also claimed: 'I read the 300 novels and no other bastard [on the panel] did' (Moss 2001).

3 Many critics, therefore, have struggled to place Kennedy within existing literary traditions, especially Scottish ones. Douglas Gifford, for example, claims that 'Kennedy's fiction is unpredictable' even while it is 'outstanding in its range of approaches and modes; from grim urban realism to surrealism, satire, and sardonic humour'. Although he claims at the same time that there is a 'unifying perspective' on class within this (Gifford et al. 2002: 945–6). Cairns Craig sees Kennedy as just one of several contemporary Scottish writers whose preoccupation with 'dubious parentages and blood relations' is a modern version of the nineteenth-century double identity. He sees this as a mediation on nationhood within which the 'ambiguity of a character's genealogy produces an absence of the self that mirrors the absent narrative of the ambiguous nation' (Cairns 1999: 199). See also Gifford 1996, McMillan 1995 and Neubauer 1999.

4 Dunnigan cites the lines 'I love these words. These words are lovely', from the short story 'Stardust' in *Night Geometry and the Garscadden Trains* as a further example of the foregrounding in Kennedy's fiction of the pleasure taken from the textures of language (Kennedy 1993a: 144). This citation is particularly relevant here, however, because these are the words of a character who is describing the way she revels in the terms that describe photographic technology: 'filters and lenses, exposure times and depths of field' (Kennedy 1993a: 83).

In other words, the terms mediate an experience of language in which the pleasure enjoyed is employed in the articulation of a primary pleasure in visual mediation.

5 See, for example, 'A perfect possession', 'On having more sense', 'The Mouseboks family dictionary' and 'Failing to fall' in *Now That You're Back* (1994) and 'Didacus' and 'The seaside photographer' in *Night Geometry and the Garscadden Trains* (1993a).

6 This is an example of what Sarah Dunnigan refers to as Kennedy's ' "expendable" temporal framework', used widely in her fiction. It involves an 'instability of tense which renders the past and present lives of characters in intimate proximity' (Dunnigan 2000: 145).

7 See also Stokes 1997 and Moyle 1995.

8 A different sort of stammering is depicted in 'Elsewhere', also in *Indelible Acts*. A family dynasty of terminal machismo is depicted through a line of men, each of whom has been named Freddie Williamson. They are comically imagined as a set of 'desperately unimaginative Freddie bloody Williamsons' who 'probably spent their winter nights together, reading the list of their forebears aloud from the family bible like one continuous, sad, baptismal stammer.' In this instance the stammer represents a preposterous dynastic self-pride with which the family imagines a smooth continuity between its past, present and future. Yet because this is merely a constant repetition (a non-generative parody of Genesis) it also identifies the lack of adaptability and imagination that will surely be the family's end. A fear of stopping, then, is reimagined here as an overconfidence in perpetuity.

9 Kennedy has also reinforced this interest in the overlap of writing and bodily pleasure in her own published reflections on writing where she has claimed that 'writing is a sensual rather than an intellectual process' (Kennedy 1995: 100).

10 A fictional echo of this occurs in the final lines of 'Star Dust' in *Night Geometry and the Garscadden Trains*. The narrator is a woman who is being pushed to the margins of her own small life as she retires, and who is given a new lease of life when she buys a camera. She also composes films in her head about her family but decides that 'there seem to be only tiny patches of my life that are at all important. There are images or moments. It's material more suited to a series of photographs' (Kennedy 1993a: 91).

References

Amis, Martin (1990) *London Fields*, Harmondsworth: Penguin.

Barthes, Roland (1986) *The Rustle of Language*, trans. Richard Howard, Oxford: Basil Blackwell.

Craig, Cairns (1999) *The Modern Scottish Novel: narrative and the national imagination*, Edinburgh: Edinburgh University Press.

Curtis, Polly (2002) 'Renowned Scottish novelist to teach at St Andrews', Education Guardian, *Guardian*, Monday, 25 November.

Dunnigan, Sarah M. (2000) 'A. L. Kennedy's longer fiction: articulate grace' in Aileen Christianson and Alison Lumsden (eds) *Contemporary Scottish Women Writers*, Edinburgh: Edinburgh University Press, pp. 144–55.

Gifford, Douglas (1996) 'Imagining Scotlands: the return to mythology in modern

Scottish fiction' in Susanne Hagemann (ed.) *Scottish Studies in Scottish Fiction: 1945 to the present*, Frankfurt: Peter Lang, pp. 17–49.

Gifford, Douglas, Sarah Dunnigan and Alan MacGillivray (eds) (2002) *Scottish Literature*, Edinburgh: Edinburgh University Press.

A. L. Kennedy (1993a) [1990] *Night Geometry and the Garscadden Trains*, London and Phoenix, Ariz.: Polygon.

—— (1993b) *Looking for the Possible Dance*, London: Secker & Warburg.

—— (1993c) *The Audition*, Edinburgh Festival.

—— (1994) *Now That You're Back*, London: Cape.

—— (1995a) *Delicate*, Motionhouse Dance Company.

—— (1995b) *Ghostdancing*, BBC TV.

—— (1995c) 'Not Changing the World' in Ian A. Bell (ed.) *Peripheral Visions: images of nationhood in contemporary British fiction*, Cardiff: University of Wales Press, pp. 100–2.

—— (1996a) [1995] *So I Am Glad*, London: Vintage.

—— (1996b) *Stella Does Tricks*, dir. Coky Giedroyc.

—— (1997a) *The Life and Death of Colonel Blimp*, London: BFI.

—— (1997b) *Original Bliss*, London: Cape.

—— (1998) *Absolutely Nothing*, Glasgow: Mariscat.

—— (1999a) *On Bullfighting*, London: Yellow Jersey.

—— (1999b) *For the Love of Burns*, BBC TV.

—— (1999c) *Everything You Need*, London: Vintage.

—— (2000a) *True [Requiem for Lucy Palmer]*, Fierce Productions/Tramway Theatre.

—— (2000b) 'A blow to the head', *Granta* 72: 157–78.

—— (2001/2) *Dice I and Dice II*, HBO/CBC TV.

—— (2002) *Indelible Acts*, London: Cape.

—— (2004a) *Born a Fox*, BBC Radio 4.

—— (2004b) *Paradise*, London: Cape.

McMillan, Dorothy (1995) 'Constructed out of bewilderment' in Ian A. Bell (ed.) *Peripheral Visions: images of nationhood in contemporary British fiction*, Cardiff: University of Wales Press, pp. 80–99.

Moss, Stephen (2001) 'Is the Booker fixed?', *Guardian*, Tuesday, 18 September.

Moyle, David (1995) 'Beyond the black hole: the emergence of science fiction themes in the recent work of Martin Amis', *Extrapolation: a journal of science fiction*, 36(4): 305–15.

Neubauer, Jürgen (1999) *Literature as Intervention: struggles over cultural identity in contemporary Scottish fiction*, Marburg: Tectum Verlag.

Stokes, Peter (1997) 'Martin Amis and the postmodern suicide: tracing the postnuclear narrative at the fin de millennium', *Critique: studies in contemporary fiction* 38: 300–11.

Tandon, Bharat (2004) 'Falling from and falling down', *Times Literary Supplement*, 27 August: 19.

Part III

Historical fictions

9 Mr Wroe's Virgins
The 'other Victorians' and recent fiction

B. E. Maidment

The intellectual origins of the 'other Victorians'

It is hardly surprising that soon after its publication in 1969 John Fowles's novel *The French Lieutenant's Woman* (Fowles 1969) provoked a round-table debate between three distinguished academics in the leading scholarly journal devoted to interdisciplinary nineteenth-century studies (Adam et al. 1972). Beyond its central interest in the philosophical conundrum of living with an existential consciousness in a repressive Victorian culture where choice was largely subordinated to manners and socially learnt behaviour, Fowles's novel was profoundly indebted to what might be called the 'moment' of Victorian studies as a broad scholarly interest. The 'moment' of Victorian studies in the late 1960s and early 1970s in fact comprised the intersection of a number of complex recognitions about the nature of the remains and records of Victorian society and the interpretative issues that these historical traces posed. Central to such changes of focus was the idea of 'history from below' – a widespread shift of attention from the grand historical narratives of wars, prime ministers, governments and economic change to the confusing variety of counternarratives provided by piecing together the fragmentary records of 'ordinary' individuals and their 'experience' of historical change. Fowles's repeated references to and quotations from *Human Documents of the Industrial Revolution* (Royston Pike 1966) is entirely characteristic of the extent and importance of this shift, but it was of course manifested widely in both academic and popular historiography, and driven on by the appointment of young Marxist scholars to the emergent 'new' universities and polytechnics. Institutionally it revealed itself in *Victorian Studies* itself, in the foundation of academic institutions aimed at fostering research into the new historical micronarratives crucial to interdisciplinary Victorian studies (such as the Victorian Studies Centres at Leicester and the University of Indiana), and in academic interest groups such as the Research Society for Victorian Periodicals.

Its published monuments were E. P. Thompson's *The Making of the English Working Class* (Thompson 1968 [1963]) Raphael Samuel's various works, including the periodical *History Workshop Journal* and the conferences and gatherings associated with it, Jim Dyos's work on urban history and the two-volume *The Victorian City*, which drew together scholars to consider urbanisation, newly established as the defining experience of the Victorian period (Dyos and Wolff 1973). Beyond using the traditional documentary sources for the study of history, the 1970s saw a massive expansion of the range of texts, records and traces available to the historian – the use of what seems now such an obvious source as photographs for the writing of urban history, for instance, was one of many new approaches emphasised or established by the publication of *The Victorian City*. Writing by working men and women, ballads and street literature, autobiographies (both formal and informal), diaries, even the oral record all resulted in major anthologies and scholarly study, led by Martha Vicinus's pioneering survey *The Industrial Muse* (Vicinus 1974) and Louis James's *Fiction for the Working Man* (James 1963). Rapt attention to obscured and liminal voices, the newly or scarcely literate and a willingness to write them back into history, characterised the Victorian historiography which Fowles sought to combine with his wider philosophical and formal interests in *The French Lieutenant's Woman*.

Central to such a broad re-evaluation of the Victorian was the topic of sexuality. Indeed, two of the key figures in the opening up of Victorian sexuality to modern appraisal had been bibliographers. Montague Summers, in quest of pornography as much as enlightenment, pursued the Victorians in his *Gothic Bibliography* (1940) into the highly sexualised and melodramatic discourses of mass-circulation fiction. Impelled by a similar impulse towards description and recovery, Michael Sadleir produced not just major descriptive bibliographies of the Victorian novel but also, drawing on his incomparable knowledge of the 'hidden' Victorian literary record, produced two novels of his own that caught the popular imagination – *Fanny By Gaslight* (1940) and *Forlorn Sunset* (1946). The latter, in its detailed knowledge of the geography of hidden desire, especially in relation to child prostitution, provided one of the key sources for the massive interest in Victorian transgression that emerged in the late 1960s and early 1970s. Important, too, in both writers was their perception that the Victorians had changed from being the moralistic and repressive grandparents of modern Britain and had become instead something more interesting – the estranged 'other', the exotic and unavailable unknown rather than the familiar and visible.

Steven Marcus's pioneering study, *The Other Victorians*, first published in England in 1966, presented itself, somewhat defensively, as an academic piece of sociological research (Marcus 1966). In a series called Studies in Sex and Society, sponsored by The Institute for Sex Research at Indiana

University and bearing the straight-faced subtitle of 'A Study of Sexuality and Pornography in Mid-Nineteenth Century England', Marcus's book nonetheless drew on sensational and detailed records of intimate Victorian sexual behaviour, and its carefully deployed scholarly credentials did not stop it being rapidly adopted by Book Club Associates. It was a book that, for the first time, gave the interested reader (rather than the specialist or antiquarian) access to the famous and emblematic 'locked cases' of sexually explicit material in the British Museum, reprinting extensive extracts from the most famous Victorian pornographic novel *My Secret Life* as well as reinstating Henry Spencer Ashbee as another key bibliographer of Victorian culture. Additionally, Marcus, by beginning his study with an account of Dr William Acton, recognised the powerful nature of social discourses such as medicine in the construction of Victorian ideology. Ronald Pearsall's *The Worm in the Bud: the world of Victorian sexuality* appeared in 1969, and gained widespread circulation reprinted as a Penguin book (Pearsall 1969). In 1970 two more books brought together ideas of sexuality and other forms of social transgression: crime in the case of R. D. Altick's *Victorian Studies in Scarlet* (cited in the *Victorian Studies* round table as a characteristically sensational popularisation of the Victorians [Altick 1970]) and the underworld in the case of Kellow Chesney's *The Victorian Underworld*, another book that rapidly became a Book Club favourite (Chesney 1970).

In 1972 Derek Hudson's *Munby: man of two worlds* was published, complete with its introductory statement about Hudson's scholarly pursuit of Munby whose records had been buried, or even conveniently 'forgotten', by their scholarly curators. *Munby: man of two worlds*, as its title suggests, was an immensely influential work in defining doubleness – a surface respectability combined with a 'hidden' and transgressive sex life – as characteristic of Victorian male sexuality. Such doubleness, beyond its immediate fascination, might be read as representative of a repressive and exploitative 'patriarchy' or, more simply, as 'hypocrisy'. Hudson's fascination with the complexity of Munby's hidden life, with its obsessive interest in working women and preoccupation with photographic scrutiny, brought together many characteristics of the interest of the early 1970s in Victorian sexuality – a recognition that records *did* exist and that they were more detailed and explicit than anyone had expected, that the Victorians both acted out and talked about their sexuality far more readily than previously acknowledged, that male sexuality was associated with power and privilege, and, crucially, that the dialogue between repression and respectability on the one hand and transgressive self-expression on the other formed the central conceptual model for the understanding of Victorian sexuality.

If one compulsion towards the kinds of interests expressed by the group of key texts from the late 1960s and early 1970s described came from 'history from below' and its broadening of scholarly sources, another clearly came from a newly felt and acknowledged sense of freedom about what could be discussed in public discourses. Angela Carter describes this process in the 'Polemical Preface' to *The Sadeian Woman* as 'repressive desublimation', that is to say, that the supposed freedom to make explicit and discuss previously taboo subjects, far from being liberating, in fact results in the construction of newer, less overtly acknowledged structures of anxiety and silence (Carter 1979: 3–7). On this argument, the supposed new 'freedom' felt in the late 1960s and early 1970s to discuss and analyse Victorian sexuality and to categorise elements of it as 'exotic', 'strange' and even 'deviant' in fact derives from a sense of what is normal and what is strange that is itself historically and ideologically specific.

Sexuality, 'other Victorianism' and recent British fiction

For the professional cultural historians who contributed to the *Victorian Studies* round table on *The French Lieutenant's Woman* the novel 'presents us with a picture of the 1860s which . . . is not bad, and . . . more than commonplace' (Adam et al. 1972: 344). One of them, Sheldon Rothblatt, argued that in its account of Charles's intellectual struggles with Darwinism the novel rose to a powerful moment of intellectual history. The central area of disagreement among the *Victorian Studies* commentators was, however, the presentation of Victorian sexuality in the novel. Brantlinger argued that:

> Perhaps the simplest explanation for the popularity of Fowles's story is that it is a product of recent interest in Victorian sexuality. It is a fictional exploration of 'the other Victorians,' although like all such explorations, including Steephen Marcus's, it raises the question of which is stranger – 'other Victorianism' or the modern interest in 'other Victorianism.' . . . Under the guise of interpretation of the Victorian age, *The French Lieutenant's Woman* is really a myth for now. One might call this the myth of the overthrow of 'Victorianism,' entailing the ritual exorcism of Duty and Work and Chastity – abstractions we like to identify with the last century, but whose diehard ghosts we must frequently lay on our own.
>
> (Adam et al. 1972: 340)

Ian Adam, disagreeing with Brantlinger over the novel's account of sexuality, argued that very few novels fail to exploit an interest in sexuality but that nonetheless 'there remains a complacency at being modern, a self-congratulation too easy to expose' (Adam et al. 1972: 346).

Such complacency, 'other Victorianism' and the 'myth of the overthrow of the Victorian' remain characteristic preoccupations in a considerable amount of recent fiction. A number of novels of the past decade or so by well-known writers have made use not just of Victorian settings but also, more significantly, of 'Other Victorianism', which is to say that they play upon our sense of who the Victorians were and how we stand in relation to them. Such a list would certainly comprise A. S. Byatt's *Possession* (1990) and *Angels and Insects* (1992), Alasdair Gray's *Poor Things* (1992), Peter Ackroyd's *Dan Leno and The Limehouse Golum* (1994), Jane Rogers' *Mr Wroe's Virgins* (1991), Victoria Glendinning's *Electricity* (1995), Matthew Kneale's *Sweet Thames* (1992) and Sarah Waters' *Tipping the Velvet* (1998) and *Affinity* (1999). All of these novels, like Fowles's, claim seriousness by focusing on potentially revealing moments of social crisis (cholera epidemics, the coming of electricity into domestic life, the impact of evolutionary theory), on institutions of revelatory importance (prisons, spiritualism, the music hall, evangelical movements) within Victorian culture. All contain some commentary on Victorian sexuality. Two of the biggest novels, in both bulk and hype, published in 2002 were Sarah Waters' *Fingersmith* and Peter Faber's *The Crimson Petal and the White* which both explored the 'hidden' intensity of Victorian sexual obsession. Of the above list, to my limited knowledge, both *Angels and Insects* and *Waterland* have been filmed, and *Mr Wroe's Virgins* and, somewhat salaciously, *Tipping the Velvet*, have been adapted into television series.

Nonetheless, despite thirty years and more of scholarly work since the pioneering work of Marcus, Hudson and the others listed above, despite the hugely more sophisticated understanding of the ideological projects of Victorian medicine and gender theory and those discourses which sustained them, recent fictional accounts of Victorian sexuality have generally reinforced models and ideas which were established thirty years ago and which have been subsequently challenged by scholars Michael Mason and Peter Gay. Victorian sexuality, it seems, still has the power to offer images of forbidden passions, of cross-class transgression and of a pervasive if hidden sexual underworld, at once both squalid and picturesque, that continues to fascinate a supposedly uninhibited and sexually liberal early-twenty-first-century readership. The assumption of 'chic Other Victorianism' allows contemporary writers to project late-twentieth-century notions of desire onto the Victorians as a means of testing the boundaries between desire and repression, the licit and the illicit, respectability and lust. Contemporary writers, however sophisticated in other respects, have tended to use Victorian sexuality as a site not so much for castigating repression and hypocrisy rather as a space for licensing their own imaginings of the transgressive. Such a process involves the construction of a repression/transgression dialectic which, far from promoting understanding of the

Victorians, uses them, crassly, as a site for the projection of contemporary preoccupations with deviance, guilt and self-fulfilment – in short, as a strange and exotic other in which deviance and transgression can be justified as a legitimate reaction to the authority and hypocrisy of patriarchy. However, I want to argue that what strikes me as the most interesting and progressive – progressive in both a formal and an intellectual sense – of recent fictions about Victorian sexuality, Jane Rogers' *Mr Wroe's Virgins*, uses the some of the formal properties of postmodernism to re-examine, and possibly even to resist, these clichés by deconstructing authority and desire as unstable entities driven by individual need rather than social norms.

Mr Wroe's Virgins and the unknowable Victorians

Mr Wroe's Virgins is avowedly a novel which seeks to write history from below, that is, to engage in the imaginative recovery of the individual experiences of the excluded, inarticulate or dumb within society. The major difficulty of such acts of recovery is that of avoiding patronising the past, of bringing to the Victorians a smug teleological certainty, as Brantlinger accuses Fowles of doing. Nonetheless, Rogers' novel proceeds initially from a desire to make the dumb eloquent both as an historiographical and political act as well as a narrative strategy. The existence of considerable documentary evidence of the activities of the real Mr Wroe is not matched by any known scrap of evidence about his 'virgins', thus providing a classical instance of the ways in which historical narratives remain essentially incomplete. *Mr Wroe's Virgins* recognises that a literary response derived from the wish to reconstruct the experience of those lost to history is also a highly polemical, even theoretical, gesture about the nature of literary 'voice', concerned with who speaks on whose behalf in a work of fiction. Accordingly, the novel is structured as the recovered if imagined narratives of four of the seven 'virgins' chosen as servants by Mr Wroe, the charismatic leader of the Christian Israelite Church in the industrial community of Ashton-under-Lyne in the Pennines. Of course the central historical 'event' in the novel – the selection and annexation of seven virgins as domestic and spiritual handmaidens of a 'prophet' – is as preposterous now as it was in the 1830s, and it is part of the achievement of the novel to imagine the experiences of those involved in anything like emotional complexity rather than to read the event simply and angrily as an example of the tyranny of men disguised by the protective rhetoric and gestures of religion.

The novel is set in the early 1830s just at the moment when the rural communities of the Pennines were being transformed into industrial towns swept over by waves of industrial unrest, early trade unionism and the transformative possibilities of Owenism and communitarianism. Despite the potentially scandalous consequences of Wroe's summons, all seven virgins have some reason to be willing to join his community in the appropriately named 'Sanctuary'. Voiced in distinctive ways as something close to diaries or internal monologues, the four interlocked narratives are used to detail the sect's struggle to establish itself as a community in the face of local mockery, shortage of money and internal divisions. The invention and sustaining of these four distinctive voices, including that of a woman who initially has no power over language, derives from the power of post-modern pastiche, as each speaks in a socially distinctive and representative idiolect. Forced to manage a large and inappropriate house on inadequate resources, much of the novel details the burdens of women's household duties. Finally, wracked by public ridicule and a sequence of scandals, the community implodes and puts Wroe on trial for drunkenness and immorality. In a melodramatic conclusion, Wroe is acquitted but ruined and flees the community, leaving the women to confront their various futures without their prophet.

Formally, *Mr Wroe's Virgins* might best be described as gently postmodern. Without any self-conscious anguish about the nature of pastiche and parody or the limitations of realist fiction, the novel draws on several realist conventions as well as the repertoire of postmodern possibilities. While the end of the novel comprises monologues which look out on to an unresolved future, there are two closures of characteristically Victorian proportions – the trial of Wroe and Joanna's death through cholera. In a more stridently post-modern text, such conventional resolutions might have become self-consciously parodic, but here they are accepted for their value in shaping a traditional text. Equally, it might be argued that the central theme of the book is the thwarted compulsion towards self-realisation and fulfilment undertaken by Victorian women, a realist convention enshrined in texts like *Jane Eyre, Shirley, The Mill on the Floss* and *Tess of the D'Urbervilles*. Again, in a more aggressively postmodern novel, such conventional textual strategies might well have been held up to critical or metafictive scrutiny of the kind Fowles so amply provides in *The French Lieutenant's Woman*. But *Mr Wroe's Virgins*, while it has a scrupulously absent author, has no metafiction at all. The carefully drawn use of naturalistic detail is similarly conventional for a historical fiction – there is, for example, a strenuously extended account of wash day that graphically depicts the detail of women's work as a collective ordeal (Rogers 1991: 97–100). The four separate speakers of the narratives through whom the novel is constructed are all given coherent identities and offer a clear account of their own motivation. In all these ways the novel might be called 'conventional' or even unself-conscious.

Yet the central theme of the novel, a deconstructive examination of a clichéd version of Victorian male sexual hypocrisy, depends on a sustained use of the complexities and ambiguities available through multiple narration, a central strategy of postmodern fiction. The central element of the narrative concerns not the history of the community but rather the changing consciousness of the four distinctively voiced 'virgins' in response to their experience of their enforced companions and, in particular, to their relationship with Wroe. Crucially, Wroe exists only as a construction of the four intersecting narrative voices, and speaks only as he is reported in these narratives. All four narratives are imbued with radical uncertainty as a consequence of each narrator's particular construction of reality. The most apparently literary and rational narrative belongs to Hannah, the orphan daughter of an engraver who is 'given' to Wroe by her uncaring guardian aunt and uncle. Hannah's fiancé has emigrated to America in an attempt to establish an Owenite community, and Hannah is left alone with her grief at her father's death, her cautious vision of the possibility of the political (rather than religious) transformation of society, and her sceptical rationalism. Joanna's voice proceeds from her fervent Southcottian religious vision, full of prognostications, signs and symbols. Driven by the possibility of women claiming their rightful spiritual roles as prophets and leaders, Joanna subjugates herself totally to the will of Mr Wroe. Leah, flirtatious and secular, and living on the hopeless possibility of ensnaring Wroe as her husband, passes off her illegitimate child as an unexpected 'gift' to the community, and strives to find ways to give her life adventure and human passion. Most complex of all, Martha has been so abused that she has lost her power over language, and spends the book slowly recovering some semblance of the conceptual and linguistic abilities she needs to order and control her sensual apprehension of the world. The three other virgins, two young and well-meaning sisters called Rachel and Rebekah and an enfeebled cripple called Dinah, are denied their own voices in the narrative. The central common theme of the four narratives is the extent to which need, desire and repression lead the four women to misinterpret their world, and to replace truth with misinterpretation or outright fantasy. The narratives share a radical unreliability that forces the reader to construct his or her own 'truth' out of the conflicting evidence, thus foregrounding the recognition that the recovery of the lost historical narratives of individuals through the imaginative energy and formal modes of fiction must recognise the uncorroborated and subjective nature, as well as the importance, of such narratives.

Central to the strategy of *Mr Wroe's Virgins* is a refusal of historiographical clichés about the Victorians, especially glib assumptions which seek to confirm a smug and knowing critique of Victorian patriarchy and hypocrisy. At a first glance, Mr Wroe's religious community seems an almost comically archetypal exposition of patriarchal authority – denied possessions and legal rights, and with even their individual autonomy under threat, a group of women are condemned to a combination of domestic drudgery, poverty and public ridicule by an unbending patriarchal regime which, under the hypocritical sanction of spiritual aspiration, is actually constructed out of male sexual and authoritarian desire. And indeed, at one level, a major achievement of *Mr Wroe's Virgins* is the imaginative realisation of this 'classic' combination of patriarchal factors, and especially the physical effects of managing a large household in the service of male need. But it is the sexualisation of the community and its activities that is most shocking. As Hannah remarks, ironically talking about Wroe's belief that Owenites opposed marriage and supported free love, 'Why is it that salacious rumours about a system of beliefs travel like wildfire, while its sober truths, and the great benefits it may confer on humanity, are ignored?' (Rogers 1991: 79). Sexuality is displayed even in the domestic furnishings of the Sanctuary. The innocent Rebekah points out the white marble figures on the living-room mantelpiece, dressed in a manner that the saintly Joanna describes as 'clearly appropriate to a climate warmer than our own'. 'At a loss to think how such things might be permitted in the Lord's house' Joanna falls back somewhat nervously on the example of Adam and Eve (Rogers 1991: 19).

A community which advertised its recruitment of 'virgins' as a central founding moment was never likely to be far away from sexual scandal, and one version of the novel's narrative would posit Wroe as merely an extreme example of a fraudulent use of religion as a cover for male desire. The male members of the community (and members is a telling word here) impose a punishment regime on themselves which involves being beaten on the buttocks while being held in place by their genitals (Rogers 1991: 58–9). The less credulous of the virgins, especially Leah, whose experience of male sexuality went considerably beyond the virginal, recognise 'the unseemliness' of such 'contact', even when 'ordained by God, through the Prophet' (Rogers 1991: 59). On one reading of the text, and way beyond these witty incidents, the Prophet Wroe might be seen not just as a religious fraud, willing to plant 'converts' in the crowd at revival meetings (Rogers 1991: 83), but as an unscrupulous abuser of women. Sexual opportunism rather than religious conviction may have been the dominant motive for Wroe's project. The gullibly pious Joanna, prepared to find and submit to God's will however oddly manifested, endures Wroe's sexual advances, hoping to fulfil her vision of a Southcottian devotional female community. Her sense of shame and violation assured Wroe of her silence, just as Martha's lack of language and mental confusion made her available to him without fear of retribution. Together with Leah's sustained attempts to seduce Wroe into marriage and to find sexual implications in even the most casual contact and Hannah's half-acknowledged attraction to the Prophet, the Sanctuary comes to represent an extreme version of the interpenetration of devotional and sexual fervour characteristic of charismatic Victorian sectarianism. *Mr Wroe's Virgins*, then, offers a classic formulation of abusive patriarchy – or it would do, without the ambiguities and counternarratives provided within the same text.

The first of these counternarratives derives from the subjective nature of the four voices through which the text is constructed, and hinges on notions of the radical unreliability central to postmodernity. The narrative gives a clear indication that the four voices may represent the internalised sexualised yearnings of the repressed through deliberately charting the way in which one incident gives rise to multiple or, more probably, *mis*interpretation. Leah, on one of her various illicit observational sorties in pursuit of Wroe's favours, and in the course of trying to listen in to a conversation between Hannah and Wroe, sees Hannah with her naked back turned to Wroe who is untying her dress (Rogers 1991: 158–9). Tormented by sexual jealousy and the undermining of her schemes to ensnare the Prophet into marriage, Leah reads the scene as proof of intimacy between Hannah and Wroe, and ascribes to Hannah all the calculation which had informed her own behaviour. In her next monologue, Hannah offers a much more prosaic account of her 'intimacy' with Wroe. In making her dress, Hannah had left a threaded needle in the fabric, which had pierced her skin and caused her to cry out. Wroe unbuttoned her dress and removed the needle, mocking her embarrassment at her nakedness in his presence. Even so, Hannah cannot exclude a frisson of sexual excitement from the incident, however proper Wroe's behaviour may have been. A slight touch wiping away drops of blood might equally, in the sexually intensified world of Wroe's presence, have been a caress. So, even in Hannah's rational and articulate version of events, a sexual ambiguity remains.

Such a carefully managed dialogue between a 'false' narrative derived from sexual jealousy and a 'true' account of banal detail raises the broader possibility that all four of the women's narratives derive from fantasised need. Joanna imagines her rape and pregnancy because of her desire to fulfil her Southcottian destiny. Leah, in her need to step beyond her promiscuous and improvisational past and find a financially secure and respectable future for herself, entirely invents Wroe's sexual attraction to her, thus misinterpreting his every gesture. Hannah, seeking intellectual stimulation and direction, positions the Prophet as an empathetic helpmate in her journey towards self-realisation rather than as a sexual predator. Martha, in her confused mental world, can only imagine Wroe in terms of her previous abuse, and projects her continuing sensual, sexual and linguistic self-recognition onto Wroe in the only way she knows how.

Gathering together these possibilities, the novel might thus be read as comment on a commonplace understanding of the Victorians – that the combined repressions of patriarchy and religious fervour forced women into becoming complicit in an entirely phallocentric narrative in which their identity is only constructed in relation to the male. The yearnings of women towards autonomy and self-realisation turn out to be another retelling of the story of the centrality of men to women's lives.

Interestingly, Rogers, rather than being fearful of this narrative, turns it to her own fictional purposes, and argues through the possibility that, acknowledging all its failings, patriarchal oppression might nonetheless operate as a source of self-definition for women. A redemptive possibility is acknowledged as being available within the preposterous and oppressive corruption of the Ashton-under-Lyne community. Indeed, subversively, *Mr Wroe's Virgins* sustains the great project of Victorian realist fiction by women in the face of postmodern uncertainty – for Hannah and Martha at least, Mr Wroe provides, however ambiguously, the appropriate permissive place (indeed the 'sanctuary') that sanctions self-recognition and self-realisation. However fraught by uncertainty, Hannah persistently acknowledges the ways in which Wroe forces her to evaluate the choices available to her. Starting from the recognition that 'he is not a fraud, I am certain of that' (Rogers 1991: 88), Hannah sustains a dialogue both with Wroe and herself over the nature of choice. Recognising that the community is 'literally a sanctuary; a construct of rules and regulations which shelter its members from the arduous world of change and choices outside' and that 'the very freedom from choice is an attraction' (Rogers 1991: 88), Hannah nonetheless perceives Wroe as not just offering her a view that choices were available but actually propelling her towards them. An early remark to Wroe about her religious scepticism evokes only the response that 'you are always free to leave, Sister Hannah. This is not a prison.' (Rogers 1991: 48). Hannah's subsequent narrative is centrally structured by her recognition of the truth of this remark, as well as by an aesthetic and, perhaps, even a sexual admiration for Wroe. She acknowledges his charismatic qualities, especially the power of his oratory, his authority (Rogers 1991: 211) and, above all, his energy: 'May it not have been such an energy, in the beginning, that tricked the round earth out of chaos; the first small notion of life from stillness?' (Rogers 1991: 84).

But above all Hannah values Wroe's recognition of her power to choose. 'When I asked him for his advice, he told me I must decide for myself' (Rogers 1991: 92), she comments while considering whether to emigrate and join her fiancé in America, and such promptings lead her to extensive meditations on the nature of women's ability to shape their own lives even within the relentless patriarchy exhibited around her in early industrialism and charismatic Christianity. Acknowledging the attractions of 'hang[ing] suspended on the edge of the promise – never having to move forward into the bald reality of days ahead' (Rogers 1991: 96), Hannah begins at first to theorise the process of self-definition (Rogers 1991: 137) and then to enact entry into the active public spheres of early trade-union politics, communitarianism and education. In this form of optimistic closure to Hannah's narrative, Rogers acknowledges the limited public space available to Victorian working women, but has nonetheless succeeded in finding a combination of factors – rational and progressive communitarianism, nascent trade unionism, working-class education – which offer a plausible or even a heroic locale for Hannah's self-seeking. Replacing the earnest intensity of, say, *Villette*, *Shirley* or *Tess of the D'Urbervilles* with the half-mocking deconstructiveness of postmodern indeterminacy has not stopped Rogers from acknowledging and reasserting the importance of the central trajectory of Brontë, Eliot or Hardy's accounts of the struggles of women.

Martha's narrative forms an even more complex discussion of self-realisation largely because it forms one of several attempts in recent fiction not just to speak on behalf of but actually to find voices for those who are literally speechless. B. S. Johnson's novel about senility, *House Mother Normal* (1971), attempted something similar using typographical as well as verbal elements to express the confused consciousness of his subjects. *Mr Wroe's Virgins* contains a prolonged and extremely interesting mediation on language, focused on the centrality of the 'Word' to notions of prophecy and religious authority. Postmodern contests over meaning of course focus on the limitations of verbal forms of communication. Rogers glosses this anxiety over language in a number of ways. Hannah, attempting to teach the retarded Dinah to read, becomes exasperated at her insistence that words are 'hieroglyphs only', intimations or 'signification of some more potent ulterior reality' (Rogers 1991: 46). Dinah's struggles with language are mirrored by Joanna's dependence on the topological reading of events as symptoms, symbols or equivalencies of God's purposes. Joanna's 'misreadings' form not so much postmodern linguistic ambiguities as a comment on the persistent religious tendency to read the world as manifest destiny or revelation. Martha learns language largely to give name to her instinctual, amoral and sensual apprehension of reality, but persistently regards words as less reliable and informative than, for example, smell (Rogers 1991: 111). Ultimately, however, Martha accepts that language is necessary as a form of self-shaping. In an extremely moving meditation on the idea of the self as a linguistic concept, Martha acknowledges not just the inevitability of language but also that words are Wroe's (or perhaps God's) gift to her:

I was a stone. He gave me life.

There are no words in the dark. If I reach back from lightness to put words on to the dark, I illumine it also. Where words light it, it is safer and more knowable than it was. If I cover it all in words like ivy growing and forcing its tendrils into the small cracks – I would gain a purchase to move on further across it. If I could force back into that stone-darkness a light from this time, language to speak the old bad life, would that be delivery?

Words forced in will not show the truth of it. Because the truth of it is wordlessness . . .

I knew nothing. I named nothing. To name it now, I invent.

(Rogers 1991: 252)

Newly armed with a vocabulary, Martha announces, in a triumphant conclusion to her narrative 'I have worlds, and worlds to discover' (Rogers 1991: 256).

Whatever ambiguities his career reveals, Wroe is named as a redemptive force in three of the four constituent narratives which form the novel. For Hannah, he created room to think and room to choose. For Joanna, he provided the focus for a life lived, against all evidence, in the certainty of transfiguration and redemption in death. Joanna's rhapsodic commentary on her own death defies cynicism if only because the rest of the novel has been so sure-footed in undermining the structures and assumptions of religious certainty. For Martha, he offered the chance to acquire the means of self-awareness, especially language, which would allow her to offset her brutalised past with a celebratory, poetic and deeply sensual apprehension of the interaction between the self and the created universe. Yet of course these three redemptive narratives do not finally construct Mr. Wroe as a benevolent patriarch with women as his transformed beneficiaries. The novel is far too deeply infused with uncertainty for this to be the case. Mr Wroe's own narrative is accordingly left unclosed, thus perpetuating the possibility that it was in spite of Wroe rather than because of him that these three women found something like closure to their narratives.

Mr Wroe's Virgins seems to me a book that combines a proper outrage at the lives lived under patriarchy with an equally proper awareness of the complexity of Victorian sexual politics. Hannah's narrative restates the analysis of women's experience provided by mid-nineteenth-century fictional figures like Lucy Snowe, Jane Eyre, Maggie Tulliver and Tess, and reinstates it into an imagined history as the experience undergone by many nameless and speechless Victorians. In this sense, the novel is a postmodern pastiche of Victorian realist fiction in exactly the manner of *The French Lieutenant's Woman*. But it seems to me that Wroe's community, for all its grotesque potential, is not constructed as an exotic exemplar of Victorian sexual hypocrisy but rather as a complex recognition of the ambiguities of gender politics and religious authority in the early industrial revolution.

References

Ackroyd, P. (1994) *Dan Leno and the Limehouse Golum*, London: Sinclair-Stevenson.
Adam, I., P. Brantlinger and S. Rothblatt (1972) '*The French Lieutenant's Woman*: a discussion', *Victorian Studies* XV 3 (March) 338–56.
Altick, R. D. (1970) *Victorian Studies in Scarlet*, London: J. M. Dent.
Byatt, A. S. (1990) *Possession*, London: Chatto & Windus.
—— (1992) *Angels and Insects*, London: Chatto & Windus.
Carter, A. (1979) *The Sadeian Woman: an exercise in cultural history*, London: Virago.
Chesney, K. (1970) *The Victorian Underworld*, London: Maurice Temple Smith.
Dyos, J. and M. Wolff (eds) (1973) *The Victorian City*, 4 vols, London: Routledge & Kegan Paul.
Faber, P. (2002) *The Crimson Petal and the White*, Edinburgh: Canongate.
Fowles, J. (1969) *The French Lieutenant's Woman*, London: Jonathan Cape.
Gay, P. (1985) *The Bourgeois Experience, Victoria to Freud.* Vol I, *The Education of the Senses*, Oxford: Oxford University Press.
Glendinning, V. (1995) *Electricity*, London: Hutchinson.
Gray, A. (1992) *Poor Things*, London: Bloomsbury.
Hudson, D. (1972) *Munby: man of two worlds*, London: John Murray.
James, L. (1963) *Fiction for the Working Man*, Oxford: Oxford University Press.
Johnson, B. S. (1971) *House Mother Normal: a geriatric comedy*, London: Collins.
Kneale, M. (1992) *Sweet Thames*, London: Sinclair-Stevenson.
Marcus, S. (1966) *The Other Victorians: a study of sexuality and pornography in mid-nineteenth century England*, London: Weidenfeld & Nicolson.
Mason, M. (1994a) *The Making of Victorian Sexual Attitudes*, Oxford: Oxford University Press.
—— (1994b) *The Making of Victorian Sexuality*, Oxford: Oxford University Press.
Pearsall, R. (1969) *The Worm in the Bud: the world of Victorian sexuality*, London: Weidenfeld & Nicolson.
Rogers, J. (1991) *Mr Wroe's Virgins*, London: Faber & Faber.
Royston Pike, E. (ed.) (1966) *Human Documents of the Industrial Revolution*, London: George Allen & Unwin.
Sadlier, M. (1940) *Fanny by Gaslight*, London: Constable.
—— (1947) *Forlorn Sunset*, London: Constable.
Summers, M. (1940) *A Gothic Bibliography*, London: Fortune Press.
Thompson, E. P. (1968) [1963] *The Making of the English Working Class*, Harmondsworth: Penguin.
Vicinus, M. (1974) *The Industrial Muse*, Brighton: Croom Helm.
Waters, S. (1998) *Tipping the Velvet*, London: Virago.
—— (1999) *Affinity*, London: Virago.
—— (2002) *Fingersmith*, London: Virago.

10 Pat Barker's vanishing boundaries

Lynda Prescott

The resurgence of the historical novel in Britain in the later decades of the twentieth century took readers into just about every phase of the past, from the Stone Age to periods within recent memory. But for some writers, including Pat Barker, the sweep of the twentieth century itself exerted a particular pull, and this is very evident in the four novels she published in the 1990s. Her acclaimed First World War trilogy, *Regeneration*, *The Eye in the Door* and *The Ghost Road* (1991–5), was followed by *Another World* (1998) in which a 101-year-old veteran of the Somme shares the fictional space with the family of his middle-aged grandson, who has just moved into a house built in 1898. But Barker's first exploration of this twentieth-century time-span came a little earlier, as she followed the memories and experiences of another long-lived character in *Liza's England* (Barker 1996). It is in this novel that we encounter the phrase 'vanishing boundaries' – a phrase that encapsulates some key features of Barker's writing. It occurs in a telling passage set towards the end of the Second World War, in a bomb-ravaged northern city, as Liza waits for her daughter Eileen to give birth:

> The sky darkened; night closed in around the woman and the labour-ing girl. As the hours passed, Liza felt herself merge into the girl on the bed. *She* had laboured to give birth like this, in this room, this bed. She became afraid of the vanishing boundaries and turned to the fire, only to feel it strip the flesh from her face and reveal her mother's bones. Eileen was not Eileen, Liza was not Liza, but both were links in a chain of women stretching back through the centuries, into the wombs of women whose names they didn't know.
>
> (Barker 1996: 211)

Here Barker describes a specifically female understanding of continuity between generations, and this kind of emphasis has tended to fuel the convenient, if simplistic, critical division between Barker's earlier writing (published by Virago and appropriated by feminists) and her subsequent novels in which she is seen as transcending the sociological limitations of the working-class female communities that provided the seedbed for her first novels. But as Sharon Monteith argues, this was always a spurious kind of division (Monteith 2002: 2), and it is clear that Barker's fiction is deeply preoccupied with the interplay between past and present as it affects both male and female characters. There is also a sense in which the phrase 'vanishing boundaries' could be applied to gender divisions themselves in Barker's novels of the 1990s, as she explores concepts of masculinity and femininity. Another kind of boundary-blurring occurs in the use that Barker makes of documented historical sources in the *Regeneration* trilogy, and the blending of fact and fiction that ensues. And although the prevailing mode of her writing is realistic, her novels also push against the boundary between the known and the unknown in ways that make that dividing line less definite than it might at first appear.

To historians as well as novelists, the 'short twentieth century', spanning the period from the First World War to the collapse of the USSR, has acquired a kind of internal coherence – not least as the bloodiest century in human history – as well as marking unprecedented change in virtually every aspect of human existence. Although the *fin de siècle* mood of the 1990s was probably compounded by the added weight of millennial awareness, it was in fact the century rather than the millennium that furnished most of the terms of reference for the retrospective tendency in the decade's cultural productions. In the Western world, at least, increasing longevity meant that it was possible for many writers and artists of the 1990s to view the century in relation to their own life experiences and memories. The historian Eric Hobsbawm, born in 1917, prefaced his 1994 survey of what he called the *Age of Extremes* (1914–91) with an acknowledgement of his sources that included not only 'wide and miscellaneous reading' but also 'the accumulated knowledge, memories and opinions of someone who has lived through the Short Twentieth Century as what the social anthropologists call a "participant observer"' (Hobsbawm 1995: x). The proliferation of written documents and visual images during the twentieth century provided more than enough material for cultural retrospection, but the testimony of those who 'lived through' particular events (especially the two world wars) was valued as perhaps never before. Veterans of the Great War, like the fictional Geordie in *Another World*, found themselves during the 1990s increasingly in demand for first-hand accounts of their war experiences:

> . . . in the 1960s, Geordie began to talk about the war. Over the next three decades his willingness to share his memories increased and, as other veterans died around him, his own rarity value grew. In the

1990s he was one of a tiny group of survivors who gathered for the anniversaries of the first day of the Somme, and most of the others were in wheelchairs. There were rewards in this for him. He was sought after, listened to, he had friends, interests, a purpose in life at an age when old people are too often sitting alone in chilly rooms waiting for their relatives to phone. But the sense of mission was genuine. His message was simple: *It happened once, therefore it can happen again. Take care.*

(Barker 1998: 82)

Geordie remains, to his dying day, haunted by the past and specifically by the death of his soldier-brother, so despite his 'public' message being a simple one Barker uses him as a vehicle for a far more complex exploration of memory. Helen, the historian in *Another World* who has recorded and written up veterans' memories of the First World War, believes that these memories are reworked over time to match changing perceptions of the war in society at large. Thus Geordie's initial repression of bitterness and pain gives way to a later articulation of his dreadful experience that is by then socially and morally acceptable, according to Helen's thesis. However, Geordie's grandson, Nick, comes to realise that the past, imperfectly remembered and leaving room for guilt, remains in the present tense for Geordie. 'For Helen, memories are infinitely malleable, but not for Geordie. Geordie's past isn't over. It isn't even the past' (Barker 1998: 241).

Nevertheless, Geordie bears witness to the horrors of the war for the benefit of the later twentieth century, and, in a more personal way, passes something of this experience to his grandson. This happens both involuntarily, as Nick follows the dying Geordie through his sleepwalking nightmares, and more consciously in their visit to the battlefields, in the winter before Geordie's illness. The monument to 'The Missing of the Somme' at Thiepval repels and moves Nick: 'Geordie was attempting to graft his memories on to Nick – that's what the visit was about – and perhaps, in spite of Nick's resistance, he'd come close to succeeding' (Barker 1998: 74). There is a distance between the two men, in terms of education and class as well as age, a distance that inevitably produces tensions within their affectionate relationship, but through sharing with his grandfather in the experience of the cemeteries and the monument at Thiepval Nick develops a new awareness, not only of the enormity of death triumphant on the battlefields of the war but also of the power of the past to leak into present.

If Geordie's experience of the First World War remains, eighty years on, an inescapable part of the present in *Another World*, when we turn back to the *Regeneration* trilogy we find that war resisting containment in its historical moment still more strenuously. Although the novels centre largely on real-life characters, such as the army psychiatrist W. H. R. Rivers and the poets Siegfried Sassoon and Wilfred Owen, this factual dimension does not generate a 'period' flavour. For one thing, the characters in the novels, both historical figures and fictional creations, speculate on time in such a way that our sense of their present being our past is repeatedly undermined. So, for example, when Wilfred Owen and Siegfried Sassoon first meet at Craiglockhart Hospital, the major setting for *Regeneration*, their tentative exploration of each other's attitudes towards the war rapidly releases more personal, and very vivid, apprehensions of time and death. Owen, who is younger than Sassoon and overawed by him, nevertheless dredges out of his own uncertainty a specific kind of insight generated by his experience in the trenches:

> '. . . Sometimes when you're alone, in the trenches, I mean, at night you get the sense of something *ancient*. As if the trenches had always been there. You know one trench we held, it had skulls in the side. You looked back along and . . . Like mushrooms. And do you know, it was actually *easier* to believe they were men from Marlborough's army than to to to think they'd been alive two years ago. It's as if all other wars had somehow . . . distilled themselves into this war, and that makes it something you . . . almost can't challenge . . .'
>
> For a moment the nape of Sassoon's neck crawled . . . 'I had a similar experience. Well, I don't know whether it is similar. I was going up with the rations one night and I saw the limbers against the skyline, and the flares going up. What you see every night. Only I seemed to be seeing it from the future. A hundred years from now they'll still be ploughing up skulls. And I seemed to be in that time and looking back. I think I saw our ghosts.'
>
> (Barker 1991: 83–4)

This brief exchange between Owen and Sassoon illustrates another feature of Barker's writing that tends to dissolve the barriers between past and present. Dialogue is always of major importance in Barker's novels, including those with a historical setting, where she handles vocabulary and phrasing in such a way that characters' speech is never tethered to an out-dated idiom. Owen's hesitations and stammering are economically rendered, and short sentences such as 'As if the trenches had always been there' match the overall crispness of Sassoon's speech. Even in this example, where each speech is, comparatively speaking, extended because of its reflective quality, we can recognise the spareness that is such a significant feature of the dialogue in Barker's novels – a spareness that feels entirely familiar to the contemporary reader.

In *Another World*, like *Liza's England*, past and present are linked not only through memories of long-lived characters but also through family relationships that bind generation to generation. These kinds of links are less prominent in the *Regeneration* trilogy, but continuity between generations is foregrounded through quasi-familial relationships. Rivers, the good doctor who becomes a father figure to the young soldiers he tries to heal, is also engaged in efforts to retrieve his own childhood memories as a way of trying to understand the fractures in his personality.

At one point, as Rivers recalls being a pupil of his speech-therapist father, he reflects that 'the relationship between father and son is never simple, and never over. Death certainly doesn't end it' (Barker 1991: 155–6). In the same passage he imagines a boy creeping up to his window at Craiglockhart and overhearing a treatment session in the same way that, as a boy, he had listened at his father's window. Rivers is acutely aware of the professional similarities between himself and his father, but acutely aware, too, that in this imaginary scenario the boy 'would not have been his son'. His childlessness hardly matters, though. The war provides Rivers with a whole family of sons – Sassoon, Burns, Prior – for whom he becomes surrogate father.

Rivers' approach to the treatment of war neuroses is influenced by Freudian methods of psychoanalysis, and the retrieval of memories is a central part of this approach. In the case of Billy Prior, who arrives at Craiglockhart without an army file on his medical condition, this is particularly difficult. But even when Prior begins to recall and communicate something of his front-line experiences he challenges Rivers' approach in the way that a clever adolescent will challenge a parent:

> This had been Prior's attitude throughout the three weeks they'd spent trying to recover his memories of France. He seemed to be saying, 'All right. You can make me dredge up the horrors, you can make me remember the deaths, but you will never make me feel.' Rivers tried to break down the detachment, to get to the emotion, but he knew that, confronted by the same task, he would have tackled it in exactly the same way as Prior.
>
> (Barker 1991: 79)

Rivers' capacity to recognise and accept a shared awkwardness is, in part, an instance of his deep humanity, but there is also a hint here of family likeness that is taken a stage further in *The Eye in the Door*. In a scene that echoes Rivers' awareness of his professional links with his father, Prior and Rivers change places during consultation and from the patient's chair Rivers finds himself 'confronted by a caricature of himself' (Barker 1993: 137) as Prior adeptly assumes the therapist's role. In the third volume of the trilogy Prior and Rivers actually meet only once, just before Prior returns to France, and Rivers reflects explicitly on the 'strong father–son element in his relationship with Prior' (Barker 1995: 98). But although this is their only meeting, all through the second and third parts of the novel their voices run in parallel. The familial bond that has been established between the characters holds in tension the alternating narratives of Prior's journal and Rivers' Melanesian recollections – the older man reliving his idyllic pre-war experiences as an anthropologist on the island of Eddystone whilst the younger man moves forward to an uncertain but probably tragic future. The interplay between past and present is thus woven into the very structure of *The Ghost Road*.

Occasionally characters in the trilogy register a particular awareness of historical change in their times. When Prior returns, temporarily, to Salford in *The Eye in the Door* he sees enormous changes in the people and places he left at the start of the war and realises that they are all living through a period when 'people *do* become aware of what's happening, and they look back on their previous unconscious selves and it seems like decades ago. Another life' (Barker 1993: 100). This recognition is prompted not only by seeing a photograph from just before the war, but also by his encounter, a few pages earlier, with the two middle-aged women who had nursed him as a baby: 'Off they went, cackling delightedly, two married women going out for a drink together. Unheard of. And in his father's pub too. No wonder the old bugger thought Armageddon had arrived' (Barker 1993: 96). For younger women, too, the war has brought sudden freedoms. Sarah Lumb, who becomes Prior's fiancée, works in a munitions factory where she earns five times her pre-war wages in domestic service, and can enjoy the independence of a single woman away from her home town and family. At first Prior 'didn't know what to make of her, but then he was so out of touch with women. They seemed to have changed so much during the war, to have expanded in all kinds of ways, whereas men over the same period had shrunk into a smaller and smaller space' (Barker 1991: 90). Although women characters play a minor role in the trilogy, Barker emphasises strongly the changes brought about in their lives by the war, often using overt comparisons with men.

Alongside this charting of social changes in relation to gender, Rivers' psychiatric work offers another set of links and contrasts between men and women. His treatment of war neuroses in men is based on a hypothesis about the connection between enforced passivity and breakdown: thus the more helpless soldiers or airmen feel themselves to be under the conditions of modern warfare, the more likely they are to break down. Although Rivers' patients are all men, his understanding of their condition depends on an understanding of *women's* lives:

it was prolonged strain, immobility and helplessness that did the damage, and not the sudden shocks or bizarre horrors that the patients themselves were inclined to point to as the explanation for their condition. That would help to account for the greater prevalence of anxiety neuroses and hysterical disorders in women in peacetime, since their relatively more confined lives gave them fewer opportunities of reacting to stress in active and constructive ways. Any explanation of war neurosis must account for the fact that this apparently intensely masculine life of war and danger and hardship produced in men the same disorders that women suffered from in peace.

(Barker 1991: 222)

Early in *The Ghost Road* we see Rivers devising a treatment for hysterical paralysis that turns, in a very literal way, on the feminisation of men in this first modern war. Ian Moffet is a young officer who had 'fallen down in a "fainting fit" while on his way to the Front, shortly after hearing the guns for the first time. When he recovered consciousness he could not move his legs' (Barker 1995: 20). The paralysis has persisted for three months, and no rational approach to treatment has had any effect. So Rivers resorts to a highly unconventional strategy, drawing thick black lines around Moffet's legs to delimit the area of sensation. Moffet himself describes the procedure:

'Well, as far as I can make out, you ... er ... intend to draw ...' Minute muscles twitched around Moffet's nose and lips, giving him the look of a supercilious rabbit. '*Stocking tops?* On my legs, here.' With delicately pointed fingers he traced two lines across the tops of his thighs. 'And then, gradually, day by day, you propose to ... um ... *lower* the stockings, and as the stockings are *unrolled*, so to speak, the ... er ... paralysis will ...' A positive orgy of twitching. 'Retreat.'

(Barker 1995: 21)

This treatment – successful, as it happens – also involves different roles for Rivers. His method of testing for sensation by means of pinpricks reminds Moffet of seventeenth-century witch-finders, and Rivers himself sees the similarities between his dramatic form of treatment and the practices of witch doctors (his pre-war experiences as an anthropologist in Melanesia have given him ample opportunity to observe such practices). But as an essential part of the treatment he also takes on the implicitly female role of nurse, washing Moffet's legs each day as he prepares to draw new lines:

Sister Carmichael . . . was shocked by his insistence on doing everything himself, including the washing off of the previous lines. Consultants do not wash patients. *Nurses* wash patients. She would have been only marginally more distressed if she'd come on to the ward and found him mopping the floor.'

(Barker 1995: 52–3)

Sister Carmichael no doubt sees this as a question of status rather than gender, but readers of the trilogy are by now well-versed in the connections between the two. The point that Margaretta Jolly makes in relation to Barker's earlier novels applies just as much to her later, historical fiction: 'Barker never sacrifices gender for class. Rather, her exploration of the unconscious of class is always measured against, and entwined with, the relations between the sexes' (Jolly 2000: 63).

One of Barker's most impressive strokes of novelistic economy is that in the *Regeneration* trilogy she embodies these complexities of class and gender in a single character, Billy Prior. Prior is a working-class officer – as one reviewer pithily expresses it, 'a native of no man's land' (Sage 1995: 9). He is not one of the First World War's 'temporary gentlemen', but more like an older, military version of the mid-twentieth-century 'scholarship boy', whose critical intelligence is accompanied by a qualified emotional detachment from his class. Prior, however, does not suffer from the lack of poise and anxiety that Richard Hoggart identified as recognisable traits of the 'scholarship boy' in *The Uses of Literacy*, despite being at 'the friction-point of two cultures' (Hoggart 1992: 292). Prior lives out the contradictions in his life wholeheartedly, often appearing to revel in his chameleon status. Another facet of his in-between nature is that he is also, energetically, bisexual, and again there is a link between sexuality and class: his parents' marriage is fraught with a Lawrentian mix of social ambition and violence, and Prior sees himself as a product of this conflict. '*He* and *She* – elemental forces, almost devoid of personal characteristics – clawed each other in every cell of his body, and would do so until he died' (Barker 1993: 90). Prior's homosexual encounters take him back into the battlefield of the English class system, especially in *The Eye in the Door*, but throughout the trilogy questions about homosexuality also overlap, like ripples on water, with questions about masculinity, war and violence.

Barker's exploration of attitudes towards homosexuality during the First World War is charged with the same kind of historical awareness that marks her depiction of changes in gender roles in this period, but she also makes considerable direct use of historical material, such as the notorious Pemberton Billing Affair, which generated considerable public hysteria on the home front in the early months of 1918. The MP Noel Pemberton Billing had put his name to a newspaper article that attempted to link homosexuality with treachery by claiming that the Germans had a 'black book' containing the names of 47,000 eminent people in Britain whose loyalty to their country was compromised by their private lives. References to this insidious campaign surface near the end of *Regeneration*, as Rivers warns Sassoon about the mounting intolerance of homosexuality that the war has produced. Sassoon's circle of friends and his public advocacy of a negotiated peace are enough to make him vulnerable, in Rivers' eyes, so he is relieved when Sassoon decides to return to the Front, despite his principled opposition to the war. It is thus through the eyes of another war-damaged officer, Prior's friend Charles Manning, that we witness, in the sixth chapter of *The Eye in the Door*, the unfolding of the central episode in the Pemberton Billing Affair.

In the spring of 1918 a private performance of Oscar Wilde's *Salomé*, authorised by Wilde's friend and literary executor, Robert Ross, took place, amidst more newspaper publicity linking subscribers to the list of 'the 47,000' and 'the cult of the clitoris' (Barker 1993: 22). This extraordinary theatrical event is knitted into the thematic concerns of the novel in several ways. The occasion brings to the fore the atmosphere of danger surrounding homosexuality, and the play itself explores the link between passion and cruelty; but Wilde's *fin de siècle* text also makes unwitting comment on the realities of the twentieth century. For example, Manning feels a spasm of revulsion at the sight of Iokanann's head on a charger, 'not because the head was horrifying, but because it wasn't. Another thing Wilde couldn't have foreseen: people in the audience for whom severed heads were not necessarily made of papier mâché.' Most of all, he feels that 'the language was impossible for him. France had made it impossible' (Barker 1993: 78). Manning's account of Wilde's dream-like, non-naturalistic play is embedded in the down-to-earth realism of the novel's overall texture in a way that not only contrasts different modes of artistic expression but also acknowledges the sheer difficulty of conveying, through art, the extremities of human experience.

Barker's way of meeting this challenge is to represent the unprecedented horrors of mechanised warfare on the western front mainly in an indirect way, through the memories of combatants, often drawing on documented sources. But the *Salomé* episode also emphasises the historical nature of the trilogy rather differently, as it gives full play to the sheer implausibility of actual happenings off the battlefield, too. The reader can consult the 'Author's Note' at the end *The Eye in the Door* for a brief summary of the (almost incredible) Pemberton Billing Affair, as well as the more freely handled 'poison plot' against Lloyd George, which becomes, in the novel, the story of the fictional Beattie Roper. It is, of course, not uncommon for a novelist, especially a historical novelist, to include such notes or even a bibliography as part of the book's apparatus, but Barker foregrounds her factual material to an unusual extent. In fact, the 'Author's Note' to *Regeneration* begins: 'Fact and fiction are so interwoven in this book that it may help the reader to know what is historical and what is not.' Although the two elements *are* sometimes separable, the factual material is blended so closely with the fictional that the boundaries could be said to dissolve in places. At the end of *The Ghost Road*, for example, Wilfred Owen's last letter to his mother (Owen and Bell 1967: 590–1) is largely transposed to the fictional Prior's journal (Barker 1995: 257–8). This is no capricious move, but a way of giving a recognisably real voice to the historically unnamed and unremembered soldiers that Prior in some ways represents.

The trilogy's historical – and structural – backbone is provided by W. H. R. Rivers. Although less well known to the modern-day reader than figures like Siegfried Sassoon or Wilfred Owen, the character of Rivers provides extraordinary opportunities for the novelist. His prominence in two fields – anthropology and psychiatry – is exploited to the full, but his real-life failure to recover his own buried childhood memory also means that, in biographical terms, a central part of his identity remains undefined. There is thus a sliver of kinship between Rivers and an invented character like Prior that allows the novelist's imagination to move fairly easily between them. But *The Ghost Road*, in particular, reminds us that there is a third category of characters between the 'historical' and the 'fictional': the people Rivers knew on Eddystone – Njiru, Kundaite, Emele and others – 'are also historical, but of them nothing more is known' beyond Rivers' unpublished notebooks (Barker 1995: 278). Interestingly, it is largely through these characters and Rivers' encounters with them that another kind of boundary between the 'known' and the 'unknown' becomes permeable, and space is created within the narrative for ghosts.

There are many kinds of 'hauntings' in Barker's novels, spanning the natural as well as the supernatural. In *Another World* the hauntings range from Geordie's indelible memories of his dead brother through to less explicable glimpses of the Victorian girl who once lived in the house that Nick and his family now inhabit and where, Nick discovers, a younger child was murdered. In the trilogy there are many more kinds of ghosts. Several of Rivers' patients are visited by the ghosts of dead soldiers, and Billy Prior turns into his own ghost when, in *The Eye in the Door*, he develops a demonic alter ego. As John Brannigan points out, 'Rivers responds to these ghostly manifestations with an impressive array of psychoanalytical and rational explanations' (Brannigan 2003: 15) and is able to make some kind of sense of them without erasing their potency as signs of general, not just personal, crisis. But whilst Rivers the war-time psychiatrist is dedicated to 'curing' his patients of their psychic disturbances, Rivers the pre-war anthropologist is increasingly obsessed by his own encounters with ghosts in Melanesia. In fact, Rivers is given a kind of alter ego, too, in the character of Njiru, the witch doctor whose practices he observed closely during his fieldwork on Eddystone.

The head-hunters of Melanesia are seen, in *The Ghost Road*, as a society in decline. Under British rule, with headhunting banned, birth rates are falling and lethargy pervades. In one of the central paradoxes of the novel, after Rivers reads a newspaper report of further bloody battles in the final stages of the First World War, he slips into a feverish recollection of Njiru performing funeral rites in the skull house on Eddystone and realises 'This was a people perishing from the absence of war' (Barker 1995: 207). The contrasts are striking, but, rather than dwelling on the question of whether or not war is an inevitable part of human life, Barker homes in on war's essence: destruction. Njiru's power, hard won and carefully guarded, includes the power to control spirits, and the most important of these is Ave, the destroyer of peoples. In the final scene of the novel Njiru appears to Rivers in his London hospital ward and speaks the words of exorcism that will quell Ave. His words are enigmatic and offer no immediate comfort, but the sense of narrative resolution is extraordinarily powerful, as Rivers' two worlds, past and present, momentarily coalesce.

The title of *The Ghost Road* comes from Edward Thomas's poem, 'Roads', depicting the road to France along which 'the dead/ Returning lightly dance' (Barker 1995: i). The echoes of other writings are often lightly present in Barker's novels, but this is not to say that she positions herself firmly within a particular literary tradition (see Monteith et al. 2004: 20). The crossing and blurring of boundaries in her fiction render most critical 'labels', including 'historical novelist', inadequate. Perhaps the most significant elements in her writing are her emphases on characters and conviction about the power of language. Billy Prior sums it up in his final courageous journal entry, where he dismisses 'Patriotism honour courage vomit vomit vomit' but notes that there *are* still words that mean something:

> Little words that trip through sentences unregarded: us, them, we, they, here, there. These are the words of power, and long after we're gone, they'll lie about in the language, like the unexploded grenades in these fields, and any one of them'll take your hand off.
>
> (Barker 1995: 257)

References

Barker, Pat (1991) *Regeneration*, London: Viking.
—— (1993) *The Eye in the Door*, London: Viking.
—— (1995) *The Ghost Road*, London: Viking.

—— (1996) *Liza's England*, London: Virago. Originally published as *The Century's Daughter*, London: Virago, 1986.

—— (1998) *Another World*. London: Viking.

Brannigan, John (2003) 'Pat Barker's *Regeneration* Trilogy', in R. J. Lane, R. Mengham and P. Tew (eds) *Contemporary British Fiction*, Oxford: Polity Press.

Hobsbawm, Eric (1995) [1994] *Age of Extremes: the short twentieth century 1914–1991*, London: Abacus.

Hoggart, Richard (1992) [1957] *The Uses of Literacy*, London: Penguin.

Jolly, Margaretta (2000) 'After feminism: Pat Barker, Penelope Lively and the contemporary novel', in A. Davies and A. Sinfield (eds) *British Culture of the Postwar: introduction to literature and society 1945–1990*, London: Routledge.

Monteith, Sharon (2002) *Pat Barker*, Tavistock: Northcote House.

Monteith, Sharon, Jenny Newman and Pat Wheeler (2004) *Contemporary British and Irish Fiction: an introduction through interviews*, London: Hodder.

Owen, Harold and John Bell (1967) *Wilfred Owen: collected letters*, London: Oxford University Press.

Sage, Lorna (1995) 'Both Sides', *London Review of Books*, 5 October.

11 Singular events

The 'as if' of Beryl Bainbridge's *Every Man for Himself*

Fiona Becket

It is the task of hermeneutics [. . .] to reconstruct the set of operations by means of which a work arises from the opaque depths of living, acting, and suffering, to be given by an author to readers who receive it and thereby change their own actions.

(Ricoeur, 1991b)

There are no singular events. Experience is process, the paradox of myriad singular events. History is the selective recording and privileging of events, organized by the dominant culture in a pattern of figuring or recession. Also, there *are* singular events, culturally, socially, constructed as punctuating experience: moments of arrest, which are simultaneously moments of transformation. Moments of regression that are also moments of progression. Amongst these are events that have intense symbolic meaning conferred upon them, to the point that they can seem 'naturally' to function as figurative within a vast cultural narrative. Such an event is the loss of the *Titanic*.

The story of the *Titanic* represents a stage of society that is past; not long past, but far enough away. That it exerts a real hold on the imagination in the present is both expected and surprising. (James Cameron's 1997 film, *Titanic*, was a box-office favourite with as many awards as the legendary *Ben Hur*, preceded by Jean Negulesco's *Titanic* [1953] and *A Night to Remember* [1958].) 'Official' histories are easy to come by. The official web site of the Titanic Historical Society offers books, pamphlets and memorabilia for sale. Articles can be located on the disaster, repeating or revising myths about the voyage and the participants. Assiduously constructed chronologies, passenger lists, deck plans, contemporary accounts and newspaper columns, and the texts of, respectively, the American and British enquiries that followed the catastrophe are available online, along with information and photographs relating to the discovery in 1985 of the site of the wreck. Details about its condition and value as a grave and monument are easily accessible. Walter Lord's reconstruction of the disaster, *A Night to Remember* (1955), was reissued in 1997.[1] We still need the story of the loss of the *Titanic*; the singular event speaks to our current interests and desires. Then, in 1912, the White Star Line's steamer was a 'miracle' of design and technology. With its sister ship, the *Olympic*, it was a sign of the prosperity and unsinkability of the economy that could conceive and produce it. Registered as an emigrant ship, many of the passengers were setting out for America. Now, it is symbolic of the end of an epoch. As a singular, iconic event, it was about catastrophe – human, commercial and national – which, or so we can claim with the advantage of hindsight, ushered in the end of the 'Edwardian summer'. In many respects, too, it anticipated the closure of the 'long' nineteenth century that was finally achieved with the 1914–18 war. An exhausted, stratified culture, with socially and economically differentiated passengers, officers and crew, for some, the *Titanic* was a pleasure dome afloat on deceptively calm waters and buoyed up by the myth of invulnerability. George Bernard Shaw uses the ship metaphor in *Heartbreak House* (1919) to describe the crisis of Western civilization.

For Bainbridge in *Every Man for Himself* (1996), the immediate value of the sinking of the *Titanic* resides in its status as 'real' combined with the fact of its important hold, still, on the popular imagination. This could also be said of the treatment of Scott's expedition to the Antarctic, which foundered in 1912, in *The Birthday Boys* (1991). In the first instance, therefore, this essay examines how reality shapes fiction as an exploration of what Paul Ricoeur, in his examination of the phenomenology of fiction ('The function of fiction in shaping reality'), calls 'productive reference' (Ricoeur 1991a: 120–1). It will suggest that Bainbridge dispenses with the classical notion of fiction as illusion (reproductive), preferring to think of it as *work* which, again in the words of Ricoeur, 'redescribes reality' (Ricoeur 1991a: 133). *Every Man for Himself* is a novel that, in beautifully understated terms, examines the transformative power of the image – its power to 'rework' the real. It is also a novel that critically examines the relation between writing and representation, truth and lie, by turning to an event in the social history of the twentieth century that almost immediately was able to accrue a symbolic significance. *Every Man for Himself* enacts all kinds of trauma (personal, political, cultural and ideological). In it Bainbridge seizes the interpretative possibilities, at the end of the twentieth century, of revisiting the wreck of the *Titanic*.

Bainbridge, Ricoeur and the 'as if' of writing

There is an affinity between Bainbridge's sense of proper material for a novel, and its effect, and Ricoeur's reinterpretation of the role of the reader re-created by the fictional work. This novel, as a supreme example of Bainbridge's interest in the interface between fiction and history, allows us to reconsider Ricoeur's approach to the encounter between experience, explanation and interpretation. The text, he asserts, 'is the paradigm of distanciation in communication. As such, it displays a fundamental characteristic of the very historicity of human experience, namely that it is communication in and through distance' (Ricoeur 1981: 131). The text, he maintains, positions the reader anew; the reader completes a process (through an act of reading) and the individual work (here, of fiction) restyles the reader's relation to event and 'world'. Challenged is the idea that to understand is 'to project oneself into the text' (Ricoeur 1981: 182). If we recall the terms of Ricoeur's essay 'Appropriation', this reconstruction of the reader is part of the role of play as a transformative aspect of aesthetic experience (Ricoeur 1981: 182–93; see especially 186–7). The particular work confers a new self that is the reader (Ricoeur 1981: 189–90), which is fundamental to Ricoeur's dissertation on mimesis. Mimesis, in his thought, is polysemic and mobile, in contrast to the classical understanding of mimesis as a process that *refers to* the world: he introduces a genuine dynamism into the concept which implicates reading. In 'Mimesis and representation', Ricoeur reminds us that writers 'do not produce things but just quasi things. They invent the "as if" '(Ricoeur 1991b: 139). However, the act of reading 'is the unique operator of the unceasing passage . . . from a prefigured world to a transfigured world through the mediation of a configured world' (Ricoeur 1991b: 151).[2] Fiction's treatment of time and experience brings about an accord between event, text and reader that is denied by history. This distinction is crucial for Ricoeur and explicated in his articulation of the multiple 'moments' of mimesis.

Consider then the kind of novel developed by Bainbridge. Few contemporary British writers are as sensitive to the 'as if' of fiction, and an examination of the approach to the real in *Every Man for Himself* can test this claim. For the greater part of the twentieth century the *Titanic* disappeared from view. It had a textual reality. The historical documents that were left to define it told partial and sometimes conflicting stories: incomplete passenger lists, press articles that made heroes of some and demonized others, the ostensibly objective accounts of the official enquiries with their futile attempts at closure, survivors' memoirs, the valedictory engraving of words on a tomb. Immediately and inevitably the disaster of the sunken ship delivers itself up to narrative treatment. It is present only in as much as it is reinscribed, represented, configured. There is much at stake in the authorial choice of the *Titanic* disaster: such an emotive and symbolic event threatens to overwhelm novelist and reader with its richness and horror. As history, an iconic significance attaches to it – and how often do we think of history as a realm of symbolic forms? In art, the 'non-metamorphosed reality' of the event is abolished, and there occurs 'the true *mimesis*: a metamorphosis according to the truth' (Ricoeur 1981: 187). Part of the astuteness of the writing in *Every Man for Himself* is Bainbridge's evident ease with this notion, manifested poetically.

The discussion can be initiated with reflections on image. The visual image as a means of access to the real is regarded highly critically in *Every Man for Himself*. The text sets itself against the visual image, and subjects it to a critique that is ultimately about perception and the ways that we habitually theorize 'world' through the eyes. Regarding plot, the narrator, Morgan (nephew to the owner of the White Star Line), has a critical relation to the image expressed at the level of events. The stranger who dies in Morgan's arms at the beginning of the novel first gives him a photograph that depicts 'a Japanese woman peeping out from behind an embroidered fan' (Bainbridge 1996: 4). This incident acquires narrative coherence only after Adele Baine's recital from *Madame Butterfly*. Dressed magnificently in Japanese costume, having sung movingly 'in character' of her loneliness, she alights on the photograph and extracts from Morgan an account of her lover's unexpected death (for he was the stranger). This scene has its own logic. Within her own story it is the moment when Adele ceases to feel distraught – with relief she learns that her lover has not abandoned her – and instead she takes refuge in the comfort of grief. As Scurra, in his guise as her protector, sardonically observes, bereavement is so much easier to bear than desertion. The Adele of the portrait, of *Madame Butterfly* – one of the versions of Adele – has more meaning (to the audience, to the reader) than Adele unadorned, the desolate woman who travels alone in steerage. Adele's presence is coherent only when it is staged. She is visible only when Rosenfelder, the tailor who aspires to make his name as a couturier, makes her so, and his moment of triumph comes later with her entrance wearing his creation. She is a vision: 'for Adele and the dress were one, and as she advanced, the splendid column of her neck circled with borrowed diamonds, those pearl-pale eyes with their strange expression of exaltation fixed straight ahead, we held our breath in the presence of a goddess' (Bainbridge 1996: 162).

The Adele of *Madame Butterfly* is, however, much more central to the debate about the logic of the icon that persists in this novel than to Rosenfelder's mannequin-woman.

So the mystery of the woman in the photograph, which is submerged from the horizon of narrative interest once Morgan boards the ship, is eventually solved via a series of straightforward deductions. Adele has been abandoned yet her lover has not tired of her, and a man has died suddenly in the street; she recognizes the snapshot as a memento given by her to

R. B.; the photographic image is explained by her manifestation on the ship's stage as Cio-Cio-San, and her account of having sung the role before. Debating the grounds of the ontology of fiction in 'The function of fiction in shaping reality', Ricoeur discusses the special quality of the photographic image in order to make a point about text: the photographic subject is not *unreal*, merely not present, except in replica form. He is interested in the 'status of absence' when it helps him determine, by contrast, the 'status of unreality' in fiction – here is his principal concern. He writes, 'what is wholly overlooked in the transition from the image as replica to the image as fiction is the shift in the referential status. This shift constitutes to my mind the critical point in the theory of imagination and the criterion of the difference between fiction and portrait' (Ricoeur 1991a: 119–20).

This foregrounds his debate about 'productive reference' described as 'the ultimate criterion of the difference between fiction and picture' (Ricoeur 1991a: 121). Ricoeur's next step is to challenge the classical pre-supposition that images are derived first from perception (Ricoeur 1991a: 121). Thinking iconoclastically, Ricoeur, as we might expect from the writer of *The Rule of Metaphor*, displaces the emphasis from perception to language. The point is then 'to show how the emergence of new meanings in the sphere of language generates an emergence of new images' (Ricoeur 1991a: 122). He is also at pains to privilege a notion of the imagination 'at work': '[i]magination at work – in a work – produces itself as a world' (Ricoeur 1991a: 123).

Ricoeur's work on metaphor, and on the key theorizers of metaphor, leads him to restate the position that language institutes a 'seeing-as' (Ricoeur 1991a: 127). The 'bound' image (the image re-worked poetically) is about 'the control of meaning' (Ricoeur 1991a: 127) as opposed to the 'free' image of word-association or dream. He concludes that the effect of imagination linked to language must be:

> a sort of *epoché* of the real, to suspend our attention to the real, to place us in a state of non-engagement with regard to perception or action, in short, to suspend meaning in the neutralized atmosphere to which one could give the name of the dimension of fiction. In this state of non-engagement we try new ideas, new values, new ways of being-in-the-world. Imagination is this free play of possibilities. In this state, fiction can . . . create a *redescription* of reality.
>
> (Ricoeur 1991a: 128)

He is fully enamoured of the paradox of productive reference, 'that only the image which does not already have its referent in reality is able to display a world' (Ricoeur 1991a: 129). Images created by the artist 'augment' reality and redescribe it in a process that positions us in a new relation to it: '[u]nder the shock of fiction, reality becomes problematic' (Ricoeur 1991a: 133).

Representation: imitation and artefact

The notion that art reduplicates the real, that which Ricoeur calls 'the closure of representation' (Ricoeur 1991a: 137) is given short shrift in Bainbridge's work. The work of fiction called *Every Man for Himself* raises interesting questions about fictional interpretations of historical realities. It also constitutes a commentary about the limitations of (visual) perception as the basis for understanding what is at stake in acts of representation. The prologue, for example, describes Scurra's last minutes before the sea sweeps him from the deck. That Morgan mistakes his actions for something they are not demonstrates precisely the unreliability of perception as a mode of understanding. The narrator is given to record that Scurra, preparing for death, 'looked directly at me, all the time buffing his glasses on the hem of that plum-coloured robe, and I admit his occupation struck me as sensual. His hand, you see, was all but hidden beneath the material and I thought he was caressing himself' (Bainbridge 1996: ix). Thereafter Bainbridge contrasts the positive power of language to produce 'world' with the ways in which visual images shape our understanding. She does so principally in her provision of a story for her narrator that is fundamentally about the twin themes of origins and belonging.

The narrator, Morgan, has only blanks for memories of his parents, his father having died before Morgan's birth and his mother having become a victim of influenza when he was three. Orphaned in Manchester and alone, the wealthy but alcoholic Miss Barrow – the face of the old woman of his nightmares – takes him in. They live in squalid conditions until the landlord murders her for her cash. Fate, and its servant Scurra, then delivers him, a boy, to his fabulously wealthy 'uncle', aunt and cousin Sissy, and a life of opulence, privilege and love. Despite his statements of contentment at his lot, Morgan's obsession is to complete the fragmented narrative of his origins (his parents being unknown to him and his experiences only palpable as dream language). Just before he leaves for Southampton and the *Titanic*, he is compelled to steal from his uncle's London house a portrait by Cézanne of his mother as a young woman. This literal appropriation of the image of the mother brings him some comfort, but it will fail to confer the self-transformation that he craves. Subsequently, on the voyage to New York, the painting (which operates like the photograph and is never of interest as a painting, merely as a representation of an absent woman) becomes a significant focal point for Morgan's several emotional and psychological needs.

On the ship it is Scurra who tells Morgan the story behind the portrait. Twenty-four years before, 'on business', Scurra had stayed with an art dealer who had taken him to see Cézanne at work. The model was 'just a girl', he says, whom he last saw 'waiting on tables' (Bainbridge 1996: 107), although when pressed he acknowledges a physical resemblance between the girl and Morgan, 'something about the eyes' (Bainbridge 1996: 106). Distinctly underwhelmed, Scurra has nevertheless enacted Morgan's dream by encountering the highly prized original. However, Morgan's real crisis in this exchange accompanies the disappointing discovery that Scurra is not his father. Despite denials, it has been perhaps Morgan's deepest wish that it might be so: 'It wasn't that I thought of Scurra as a father-figure or looked up to him – how could I, seeing I scarcely knew him – simply that in his presence it was possible to attach the word love to what one felt, and not wriggle at its implications' (Bainbridge 1996: 66).

Scurra is a useful contrast to Morgan. The latter defines himself as incomplete, convinced that his mother's face combined with her history will anchor his identity in something true and enduring. The figure Scurra, however, revels in generating only conflicting and various narratives about his 'true' identity so that it remains productively hidden, hence the multiple versions of how Scurra's lip was deformed, the nature of his business and just who he is. With the fantasy of Morgan's imaginary family impaired – whoever or whatever he might be, Scurra is not his father – the painting of the mother begins to lose its value for its abductor. Morgan almost throws it overboard on discovering that the beautiful, bored Wallis Ellery, for whom he has a painfully unexpressed infatuation, is in a grown-up, mutually grati-fying relationship with Scurra. Forced by circumstance to become the silent witness to their sexual play, Morgan childishly scrawls '*fuck*' on Wallis's bathroom mirror and retreats to his stateroom where the first victim of his anger is the portrait. Unable to bear 'my mother's painted eyes' (Bainbridge 1996: 143) he rushes to the side of the ship, but confesses:

> I don't know whether I really intended to throw the painting of my mother into the waves. True, I wanted to cast her from me. It was she, not the fetid old woman who counted gold each night, who had bound my wrists with string and tied me to the iron bolt of those half-closed shutters overlooking that stinking worm of water.
>
> (Bainbridge 1996: 143)

When the family fantasies die, so too does the reality value of the image. The Romantic vision of the mother is replaced by a sense of her malevo-lence; she is responsible for his earliest trauma defined by the experiences of displacement, abandonment and identity loss. Initially so highly prized by him for its emotional resonance rather than for its market value, the picture is finally accounted for, without additional comment from the narrator, as simply one item amongst the detritus left on the surface of the waters after the ship has gone down: 'chairs and tables, crates, an empty gin bottle, a set of bagpipes, a cup without a handle, a creased square of canvas with a girl's face painted on it' (Bainbridge 1996: 214).

Elsewhere, with the personal dimension shelved, the narrative has underlined primarily art's cultural meaning and economic value; that is to say, its investment potential. Morgan's luggage includes 'a consignment of theatrical manuscripts in the name of J. Pierpont Morgan' (Bainbridge 1996: 43). The only time he seems to attract Wallis's attention in any flattering context is when she mistakenly thinks that he is responsible for the transportation to America of his uncle's European art collection:

> 'You mean to tell me,' she cried, 'that all those wonderful Rubenses and Rembrandts are down in the hold this very moment?'
> 'No,' I said, 'There was a postponement due to the miners' strike. The shipment will follow later.'
>
> (Bainbridge 1996: 40)

Later, Morgan, Van Hopper and Charlie Melchett kill time in the hold looking at the high-status possessions of their friends and fellow passengers: Dodge's father's new Lanchester, and Seefax's Wolseley, and Morgan notices a package '*Portrait of Garibaldi, Property of C. D. Bernotti*' (Bainbridge 1996: 76). It has earlier been Charlie's role to voice what the first-class passengers are permitted to inhabit, which is the vision, the visionary nerve, that the ship represents:

> He was enthusing over the magnificence of the ship, comparing it in concept and visionary grandeur to the great cathedrals of Chartres and Notre Dame. 'A cathedral,' he reiterated, waving his cheroot in the direction of the stained glass above the bar, 'constructed of steel and capable of carrying a congregation of three thousand souls across the Atlantic.'
>
> (Bainbridge 1996: 23)

Despite his merging of the sacred and the secular, it is their confrontation with the vessel's monumental modernity that eventually reduces Charlie and Morgan to an awe-filled silence, and allows Morgan to reflect (with Ricoeurian optimism),

> it was the sublime thermodynamics of the *Titanic*'s marine engineering

that took us by the throat. Dazzled, I was thinking that if the fate of man was connected to the order of the universe, and if one could equate the scientific workings of the engines with just such a reciprocal universe, why then, nothing could go wrong with my world.

(Bainbridge 1996: 28)

These words, however, must constitute for the reader an ironic elegy for the ship and the self-assured class to which Morgan belongs. As we all know, sublime thermodynamics will not save the *Titanic*. Self-confident modernity is vulnerable, and it will not be long before the survivors of this catastrophe will be plunged into world war (tensions in the Balkans began to manifest in earnest in 1912). The faith placed here in science and technology, a faith which characterizes the monster economies of the twentieth century, has its frailty exposed in the collision with the iceberg and the intransigent presence of nature in arresting man's designs. For Bainbridge, the *Titanic* is the image of the achievement of modernist engineering – recalling the idea of Britain as the engine room of progress (and America as its banker) – and a museum ship.

The creation of symbols

The end arrives rudely, by disturbing a card game. Morgan, Charlie and Hopper race to the starboard deck to see steerage passengers larking about with pieces of ice that have shivered off the iceberg. The narrative insists on the ordinariness of the moment – men return to the smoking-room 'in boisterous mood' (Bainbridge 1996: 172), laughter comes from the bar and from the groups of disturbed sleepers who stand around in their night attire and incongruously mated gloves, scarves and coats. Morgan clings to heroic, boyish narratives of a pictorial kind:

Somewhere in my mind I pored over an illustration, in a child's book of heroic deeds, of a rescue at sea, ropes slung between two heaving decks and men swinging like gibbons above the foaming waves. How Sissy would gasp when I recounted my story! How my aunt would throw up her hands when I shouted the details of my midnight adventure! Why, as long as I wrapped up well it would be the greatest fun in the world.

(Bainbridge 1996: 176)

At the critical moment he takes refuge in a comforting model of certainty – the conviction that the narrative of a ship in trouble concludes with rescue and shows of manly valour. This is entirely in keeping with the way he has formerly theorized his self-positioning. Morgan, when he relates the effects of first learning unpalatable details about his childhood, informs the reader that: 'they merely confirmed a growing belief that I was special. I don't care to be misunderstood; I'm not talking about intellect or being singled out for great honours, simply that I was destined to be a participant rather than a spectator of singular events' (Bainbridge 1996: 7).

The events that he relates describe his encounters with death – the suicides of Amy Svenson and Israel Wold, and the death of the stranger in his arms at the beginning of *Every Man for Himself*. To Morgan this is proof that he participates; that he is not naturally the forgotten onlooker (as he is in Wallis's rooms on the night that his illusions about her interest in him are shattered). He takes refuge in a genealogy of intimate histories to replace the certainty, the stability that was threatened at birth. Of his uncle he says, 'We were linked by events, not blood, and he viewed me as if through a microscope, the *infusoria* of his long-gone past wriggling before his magnified gaze' (Bainbridge 1996: 57).[3] Such linked narratives are apparently reassuring guarantors of personal survival.

But in what does he participate? His survival obeys the imperative of the novel's title, if not its spirit, and the solipsistic sentiment of the title is repeated throughout. Just before Scurra orders Morgan to look out for himself he treats him to a synopsis of his personal philosophy: 'A man bears the weight of his own body without knowing it, but he soon feels the weight of any other object. There is nothing, absolutely nothing, that a man cannot forget – but not himself' (Bainbridge 1996: 210). Scurra is the originator of every reminder to Morgan that it is every man for himself in this world, and the world of the *Titanic* is that of the elite bourgeois culture, literally occupying the upper levels, sustained by the unequal and barely regulated labour of the workers below. The stricken stoker unexpectedly encountered by Morgan in a corridor has worked a double shift without a break; Morgan's patronage of seaman Riley is treated with contempt, and as the ship sinks Riley observes that at least now, 'you with your millions and me with me half-crown, we're both in the same boat' (Bainbridge 1996: 208). Rosenfelder, the *arriviste*, is desperate for the patronage of Lady Duff Gordon and can accommodate two views of Adele Baines, as his ideal model and his meal ticket: 'Since when did a woman with two pounds in her purse and no buttons to her coat know such a thing as choice?' (Bainbridge 1996: 91). The passengers in steerage are kept in their place. 'They know how to enjoy themselves' (Bainbridge 1996: 45) when viewed from a deck above, although during the Divine Service on Sunday, 14 April, they offend Morgan first by 'gawping to find themselves in such opulent surroundings' and then by having stinky and unruly children (Bainbridge 1996: 149–50).

Public modes of transport, all modes of transport, are far from being socially neutral. The automobiles in the hold are high-status possessions signifying aspiration or, no pun intended, arrival. An oceangoing liner manifests class divisions in its design and layout, in its passage costs and in the services it offers. Throughout the narrative Bainbridge expresses a fascination with the ways in which the *Titanic* was designed to reduplicate and preserve existing class divisions, and to present them as natural. Within the enclosed world of the ship the social values of terra firma effortlessly establish themselves; all the protocols that dictate the relations of the city, the country and the suburbs are observed. Against the images and signs that sustain social illusions in the world that feels natural to Morgan and his peers, Bainbridge then sets the unregulated unknown of the non-human world with its capacity to alter human horizons. The dramatic significance of the *Titanic* catastrophe, at least for this novel, does not only reside in the loss and preservation of lives, or the destruction of a beautiful and grand design. Equally poignant are the ways in which the disaster derives from a fatal indifference, at the eleventh hour, to the wilderness. It is quite fitting that the elemental sea barely moistens the consciousness of the passengers, or Morgan's narrative, until the moment of crisis. The occasional warning note is sounded about a fire in the hold, and a list to port; and when the crew stumble into view, exhausted and dirty from the firefight, they are quickly stowed away out of sight. Bainbridge attempted something similar in *The Birthday Boys*, in the representation of the rigid class distinctions that persisted between officers and men even in the extremity of the Antarctic wilderness, an adventure that was practically contemporaneous with the sinking of the *Titanic* and, like it, has acquired the iconic status of the doomed event. In *Every Man for Himself* it is strategically crucial that the environment is not foregrounded. It is never going to be a narrative shock, a fact held in abeyance, or a revelation that the ship hits an iceberg and goes down. What must be invented is the overwhelming sense of disbelief, on the part of those who run the vessel, as well as those who allow themselves to be carried, that the wild world that buoys them up could also intrude. The random indifference of natural forces enables the *Titanic*'s movement from modernity to eternity, from the historic to the symbolic. The ship is, as Charlie Melchett recognizes, an architectural as much as it is a nautical form, that is to say it is understood first as social space, and Melchett's metaphor ('cathedral') underlines its capacity to be perceived as sacred. This is true also of the camps and bases of *The Birthday Boys* with their carefully regimented communal areas: they keep the non-human world at a distance, psychologically remote. In both cases the narrative imperative is to contrast the illusions of security and salvation, derived from regulated social spaces, with the unmanufactured 'real'. It is the temporary shattering of those illusions in which Morgan participates.

Conclusion

Writing, Ricoeur asserts in 'Mimesis and representation', is fulfilled in read-ing (Ricoeur 1991b: 151). The Reading is the operation that (after Roman Ingarden and Wolfgang Iser) 'completes' the work of fiction resulting in (after Roland Barthes) the pleasure of the text. More than that, the trans-figurative operation of fiction is so because it alters the reader who partici-pates in the remade world. We are returned again to the dynamism of Ricoeur's analysis that talks of 'the conjoint work of the text and its reader' (Ricoeur 1991b: 151) in the context of his rejection of the mimesis of 'representative illusion' (Ricoeur 1991b: 150). The reader cannot be con-ceived as 'outside' the work, but on the contrary as a player and a construct of the multiple operations of mimesis freshly articulated by Ricoeur. Towards the end of the last century Bainbridge's 'as if', constructed in relation to the *Titanic* disaster, takes on a defining moment of dashed con-fidence, a historical event that is always already unconditionally symbolic, and finds a way of reworking it in such a way that the operations of repre-sentation are themselves brought into view. It is in these terms that the novel, in her hands, critically and responsibly examines the parallel paths of language and imagination, in the defamiliarization of the utterly familiar, and turns history over to the reader.

Notes

1 The book inspired the 1958 film of the same name.
2 'Mimesis and representation' in *A Ricoeur Reader*, pp. 137–55. I have chosen to work from this essay rather than from the sometimes problematic elaboration of its thought in *Time and Narrative*. Ricoeur's work on mimesis is most often cited in relation to fiction and in particular the novel. Andrzej Gąsiorek's dis-tinguished analysis of literary realism after 1945, *Post-War British Fiction: realism and after* is a case in point, but there, to my mind, as in other instances, Ricoeur's emphasis on the reader, the operations of reading – without which, no hermen-eutics – is minimized despite its centrality to his analysis of the phenomenology of fiction.
3 It is a nice textual detail that this expression evokes the opening of H. G. Wells's *The War of the Worlds*, the Victorian catastrophe narrative par excellence.

References

Bainbridge, Beryl (1991) *The Birthday Boys*, London: Duckworth.
—— (1996) *Every Man for Himself*, London: Abacus.
Gąsiorek, Andrzej (1995) *Post-War British Fiction: realism and after*, London: Edward Arnold.
Lord, Walter (1997) [1955] *A Night to Remember*, New York: Bantam Books.
Ricoeur, Paul (1981) *Hermeneutics and the Human Sciences: essays on language, action and*

interpretation, ed. and trans. John B. Thompson, Cambridge and Paris: Cambridge University Press and Éditions de la Maison des Sciences de l'Homme.

—— (1991a) 'The function of fiction in shaping reality', in Mario J. Valdés (ed.) *A Ricoeur Reader: reflection and imagination*, Hemel Hempstead: Harvester Wheatsheaf, pp. 117–36.

—— (1991b) 'Mimesis and representation', in Mario J. Valdés (ed.) *A Ricoeur Reader: reflection and imagination*, Hemel Hempstead: Harvester Wheatsheaf, pp. 137–55.

Shaw, George Bernard (1964) [1919] *Heartbreak House*, Harmondsworth: Penguin.

Wells, H. G. (1946) [1904] *The War of the Worlds*, Harmondsworth: Penguin.

Part IV
Narrative geographies

12 Iain Sinclair's millennial fiction

The example of *Slow Chocolate Autopsy*

Julian Wolfreys

'WANTED: INTERPRETER. UNEDITED CITY.'

(Sinclair and McKean 1997: 84)

'Treat London like an autopsy catalogue.'

(Sinclair and McKean 1997: 90)

'SURVEILLANCE IS THE ART FORM OF THE MILLENNIUM.'

(Sinclair and McKean 1997: 91)

Touching on the truth

This essay considers Iain Sinclair's collaboration with Dave McKean, *Slow Chocolate Autopsy* (Sinclair and McKean 1997), doing so by way of certain 'detours'. I do not propose to offer anything amounting to a reading. Instead, I wish to highlight ways in which Sinclair's writing is traced by, responds to and is illustrative of millennial interests. In focusing on this particular text as the singular expression of Sinclair's millennial fantasies, as these in turn are read and written around the subject of London and its occluded histories, the essay orientates itself by addressing a series of contiguous relationships. In attempting to understand Sinclair's writing and its representations of London, it has to be said that such a project is fraught with difficulties, not least because no critical language is adequate to Sinclair's excessive texts, even if one does delimit, however violently or unreasonably, the scope of one's inquiry to the consideration of such excess as it is informed by, or may be read through, the notion of the millennial. Indeed, I would like to begin by making the remark that a sign of the millennial is a certain excess, while observing reciprocally that that which we perceive as excessive is but one aspect of the millennial.

The problems I am describing here are more than adequately commented on by Iain Sinclair, in an earlier publication, 'Nicholas Hawksmoor, His Churches': 'The scenographic view is too complex to unravel here, the information too dense: we can only touch on the truth . . . It is enough to sketch the possibilities' (Sinclair 1989: 60). Sinclair is commenting on perceived encrypted and hieratic patterns that the churches of Nicholas Hawksmoor, along with other obelisks and coordinates, trace on London, when he remarks that 'the web is printed on the city and disguised with multiple superimpositions' (Sinclair 1989: 60). Each of Hawksmoor's churches is read in the same fashion, for they are 'incredible culture grafts, risky quotations studded into a central and repeated image of strength, key symbols that remain secret' (Sinclair 1989: 57–8). This apparently Rosicrucian fantasy focuses for me both the seductiveness and the frustration of Sinclair's writing as well as the equally endless appeal and disappointment of the city for Sinclair; it plays with the ghost of the millennial encryption that it ultimately refuses to assign with any surety.

With this in mind this essay proceeds. Initially, I explore the relationship between the notion of the millennial and writing, the temporal connections between the two, and the iterable pulse that is at work in this connection. From this, I turn to a brief consideration of London as a city of the dead and what Sinclair calls its 'necropolis culture' (Sinclair 1989: 61). London seen in this light is a haunted ground in his writing. The dead of the city, and the city as a necropolis, is what connects Sinclair to a discernible millennial and millenarian tradition in English letters. From this, the final part of the essay considers particular aspects of *Slow Chocolate Autopsy*, with passing reference to other texts by Sinclair. In particular, I concentrate on three figures or motifs that impose themselves insistently: editing, autopsy, surveillance, and their relationship to Sinclair's time-travelling narrator, Norton.

Writing and the millennial

If one refers to the millennial obviously one is acknowledging either a span of 1,000 years, or, more poetically, an epochal shift anticipated or envisioned as an irreversible, possibly messianic instance of transformation. Occasionally, 'millennial' refers to an epochal and perhaps eschatological moment, the thinking of which is akin to the idea of a *fin de siècle*, with all that such a notion implies. To consider a novelist, or particular novels, as the figure or figures of the millennial implies or suggests acts of writing that make manifest, giving provisional form to, the millennial hope in the guise of prophetic visionary narratives, images and symbols. There is a temporal dimension to millennial fiction, therefore, announced in anticipation, prolepsis, and, it might be argued, desire or obsession. Writing the millennial involves a process of simultaneously imagining *and* staging a future, however utopian or idealist such a future might be considered, in the present time of writing. As the theological overtones and uses of the term 'millennium' admit, the very idea of a future, of possible futures and the possibility of envisioning, projecting or imagining such futures, is one predicated on the anticipation of an act of revenance, of a transformative return, wherein the singularity of an event from a past that we can never recover is apprehended by the merest chance of its iterability. This iterability is announced every time the expectation it bears within it is inscribed, traced and encrypted, as a potentially infinite series of *now* . . . *now* . . . *now*.

Writing such revenance entails both a response and a responsibility, in which one risks an apprehension of the event and the haunting legacy of its trace. It announces within itself the possibility 'to transmute' its subject matter, 'to begin with precisely observed particulars and to open them out' (Sinclair and McKean 1997: 21). In responding and thereby opening itself to the singular, writing thus puts in place the displacement of iterability and difference as the hope for the telecommunicative relay *and* its ruin. This relay is performative. For every time the trace takes place the double, and doubly reduplicating, dividing figure occurs, simultaneously remarking a past and what Iain Sinclair has called an 'unscripted future' (Sinclair 1999: 7), which will never arrive as such. In the figure of the millennial there is no time like the present; there is only ever the endless loop of the immanence of revelation articulated from within the anamnesis of the 'always already'. The millennial names, therefore, a 'phantasmic dimension' (Hamacher 1998: 5), and in this, admits to that which of course haunts all reading and writing. Disfiguring this just a little, we might risk the proposition that 'millennium', the 'millennial', name all writing and reading, whilst also admitting that both are untimely, and we will never have done with them. This is the promise, and the gift, of reading and writing.

The temporality and concomitant temporal disruption of revenance occasioned by reference to, and encoded within, the idea of the millennial is also serially structural, or spatial, as the relation between reading and writing makes apparent. There is clearly no closure to such structure. Rather, the movement by which the millennial structure maintains itself, remaining open and remaining as an abyssal opening (whereby the remains, in returning, remain to be read), is a motion involved in substitution: one figure in the place of the other, of every other, though without the possibility of subsuming the other, hence the openness. The occasion of opening is announced by Norton, the narrator of *Slow Chocolate Autopsy*, when he reflects that 'night football was just my way of coming to an understanding with the magnitude of London, seeing it as an anthology of green scraps, fragmented meadows, wastelots, school yards' (Sinclair and McKean 1997: 35). This openness, by which is signalled a separation, 'the one separated', as Levinas describes it, 'from the other by the interval or the meanwhile of difference' (Levinas

2000: 186), imposes or, more precisely, bears within it responsibility, of a kind akin to that responsibility already announced. Clearly, from particular conventional perspectives if one is talking of responsibility, football might seem an innocuous figure at best, fatuous at worst. Yet it must be observed that it is announced as singular, as 'just my way of coming to an understanding'. An instant of catachresis, it is as arresting as it is improper in gesturing towards, and thereby opening onto, the chance of understanding London's magnitude. It is in the risk of failure, the failure to communicate or to be taken seriously, that the responsibility is announced.

Furthermore, in being such an estranged and estranging trope, whatever there might be of understanding for the narrator in this is, I would aver, not transmitted. I cannot understand the city's enormity, and so both the figure and the narrator's apprehension – and also the city – remain other. In this responsibility does not end, but instead is transmitted to the reader in the very transmission *and* the failure of the figural. As Levinas suggests therefore, this responsibility, which never ceases, is not knowledge, it does not amount to an understanding (Levinas 2000: 186). In affirming my inability to understand, I acknowledge myself as passive: I am passive in my reception of the image, the otherness, and the being of the city. This is confirmed by Sinclair who informs us, of Norton's reception of the city-as-other, 'He has no claim on what he sees' (Sinclair and McKean 1997: 48). Comprehending the other through the image and the apparitional being that is thus announced is not a gradual process of acquisition; one does not apprehend the other, and apprehension does not mean ontologising it. Instead, as the open structure embodied in what I would like to read as the trope of the millennial reveals, responsibility to the other entails the endless work affirming a kind of radical passivity – of being open to the other, thereby allowing the other to return, in Sinclair's case this 'other' being 'another London, peopled by invisibles' (Sinclair 2004: 104). In *Slow Chocolate Autopsy* Sinclair affirms the significance of passivity – acknowledging 'all the strands of urban society' (Sinclair 2004: 77) – in the figure and motion of Norton's aleatory wandering, through both the times of London and its spaces: 'He lets it all drift, unedited, unreformed' (Sinclair and McKean 1997: 48). Through such passivity comes the chance to affirm, bearing witness to the revenance of the other without seeking to capture it and, in this manner, to stage a writing that is millennial in its hope for the persistence of the millennial-to-come. Being radically passive therefore suggests that the arrival of the other transforms one's subjectivity, as Thomas Carl Wall asserts in his reading of radical passivity in Levinas, Blanchot and Agamben (Wall 1999). It is this subjective 'translation' that Sinclair's narrator in *Slow Chocolate Autopsy*, Norton, undergoes constantly, even as he nominally remains himself – this is the experience of the millennial.

To understand this is to comprehend that millennial writing is not merely utopian or messianic. It is not that a millennial fiction projects an imagined moment in the future of millennial revenance. Rather, as the figure of Norton might give us to understand, in every gesture of writing – which is simultaneously haunted, at every step, by that gesture of reading that responds to the trace of the 'always already' – there is, without being present, without a presence, the phantasmic givenness of the millennial-to-come. This is caught perhaps in certain imagistic concatenations on Sinclair's part. Images or objects from different, irreconcilable historical times affirm themselves as they arrive with a reverberating echo. We read, for example, how in London's East End, 'the tweeting of cellphones replaced the Huguenot canaries' (Sinclair 2004: 94); elsewhere, 'recording devices hummed like birds-of-paradise' (Sinclair 1994: 138); and the interpretative response of dowsing is equated with, even as it is opposed to, the interrogation of 'satellite scans' (Sinclair 2004: 116). In the defamiliarising, uncanny recognition of the arrival of the other trace within and as ghostly counterpoint to modernity's tele-technologies, the present is solicited. Its identity shaken, its certainty and hegemonic tyranny is undone; or, as Sinclair puts it, through being open to such oscillations in any given site, the site is set 'adrift in time, unanchored' (Sinclair 2004: 88).

The millennial pulse thus *lays claim* to me, as Levinas puts it. It is not a matter of revelation or disclosure; it is a question of the exposure of 'me' to another (Levinas 2000: 187). By this, according to Levinas, the subject comes to be *animated* or *inspired*: 'this psyche is that animation and inspiration of the Same by the Other; it is translated into a fission of the core of the subject's interiority by way of its assignation to respond, which leaves no refuge and authorises no escape' (Levinas 2000: 187). To employ Levinas's language, the other *elects* me, *despite* my self. In the radical passivity of bearing witness, I am open to the chance of the other, to what gives in the possibility of the arrival, a possibility that an 'unseen, shapeless [*informe*] material . . . yet to be seen' takes shape, as Jean-Luc Marion has argued (Marion 2004: 26). The shape it takes however is not its own 'proper' shape, for there is no proper shape to the millennial. It arrives 'only by analogy with the form that it is not' (Marion 2004: 26), hence the irremediable condition of the millennial, the secret of its disclosedness being in its remaining hidden and yet everywhere. This movement, 'by analogy', offers the glimpse of synecdochal singularity, by which the other remains other. The fleeting transmission is caught by Sinclair in certain images, not only in the citations given in the previous paragraph, but also when he reads the city's blue plaques as 'satellite dishes for the heritage classes (commissioned from Wedgwood)' (Sinclair 2004: 89–90). Despite, or perhaps because of the transmission's transience, in being intimated through the synecdochic pulse, that momentary visible efflorescence on a radar screen or heart monitor, the iterable pulsation offers to renew, in every instance, the millennial, and with that the hope for the millennial-to-come. Thus what I am addressing here as 'millennial writing' and 'millennial fiction' responds in tracing this trace, assuming the burden of responsibility that cannot be fulfilled, in the admission that it is no more, itself, than an instance of synecdoche, by analogy.

'Necropolis culture': the millennial, the city, the dead

As Michael Moorcock has argued, in the millennium's *fin de siècle* 'London fiction has . . . become characteristically a visionary medium' (Moorcock 1995: 3). As other to its writers, it calls for and demands what Iain Sinclair calls, with reference to Rimbaud's writing, 'occult awareness' (Sinclair 1995: 131). The city insists on fictions, narratives and poetic explorations appropriate to the millennial condition as explored above, whether in the form of novel or poetry. Such texts may imagine London as being haunted from within by the immanent promise of the New Jerusalem. They may visualise the millennial aspect of the city through meditations on the haunting recurrence, the iterability, of violence and power; in such moments of vision London is understood, millennially, both as having 'been one of the dark places of the earth' (Conrad 1995: 49) and also persistently throughout its history as 'the most darkly encoded enclosure in the western world' (Sinclair 1995: 130). They may envision London as the site through which wander the ghosts of its dead, whereby any temporal or material certainty concerning the present is undone. Such acts of writing the millennial spirit of the city, in which the traces of the past erupt as an unexpected event, disturbs representation. There is thus a dialectic in the millennial urban fiction between mere material sight and vision, by which narrative imposes 'an ordeal [*une épreuve*] of sight', which 'plays itself out in a unique act: vision as reception of a gift made to eyes that did not expect it' (Marion 2004: 43–4). This often involves forms of anachronistic and disquieting representation and, in response therefore, narrative instances of bearing witness to that which previously invisible suddenly manifests itself in shocking and unexpected visions. In the production of such visions, Sinclair (to cite Moorcock once more) 'drags from London's amniotic silt the trove of centuries and presents it to us, still dripping, still stinking, still caked . . . with a mixture of relish and horror' (Moorcock 1995: 3).

In responding to this, in being open to the inspiration or animation that is the response to *election* as Levinas has it, millennial writers such as Sinclair are most appropriately understood as 'mediums'. What such writing articulates is expressed in temporal terms in *White Chappell Scarlet Tracings*; it gives 'a shape to some pattern of energy that was already present' (Sinclair 1995: 129), while figuring also the '*gigantic shadows which futurity casts upon the present*' (Sinclair 1995: 131; emphasis in original). In such a response, different times, differing narratives arrive, so that one catches the merest apprehension how, through the act of writing, 'all the times of London'[1] may be implicated through this synecdochic image, even though, as the random concatenation implies, this is not, cannot be, all the city, all its times, all its manifestations – for the city gives one to understand what Sinclair calls 'the escape of the other' (Sinclair 1995: 129). The intimation of an otherwise ineffable totality only serves to announce failure, the ruin of representation, representation in ruins, and thus, the withdrawal of millennial alterity in the instant of its being registered. Thus the millennial city, as it is perceived through its millennial fictions, is apprehended in only the most indirect, fleeting manner, as we have already suggested. However, it is precisely in the condition of being open to the temporal dimension that marks the millennial, that the millennial city, its 'phantasmic dimension', is registered, through an inscription of the future promise at every moment of the possibility of revenance, of the becoming visible of the invisible, and of the chance of event and epiphany attendant on such irrevocable, irreversible transformation and translation. In this manner, the writer assumes responsibility, as Sinclair has it, to bear witness to 'the already dead who can die no more' (Sinclair 1994: 138).

In millennial discourse, this is not simply a question of telling histories, recording facts. It is perhaps more appropriately grasped as a matter of seeking 'to recover the dream / of an aboriginal dynamism' ('Frog Killer Memorial (Whitechapel)', Sinclair 1989: 52) as this comes to appear through the narrative reshaping of historical proceedings and the stories that are told of districts, neighbourhoods and other London locations. This has become all the more urgent in Sinclair's writing from *Lights Out for the Territory* (1997) onwards, as the millennial impulse seeks to respond to the recognition that 'global capitalism had nowhere left to invade – except the past' (Sinclair 2004: 99). In both the fiction and non-fiction, Sinclair – or his narrators at least – rage against first Thatcherite and, subsequently, Blairite heritage projects, such as the moving of the Aldgate Pump – 'a heritage token shunted and shifted for the convenience of developers' (Sinclair 2004: 98) – or 'the invention of that entity now known as Jack the Ripper' (Sinclair 2004: 99). Of course, it is well known that Sinclair himself has more than once invented the Ripper narrative, but from this one example it can be understood how the contest between what might be termed a millennial sensibility and the official version of the past is fought not solely by unearthing that which authorised narratives fail to acknowledge, or what

Sinclair has described as the 'real memory traces of London, lost lives, greasy suits with the imprint of dead bodies still in them' (Sinclair 2004: 59).

The problem is one also of contesting the very ways in which one gives testimony, how the same story might be told with a difference, so as to bear witness to the dead, without simply making them subservient to some present political narrative of progress and historical sanitisation. In this struggle, earlier literary manifestations are significant, their mapping of the city and its dead, its ghosts vital: 'imaginary creatures, borrowed from Stevenson and Machen, beckon you from doorways . . . London . . . become[s an extension] of your immune system. But you are not immune, you are wide open to all the viruses, syndromes, germ cultures: you twitch and fret, rant, sweat, ravish' (Sinclair 2004: 94).

Sinclair's language of openness and contamination details the extent to which the subject is made to experience, and so to suffer, that which the city communicates to the self, and which the self takes up in being *moved* through the openness of its radical passivity, which, as the quotation illustrates, is 'purely passionate' (Wall 1999: 1). In becoming infected by the city's dead, you have also become *elected*, despite yourself, to recall Levinas once more. Election by the other becomes a matter of getting it 'straight' as Sinclair has it (Sinclair and McKean 1997: 154), of being open to the inevitable, to what is 'bound to happen' (Sinclair and McKean 1997: 154). Once you 'get into the zone . . . your book writes itself' (Sinclair 2004: 94), 'words have a kind of magic' (Sinclair and McKean 1997: 154). But getting into the zone involves no activity that I can take upon myself. Acknowledging that the subject must remain open through radical passivity, and therefore situating myself in relation to the city, by analogy, *as if* I were dead, I have then 'finally to wait to see what gives' (Marion 2004: 45).

Editing, autopsy, surveillance and the trans-temporal narrator

The three epigraphs that open this essay come from *Slow Chocolate Autopsy*. Taken together they offer one possible access code, through the motifs of 'interpreting' or 'editing', 'autopsy', and 'surveillance'. All three are taken from Chapter 6, 'The griffin's egg' (Sinclair and McKean 1997: 82–93). Each line is chosen because it maps those coordinates with which we are presently concerned. The discontinuous narrative of *Slow Chocolate Autopsy* presents a series of encounters with particular aspects of the city's darker histories. In this manner Sinclair weaves into the narrative the act of bearing witness to chance relations. As the expression of a quasi-phatic snapshot, witnessing thus makes explicit the interrelation of the spatial and temporal, of topography and time. In doing so, every act, every in(ter)vention in the city offers a fleeting 'edit', a brief moment of 'surveillance' (or perhaps more appropriately countersurveillance, as I shall explain immediately below) and 'autopsy', that process of examining the dead, and which means, as Sinclair reminds us, the 'act of seeing with one's eyes' (also the title of a film by Stan Brakhage and referred to on more than one occasion by Sinclair [2004: 347; 'Frog Killer Memorial (Whitechapel)', 1989: 53; 'Rites of Autopsy', 1989: 82]). The injunction, to 'treat London like an autopsy catalogue' (Sinclair and McKean 1997: 90), admits to the importance of seeing with one's eyes and translating the materiality of vision into that of the letter.

Doubtless, from particular perspectives, the three motifs or metaphors, brought into alignment with Sinclair's textual configurations of the city, can be taken as understood in their operation. Sinclair's repeated use of 'autopsy' and his equally insistent announcement of the word's meaning leaves the reader little doubt as to the fact that the materiality of the text is intimately enfolded with the materiality of vision (as I have just indicated), as both conjoin to receive and record a third and fourth materiality, those of the city's sites and those of its histories, its events. In this connection between sight and writing as the conjunction necessary to bearing witness, the process of surveillance is also announced, and what comes to be produced thereafter is not so much creative as it is editorial. Invention takes place, but it is the invention of nothing new. It is instead the act – and art – of invention as finding what is already traced and yet forgotten.

Of our three figures, surveillance is the most problematic because of its connotations with matters of policing and forms of power. Surveillance, in its conventionally understood sense, and specifically with regard to the use of CCTV cameras in and around corporate buildings and specific districts, is a subject that Sinclair addresses in a number of places, not least throughout *Lights Out for the Territory*, in which he connects corporate and multinational interests with the political agendas of Thatcherism in its various manifestations (Sinclair 1997).[2] However, as that text attempts to recuperate the idea of stalking from its overdetermined relationship with sexual predation, so, I would like to argue, the idea of surveillance is also forced into double service in Sinclair's text. For, against the critique of anonymous electronic surveillance associated immediately via the synecdoche of 'forests of surveillance cameras' (Sinclair 1997: 105) with a globalised political-economic machinery,[3] there is the act of lone countersurveillance, of watching – and recording – the watchers (Sinclair 1997: 106). In King William Street, for example, near the Bank of England, Sinclair and Marc Atkins photograph 'a major complex of camera poles', whose 'interference', 'alien consciousness' and 'unceasing attention' disrupt the 'time-stream' (Sinclair 1997: 106). 'Legal' or 'official' surveillance is read by Sinclair as '*erasing* truth', it 'abuses the past while fragmenting the present' (Sinclair 1997: 106). While Sinclair and Atkins record the recording devices, and thus offer themselves as the 'subversive psyche' (Sinclair 1997: 106) of countersurveillance and its memory work, this process is embodied in *Slow Chocolate Autopsy* by Norton.

Orientating ourselves more precisely to the notion and possibility of countersurveillance, we would do well to consider Norton's role carefully. Norton, although he can never leave the city, is witness to a number of events, from the murder of Christopher Marlowe, 'poet and espion' (Sinclair and McKean 1997: 11), to occurrences in the 1990s. Norton happens by chance upon events, violent occurrences, moments from the city's history. In coming back repeatedly, he arrives, and presides over, thereby maintaining the memory of location and event as the spectral bystander in an iterable series. Thus, if surveillance is, indeed, the art form of the millennium as Sinclair has it (Sinclair and McKean 1997: 91), in the pulsing iterations of revenance, then the millennial is affirmed in every moment of countersurveillance. Norton's acts of spying are both open to, and open onto the abyssal in the name of the city, and thus echo with the millennial and the millennial-to-come (to bring back the understanding of the millennial articulated above). There is also the sense that Norton's acts of surveillance are themselves double. For he both watches over the scenes of London and, in remembering the city, bearing witness to its darker, more obscure moments, he looks after these, in memory and in narration, as both of these are forms of record or testimony. There is therefore a movement from empirical event, to phenomenological perception, to anamnesiac inscription: from history, to the gaze, to writing. Thus, while remaining other to the city's serial alterity, Norton assumes, albeit unwillingly, that responsibility identified by Emmanuel Levinas to the city-as-other, to its histories of violence and to the violence of the city's historicity. It is this role to which he is elected, and in which reluctant function he bears witness to traces of London's pasts, to 'London as a millennial landscape' (Sinclair 1999: 7), and to the persistence of the capital's 'millennial fear, the flood at the end of time' (Sinclair 1997: 98).

But of course, despite the fact that Norton is in on the murder of Christopher Marlowe, one always has to remember that 'there is no Norton' (Sinclair and McKean 1997: 10). This name, we are told, is 'an invented name to rechristen a dead man' (Sinclair and McKean 1997: 10); in the light of which salutary remark, it is necessary to consider Norton's purpose. One must ask why the persistence of this figure, throughout the time of the city in *Slow Chocolate Autopsy*, and as a recurrent revenant in Sinclair's writing. At the same time one must avoid attributing to 'him' any being, giving 'him' a life he never possesses, seeing him mistakenly as a more or less 'real', albeit fictive character who is paradoxically only 'alive in crude print' (Sinclair and McKean 1997: 10). The clues for how we do this are already there, in all that has been said thus far, and in Sinclair's writing of course. A transhistorical ghost, one more pulse in the city's network, Norton engages in acts of witnessing that are, in essence, so many acts of autopsy. Crossing time, but remaining within the precincts of London, Norton's function is to maintain what I have called countersurveillance. This is his curse, the inescapable responsibility dictating that he 'has lost his chance to escape' London. As Sinclair remarks, 'the witness pays the reckoning' (Sinclair and McKean 1997: 11); though inescapably the debt can never be paid in full. It is thus a function of Norton's ghostly existence to abide (although he finds his condition unabidable) and thus, at the end of the millennium, to register the millennial in every event – to act as a medium, a conduit or relay, or what Sinclair might call a psychic satellite dish for the reception and transmission of the merely a few of the city's signals. In this fashion Norton, much less than human, has no existence for himself. As Sinclair informs us, he is merely 'a paragraph in a pulp novel' (Sinclair and McKean 1997: 10). Norton is double, he is a 'spook' (Sinclair and McKean 1997: 9), both ghost and spy, a 'time surfer' (Sinclair and McKean 1997: 9). In this role he is translated into an editing-machine receiving 'surveillance acoustics' (Sinclair and McKean 1997: 9), as well as being a tele-technological device for transmitting the city's signals in some semi-coherent, yet still fragmented manner. In effect, through his revenant shadowy witnessing at particular sites and subsequently through his memory work, Norton edits. Acts of autopsy, of seeing with one's own eyes, thus become transformed into narrative ruins, from which it still remains impossible to assemble the city. Norton interprets; Norton translates; 'Norton' names a junction box, a neural nexus. 'Breaking time into a stutter of single frames' (Sinclair and McKean 1997: 11), Norton, a 'seismographer of the unseen' (Marion 2004: 37), names, if you will, a programme that, if you click its icon, appears to promise to 'economise on the abyss' (Derrida 1987: 37) that is London, offering momentary configurations, articulations for the 'otherwise undocumented past' (Sinclair and McKean 1997: 25) of the 'unedited city' (Sinclair and McKean 1997: 8).

However, things are not quite so simple. As Norton is forced to concede early on, the images of the city 'set up their own force field' (Sinclair and McKean 1997: 6); there seems 'no way of accessing the data' (Sinclair and McKean 1997: 8). A tension is discernible, then, between the traces of the city, perceived in their inaccessibility as hieratic, and the desire or obsession to narrate and thereby create the illusion of mastery over London. The problem is that, initially at least, Norton appears to believe mistakenly that responsibility to the city involves a cognitive gathering of the traces of the other into representation. To borrow once more from Levinas in his discussion of the relationship between the passive self and the other, Norton's error, his misperception, is in the belief that, in seeking a 'relationship that might be *meaningful*' (Levinas 2000: 187) between his being and the alterity of the city, there has to be a transformation 'into knowledge' in more or less stable forms of interpretation. Yet, as Norton will realise, what comes to be disclosed in the random encounters with the city's traces is not the truth, the permanence, of the city's identity (there is no such thing, as we have argued). Disclosure takes place for Norton, but it is a disclosure through the encounter with the various times and events of the city of a 'trauma at the heart of my-self', the 'exposure of the "me" [*moi*] to another, prior to any decision' (Levinas 2000: 187). The city, defined provisionally by Sinclair elsewhere as 'an absence, a tremble visited on the neurotically sensitive' (Sinclair 2002: 18), thus discloses Norton to himself, to his condition of being written by, and as a trace of, the city. Here is the millennial revenance, filtered through all the 'arcane pulp images of terror, and my own crippling sense of psychogeography' (Sinclair and McKean 1997: 41), until Norton pauses to ask: 'was he proposing a journey already made? Or casting a future excursion?' (Sinclair and McKean 1997: 102). His task is, of course, 'to balance the millennial elements, narcissism and melancholy' (Sinclair and McKean 1997: 148).

It is all a question of unexpected convergent flows. Sudden appearances mark and transform, even as the city is itself changed in the process of being witnessed in 'its own constant transformation, its becoming different images and different minds' (Arsic 2003: 9). Traces appear unexpectedly from within the visible and the material; in doing so, the gaze does not choose what it witnesses. It is passive, and suffers accordingly. Norton and London inform one another; he is 'adrift in a city that altered as his understanding of it altered. That grew, developed, branched out in fractal abundance' (Sinclair and McKean 1997: 109). The subjectless second sentence appears to grow out of, graft itself onto that first 'That' of the previous sentence, so that we are meant to understand that it is the city which grows, branches out in fractal abundance; however, by a forceful reading, applying just a little torque, we might take the sentence to refer to Norton's understanding of the city, which is one more in a series of versions of London. Whichever way we do take this however, the image of fractal abundance catches significantly that which cannot otherwise be captured, either about the city or in any representation of London. Such depiction involves Norton in what Sinclair refers to 'archaeological retrievals, memory games' (Sinclair and McKean 1997: 104), in which London is revealed indirectly at the same time as it withdraws in its unorderable totality, even in the process of mapping 'this liquid provisional book' (Sinclair and McKean 1997: 102), as Sinclair calls the city. That the city offers such superabundance in a series of potentially infinite rearrangements is apprehended when it is realised that all at once the streets are 'unknown, over-familiar. They took too much on themselves, replete with bad script, excessive narrative' (Sinclair and McKean 1997: 135). And so London escapes, 'an infinite image composed of innumerable images' (Arsic 2003: 4), in a fiction where the millennial might best be conceived as belonging to a 'logic of infinite [and therefore abyssal] mirroring' (Arsic 2003: 4). Such a logic gives us to know that in the revelation of truth concerning the city is the disappearance or withdrawal of the city's ineffable totality. The millennial fiction of Iain Sinclair acknowledges the logic of the mirror in its endless tropings, its constant repetitions; Norton may not, but he at least gives the logic of the millennial narrative a name.

Notes

1 The phrase belongs to Charles Williams, from his novel, *All Hallows' Eve* (1948) intro. T. S. Eliot (New York: Farrar, Strauss, Giroux, 1979), p. 145.
2 On surveillance and the city, see particularly the third essay, 'Bulls & bears & Mithraic misalignments: weather in the city', pp. 89–132.
3 See the citation on global capitalism and its colonisation of the past, above (Sinclair 2004: 99).

References

Arsic, Branka (2003) *The Passive Eye: gaze and subjectivity in Berkeley (via Beckett)*, Stanford, Calif.: Stanford University Press.

Conrad, Joseph (1995) *Heart of Darkness*, in *Youth; Heart of Darkness; The End of the Tether*, ed. John Lyon, London: Penguin, pp. 47–148.

Derrida, Jacques (1987) [1978] *The Truth in Painting*, trans. Geoff Bennington and Ian McLeod, Chicago, Ill.: University of Chicago Press.

Hamacher, Werner (1998) *Pleroma*, Stanford, Calif.: Stanford University Press.

Levinas, Emmanuel (2000) [1993] *God, Death, and Time*, trans. Bettina Bergo, Stanford, Calif.: Stanford University Press.

Marion, Jean-Luc (2004) [1996] *The Crossing of the Visible*, trans. James K. A. Smith, Stanford, Calif.: Stanford University Press.

Moorcock, Michael (1995) 'Introduction', in Iain Sinclair, *Lud Heat and Suicide Bridge*, London: Vintage, pp. 3–6.

Sinclair, Iain (1989) *Flesh Eggs & Scalp Metal: Selected Poems 1970–1987*, London: Paladin.

—— (1994) *Radon Daughters: a voyage, between art and terror, from the Mound of Whitechapel to the limestone pavements of the Burren*, London: Jonathan Cape.

—— (1995) [1987] *White Chappell, Scarlet Tracings*, London: Vintage.

—— (1997) *Lights Out for the Territory: 9 excursions in the secret history of London*, London: Granta.

—— (1999) *Sorry Meniscus: excursions to the Millennium Dome*, London: Profile.

—— (2002) 'Letter to Prague', in *Saddling the Rabbit*, Buckfastleigh: Estruscan, pp. 18–19.

—— (2004) *Dining on Stones, or, the Middle Ground*, London: Hamish Hamilton.

Sinclair, Iain and Dave McKean (1997) *Slow Chocolate Autopsy: incidents from the notorious career of Norton, prisoner of London*, London: Phoenix House.

Wall, Thomas Carl (1999) *Radical Passivity: Levinas, Blanchot, and Agamben*, Albany, NY: State University of New York Press.

Williams, Charles (1979) [1948] *All Hallows' Eve*, New York: Farrar, Strauss, Giroux.

13 Hedgemony?

Suburban space in
The Buddha of Suburbia

Susan Brook

It is hard to find anyone with a good word to say about suburbia. The image of suburbs as homogenous and conformist is pervasive, not only in popular culture but also in contemporary literary and cultural criticism, where the suburb tends to feature negatively, if it features at all. Instead, attention has been focused on 'the city', which in practice usually means the inner city, and which, following Charles Jencks, David Harvey and Fredric Jameson, has become central to the analysis of postmodernity. The belief that we must turn to the city in order to examine the distinctive conditions of contemporary life seems to be borne out by the number of British novelists who have taken cosmopolitan, fragmented, urban space as their subject, from the psychogeographies of Peter Ackroyd and Iain Sinclair, to the metafictional treatments of London in Salman Rushdie's *The Satanic Verses* (1988) and Martin Amis's *London Fields* (1989), to recent work by Zadie Smith (*White Teeth*, 2000) and Monica Ali (*Brick Lane*, 2003).

However, if, as Roger Silverstone has suggested, the suburb is 'the hidden underbelly of modernity' (Silverstone 1997: 3), the same is true of post-modernity. For millions of people in contemporary Britain, their experience of postmodernity is not the strip in Las Vegas, but the out-of-town shopping centre; not the Bonaventure but the Travelodge; not just the surveillance of CCTV in the central city, but also the invisible gaze of the Neighbourhood Watch. Recent work in urban studies has suggested that the traditional idea of the suburb may no longer be relevant, as new urban forms such as 'edge cities' blur the distinction between city, suburb and country.[1] And, of course, the archetypal postmodern, decentred city is Los Angeles, in which boundaries between city and suburb are also blurred. Yet nevertheless, the suburb is still an important cultural reference point in both the USA and Britain as the (often demonized) other of city life: safe where the city is dangerous; conformist where the city is heterogeneous; monotonous and enervating where the city is diverse and stimulating; the site of heterosexual family life where the city opens up the potential for sexual experimentation and possibility.

In this chapter, I explore and question such distinctions between the urban and the suburban with reference to Hanif Kureishi's 1990 novel, *The Buddha of Suburbia*, in which the suburb contains not only the ills of postmodern life but also its possibilities. I begin by outlining some of the reasons to be suspicious of the common assumption that suburbs are homogenous and dull at best, deadly and repressive at worst (the position I am calling 'hedgemony'[2]), and go on to explore an alternative idea of the suburbs as sites of surface and of display, where the boundaries between public and private are both installed and constantly undermined. These ideas are developed through a reading of *The Buddha of Suburbia*'s ambivalent representation of suburban space, which argues that the novel presents a more complex notion of the suburb than critics have tended to recognize, as the suburb emerges as a site that is camp and potentially queer. The very emphasis on surface and façade associated with the lower-middle-class suburb opens up the possibility for experimentation with appearance, and for a potentially radicalized relationship to surfaces and style. In addition, the suburb emerges as literally eccentric: the straight lines of the commute to the centre are supplemented by lateral movements across and through suburban spaces. My larger argument, which cannot be fully developed here, is that recent British writing, from Graham Swift to Jonathan Coe to Bernadine Evaristo, represents the suburb not just as a cage to be escaped but also as a resource to be mobilized – and often as both at the same time. If we want to understand the city from below as well as from above we must look not just at de Certeau's oft-cited pedestrian walking the streets of Manhattan (de Certeau 1984), but also at the multiplicity of ways in which people negotiate, mobilize and map the everyday space of suburban avenues.

Criticism of suburban architecture and of suburban life unites those at opposite ends of the political spectrum. The British philosopher Roger Scruton, in an account of the reasons he became a conservative, explains: 'I suppose that, in so far as I had received any intimations of my future career as an intellectual pariah, it was through my early reactions to modern architecture, and to the desecration of my childhood landscape by the faceless boxes of suburbia' (Scruton 2003: 7).

Architecture critic Jonathan Glancey, unlike Scruton a champion of modernism, suggests that British suburban sprawl should be replaced by more compact urban spaces, home-grown versions of Tuscan hill towns. He writes:

> Suburbia, as we know it – cropped and sprinkled lawns, lovingly polished cars, video rental shops, neo-Georgian and mock-Tudor homes spread like inkstains across former meadows, farms and market gardens – is a recent phenomenon . . . the new suburbs spread out from

towns and cities south of the Humber-Severn divide like the tentacles of some humungous brick and breeze-block octopus. Today, we build suburbs from scratch in the middle of nowhere. Not a town or city in sight.

(Glancey 2002: 10)

Scruton contrasts suburbia with a nostalgic version of the pastoral, Glancey with a utopian vision of urban density. Yet despite their differences, both writers give us a similar picture of suburbs. Suburbs are homogenous, full of undifferentiated boxes and identical brick and breeze-block tentacles, and in their homogeneity also inhuman: 'faceless' in Scruton's words; for Glancey, like a devouring octopus. For both writers, suburbs are character-ized by surface over depth and pay the price of inauthenticity: Scruton's faceless boxes are all inorganic surface, while Glancey lingers on the 'neo-Georgian' and 'mock-Tudor' façades of suburban houses, which mark them out as pretentious copies.

Similar language also pervades many academic discussions of suburbs, certainly in literary and cultural studies, and dislike of the suburbs brings together some equally unlikely bedfellows, as queer theorists echo the concerns of conservative modernist critics, for example in the depiction of suburbs as sexually and socially repressed and repressive. The film-maker and critic Isaac Julien has said: '[Suburbia is] something I can't really take seriously – especially in relation to "gay culture" – what would be my investment in appealing to suburbia or countryside places?' (Julien 1993: 127). In his contribution to the edited collection *Visions of Suburbia* (1997), the critic Andy Medhurst criticizes T. S. Eliot who 'so loftily despised' sub-urban commuters – in Eliot's *The Waste Land*, it is the suburban commuters pouring over London Bridge who come to represent the 'Unreal City', and the inauthenticity of urban life. Yet the rest of Medhurst's article, which analyses sitcom representations of the suburbs, mobilizes suburbia as an overwhelmingly negative category, as it praises programmes that 'shake the certainties on which suburbia depends' (Medhurst 1997: 254) and that attack 'traditional suburban values' (Medhurst 1997: 258). Medhurst admits 'In matters of sexuality . . . the suburbs are so deadly that I almost find myself siding with the architects and literary types [such as Eliot]' (Medhurst 1997: 266). Roger Silverstone echoes Medhurst's comments about the sex-ual repression and social homogeneity of the suburbs in his discussion of American sitcoms: 'In images as in life . . . what was being asserted was – and palpably still is – an ethic of exclusion – insistently homophobic, consistently racist' (Silverstone 1997: 22).

However, the critique of homogeneity in much of this criticism is itself dependent on an undifferentiated, homogenous notion of 'the suburbs', as though there were no distinctions between different kinds of suburbs. The binary opposition between the city and the suburb persists because of the vagueness of the idea of 'the suburbs', which enables it to function as the other of a range of urban experience. 'Suburbia' is an almost infinite category: it can refer to upper-middle-class exclusivity and to lower-middle-class monotony, to Purley or Penge, to Wilmslow or Wythenshawe. The classification of an area as 'suburban' therefore conceals difference within its judgement of homogeneity. As John Carey has suggested, 'Like "masses", the word 'suburban' is a sign for the unknowable' (Carey 1992: 53).[3]

Following Raymond Williams, then, we might say that 'there are no suburbs: there are only ways of seeing places as suburbs' (cf. Williams 1958: 289). And in practice, despite the term's slippery potential, to see an area of a city or town as 'suburban' in Britain is usually to classify it as lower middle class.[4] Judgements about the homogeneity and repression of suburban life are often judgements aimed at the lower middle classes. The icons of suburbia are garden gnomes, houses on dual carriageways called Bellevue, net curtains, mock Tudor façades: whether aspirational or simply naff, definitively lower middle class. Rita Felski has recently pointed out that in general, the experience and representation of lower-middle-class life is ignored in academia (Felski 2000). It is also in a shared antipathy towards lower-middle-class culture that we see the root of the parallels between the queer and the modernist dislike of the suburb, which helps to explain the Medhust–Eliot concord. Jon Binnie helps to explain this alliance when he suggests that: 'coming out and developing a gay identity has commonly gone hand in hand with becoming a sophisticated urban dweller at ease with urban life' (Binnie 2000: 172). As a result, although queer theory has thoroughly problematized the modernist category of authentic identity, it has only just begun to question the basically modernist privileging of urban authenticity over the suburban inauthenticity. This distinction became established in the early twentieth century: by 1923, Luis Buñuel compares the 'feverish movement' of the city to 'the endless yawn of the suburb, its fringed and withered eyes' (Buñuel 1999: 239), and Le Corbusier was another critic of suburbs, describing them as the scum of the city. Yet objections to suburbs as homogenous and stultifying emerge at the moment where suburbia is opening up, expanding and diversifying to include the lower middle classes and the upper working classes.[5] The idea of the monotonous suburb, which has persisted throughout the twentieth century, tells us less about suburban life and experience than it does about those who make such judgements, often intellectuals or the socially mobile.[6]

Antagonism towards 'the suburbs' is generated not just by class anxieties, but also by the link between suburbs and femininity. Women are frequently the targets in satirical portraits of the suburb, where they are shown to be obsessed with conspicuous consumption and display; the most famous suburban monsters are women, from Hilda Bowling in George Orwell's *Coming Up For Air* (1939), to Hyacinth Bucket in *Keeping Up Appearances* and Margot Leadbetter in *The Good Life*.[7] Suburban display is usually seen not only as inauthentic but also as feminine, like mass culture. It is doubtless the history of the development of suburbs as spaces for private family life delineated from the public sphere of work in the inner city that has meant that suburbs have invariably been associated with femininity and therefore with consumption and display.[8]

But spaces often exceed their intended purposes, and in many cultural representations the suburb emerges as a strangely disturbing place, associated with the private made public, with enclosure *and* with disclosure, raising the unsettling possibility that, as the net curtains twitch, the boundaries between what is public and what is private break down. It is precisely the way in which suburban life installs boundaries between public and private, and breaks them down at the same time, that leads Jürgen Habermas (1989) to identify suburbanization, as well as new patterns of consumption and media, as a key component in the breakdown of a public sphere which contained the possibility of civil society and political debate. Habermas points to the picture window of the ranch-style suburban bungalow as symbolic of the increasingly vulnerable private sphere. Habermas's conception of such a public sphere, which he famously associates with eighteenth-century coffee houses, depends also on a separate private sphere where thought and reading take place; he sees in twentieth-century life a breakdown of the distinction between the two spheres with the result that the public sphere is no longer the site of political critique. Yet against Habermas, it could be argued that the unstable distinction between public and private life that characterizes suburban life reveals the contradictions of liberalism, and the way in which the supposedly neutral public sphere is always permeated by the 'private' sphere of sexual life in its heteronormativity. The idea of a potentially queer suburb emerging out of the blurred boundary between public and private is one we shall see in Kureishi.

The tension between private life and public display, as well as the suburb's association with femininity, also allows for the possibility of what might be called suburban camp. Susan Sontag famously writes that camp is: 'one way of seeing the world as an aesthetic phenomenon. That way, the way of Camp, is not in terms of beauty, but in terms of the degree of artifice, of stylization' (Sontag 1982: 106). She adds 'The pure examples of Camp are unintentional; they are dead-serious' (Sontag 1982: 110). Sontag's description of camp has been criticized for privileging aesthetics at the expense of the political, and it would be difficult to argue that suburban camp was necessarily radical. Nonetheless, it is unmistakably *there*, whether in Margot

Leadbetter's outfits and her fondness for musical theatre, or Hyacinth Bouquet's fetishizing of table-settings and toilet-roll covers, as she performs a middle-class identity which is always about to slip. It is visible in the 1997 film *The Full Monty* in the suburban house and garden of the lower-middle-class foreman, Gerald, with its garden gnomes which become symbolic weapons wielded against him at his job interview by his former employees, Dave and Gaz, who parade the gnomes distractingly behind the interviewers' backs. Yet, if in the film suburban camp is initially mocked, the house later becomes the space of reconciliation in which the men both unite together and embrace their femininity, as they use the sunbed, read women's magazines and learn to dance.

Of course, 'the suburb', or more precisely the lower-middle-class suburb, is not inherently queer or camp: while space is more than simply a container for activities, and instead helps to produce social relations, it is dangerous to assume an isomorphism between space and culture. Instead, it might be possible to think of the queer or camp possibilities within suburban life that certain writers activate or draw on, but others disregard. Frank Mort has pointed out that 'the sexual body is . . . marked by all of those forms of hyperindividualization – through dress and personal adornment, stylized forms of movement, display and visual spectacle – which lie at the heart of urban self-presentation' (Mort 2000: 313). In the work of several contemporary writers, the qualities Mort describes are associated not only with the inner city, but also with suburbia. From Anita Brookner to Julian Barnes to Hanif Kureishi, the suburb arguably emerges as a space of camp and artifice. In Kureishi the suburban aesthetic of display is also specifically linked to new possibilities for the display and performance of personal identities, whether sexual, ethnic or class.

Suburban space in *The Buddha of Suburbia*

The suburb features as a camp and queer space in Hanif Kureishi's screen-plays from the 1980s, particularly in *My Beautiful Laundrette* (1987), where the south London suburbs are the setting for the affair between Omar and Johnny. But the camp potential of the suburb is seen most clearly in Kureishi's first novel, *The Buddha of Suburbia*, however much this book is seen by critics as a sally fired against the smug monotony of suburban life. Now canonical in surveys of recent fiction, the novel and its mixed-race narrator, Karim, are often celebrated as examples of post-colonial hybridity, or queer transgression, and readings emphasize Karim's bisexuality, performativity and his description of himself as an 'odd mixture of continents and bloods, of here and there, of belonging and not' (Kureishi 1990: 3).[9] Karim's sexual and ethnic difference, along with his refusal of fixed identity categories, is often associated with urban cosmopolitanism and seen as a challenge to suburban sameness. Matthew Graves's article on the novel is entitled 'Subverting suburbia'; Berthold Schoene argues that it shows 'the gaping void at the disheartening core of middle-class suburban Englishness' (Schoene 1998: 115); Anthony Ilona suggests that 'London is celebrated as a location of cultural diversity without the stifling tensions seen in the suburbs' (Ilona 2003: 101).

Even critics who have tried to question such readings rely on a standard notion of the suburban as consumerist and conformist. James Procter gives one of the most interesting and provocative accounts of the novel, arguing that it is 'about becoming local, about a turn away from cosmopolitan versions of migrancy' (Procter 2003: 126), and that suburbia is central to the novel's claim to the local. However, Procter's reading does not funda-mentally complicate the distinction between multicultural inner city and tedious suburb, as he argues that the novel's suburbia 'display[s] a staid provincialism, a shrinkage from the (post)modernity and the multicultural-ism of the metropolis' (Procter 2003: 155).[10] Dominic Head has argued that the novel demonstrates 'an enriching conflict between urban and suburban experiences' (Head 2002: 223), yet his reading still identifies the novel's representation of suburbia with conformity. David Oswell goes further, claiming that Karim 'foregrounds the suburban as a space of performance and hybridity' (Oswell 2000: 81). Yet Oswell also argues that the novel challenges and deconstructs 'contemporary straight suburban masculinity' (Oswell 2000: 85), finishing his article by describing the negative media response to the novel's televised version: 'this tabloid blast of disgust rico-cheted within the wedding-cake walls of suburban England' (Oswell 2000: 85). There is an interesting tension here, as Oswell rehabilitates suburbia as hybrid within the novel, but criticizes it for being narrow-minded and straight in reality. Like Medhurst, Oswell is willing to grant *representations* of suburbia some subversive potential, but suburbs themselves are once more constructed as homogenously conservative, rather than as anything more interesting. For Oswell, hybridity becomes purely textual, something which can be found only in 'the *imaginary* space (or the imagined communities) of the text' (Oswell 2000: 84; emphasis in original). Both Oswell and Head see Kureishi's novel as outside of or beyond the limitations of suburban life, either engaging with the suburb in a dialectic between urban and suburban, or constructing an alternative and superior textualized suburb.

It is true that, to some extent, the novel does rely on a familiar distinction between the urban and suburban, for which the inner city represents a world of escape and sexual possibility in contrast to the stultifying suburbs. Karim describes the suburbs as 'all familiarity and endurance: security and safety were the reward of dullness . . . It would be years before I could get away to the city, London, where life was bottomless in its temptations' (Kureishi 1990: 8). The narrative of escape from the suburb to the city is written into the novel's *Bildungsroman* structure: the first half of the novel is entitled 'In the Suburbs', and describes Karim's life growing up in Beckenham in south-east London; the second half of the novel follows his career in the theatre after he moves with his father and his father's mistress, Eva, to central London. Yet over the course of the novel, this distinction is often contradicted, modified or rendered unstable (as Head 2002 also notes).

The novel engages with the possibilities of suburban life as well as its limitations, and these possibilities take the form of particular kinds of movement and self-presentation that can be seen as (at least potentially) queer. Karim's move from the suburbs to the city is complicated by a series of trips he makes back to the suburbs. More broadly, the differences between the inner city and the suburb are increasingly unclear: the sexual excitement Karim seeks is available in the suburb as well as in the city, just as he encounters 'suburban' racism and snobbery in the inner-city milieu of the theatre. The suburb, more specifically Beckenham, emerges as a space of in-betweenness, albeit of an unfashionable kind – of the lower middle classes, of middle England, of the private and domestic also partially open to public display.

The novel often returns to the importance of decoration and of the display of private life within suburban life, particularly in the site of the suburban house. The predominant obsession of the suburbs is not sameness, but difference and distinction as exhibited through such display. Walking to the pub down a suburban street, Karim observes:

> All of the houses had been 'done up.' One had a new porch, another double-glazing, 'Georgian' windows or a new door with brass fittings. Kitchens had been extended, lofts converted, walls removed, garages inserted. This was the English passion, not for self-improvement or culture or wit, but for DIY, Do It Yourself, for bigger and better houses with more mod cons, the painstaking accumulation of comfort and, with it, status – the concrete display of earned cash. Display was the game.
>
> (Kureishi 1990: 75)

Display marks distinctions between houses in a suburb, and it also points to differences between suburbs. Karim's uncle and aunt live in more middle-class Chislehurst, where the houses have 'greenhouses, grand oaks and sprinklers on the lawn' (Kureishi 1990: 29). Houses, here, are not just spaces of private life, but blur the lines between privacy and display, as identity is shown to be constituted more through public performance than through inner essence. Karim asks at the beginning of the novel 'why search the inner room' (Kureishi 1990: 3), and the novel persistently privileges notions of surface rather than depth in its exploration of identity formation.

Throughout the novel, the house and its surfaces are important sites for the construction of identity, particularly for female characters. Karim's mother redecorates as she re-establishes her sense of self in the wake of Haroon's departure. Crucially, Eva, who in many ways acts as Karim's double, gets the money to move to West Kensington through DIY, renovating and selling her house, and later establishes herself as a professional interior designer. Like Karim, in London Eva is 'constructing an artistic persona for herself' (Kureishi 1990: 150), and she enables Karim's escape from the suburbs financially. Eva bears witness to the performativity of ethnicity and gender through her interiors, which are displayed to the public. In one passage, she shows around a journalist from an interiors magazine:

> 'As you can see, it's very feminine in the English manner,' she said to the journalist as we looked over the cream carpets, gardenia paintwork, wooden shutters, English country-house armchairs and cane tables. There were baskets of dried flowers in the kitchen and coconut matting on the floor.
>
> (Kureishi 1990: 261)

Englishness and femininity are here shown as surfaces to be displayed, or the sum of commodities to be assembled and rearranged. Bart Moore-Gilbert has pointed out that many of these commodities, such as the cane work, the shutters and the matting, 'reflect the incorporation of foreign, more specifically eastern, items within "English" décor' (Moore-Gilbert 2001: 129). Interiors bear witness to the fiction of Englishness as ethnic purity just as suburban inhabitants do, and can be excavated for traces of the colonial otherness at the heart – or more precisely, on the surface – of Englishness.

There are parallels between the novel's treatment of the house and of the body. If Eva and Margaret redecorate their homes to construct new identities, their sons Karim and Charlie redecorate their bodies, using clothes to mark out their subcultural identities, and frequently changing images to signal a change in their musical and cultural allegiances. As many critics have pointed out, the novel constantly questions the notion that the body provides any essential ground for identity, associating such an idea with dubious and often racist practices. The director Shadwell, for example, tells Karim that he was cast in a version of *The Jungle Book* 'for authenticity and not for experience' (Kureishi 1990: 147), assuming from the colour of Karim's skin some mystic connection to Indianness – though ironically Karim's body is not brown enough, and he needs to be covered in make-up in order to look truly authentic. If throughout the novel race and ethnicity are associated with surfaces and malleability, in a key passage space is linked to identity more closely than race. Karim could be describing himself when he says of Eva 'I saw that she wanted to scour that suburban stigma right off her body. She didn't realize it was in the blood and not on the skin; she didn't see there could be nothing more suburban than suburbanites repudiating themselves' (Kureishi 1990: 134). Here notions of depth and surface are ironically reversed, as the language of blood and belonging is used to signal the persistence of suburban identity, an identity constituted through surfaces, and through the desire to recreate oneself, to reshape or repudiate past identities. Rather than being antithetical to his identity, it is the suburban concern with display and surface, and with the private made public, which provides Karim with strategies to reshape himself – as politico, as urban sophisticate, as Englishman in New York.

In other ways, too, the novel shows the way in which suburban life blurs the boundary between public and private, allowing for the possibility of what could arguably be called queer space. The history of the suburb is imbricated in the history of attempts to delineate a supposedly neutral and non-sexual public space. However, critics such as David Bell have pointed out that an implicitly heteronormative public sphere condones the display of numerous cultural expressions of heterosexual coupledom, from hand-holding to opening bank accounts, but not of homosexual or lesbian (see, for example, Bell 1995). Queer activism has included attempts to 'sexualize' public space (through kiss-ins, for example) as a way of challenging the division between public and private that helps to police the heteronormative public space (whereby non-heterosexual behaviour is categorized as 'sexual' and therefore 'private' and rendered invisible). In *The Buddha of Suburbia*, the boundaries between public and private are similarly disturbed through numerous examples of the 'private' sphere of family and sexual life becoming at least partially public, as the privacy of suburban spaces are shown to be always already a fiction.[11] Throughout the novel, people stumble across other people having sex. At a party, Karim sees his father and Eva making love outside on the garden bench, a liminal space between public and private: 'I knew it was Daddio because he was crying out across the Beckenham gardens, with little concern for the neighbours, "Oh God, oh my God, oh my God" ' (Kureishi 1990: 16). His father in turn comes across Karim giving Charlie a handjob in the bedroom; Changez discovers Karim having sex with his wife, Jamila; Jamila and Karim also have a history of having sex in public toilets. This could be seen as a way in which the novel questions the desirability of 'the organization of love into suburban family life' (Kureishi 1990: 26) and subverts the straight space of the family home, queering private domestic space. But equally, such images suggest that the 'metropolitan' orgy scene between Pyke, Marlene, Karim and Eleanor is not so much antithetical to suburban life as a continuation of it.

These sexual episodes might be seen as showing the way in which the 'straightness' of suburban space becomes an eroticizing fetish for Karim and others, but they also tell us something about the way in which suburban architecture and space blur the lines between privacy and display. Throughout Kureishi's work, doors and windows are images of the permeability of the boundaries between public and private. In *My Beautiful Laundrette*, Omar sees Tania through the suburban french doors as she pulls up her top and displays her breasts, enticing him to leave the family gathering and join her in the garden. In another scene, Omar and Johnny make love in the back room of the laundrette as the camera shows through the one-way mirror behind them Omar's father and his girlfriend dancing in the laundrette to celebrate its opening. This scene both reveals and subverts the public space of the heterosexual couple and the private, invisible space of the homosexual couple, as the mirror/window both divides and joins these spaces. Similarly, in *The Buddha of Suburbia*, windows and doors are images of the private made public: Changez looks through an open door to observe Jamila and Karim in bed together (Kureishi 1990: 109); when Karim's mother asks him to pull the curtains to hide his father's half-indecent yoga display, he tells her 'It's not necessary, Mum. There isn't another house that can see us for a hundred yards – unless they're watching through binoculars', to which she responds 'That's exactly what they're doing' (Kureishi 1990: 4). Windows and doors throughout the novel are images of the porousness and permeability of 'private' space, yet whereas for Habermas this signals the erosion of an autonomous public sphere, in Kureishi it potentially paves the way for a politics that refuses the relegation of minority sexualities to the private sphere.

The novel's treatment of movement is another way in which suburban space is associated with the blurring of the lines between public and private. There are two kinds of movement across the city in the novel: vertical journeys from the suburb to the centre, and lateral journeys across suburbs. The first category includes Karim's upwardly mobile trajectory, from Beckenham to West Kensington, where Karim gets his acting break and meets his upper-middle-class girlfriend Eleanor, whose friends are called 'Candia, Emma, Jasper' (Kureishi 1990: 173); it also includes his father Haroon's daily commute between Beckenham and Whitehall. These journeys from periphery to centre enforce the separation of the public and private, leaving the hierarchical relationship between the two untouched, as the world of domesticity is separated from the world of work, and Karim's home life in the suburbs is subordinated to his burgeoning career in the city. Another example of movement in this category is Uncle Ted's journey with Karim on the train to see Spurs play at home to Chelsea, a trip that mirrors 'the journey Dad made every day' (Kureishi 1990: 43). On this trip, Ted is transformed from mild-mannered suburbanite to football hooligan, smashing up the carriage, and racist, as he tells Karim that Brixton is where 'them niggers live' (Kureishi 1990: 43). The division of spheres enforced by this trip in this case is not between work and home, but (masculinized) leisure and (feminized) domestic life, as Ted returns to his normal mild-mannered self back in Chislehurst.

In the second category are the horizontal journeys between and across suburbs that both Karim and his father undertake. Haroon dresses in a suit to go to Whitehall, but in his Buddha costume he travels laterally from Beckenham to Chislehurst, making money from offering his performance of eastern spirituality to the white middle classes who see him as an embodiment of the authentic Other. It is this sideways journey that also provides Karim with sexual and social excitement as he goes to visit Charlie, dressed up in his shiny pink shirt and purple flares. Karim cycles around Beckenham, and from Beckenham to Penge and Forest Hill to visit Jamila. In this respect, he is an inheritor of H. G. Wells's Mr Polly, also an inhabitant of south-east London, who cycles his way out of his occupation as clerk; yet cycling for Karim is not a straight line of escape, but a much more meandering journey of exploration.[12] Karim describes his cycle trips in terms of rule-breaking and dangerous excitement: 'So I was racing through South London on my bike, nearly getting crushed several times by lorries . . . sometimes mounting the pavement, up one-way streets, accelerating by standing up on the pedals, exhilarated by thought and motion' (Kureishi 1990: 63). Similar lateral journeys are also taken by bus: after his parents separate, Karim moves between their houses and also stays with friends, saying 'I was not too unhappy, criss-crossing South London and the suburbs by bus, no one knowing where I was' (Kureishi 1990: 94).

Here Karim's horizontal journeys are images of individual freedom and exploration, as he becomes a suburban *flâneur* as well as a dandy, travelling not by foot but by bus and by bike. These journeys are not structured around the distinctions between public and private, work and domesticity, masculine and feminine; they could be seen as examples of the way in which space is queered in the novel, in contrast to the straight journeys of the daily commute. Similarly, the form of the novel could be seen as a corollary of these lateral journeys; although structured around an apparent journey of one-way mobility, from the suburbs to the city, the novel returns to the suburbs on numerous occasions, including in the novel's final chapter when, after Karim's return to London from New York, he 'got the bus down to South London' (Kureishi 1990: 266). At the end of the novel, various characters gather for dinner on the night of the 1979 elections; in the BBC television adaptation of the novel, whose screenplay was co-written by Kureishi, Karim states 'Nobody is going to vote for that cow. She's too suburban', to which Eva responds 'Don't we live in a suburban country?' If suburbia, rather than race, unites the imagined national community, suburbia forms a point of return as well as of departure for the novel, disrupting a simple linear structure.

Robert Seguin's recent study of post-war American middle-class identity argues that in the dominant tropes of such identity, including in representations of suburbia, 'imagined mobility fuses with stasis' (Seguin 2001: 11); he describes the sense of instability that results from images and forms that combine fixity with movement.[13] A tension between mobility and stasis also characterizes Kureishi's representation of suburbia, seen both as limit ('If the secret police ordered you to live in the suburbs for the rest of your life, what would you do? Kill yourself? Read?' [Kureishi 1990: 45]) and as the motor for movement ('it was obviously true that the suburbs were a leaving place, the start of a life' [Kureishi 1990: 45]). Such liminality is also shown to characterize the immigrant experience, as Karim notes: 'Now, as they aged and seemed settled here, Anwar and Dad appeared to be returning internally to India, or at least to be resisting the English here. It was puzzling: neither of them expressed any desire actually to see their origins again' (Kureishi 1990: 64). It is in its suspension between movement and fixity that suburbia perhaps best characterizes many of the larger tensions around identity which Kureishi addresses, including that of immigrant identity.[14] As John Clement Ball (1996: 21) has argued, the novel's distinction between suburb and city is a counterpoint to the distinction between colonial periphery and metropolis, and if suburbia is the heart of England and English racism in contrast to the multicultural inner city, it is also the periphery that in many ways is marginal to the cosmopolitan centre.

This unexpected link also helps to modify some of the claims made about the politics of suburbia by a critic such as Roger Silverstone, who states that suburbia offers a 'new kind of neo-participatory politics based on self-interest and grounded in defensive anxiety' (Silverstone 1997: 12). To some extent this describes the politics of Karim, surely one of the most egotistical (if also charming) characters in contemporary British fiction. Karim shamelessly acknowledges the way in which self-interest drives him, both in his desire for Charlie ('I coveted his talents, face, style' [Kureishi 1990: 15]) and in his willingness to use others to get what he wants. But Karim's selfishness, as well as his materialism, is interrogated by various characters, as the novel stages a political dialogue between Karim and Terry, Jamila and Karim's father, among others. This dialogue reflects a tension throughout Kureishi's work between celebrating the possibility of individual self-invention, on the one hand, and criticizing the cruelty of entrepreneurial culture and the costs for those left out of it, on the other. Yet if suburbia promotes the interests of the individual, in its tension between stasis and movement it also stages the unstable process of the formation of any individual identity.

Similarly, if the novel criticizes aspects of suburban life for its mundanity and materialism, in its depiction of the figure of the suburban eccentric, and in horizontal, queer journeys between and around suburbs, suburban space is shown to produce non-conformity and self-invention. The suburb not only contains but produces its opposite. Within the novel, the very emphasis on surface and façade associated with the suburbs opens up a place for experimentation with appearances, and for a potentially radicalized relationship to surfaces and style. *The Buddha of Suburbia* suggests that it is precisely the suburbs' camp emphasis on display and artifice that give them their potential as sites for the performance and invention of alternative sexualities outside of heteronormativity.

Karim's queer trajectories and his camp aesthetic therefore should not be seen a reaction against suburban homogeneity, but instead as drawing on and activating the possibilities found in suburban space. Through the novel's exploration of the suburb as a space of display and lateral movement, a space that complicates distinctions between public and private space, and as a space of artifice and self-invention, it suggests a sympathetic as well as antagonistic relationship between Karim and the suburbs. The novel problematizes the simple distinction between urban cosmopolitanism and suburban monotony and conformity, and suggests that beneath the received idea of suburbia lurks a more disturbing, and more differentiated kind of urban life that deserves further exploration.

Notes

1 See Garreau (2001) for an analysis of this phenomenon.
2 A term I have borrowed from John Hartley.
3 Carey argues that this is true from the late nineteenth century onwards. He points out that a 1905 critic of suburbia, T. W. H. Crosland, included within that category virtually the whole of the population, except for manual workers (and, one presumes, aristocrats) (Carey 1992: 57–8).
4 The term has somewhat different connotations and meanings in the USA, where suburbia is often associated with upper-middle-class enclaves, such as Westchester or Orange Country, and with 'white flight' from the inner city. Yet even in this context, we might consider that the multiplicity of suburbia is concealed within a single judgement. In her recent study of representations of suburban life in twentieth-century America, Catherine Jurca (2001) focuses almost exclusively on the upper-middle-class white suburb, which – although it

may the dominant image of suburbia in US life – is certainly not the only form of suburb.

5 See Gaskell (1977), Crossick (1977) and Carey (1992) for fuller accounts of this process.

6 Julian Barnes's first novel, *Metroland* (1980), is structured around the links between intellectual pretension, social mobility and disdain for suburbia.

7 As Felski argues, 'many of the values and attitudes traditionally associated with the lower middle class are also identified with women: domesticity, prudery, aspirations toward refinement' (Felski 2000: 43). Yet even solidly middle-class suburban women such as Margot Leadbetter are associated with such qualities by virtue of their *suburban* identities, above and beyond their class position.

8 See Robert Fishman's excellent study *Bourgeois Utopias* for a full account of the process of suburbanization, which took from the early nineteenth century in London and Manchester, influencing city planners in the USA as well.

9 See Moore-Gilbert (2001) for a useful account of debates around hybridity in *The Buddha of Suburbia.*

10 As will become clear, I disagree with various aspects of Procter's reading of the novel, including his claim that its representation of DIY is synonymous with white Englishness (Procter 2003: 147), and his reading of Karim's journeys throughout the city both as politically evasive, and as mirroring the commuter's desire for return (Procter 2003: 155).

11 Here, again, I disagree with James Procter who accepts the standard reading that suburbia, in the novel as in the world, is synonymous with a 'larger retirement from the public or political realm' (Procter 2003: 147).

12 This literary debt is acknowledged in the text: 'I got off my bike and stood there in Bromley High Street, next to the plaque that said "H. G. Wells was born here" ' (Kureishi 1990: 64).

13 I am indebted to the excellent review by Susan Edmunds (2003) that brought this book to my attention.

14 In this respect, my reading of the novel contrasts with the conclusions drawn by Catherine Jurca in her analysis of American suburban literature. Jurca also analyses tropes of movement, stating that suburbanites are 'transients who will never get to move' (Jurca 2001: 147). Yet Jurca views such tropes suspiciously, as evidence of unconvincing and implicitly racist claims by white suburbanites to alienation and victimization, and therefore as fictions that need to be unveiled. Kureishi's use of similar tropes suggests instead a certain homology between British suburban life and the experiences of racial minorities in Britain.

References

Ali, M. (2003) *Brick Lane*, London: Doubleday.

Amis, M. (1989) *London Fields*, London: Cape.

Ball, J. C. (1996) 'The semi-detached metropolis', *Ariel* 27 (4): 7–27.

Barnes, J. (1980) *Metroland*, London: Cape.

Bell, D. (1995) 'Perverse dynamics, sexual citizenship and the transformation of intimacy', in D. Bell and G. Valentine (eds) *Mapping Desire: geographies of sexualities*, London: Routledge, pp. 304–17.

Binnie, J. (2000) 'Cosmopolitanism and the sexed city', in D. Bell and A. Haddour (eds) *City Visions*, Hemel Hempstead: Longman Press, pp. 166–78.

Buñuel, L. (1999) [1923] 'Suburbs', in Vassiliki Kolocotroni, Jane Goldman and Olga Taxidou (eds) *Modernism: an anthology of sources and documents*, Edinburgh: Edinburgh University Press.

Carey, J. (1992) *The Intellectuals and the Masses*, London: Faber & Faber.

Crossick, G. (ed.) (1977) *The Lower Middle Class in Britain, 1870–1914*, London: Croom Helm.

de Certeau (1984) *The Practice of Everyday Life*, Berkeley: University of California Press.

Edmunds, S. (2003) 'Accelerated immobilities: American suburbia and the classless middle class', *American Literary History* 15 (2): 409–20.

Felski, R. (2000) 'Nothing to declare: identity, shame and the lower middle class', *PMLA* 115 (1): 1–25

Fishman, R. (1987) *Bourgeois Utopias*, New York: Basic Books.

Garreau, J. (2001) *Edge City: life on the new frontier*, New York: Doubleday.

Gaskell, M. (1977) 'Housing and the lower middle class, 1870–1914', in G. Crossick (ed.) *The Lower Middle Class in Britain, 1870–1914*, London: Croom Helm, pp. 159–83.

Glancey, J. (2002) 'Visions of Utopia', *Guardian*, G2, Wednesday October 30, 10.

Graves, M. (1997) 'Subverting suburbia: the trickster figure in Hanif Kureishi's *The Buddha of Suburbia*', in F. Gallix (ed.) *The Buddha of Suburbia*, Paris: Ellipses, pp. 70–8.

Habermas, J. (1989) *The Structural Transportation of the Public Sphere*, Cambridge: Polity.

Hartley, J. (1997) 'The sexualization of Suburbia: the diffusion of knowledge in the postmodern public sphere', in R. Silverstone (ed.) *Visions of Suburbia*, London: Routledge, pp. 180–216.

Head, D. (2002) *The Cambridge Introduction to Modern British Fiction, 1950–2000*, Cambridge: Cambridge University Press.

Ilona, A. (2003) 'Hanif Kureishi's *The Buddha of Suburbia*', in R. Lane, R. Mengham and P. Tew (eds) *Contemporary British Fiction*, Cambridge: Polity, pp. 87–105.

Julien, I. (1993) 'Performing sexualities: an interview', in V. Harwood, D. Oswell, K. Parkinson and A. Ward (eds) *Pleasure Principles: politics, sexuality and ethics*, London: Lawrence & Wishart, pp. 124–35.

Jurca, C. (2001) *White Diaspora: the suburb and the twentieth-century American novel*, Princeton, NJ: Princeton University Press.

Kureishi, H. (1990) *The Buddha of Suburbia*, London: Faber & Faber.

Medhurst, A. (1997) 'Negotiating the gnome zone', in R. Silverstone (ed.) *Visions of Suburbia*, London: Routledge, pp. 240–68.

Moore-Gilbert, B. (2001) *Hanif Kureishi*, Manchester: Manchester University Press.

Mort, F. (2000) 'The sexual geography of the city', in G. Bridge and S. Watson (eds) *A Companion to the City*, Oxford: Blackwell, pp. 307–15.

Orwell, G. (1962) [1939] *Coming Up for Air*, Harmondsworth: Penguin.

Oswell, D. (2000) 'Suburban tales: television, masculinity and textual geographies', in D. Bell and A. Haddour (eds) *City Visions*, Hemel Hempstead: Longman.

Procter, J. (2003) *Dwelling Places: post-war black British writing*, Manchester: Manchester University Press.

Rushdie, S. (1988) *Satanic Verses*, London: Penguin.

Schoene, B. (1998) 'Herald of hybridity: the emancipation of difference in Hanif Kureishi's *The Buddha of Suburbia*', *International Journal of Cultural Studies* 1 (1): 111–30.

Scruton, R. (2003) 'Why I became a conservative', *New Criterion* 21 (6) February: 4–13.

Seguin, R. (2001) *Around Quitting Time: work and middle-class fantasy in American fiction*, Durham, NC: Duke University Press.

Silverstone, R. (1997) 'Introduction', in R. Silverstone (ed.) *Visions of Suburbia*, London: Routledge, pp. 1–25.

Smith, Z. (2000) *White Teeth*, London: Hamish Hamilton.

Sontag, S. (1982) *A Susan Sontag Reader*, New York: Farrar, Strauss, Giroux.

Williams, R. (1958) *Culture and Society*, London: Chatto & Windus.

14 Iain Sinclair

The psychotic geographer treads the border-lines

Peter Brooker

Leaving London

It's difficult to keep pace with Iain Sinclair. His most recent 450-page book, *Dining on Stones*, follows the equally hefty *London Orbital*, which at its close anticipates the soon-to-be published walk in the footsteps of poet John Clare from Essex to Northborough and was itself accompanied by the co-authored illustrated prose and poetry text *White Goods*. These main-line and sup-plementary texts have run alongside the publication of selections of poems, the volume titled *Verbals* of conversations with Kevin Jackson, a co-walker in *London Orbital*, and two Channel 4 videos, *Asylum* and *London Orbital*, made with Chris Petit and other familiar collaborators. All these works appeared between 2002 and 2004, and followed, in what we might think of as a London sequence, a little tug boat of a book *Sorry Meniscus*, pulling a flotilla of articles on the Millennium Dome, and three other books, includ-ing a study of J. G. Ballard's *Crash*, all published in 1999. If this is *flânerie* it's *flânerie* on fast forward; Sinclair more roadrunner than urban stroller.

The novel *Landor's Tower* appeared as long ago as 2001. This, says Sinclair, in one of the designs given his burgeoning project, should be understood as the second in a quartet of novels beginning with *White Chappell* in the late 1980s. The two volumes, which will complete this quartet, will emerge alongside a future projected volume titled *Sixty Miles Out*, the third in a trilogy with *Lights Out for the Territory* and *London Orbital*. This new book will circle London from the outer distance of a route passing through Southend, Cambridge, Northampton, Oxford and Hastings, where Sinclair has recently established a bolt-hole (Jackson 2003: 136–7; Jeffries 2004: 23).

It's from *Landor's Tower* that I want to take my bearings. This is, as its readers will know, a very busy text, occupied as much as anything with its own composition or, what amounts to the same thing, its de-composition as a novel. At one point groaning under the excess baggage of his novel in progress, Sinclair comments 'Redundant . . . unless there is intervention by that other; unless some unpredicted element takes control, overrides the pre-planned structure, tells you what you don't know' (Sinclair 2001: 31).

This commitment on the part of the narrator and Sinclair persona, named Norton (derived from William Burroughs' *Junkie*) to the unpredictable, to chance, and the accidental, is indebted, we might think, to the Situationist tactic of the 'dérive', a way of traversing the modern city which begins from a known or stable point, but remains determinedly open to the contingent and unexpected.[1] It is, I think, the characteristic mode of energetic, dogged, digressive movement in Sinclair, by foot, of course; one which starts literally from 'home', in Albion Place, Hackney, and moves off in quadrants, triangles and circles to explore the unknown, or recover the forgotten and report back to base. It is a physically structured, and, we might say, psycho-geographically enacted form of the 'uncanny' by which the strange and repressed in the cultural memory of the city are invited into the normative homely habitat which is also the place of writing. My interest in what follows is in what notion of 'otherness', as in the above quotation, hence of estrangement, difference and newness this strategy produces beyond conventional notions of single autonomous selves, chronologically ordered times and familiar places.

We think, I dare say, of the other in Sinclair's London writings predominantly as the 'other London', the Gothic and occult soundings taken in the city's sacred and profane places, its liminal passages, crypts, remains and substrata seguing into an East End criminal or vagabond underworld and subcultural artistic networks. We do not think of Sinclair's London as associated with the proletariat, women, ethnic or other oppressed and oppositional social groups. 'There's an unreformed residue of the 1960s in him' reports Andy Beckett (1997: 25; and see Brooker 2002: 96–105). Sinclair does not provide us with a politically correct cognizance of the newly differentiated multi-ethnic global city. He does, however, represent, if there is a core to his position and politics, the spectre that haunted Margaret Thatcher, of a 1960s counterculture, in all its white, masculinist imperfections from one perspective, and all its provocation, permissiveness and anarchic disturbance from another.

As a London novelist Sinclair is pulled in by the city's gravity through the chamber of the East End and the historic financial City of London, but also pulled away from the city, I suggest, on the river's current, for example, to the nowhere lands of the novel *Downriver* (1991), the graphic novel, *Slow Chocolate Autopsy* (1998) and the text *Liquid City* (1999) to Tilbury, the Isle of Sheppey and the mouth of the estuary. The earlier *Lights out for the Territory*, Sinclair confirms, surprisingly, too, but in the spirit of its title, was 'the end of the London project' (1997c: 16). The novel *Radon Daughters* shifts from East London to the Isle of Grain and eventually to the west of Ireland.

Elsewhere, he is drawn to the story of the inexplicable disappearance of David Rodinsky, the isolated Jewish savant and misfit, whose sad end, once discerned, is testimony to his extreme alienation and the gradual erosion of Jewish settlement in the East End. Sinclair's contribution to the co-authored *Rodinsky's Room* recycles old tropes in ruminations on Pinter's *Caretaker*, the cult film *Performance*, the West End playboy, East End hustler David Litvinoff; while the supplementary text *Rodinsky's A-Z* takes him north and east along Rodinsky's own walks, ready to hit the line of zero longitude, to Waltham Abbey, the elected starting place for the *London Orbital* (Sinclair and Lichtenstein 1999: 273).

The opening of this latter work is threaded with a grumbling jeremiad: escalating house prices, prolonged building work, the demolition of 1960s tower blocks, the closing of the Whitechapel library and simultaneous opening of a Jewish heritage exhibition; 'developers and visible artists, explainers and exploiters' – all tell Sinclair it is 'time to move on, move out' (2002a: 11).[2] So he lights out for the outer rim, marking the circumference that will encircle and define the city's boundaries. Inside at its hub sits another circle, the flat white blob of the Teflon millennium dome, a continuation for Sinclair of the Thatcherite project under a new name, and an unmitigated failure. The emptiness and vanity of this folly moves him in a mood of comic satire and bardic spleen to invoke an earlier pre-industrial London: 'tear down the fences', he rails, 'return the poisoned land to use. No circuses, no tent shows, but the kind of workaday fields that once existed outside the walls of the city. Somewhere to practice archery, to operate market gardens, to listen – as entertainment – to the threnodies of hucksters, hedge priests and visionary madmen' (Sinclair 1997b: 10).[3] His self-appointed task in *London Orbital* is to exorcise the spell of the dome, weaving a circle round it twice, if not thrice, by foot and by car, in word and on film. So too in distempered, visionary tones he surveys the new sights and proposed planning changes; the London Eye 'is deemed to be a success' (2003: 60); the river's working life is over, thrown now onto the M25; the Thames Gateway, the site of new Labour's New Jerusalem courtesy of John Prescott & Co. is a 'heritage experiment' that presents 'squirts of housing' in a dead industrial landscape (Jeffries 2004: 20; Sinclair 2004).

In much of this Sinclair addresses 'central' aspects of the new city. Nevertheless, the works and their political animus follow a logic of withdrawal; away from the routine neighbourhood experiences of petty crime and failing councils to the wider failures of humdrum planning and vacant memory. To live in this city is to live in tension with it, therefore, in a dual focused, double existence as actor and spectator, pulled simultaneously deep inside and centrifugally out to a curmudgeonly distance, speaking from another place and in another discourse upon the interior.

In all this, though Sinclair, as we shall see, rejects the compromises of a modernist aesthetic, calling rather upon the power of the high Romantic imagination, he nonetheless inherits the modernist ambivalence towards modernity, of which the metropolis remains the prime expression. Like Walter Benjamin's angel of history he too faces backwards, attempting in vain to gather in the accumulated wreckage of the past while whipped forward by the storm of progress. There is only one way to go in fact: to the perimeter, to orbit the city, to move out along the A13, to cast the circle wider at sixty miles out and to slip off the circuit at a town such as Hastings, alongside the asylum seekers and the 'dispersed of Hackney and Tottenham'. It's 'exactly like Hackney in the 1960s', Sinclair enthuses (Jackson 2003: 136).

Or there is Wales, specifically the Welsh borders and the region of Sinclair's first childhood home in Maesteg, near Cardiff, and his early divided life as a Welsh boy at an English prep school and then public school at Cheltenham where he discovered film, the Beats, and the beginnings of the counterculture than would sustain his later career (Jackson 2003: 21–4).

Welsh borders

The London project allows for a comfortable method of walking, meditating and circling back home to write. 'Lovely', says Sinclair, 'but you can't do that with Wales' (1997c: 16). So Wales, on the other side of England, pulls him back eventually across space and through time to a second home which was his first boyhood home. *Landor's Tower* is the Welsh novel and it delivers all manner of couples, doubles and twins out of the fertile notion of the borders, gathering these at times in constellated, heterotopic sites such as the Aust service station which looks back over the Severn from just inside England on the motorway that leads to London. Similarly, the 'accidental parking spot' on the borders, at Arthur's quoit where the novel opens, 'was a place of revelation, off-piste, but sited at a notable conflux of energies', the beginning point, he says, of 'all my narratives' (Sinclair 2001: 10).

The novel's ostensible purpose originates in a commission to investigate the Tower or mansion built by Walter Savage Landor in the Ewyas valley in the early nineteenth century. Nearby stands the remains of Llanthony Abbey – a facsimile of an earlier priory – established by the bogus Father Ignatius in 1870, the year too of the beginning of the diary by his contemporary and neighbour, Francis Kilvert. The parts of this tale, or tails of this part, run into an account of Coleridge's proposed utopian 'pantisocracy' and later attempts to establish utopian communities, at the same site in the Ewyas valley by the sculptor Eric Gill, his family and the artist and poet David Jones, and a present-day attempt to found a utopian settlement in

Neath valley by the poet named Gwain Tunstall who is, at a guess, the real-life Chris Torrance. The magnet, then, that draws Sinclair to the Welsh borders is the utopian no-place, the 'other' place to the oppressive here and now of the dystopian metropolis.

In the event, these settlements present a story of conceit, fraud and failure, told in scraps and fragments, half pages and broken collage sketches by David McKean which form the novel's endpapers. The novel opens with a multi-text of drawings, a dedication, citations and allusions, of whom the authors and beneficiaries are Chris Petit, Chris Torrance, Foucault, the critic Patricia Duncker and Wordsworth. These fragments compose from the outset the ruins of the tumbledown anti-novel and as such match the story of failed utopias, known only through their surviving remnants.

Sinclair's plan had been to follow *White Chapell* with *Landor's Tower* as the second book in an intended quartet (Jackson 2003: 113–14). This plan was diverted first through *Downriver*, then *Lights Out for the Territory* and subsequently *Radon Daughters*. He had in the late 1980s begun the research in Wales for what becomes the first part of *Landor's Tower*, working then, as the novel relates, in a cottage haunted, as the writer-narrator, Norton, believes, by its previous occupant, the hostage Terry Waite (Sinclair 1997c: 14; Jackson 2003: 128). The project at that point breaks off, for character and author. They return to London only to return again to Wales, in fiction as in life, after *Downriver*, on the death of Norton/Sinclair's father and then a third time after *Radon Daughters* (Jackson 2003: 120, 128).

This sequence of diversions and interruptions upon interruptions across a period of twenty years from the late 1980s to 2000s confirms how the London texts are consistently woven with the apparently peripheral non-London novel. This is the characteristic movement, once more, here writ large, of the tactic of *dérive* within the novels, whereby the planned journey from A to Z steps off track into occultist byways, pulp fiction or Gothic tangents and parodies in a jumbled abracadabra. In *Landor's Tower* this digressive movement becomes the material of the book itself, providing Norton with the meta-novel or anti-novel which reports on the impossibility of the intended project.

In an early digression Norton reads a novel by Barbara Vine, the pseudonym of Ruth Rendell. Her impressive sense of place, user-friendly references and control of plot kills the idea of his own Welsh novel, he feels. Still he dumps her book because of its predictability. On his own uncontrollable material, he reflects:

> All of it to be digested, absorbed, fed into the great work. Wasn't that the essence of the modernist contract? Multi-voiced lyric seizures countered by drifts of unadorned fact, naked source material spliced

into domesticated trivia, anecdotes, borrowings, found footage. Redundant. As much use as a whale carved from margarine, unless there is intervention by that other; unless some unpredicted element takes control, overrides the pre-planned structure, tells you what you don't know. Willed possession.

(Sinclair 2001: 31)

Sinclair will deliver neither a modernist totality, nor the thrill of the formulaic crime novel. Instead he produces a many-branched narrative which disappears the novel in a frazzled concoction of biography, documentary, conspiracy theory, and fabulation, stretching from sub-Dante to spoof Micky Spillane. The result is a jostling mêlée of doppelgängers, twins and repeats across time, which shuffle events out of sequence and in and out of place.

All this is strung along some shaky plot lines. Rogue booksellers, mythologized out of Sinclair's past, dive in and out of Hay-on-Wye, like manic music-hall acts; a freelance researcher hunts down the forgotten scandal surrounding the one-time Liberal Party leader, Jeremy Thorpe, now disappeared into ghoulish silence somewhere in Barnstable. The novel's one woman, Prudence, is three women in one: 'wild woman of the woods, moon goddess, figure of death leading virgin males down into darkness' (Sinclair 2001: 255), an insane reincarnation of the woman Prudence Pelham who obsessed the artist David Jones. She appears and disappears. The Sinclair/ Norton figure is accused of her murder. And so on.

The remarkable thing is how this excess and plenitude tumbles into a familiar code. We've been here before and have come to know what to expect: lost texts, lost people, lost plots. The risk therefore is that all the frantic comedy of splitting and doubling produces not the strangely other but the familiar, a box of recycled tropes which set the same old Sinclair buddies and standbys running around in circles.

The risk is voiced in the novel through Marina Warner; author, says Sinclair, of a wonderful essay 'Persephone and the legend of the acoustic double' which 'brought tears to my eyes' (Sinclair 2001: 252). Marina Warner appears too in the Channel 4 film *Asylum* made by Sinclair and Chris Petit. Here she refers to the danger that a first twin may lead the second into captivity not liberation. The Sinclair 'other' risks just this: being trapped, character after character, book after book, under the roof of the one swirling dome.

The chances for newness and difference are therefore slim. As the character Silverfish puts it: 'We're trapped within the spiral of a posthumous fable. The circularity imposed upon us is temporal not spatial. "Here" doesn't matter. "When" does. We're returned to the point where we started, but we're not who we were' (Sinclair 2001: 256).

My dead self

There is 'something in this borderland . . . that haunts me', says Sinclair (Sinclair 2001: 13); it turns out this is 'a landscape of childhood' (Sinclair 2001: 87). Driving back to Wales he is accompanied by his dead father. The novel henceforth carries its earlier cast of characters and scraps of plot across this other borderline into a personal past and the source, we discover, for some of the story's allusions and obsessions. Intermittently it produces a younger self in this same place though neither person nor place are quite now where or 'who we were'.

In one complicated sequence, Norton, by now more evidently Sinclair, remembers coming in the early 1990s upon a set of photographs by the Swiss-American photographer, Robert Frank. He realizes that one of the photographs was of himself at a time when Frank visited Wales in the early 1950s and took a shot of Sinclair and a gang of boys above the colliery at Caerau. Here, says, Sinclair/ Norton, was, 'The child I never was . . . Frank successfully photographing an invisible person, my dead self, undid every-thing I knew of the workings of culture and memory. From that moment, my story was misaligned; revising a singular instant meant seeing myself from another angle' (Sinclair 2001: 126).

This younger self is a 'dead self', from simultaneously a previous life and an after-life. Time, place and person are out of joint. This sensation of misalignment, we realize, is the sensibility Sinclair entertains in the practice of *dérive*. We might think we are in the deranged, nomadic textual world of surrealism of Deleuze and Guattari. However, while Sinclair's text embraces misalignment it is in the grip of strategies which seek to order, map and *re-align* what is perceived as chaos. The return home is one. Characteristically too, while busy losing the plot, Sinclair produces the plot as conspiracy, a reduction of unfathomable complexity to one all-knowing, all-controlling agency. And there is, notoriously, in Sinclair's work, the usable fiction or revealed truth, as he chooses, of leylines, connecting Nicholas Hawksmoor's East London churches, or, as here, intersecting the sites of traditional sanctity across the Welsh Marches. The postmodern Sinclair relaunches the modern and pre-modern quest for order, as eccentric in this respect, if you will, as William Burroughs, William Butler Yeats and William Blake.

There is a further, more intriguing and far more sustained type of connection, however. This appears in the mapping of sequences of books as trilogies, quartets and life-time projects and in the networks which run in rhizomatic fashion through their interiors, dropping allusions, echoes, repeats and doubles of places, people and stories, as they go. We might see here an aesthetic of recycling which tries at once to recover and sustain a valued but disappearing past and to extend or 're-function' this in the present, beyond a circle of self-reference.

Thus Frank, for example, Sinclair reminds us, made the film *Pull My Daisy* on the Beats, and made films with Rudolph Wurlitzer who wrote *Pat Garrett and Billy the Kid* for Sam Peckinpah, the subject of a television profile by Jamie Lalage, a running reference in this book. On one occasion wanting to rough up some prints, Frank wrote 'Like a dog' across one, borrowing a phrase, which Sinclair also uses in *Downriver*, on the death of K. in Kafka's *The Trial*. 'So all my interests', says Sinclair, 'Beats, Hollywood, utopian communities, the austere European cinema of Lalage, knew each other, interacted' (Sinclair 2001: 125).

Once released, the references segue across Sinclair's work by way, for example, of Wurlitzer's screenplay for *Two Lane Back Top* to the canon of cult road-movies, films and car crashes of movie stars and celebrities invoked by Ballard's *Crash*. David Cronenberg's film of *Crash* followed his film of Burroughs' *Naked Lunch*. Chris Petit's film *Radio On* Sinclair sees as 'a kind of translation of *Crash*' (1999c: 35). Petit's work takes us into the 'austere European cinema' of Godard and Chris Marker, which Ballard conceived as parallel to his own work. And so on, travelling through nodal points in Sinclair's landscape. Memory regenerates and pulls these figures and texts into alignment, and ticks on to others, parts of an expanding 'field of force' or confluence of energies (Sinclair 2001: 124).

If the face of the future is an unscripted blank in Sinclair, the past is thumbed and written over, his works a kind of montaged scrap book. City and country alike are perceived consequently as a kind of layered palimpsest across the ages: 'You can't *not* go back into the past', he says, of London: 'its echoes come into you as you set off on a mood, at an angle to come upon the past at all turns by accident, inevitably like the fossils in London's Portland stone the byways and memories of Mycenae and Romans in the city' (Sinclair 2000).

Sinclair means neither to 'make it new', then, nor reconstruct the past in the false *aides-mémoires* of the heritage industry. Rather his mission is to chronicle decline, ruin and disappearance, and he takes this on with relish. Thus the newness of Docklands meant 'the back-story was being eliminated in front of my eyes. Buildings disappearing overnight . . . couldn't have been better . . . Things were so bad, they were really great to write about' (Jackson 2003: 121).

'Thesis writers', Sinclair moans, 'drag in chunks of Walter Benjamin . . . unknown to the victim' (Sinclair 2001: 286). And so of course do writers of essays. There are two respects at least in which we could drag in Benjamin. The first is the motif of disappearance. For Benjamin writes how it is in the arc of decline, captured in Baudelaire's depiction of the Paris arcades, that historical time is best understood. What haunts Sinclair, I think, a century or more later, is memory loss, the kind of slippage and misalignment in time which his mother, he tells us in *Landor's Tower*, came to suffer from and which he fears (Sinclair 2001: 314–15). Now contemporary society at large is marked by a kind of creeping Alzheimer's, for it is not only buildings but also the mind and memory which stand in ruins.

His remedy is, I think, essentially books – and here is the second connection with Benjamin. Books and films: words, names, images and texts held in the memory vault which once recalled stir their near neighbour or distant cousin or double into life. His own books therefore open up and replay the repertoire stored in the Sinclair archive, connecting and realigning the items in a valued avant-gardist, cult and popular catalogue. And it is this recycled culture of risk and wild imagination, headed by an elect of 'illuminati' who preserve the forgotten in the cultural memory, which he sets against the non-culture of Thatcher regeneration and Blairite spin.

Sinclair began his career in London in the 1970s as a book dealer in rare Victorian and pulp titles, working off a stall in Islington or 'charging around looking'. He kept company with 'runners and ragpickers, glowering eccentrics like the now vanished Driffield' (Sinclair 2002b: 14), and these figures of grotesque comedy and legend in the trade reappear, renamed in *White Chapell, Downriver* and again in *Landor's Tower*.

Thus he entered the double life, as he describes it, of writer and dealer (Jackson 2003: 139). Only now the bookseller, Iain Sinclair, has come to fame as the writer of his own books for sale. Nothing is abandoned en route: a lock-up in Whitechapel holds stacks of early writings he jokingly hopes an American University will buy (Jackson 2003: 30). And each book imagining the city like some massive archive pursues the book dealer's harried, addicted search, waylaying the author, hunting down the rare find, clearing away the pulp and remainders to reveal, perhaps, the jewel of a first edition.

'[T]o a true collector', writes Walter Benjamin, 'the acquisition of an old book is its rebirth'; his 'deepest desire' is to 'renew the old world' (Benjamin 1970: 61). He catalogues confusion and chaotic plenitude; he walks the borderline of disorder and order bringing all into the 'circumscribed area' of the 'magic encyclopedia' (Benjamin 1970: 60). There is much here that I have wanted to draw out – and there is another circle, the circumscribed area of the 'magic encyclopedia'. Inside the circle is knowledge: the culture of texts, the detail of their period, region, craftsmanship, the former ownership, the whole background of an item, as Benjamin describes it. As he looks too at the items in his glass case and holds them to his hand, the collector 'seems to be seeing through them into their distant past as though inspired' (Benjamin 1970: 61). The world of the collector too, moreover,

Benjamin, and Sinclair, in his own time, understand as a receding one. 'Only in extinction', Benjamin reflects, 'is the collector comprehended' (Benjamin 1970: 1967). Only at the point of disappearance, similarly, is the valued text reclaimed and comprehended, known in its catalogued place in the magic encyclopedia.

Magic, vision, imagination are Sinclair's tools and weapon. The questions this raises are as obvious to him as to ourselves. 'I thought it would work then', he says of his anti-Thatcher novel *Downriver* (2002c: 19). But did it work? And will it work now? For something, after all, has happened to the author and his book. Now the dealer has book deals for himself, and book and author are a united product trawling the market. Sinclair has become a cult, a brand, the 'psycho-geographer' on call (Jeffries 2004: 22);[4] from small presses he has moved to the *London Review of Books*, weekend supplements and gigs on BBC Radio 4. He does outlandish copy. And then there are the films and videos and friends, collaborators from the vault of the 1960s and 1970s: Chris Petit, Marc Atkins, Brian Catling, Dave McKean, J. G. Ballard, Michael Moorcock, attended by young scholars and situationists, old hippies and honoured guests. The kind of company for example assembled at the Barbican for a multimedia performance inspired by *London Orbital*. 'A parallelist performance in three lane theatre', presented readings by Sinclair, J. G. Ballard, Bill Drummond, Ken Campbell and Kevin Jackson, music performed live by WIRE, Scanner and Jimmy Cauty to a backdrop of Chris Petit's Channel 4 M25 film (Sinclair 2002c). Ballard unfortunately was represented by a cardboard cut-out. It was magic, but magic has a market cachet like never before. Sinclair can play Gandalf to Harry Potter in Charing Cross Waterstones. There is a danger then of self-parody and of typecasting: the hack personality who talks a good walk. What next: product endorsement? Sinclair rucksacks and trainers?

You get my drift. Sinclair highlights the aggravated plight of the avant-garde, nostalgic for the 1960s or 1920s, in a present-day wrap around media culture. The struggle to be some other in some other better place and earlier time than we are – the core of Sinclair's critique of prevailing political culture – risks becoming a spectacle of the very culture it seeks to outrage: the twin who is led into captivity not liberation, his 'imagination' against their 'imagineering' (Sinclair 2002a: 11). The contest is as close as this sounds. Does it work? Can it work?

Notes

1 Associated with Guy Debord (1931–94), political theorist and activist and co-founder of the Situationist International. His 'Theory of the *dérive*' was published

in 1956. Translated literally 'dérive' means 'drifting' but entails a more active and purposefully disorientating strategy that this suggests. As defined by Debord it is 'An experimental mode of behaviour linked to the conditions of urban society: a technique of transient passage through varied ambiances' (Knabb 1981: 45) 'Drifting purposefully is the recommended mode . . . in alert reverie' writes Sinclair (1997a: 4); and again 'Drift was the preferred mode' (Sinclair and Lichtenstein 1999: 259).

2 'I can't live in Hackney', he complains two years later, reacting to a murder, a drug-related killing on his street and the closure of the local baths. There's 'nothing working' (Jeffries 2004: 23).

3 The equivalent passage in the later collected essays on the dome, *Sorry Meniscus*, is noticeably more moderate: he calls here for

Somewhere to listen to the riffs of ranters and unsponsored visionaries; soothsayers, however distracted, who understood that this was a place with a long and complicated history, industrial and geological, that would never take its allotted role in the national cartoon without delivering an angry sense of its troubled past and its uncertain future.

(Sinclair 1999a: 44–5)

4 Originally associated with the Situationist International, psychogeography was given popular currency in England in the 1990s largely by the works of Sinclair, Peter Ackroyd and Stewart Home. 'It took off', Sinclair comments, but adds that he thinks of it rather 'as psychotic geography – stalking the city' (Jackson 2003: 75. See also Sinclair 1997a: 77 and Brooker 2002: 99–100).

References

Beckett, Andy (1997) 'In from the cold', *Independent on Sunday*, 12 January: 24–5.

Benjamin, Walter (1970) *Illuminations*, London: Fontana.

Brooker, Peter (2002) *Modernity and Metropolis*, London: Palgrave.

Jackson, Kevin (2003) *The Verbals: Kevin Jackson in conversation with Iain Sinclair*, Tonbridge: Worple.

Jeffries, Stuart (2004) ' "On the Road": profile of Iain Sinclair', *Guardian Weekend*, 24 April: 20–3.

Sinclair, Iain (1997a) *Lights Out for the Territory*, London: Granta.

—— (1997b) 'Mandelson's Pleasure Dome', *London Review of Books*, 2 October: 7–10.

—— (1997c) ' "Unfinished Business": Interview with Iain Sinclair', *Entropy* 1(2): 14–18.

—— (1999a) *Sorry Meniscus: excursions to the Millennium Dome*, London: Profile.

—— (ed.) (1999b) *Crash: David Cronenberg's post-mortem on J. G. Ballard's 'Trajectory of fate*, London: BFI.

—— and Rachel Lichtenstein (1999) *Rodinsky's Room*, London: Granta.

—— (2000) 'Forum on London', *In Our Time*, BBC Radio 4, 28 September.

—— (2001) *Landor's Tower, or The Imaginary Conversations*, London: Granta.

—— (2002a) *London Orbital: a walk round the M25*, London: Granta.

—— (2002b) ' "Reader, I was that beret", Review of John Baxter, *A Pound of Paper Confessions of a Book Addict, Independent on Sunday*, 13 November: 14.

—— (2002c) 'On the Road', *Guardian Weekend*, 19 October: 18–19.

—— (2003) 'Beyond Bow Bells', *Royal Academy Magazine* 78 (spring): 58–61.

—— (2004) Contributor to 'The Sunday Feature: The Thames Gateway', BBC Radio 3, 9 May.

Index